The Other Language

The Other Language

STORIES

Francesca Marciano

Pantheon Books · New York

Copyright © 2014 by Audenspice Ltd.

All rights reserved. Published in the United States by Pantheon Books, a division of Random House LLC, New York, and in Canada by Random House of Canada Limited, Toronto, Penguin Random House companies.

Pantheon Books and colophon are registered trademarks of Random House LLC.

"Chanel" first appeared in *The Common* (April 2014).

Grateful acknowledgment is made to Alfred Music for permission to reprint an excerpt from "Carey," words and music by Joni Mitchell. Copyright © 1971 (Renewed) Crazy Crow Music. All rights administered by SONY/ATV Music Publishing. Exclusive print rights administered by Alfred Music. All rights reserved. Reprinted by permission of Alfred Music.

Library of Congress Cataloging-in-Publication Data
Marciano, Francesca.
[Short stories. Selections]
The other language : stories / Francesca Marciano.
pages cm
ISBN 978-0-307-90836-0
I. Title.
PR9120.9.M36A6 2014 823'.914—dc23 2013030931

www.pantheonbooks.com

Jacket design and illustration
by Ben Wiseman
Book design by Betty Lew

Printed in the United States of America
First Edition

1   3   5   7   9   8   6   4   2

To change your language
you must change your life.

—*Derek Walcott*

· CONTENTS ·

The Other Language

The Other Language

In those days getting from Rome to Greece took forever. The highway ended abruptly in Naples and to get to Brindisi on a local road full of potholes was an exhausting ordeal. The journey took two full days but the children were too excited to complain, as this was their first time abroad. That was the idea: to go on a real adventure in order to take the children's minds off what had just happened.

For the occasion the father had bought a new car. Looking back now it was just another tiny red Fiat, though at the time it felt like a grand, modern vehicle. It impressed the children and seemed to cheer them up as if this time of their greatest loss would coincide with the promise of a richer and more exciting life. As if, by losing their mother, they had been promoted to a higher level of lifestyle.

Emma was twelve, Luca was a year older, and Monica only nine. Their feelings were muddled; they were not sure what they were expected to feel. It was the early seventies, before cell phones, before the Web, when children were still children and didn't know about designer labels and makeup, there were no reality shows, and no easy access to information about sex.

Their upbringing had been disciplined and they had turned out to be good kids; today one would say they were low maintenance. Even as very small children, their requests to Santa Claus had been modest: a puppet, a red car, a box of watercolors were all they had wished for. But after the accident, they were inundated by an unusual attention. Schoolteachers, neighbors, parents of their school friends—all kinds of grown-ups—had offered to have them spend the night, insisted on taking them to the cinema or puppet shows, fed them chocolate cake and ice cream, presented them with toys and new books to read. This overwhelming sympathy had soon become a nuisance, but because they were so well mannered they didn't recognize what the uncomfortable feeling they felt really was, so that suddenly the prospect of a foreign land in which to be alone with their father, in which they would not have to say the whole time thank you, yes, please, sorry, to strangers, seemed a liberation.

Emma doesn't remember exactly when, during the trip, Monica began to cry in the middle of the night (was it in the little hotel on the way to Brindisi or was it in their cabin, on the boat crossing over to Greece?). "I want Mamma," she kept saying, almost choking between sobs so that Emma and Luca had to wake up their father, who was sleeping next door. He seemed helpless and scared. He had never been alone with his children, at least not like this, in the midst of a drama, on the way to another country. Maybe he had been too confident, maybe it had been a mistake to drive them so soon this far away from the familiar. He managed to have someone brew a chamomile tea sweetened with honey, and after a few sips of it, Monica fell asleep again. Emma worried that if Monica cried once more they would have to turn back and go home. More than her brother and little sister, Emma wanted to get away as far as possible from what had happened so she could pretend it never had. No accident, no funeral, and no mother.

· • ·

The village was nothing much. At first Emma felt it didn't make a lot of sense to have come such a long way to find a village cut in half by a single road. A village with no particular charm, with just one bakery, one café, and two tavernas on the beach, the only places offering any kind of accommodation. The tavernas were identical, except for the colors of the chairs and tables. The first one, called Iorgo's, had them painted blue, the second one, Vassili's, were painted a yellow mustard. Just a few hundred meters across the beach was a tiny islet, made of two hills connected by a low strip of land. Its terrain was bare and rocky, save from a few thorny bushes, shaped like two humps on a camel's back. It looked deserted except for a few goats that one could spot from the beach with the naked eye. The children were excited to find that it was so close. After all, this was—despite its size and closeness to the mainland—the first deserted island they had ever come across other than in adventure books.

The father had rented two rooms on the first floor of Iorgo's taverna, after the children had expressed their preference for his blue over the yellow of Vassili's. Emma and Monica slept together in one, the father and Luca shared the other. The rooms were simple but had flair: the floors were creaky wide planks of wood and the beds of old cast iron, painted in white, with thick, coarse cotton sheets. On the windowsills were pots of basil to keep the mosquitoes away. The children fell asleep to the sound of the waves.

They woke up early in the morning when the light was still soft, the water glassy and clear and one could make out every pebble on the bottom. They ran downstairs in their swimsuits, sat at the blue table on the beach and ordered breakfast. The only sounds were donkeys and roosters waking up and the low chatter of the fishermen intent on disentangling their nets. They devoured yogurt and honey, crisp sesame bread still warm from the bakery, shuffling their bare feet in the cool sand, under the frazzled sunlight streaming from the bamboo roof. Each one of them secretly believed this might be the end of the tears, and they marked that beach as the place where pain had ended and a new life could begin. Their father was quiet but watchful, eager to notice any progress his children made. He never asked them whether they had washed their faces, brushed their teeth; he never demanded they put their sandals back on. To see them chatting again, enjoying the different food, the light, was more than enough for him.

. • ·

At lunchtime one was supposed to go straight into Iorgo's steamy kitchen, check what was cooking on the stove and order whatever looked good. This was the children's favorite moment of the day. To be able to lift the lids off the huge aluminum pots and peek inside had been unthinkable at home (never ever rummage inside a lady's handbag, their mother had warned them, as if ladies could be hiding a hand grenade in there).

Moussaka, chips, *keftedes:* the pots always held the same food. But the children loved ordering it, picking it, rummaging as they pleased.

. • ·

The women of the village were mainly dressed in black and neither swam nor sunbathed; most had the faint shadow of a mustache darkening their upper lip. But Nadia was different. She was Greek but she came from Athens: a city girl. Her extended family—a large group of aunts, cousins and big men with gold chains and bracelets—came to the village every year in the summer and always lodged at Vassili's. She must have been fourteen at the most but she looked more like a woman in her bikini, showing off her full breasts and round hips. She always wore mascara and pouted her lips whenever she swam in her uncertain breaststrokes, always careful to keep her head above the water like an old lady who doesn't want to get her hair wet. In their one-piece striped swimming costumes, flat-chested and skinny like shrimps, Emma and Monica x-rayed her every day with a mix of awe and contempt while Luca watched her with hormonal greed.

At meal times they couldn't avoid hearing Nadia and her parents, cousins and aunts hissing their *s*'s and rolling their *r*'s, always at the top of their lungs as they ate large portions of moussaka and chips.

"Why are they always screaming? Are they having an argument?" Emma asked her father.

"It's just the way Greek sounds. Be grateful that there is one place where people are louder than Italians."

He gestured toward Nadia.

"You should go and try to talk to that girl, Emma. She's about your age."

Emma shook her head.

"She's not. She's much older."

Emma didn't want to make friends with anybody new. She didn't want to have to answer when they'd ask, "Where is your mother?"

. . .

The children had been spared the details of the accident: where it had happened, how badly crushed the car was, how long before she died, whether on the spot or at the hospital. The adults had decided they were too small to be told such dreadful particulars, as if their mother's death was just another protocol they had to observe, like never ask for a soft drink unless they were offered one and never fish inside a lady's handbag. But Emma, Luca and Monica misunderstood. They assumed death must be an impolite subject to bring up in conversation, a disgrace to be hidden, to be put behind.

. . .

Luca was the first to befriend Nadia. She didn't speak any Italian and he didn't speak any Greek. And though it was unclear how they managed to communicate at first, soon he'd deserted his sisters in favor of Nadia and her entourage. He was given permission to hang out on the beach after dinner, sitting around a fire with Nadia and her large group of cousins and friends, who played long, repetitive Greek songs on the guitar. They were called either Stavros, Costa or Taki, as if their parents had made no imaginative efforts as far as names went. Emma found their hairy calves and armpits daunting and their manners coarse. She didn't like the way they dressed and not even the songs they sang.

. . .

The ruins of King Agamemnon's palace in Mycenae were only a couple of hours away, perched on a steep hill overlooking the Argolic plain. The father and the children drove there on an unusually gray afternoon, and on the way, on a steep rocky road, he recounted the story of the king and his daughter Iphigenia. How, because of lack of wind, the king couldn't sail to Troy and join the war. An oracle had told him the hunting goddess Artemis was punishing him for his arrogance and to calm her rage he'd have to offer a sacrifice to the deity.

"So he had to sacrifice the dearest thing he had," he said.

"What?" Monica asked, peeking in from the backseat.

"Iphigenia, his beautiful daughter. He summoned her and she was put on the altar, to be slaughtered."

But luckily, he said, just as the king was about to cut her throat, the goddess saved the girl by transforming her into a beautiful deer that slipped away.

When they arrived at the site, it had begun to drizzle, and a cold wind had begun to blow. The ruins—the imposing lion's gate, the tomb of the king, built like a dome with gigantic lintels—were deserted. Emma kept asking where the altar on which Iphigenia had stood was, but her father told her the guidebook wouldn't mention it because the story was only a myth.

She wandered around in silence, touching the surface of the ancient stones with her fingers. After a while she sat on a step and said she felt cold and tired. The father found an old sweater in the back of the car and wrapped her up, but the atmosphere of the place was having a strange effect on all of them. It was dark and sinister, compared to the bright colors of their village. They didn't stay long and on the way back in the car Emma kept asking her father how it was possible that Agamemnon would agree to kill his own daughter.

"He was a warrior. He had to join the war at all costs," the father said.

But Emma wouldn't relent. How could he? And what about the queen? Why didn't she do anything to stop him?

"*Basta,*" Luca interrupted her, annoyed. "Papà told you already. She doesn't die in the end, she becomes a deer."

"Yes," Emma said, "but what about the mother?"

· • ·

She was sucking the last drop of her lemonade through a straw, watching Luca play a game of cards with Nadia in her yellow bikini, when she saw the two boys for the first time. They were standing on the jetty, one tall, blond, thin as a reed. The other one smaller, darker, younger. Nadia lifted her eyes from her cards and made a face, as if the sight of them annoyed her. She said something to Luca in Greek.

"What was that?" Emma asked Luca. She hardly ever paid attention to Nadia, but this time she wanted the information.

"They are English. Two brothers," said Luca, uninterested.

"How do you know that's what she said?"

"I just know. I've learned the words. So what?"

Emma didn't say anything. Luca looked at her with hostility.

"Stop sucking that straw. You are driving me crazy."

Nadia giggled. Apparently, she was beginning to pick up some Italian.

· • ·

The English brothers, it turned out, came every summer, because their parents owned a house in the village.

They came and went to the beach every morning, barefoot

and silent. Their cutoffs were bleached by the sun, their T-shirts ripped, their perfectly hairless legs were long and scratched, their longish hair tousled. Emma found the casualness of their wardrobe fascinating. She had never come across a similar style before—the Italians looked too dainty while the Greeks were so unsophisticated. She observed the boys as they put on flippers and masks and watched them as they swam slow and steady all the way to the island.

Emma gathered the details from one of Nadia's aunts who spoke a little Italian.

"The mother and the father buy our cousin's villa. Rich English people," the woman said, fanning herself with a newspaper.

Emma asked her which villa it was; she hadn't seen any building worthy of that word.

"In front of the souvlaki place. The big villa, you cannot miss. The biggest in the village."

She shook her head with irritation as if the loss of this piece of family property had been a personal affront.

That same afternoon Emma spotted it. *Villa* was a big word for what it was: a plain two-story house on the main road, just across from the bakery and the souvlaki stall. The dark blue shutters had been newly repainted and gave it an air of nobility, but that was about it. There was a car with an English license plate parked outside. Emma ate her souvlaki in silence, staring at the house for a long time.

· • ·

Nadia was lying on a towel in her bikini, flipping the pages of a comic book, her skin shiny with tanning oil, her hair done up in a twisted bun.

"Come on, why don't you go talk to her?" said the father again.

Emma shrugged; Monica imitated her.

"I don't speak any Greek," she said.

"We can't understand her," Monica echoed.

Emma turned her gaze to the English boys in the distance as they were putting on their flippers, getting ready for their swim to the island. She loved the hushed, clipped, refined sounds of their language, the way they exchanged quick sentences, hardly moving a muscle in their bodies. Emma wished she could speak the boys' language instead. It sounded authoritative, distinguished, exact.

"What's wrong with you two?" said the father.

"Nothing is wrong. We're fine," said Monica, suddenly defensive.

"We're fine playing with each other, Papà," Emma said.

She observed Luca and Nadia splashing each other in the shallow water. They no longer needed a common language to get along.

· · ·

Come the start of August, there was a new arrival, a group of well-groomed adults. The women were tall and slender, and wore similar sleeveless linen dresses way above the knees and flat Capri sandals. The men showed up for dinner in soft loafers, pastel-colored sweaters wrapped around their shoulders and tied by the sleeves, their wet hair parted on the side.

"Milanese," said Luca disapprovingly.

Emma, her brother and sister had become proprietorial by now, as if they had always owned the place, so used had they become to their particular sunbathing spots, their favorite rocks, their table at breakfast, their access to the kitchen where Iorgo's wife, Maria, erect, hands on hips, would holler the name of the dish each time they lifted the lid. Nadia and her family also watched the new group with an air of superiority.

The Italians ignored their stares, and pretty soon were all over the kitchen lifting lids from the pots just like the rest of them. They too were early risers and breakfast was no longer a quiet affair of tiny waves lapping the shore, birds, breeze, hushed voices and Papà quietly flicking pages of his book while they ate bread and honey. The Milanese were loud and jolly and never stopped talking. It felt so unfair to have come out such a long distance, undertaken such a perilous voyage, having had to learn the Greek words for *milk, honey, bread, cheese, good morning, thank you, please,* to have actually established a silent complicity with the English boys by the mere fact of sharing the same beach, and now, with the intrusion of the Italians, to have this sense of foreignness and adventure be disrupted. Emma resented their calculated stylishness as if it didn't make any difference to them to be in Milan or in a tiny village of the Peloponnese. She had made sure not to speak Italian in their presence, confident that by lying low, she, Monica and Luca would be able to shroud their identity.

But only a few days later Emma and Monica came back from a swim just before lunch and saw that their father had joined the Milanese's table and was drinking iced retsina in an amiable mood. He called the girls over and introduced them to the group. They had to shake everyone's hand, giving their names as they had been taught to do. The grown-ups sized them up with circumspection, squeezing the children's hands longer than necessary. Emma knew right away what that expression of pity meant and felt doubly betrayed.

She felt ashamed, as if the loss of her mother had made her a lesser person in the eyes of the world.

· • ·

It was way past noon, and Emma was dozing off on a rock in the bay of Kastraki. The cove was on the north side of the village, a perfect half-moon shape. She and Monica had discovered it one day during one of their explorations and decided that they preferred to swim there, away from the loud Greek families always yelling and shouting at their children. She felt a shadow come between her and the glare of the sun behind her closed eyes. It was the younger English boy. He said something to her in his clipped, authoritative language. His voice was surprisingly hoarse and Emma sat up, her heart pounding. His eyes were of a warm brown, speckled with gold flakes. His lips, a dark pink, were cracked and crusty. She noticed how his sinewy arms were rounded by snaky tendons and muscles, and the way his chestnut hair—a mass of salty curls bleached by the sun—fell over his eyes. Emma felt an unfamiliar sensation: the first perception, of something as yet unknown to her and still unnamed. She shook her head and raised her palms up. The boy repeated his question. He waved a hand, as if to prompt an answer, encouraging. Emma remained mute, so he gave up, turned back and left.

· • ·

That same day, as she was heading back toward the blue taverna, she noticed her father in the distance walking on the beach side by side with one of the Milanese women. They were engrossed in conversation and it struck Emma how at ease with each other they seemed, as if they had known each other a long time. An image of this woman—or any woman—replacing her mother insinuated itself. In the days that followed Emma kept an eye on her father and the woman. There was nothing out of the ordinary happening between them: her father kept joining the Milanese's table after dinner for a card game, there were laughter and jokes, chilled bottles of retsina and cigarettes, but she never caught him alone with the woman again.

· • ·

By the end of August days were getting shorter and the light was changing. Soon her father started talking about getting ready to go back home. Emma realized that returning meant facing changes they'd all been postponing. Their tans would fade quickly; so too the brilliance of the endless summer and the whir in her chest at the thought of the younger, dark-haired English boy. She was afraid to ask her father whether he intended to bring them back again to the village the following year. She had been taught that children should never ask for things, but were supposed to wait and be offered.

She felt a terrible regret for not having been able to speak to the English boy when he had materialized that afternoon at the beach, looming above her against the sun. Emma was certain that his friendship would have produced a drastic transformation in her. His nature—so opposite to hers, so attractive—seemed to exude a power and a strength that she needed for herself. She wanted to learn how to swim to the island and back, wanted to speak in that same voice, wear bleached cutoffs and faded T-shirts and never have to wear the same clothes as the Milanese women or see her father ever wrap a sweater around his shoulders, tied at the sleeves. Everything she had experienced during that short holiday had been a discovery: from the sound of his language, to the endless possibilities of her hopes and aspirations. That was the summer when Emma understood that one of the many ways to survive the pain buried inside her was to become an entirely different person.

· • ·

The children went back to the city to what they assumed was home only to realize how unfamiliar it had become. Everything was the same but nothing was the same anymore. Their mother's bathrobe was still hanging behind the bathroom door (probably left behind by mistake by the aunts who had cleared the apartment like policemen removing evidence). Her hairbrush, which Emma found in a drawer, still had a few strands of her blond hair caught in it. These objects, innocuous, ordinary, had acquired an ominous nature. And so had the apartment: the dent on the sofa where she had sprawled when reading, her favorite coffee cup that had a crack but never broke, now frightened them.

A couple of weeks later Emma, making sure nobody saw her, threw away the cup and the brush; soon thereafter someone took care of the bathrobe.

· • ·

In January Rome was hit by a freakish snowstorm. Luca, Emma and Monica woke up to a stunning white landscape—a wonder they had never seen before. The whole city had come to a halt and a childish euphoria had descended upon everyone as if a miracle had taken place. The children were allowed to stay home from school, and all the offices shut down, so that it felt as if the whole world was on holiday with a splendid playground at their disposal. The father took the kids for a walk along the Via dei Fori Imperiali, all of them bundled up in scarves, wool hats and thick gloves. He took several pictures of the Forum and the Colosseum shrouded in white with his new Olympus. He kept saying what an amazing spectacle this was, a once in a lifetime occurrence—Rome covered in snow was something he had hardly ever seen himself. When Monica and Luca started a snowball fight under the Arch of Costantino, he clicked away and turned to Emma, gesturing for her to join in. But she shook her head. She didn't have it in her to play. For the first time in months she felt a burst of longing, like a sharp ache piercing her lungs. Shouldn't her mother be in the photograph with them, throwing snowballs and screaming with laughter? Where else could she belong? The injustice of her loss manifested itself in all its cruelty. Emma burst out crying, as if a hidden button had been pushed, and the tears she had withheld for almost a year found their way out at last. She turned her back on the snowball fight and walked a few steps away so that her father wouldn't notice. She was too small to understand how such a pain could gush up to the surface without warning, but, as she felt the tears stream down her cold cheeks and she quickly wiped them away with her gloves, she somehow knew she shouldn't be afraid of them.

· • ·

The winter was hard on the father. He felt lonely and at times even desperate. To find himself suddenly responsible for the three children turned out to be more than he could handle. He had no time to grieve, busy as he was taking the kids to school before the office, picking them up, making sure they ate proper meals and got new shoes whenever their feet went up one size. In the spring he consulted with friends and family and he recalled for them how the Greek holiday seemed to have had such a beneficial effect on the children—so much so that it seemed worth repeating. The younger aunt, their mother's sister, told him the kids had talked all winter about the friends they'd made in the village. Apparently Luca had exchanged a few letters with Nadia, whereas Emma kept talking about the two English boys. The father asked, puzzled, Which English boys? He had hardly noticed them.

· • ·

They took off again the following July. The children couldn't wait to arrive; their excitement mounted to a frenzy when they got off the ferry and started hearing Greek being spoken again. All winter long they'd fantasized about this moment: the memory of the village—of their immaculate rooms, of the deserted island across the beach—had haunted them, and they couldn't believe the place still existed as they'd left it.

It was a relief to find that not much had changed during their absence. Iorgo and Maria's taverna looked identical, except for a new coat of slightly darker blue paint. Nadia and her large family had just arrived from Athens a few days earlier, and she was already positioned on her towel working on her tan. The two humps of the island were there, so were the goats; in the kitchen, under the lids, pots and pans disclosed the same moussaka, *keftedes,* and chicken with chips. Nothing had changed. If anything, it was the children who had.

Luca's voice had turned into a mix of hoarse and strident trumpeting, his legs were now just as hairy as the Greek boys'. Monica's face had rearranged itself in a different order, the tip of her nose had settled into a slightly more rounded shape, she didn't look like any of the pictures from the previous year. Emma's figure, too, had reassembled itself. She had just gotten her period and with it a new softness around her hips, so now she had a waist, small breasts and a bottom. She looked at Nadia with overt suspicion: the roundness of her curves and bosom were an anticipation of what was yet to come. Luca was besotted more than ever by Nadia but soon realized the new guy from Athens who smoked Marlboros and played backgammon with her every afternoon must be the new boyfriend. This was at first a disappointment but Luca quickly devised a new strategy: he had no hope against such a masculine antagonist and so pursued the role of harmless admirer, in order to maintain his privileged position with the queen. Nadia organized her usual after-dinner singing around the bonfire, which allowed furtive kisses among her teenage friends to be exchanged thanks to the dark. She also encouraged her court to join *sirtaki* dancing with the locals under the string of lights hanging across the taverna's roof. She led the dance with the old fishermen—her jet-black hair loose on her shoulders, allowing glimpses of her soft cleavage to show—and insisted on teaching Luca the steps. When the dance reached a climax, the fishermen would each grab a plate from one of the tables and smash them on the floor, which sent the audience into a frenzy of applause and cheers. Emma found this form of entertainment irritating and refused to join in, declaring Greek music repetitive and too loud for her.

The previous winter at school Emma had been taking a weekly English class, but the teacher, an elderly woman from Palermo, spoke it with a thick Sicilian accent and the sentences she gave the class to translate didn't go beyond "the pen is on the desk" or "Mary is a very good student." Emma had higher ambitions: she needed to pry open the secret of the language she longed to master in view of her forthcoming—she hoped—encounter with the dark-haired English boy. She had been playing the Beatles' *White Album* and Joni Mitchell's *Blue* incessantly in her room, making a point of learning the lyrics by heart and singing along. She had looked up every single word in the dictionary and had painstakingly attempted to paste the pieces together in a way that would produce an intelligible sentence. She found out from a magazine that one of Joni Mitchell's songs, "Carey," was about a hippie girl living on Crete.

The wind is in from Africa
Last night I couldn't sleep
Oh, you know it sure is hard to leave here Carey
But it's really not my home

There was so much joy and excitement in Joni's voice. Emma sang the lyrics over and over in an endless loop. There was something so seductive in the image of a free-spirited young woman on a Greek island, a wind coming all the way from Africa. One day soon, might that person be her?

· • ·

Once back in the village Emma had checked right away for signs of the English boy's presence but the villa's blue blinds were always shut, no car with an English plate was parked in front of it, and she began to sulk.

In the meantime she'd been practicing her swimming technique; she wanted to be ready. Emma went every day to Kastraki by herself and now she could easily swim halfway to the island and back. It was her secret, which she had kept even from her siblings. She didn't want her father to know she was training for the crossing; he would not allow it because he still didn't trust her as a swimmer. It was true, she wasn't very experienced, but she saw that each day she managed to reach a bit farther; her strokes were getting more powerful and her breathing more controlled. All she needed was time, and in a week or two she might be able to reach all the way.

After the swim she sat on a rock, listening to her accelerated heartbeat, to the blood pulsing in her temples and to her shortened breath, until it all slowed down and the drying salt tightened her skin. These were the moments that would stick in her memory for years to come, those instants of perfect bliss that nothing else would ever match again.

One afternoon she was walking in the blistering sun, heading back from her swim. As she approached Iorgo's taverna she could make out her father sitting under the bamboo roof in his shorts and open shirt, covered with zebra stripes of light and shade. She liked those hours of quiet, when it was too hot to speak and everything stood still, a suspension in the glare of the day. As she got closer she saw he wasn't alone. The Milanese woman from the previous summer was sitting across from him, looking urban and pasty, her white linen dress stuck to her damp skin. He waved.

"Emma, come say hallo to Mirella."

He looked uneasy. He urged her to go and chase up Luca and Monica wherever they were and join them for lunch. Mirella didn't look as attractive as she had the year before. Now she seemed to Emma somehow powerless, tense.

"Where are the others?" Emma asked her.

"Which others, dear?" Mirella strained to smile.

"Your friends from last summer."

Mirella put a hand in her hair absentmindedly, not quite meeting Emma's eyes.

"Friends? Oh. I don't know. I came alone, this time." Another awkward silence followed, as though Emma had asked the wrong question.

· • ·

Monica was the first to broach an exploration of the potential consequences of Mirella's arrival.

"Why does she have to sit with us all the time? Can't she eat at her own table?" she blurted out, completely out of context, while she and Emma were looking for green glass pebbles on the beach. Since Mirella had arrived, if Emma had become sulky, Monica had turned morose. The woman's presence had made their mother rise from the dead, and they felt frightened in ways that they couldn't decipher, let alone discuss. Meanwhile, this summer Luca had abandoned them for good, in favor of his new group of teenage friends from Athens; he was to be counted upon neither for solidarity nor for help.

Emma shrugged, pretending not to know the answer to her sister's complaint, but Monica wouldn't let her off the hook.

"She is in love with Papà. Otherwise why is she here again, all by herself?"

Emma handed Monica a dark blue pebble. Blue was a rare color. Monica put it in the jar without looking. She persisted.

"Why do *you* think she came back?"

"I don't know. I doubt Papà is interested in her."

"How do you know? He lets her eat with us every day. They play cards at night. They are always together."

"I think he's embarrassed that she came back but is just trying to be kind to her."

"Why should he be kind?"

Emma didn't answer, which made Monica more anxious and angry.

"Why does he have to be kind? Because of what? Huh?"

"Stop it."

"Stop what?"

"You are screaming."

Monica lowered her voice.

"Why does he have to be kind to her? She's nothing to us. She's just a stranger."

"Because he's feeling sorry for her, okay?" Emma said calmly, although she felt this wasn't the best answer. She looked at Monica. She was as dark as the fishermen, and her curly brown hair hadn't been brushed in weeks. Her little body had grown sturdy and strong, a bomb ready to explode.

· · ·

Then one early morning Emma looked up from her yogurt and honey and there they were, the English boys, back on the jetty in their canvas shorts sitting low on the hips, slipping on flippers, ready to dive in. They too had grown up since the previous summer, in that shocking Alice in Wonderland way that happens between the age of twelve and fifteen: they were much taller, sturdier, and their hair had reached their shoulders. She followed the trajectory of their arms and fins breaking the stillness of the water like two dolphins behind a boat till they reached the shore of the island and turned into two tiny vertical figurines, jumping from rock to rock just like the goats.

"What are you looking at?" the father asked.

"Nothing," she said, smiling at him.

He was such a handsome man, her father, still so young and lanky, his sandy hair falling across his face. He wore a white shirt with a threadbare collar over what he called his Bermuda shorts, the sleeves rolled up to his elbow. No wonder women fell in love with him. He was so quiet, and—by then she could tell from his enduring silences—lonely.

· · ·

Emma doesn't remember now how the magic happened. Who said what first, which words were exchanged. All she knows is that the memories of that summer turned into English because that's what she found herself speaking. It was like an infant going from blabber to complete sentences in just a few weeks, letting the brain do the job in its mysterious way. It came like a flow, an instantaneous metamorphosis she was completely unaware of. All she remembers is that one summer the younger boy was speaking incomprehensible phonemes, and the next—thanks to the Beatles, to Joni Mitchell's lyrics, to the promise of love?—the same clipped syllables turned into verbs that described actions, adjectives that specified attributes and nouns she now grasped as if in her hands and succeeded in using them all, ordering them in the right sequence to make herself understood.

That summer forever marked the moment when she swam all the way to the island and landed in a place where she could be different from whom she assumed she was. There were so many possibilities. She didn't know what she was getting away from, but the other language was the boat she fled on.

· • ·

It turned out that Jack and David longed for company too, and an Italian girl their age was probably an equally exotic novelty for them. David, the older of the two, had deep blue eyes, lighter hair and the look of a melancholic troubadour. He told her she should listen to the Rolling Stones instead of the Beatles and twisted his lips when she quoted from *Blue*. He asked her whether she liked Pink Floyd, the Doors, Frank Zappa or Led Zeppelin. Emma nodded but didn't make any specific comment, not wanting to reveal what a beginner she was in terms of rock bands. Jack, the dark-haired one who had spoken to her the previous summer in Kastraki, seemed in awe of his older brother and waited for him to end the interrogation, nodding from time to time. When David was finished, Jack stepped forward and without any preamble asked her whether she'd like to follow them home for tea.

Inside the villa, things were scattered all over the place without logic, as if by a tornado. The kitchen table was covered with breakfast leftovers, potted plants, gardening utensils, masks and flippers, wet swimsuits, baskets filled with tomatoes and onions and stale bread, piles of magazines and newspapers. On the floor there were tools, the wheel of a bicycle, a huge carton concealing a mysterious appliance. An English pop song blared cheesily from a small stereo, and a diffused smell of burned garlic hovered in the air.

The boys' mother walked into the kitchen barefoot and bra-less, wrapped in a floral tunic. She had a pyramid of frizzy hair, a shining halo of gold. She stroked Jack's curls, introduced herself as Penny and asked Emma whether she was going to join the boys for tea.

"Peter, come meet lovely Emma!" she sang to her husband.

A balding man with a paunch and a deep tan, intent on dig-ging a hole in the backyard, waved his hand with a musical "Hallo there!"

Emma was impressed by their ease. Nobody seemed to mind or even notice the mayhem, as if this was simply their habitual standard of life.

The boys took Emma to their room—more clothes and wet towels rolled up on the floor—and put a Frank Zappa LP on a small record player full blast, overpowering their parents' music from the next room. They made Emma listen in religious silence, scanning her face for a reaction. David laughed when she said she wanted to learn how to play the guitar.

"Why you laugh?" she asked.

David blurted out something unintelligible.

"Because you said gh—tahr." Jack repeated for her, slowing down the words, his dark eyes holding hers.

"It's 'guitar.' Try," David said.

She tried a few times, wishing she had never pronounced that word. The feeling of those ungovernable sounds sliding and slush-ing out of control between palate, teeth and tongue embarrassed her.

"I can't," she pleaded.

"It's okay," David said. "I like your Italian accent."

His remark displeased her, because she had no idea she had an accent, and figured it probably made her sound stupid.

"It's very cool, actually," Jack added with sudden fervor and smiled at her. Emma blushed, unprepared as she was to receive a compliment from him. It was such a surprise to feel that he could find her interesting.

Then Penny called from the kitchen in a soprano voice and made room on the table for a teapot, toast and butter. Emma looked at a small round jar filled with a dark brown, sticky-looking substance.

"What is this?"

"You don't know Marmite?" Jack asked, incredulous.

Penny turned from the sink, where she was busy washing something.

"Jack darling, Marmite is a British peculiarity, mostly ignored by the rest of world."

She came to the table and swiftly spread butter and the brown sticky stuff on a piece of burned toast. She handed it to Emma.

"Here, my love, try your first Marmite sandwich and make a wish."

Emma bit into it with her eyes closed. The taste was so different from anything she'd ever tried before. The sticky, salty substance married the bitter taste of black tea deliciously. She made her wish. If Peter died of a sudden heart attack, then her father could marry Penny and their life would be filled with pop songs in the kitchen, colorful hippie clothes, Marmite sandwiches and more words in English.

· · ·

Walking back on the beach toward Iorgo's, Emma practiced saying the word *guitar*, repeating it again and again all the way there. Just like a fugitive in a detective story, who needed to erase any trace of his past before getting caught, it was imperative to get rid of any trace of accent for her transformation to be complete. The visit to the boys' house, the way she'd felt at ease with their parents, understanding every word of their conversation, had made her extremely proud of herself and excited. She had stepped through a curtain into another realm, a wide, mysterious landscape that she had only begun to explore.

Her father, Luca and Monica were already sitting at their usual table under the string of tiny lightbulbs with Mirella next to her father wearing a blank canvas face and absent smile.

"Papà said we didn't have to wait for you. We ordered our food already," Monica said emphatically, as if this were some kind of privilege their father had just bestowed on her and Luca.

"Emma, just go and order your food in the kitchen," her father said.

"I'm having a cheese omelette," Emma announced when she came back.

"They don't make omelettes for dinner," Monica objected.

"Maria is making me one especially. I'm tired of eating Greek salad and meatballs." After her tea and Marmite toast experience she felt her food choices should be more idiosyncratic.

"You are such a snob," Luca said.

"Shut up and mind your own business," she snapped back.

"Why are you saying that, Luca?" the father asked.

"Emma thinks the Greeks are all peasants." Luca had acquired a dense cluster of blackheads on his nose. At times Emma felt she could never love her brother again because of them.

"That's ridiculous, Luca. Don't make assumptions about what other people think." The father sounded annoyed.

"She thinks she is so—"

"Stop it, I said."

The father was beginning to grow impatient with them. It had been more than a whole year now of taking nonstop care of them and of an empty bed at night. He was beginning to think he too had a right to his share of happiness. Although Mirella was not the answer—he wasn't even attracted to her—he was beginning to appreciate her tenaciousness. Sometimes, especially in the middle of the night, during the hours when dreams and insomnia merge into a spiral of gloom and paranoia, he worried his children might end up growing into indifferent, self-centered adolescents, and he realized he had no idea how to prevent this from happening. The exteriors of their bodies were changing so rapidly—every day another bulge, a new ripeness—and soon he wouldn't be able to look at his daughters in their underwear. How could he foresee what was to happen underneath the surface? But more than that, who—now that their mother was gone—was going to help him shape or straighten their personalities in the event they veered in the wrong direction? What if the terrible accident had forever frozen them? And what if he ended up disliking them, once they would be set in their ways? What did he need to do or learn to raise emotionally sound children, who would turn into generous, independent and confident adults? In the morning these fears dissolved and his children went back to looking like lovely normal kids. He felt guilty and blamed his angst on difficult digestion, knowing, however, that those thoughts would be waiting for him until he found some answers.

Mirella had been waiting for the tension to dissolve. When she thought it had cleared, she recited the lines she'd been preparing all evening.

"I was thinking we could all go on a little trip tomorrow and visit the ancient amphitheater in Epidaurus." She looked at the children expectantly. It felt as if this idea was part of a bigger plan that involved doing things all together—as if she were now part of the family.

Monica and Luca exchanged a look and remained silent.

"Would you like to do that, children?" she added, perhaps a bit too loudly.

Monica and Luca turned to Emma, but she kept looking at her plate.

"Mirella has asked you a question," the father prompted them.

They kept a stubborn silence.

The father raised his voice.

"I said answer the question!"

"It's all right, leave it . . . if they don't feel like—" Mirella reached for his arm but he shook her hand away.

The kids stared at the father, mute. Emma felt his fury, like a heat wave slapping her face. It was the first time he was siding with a stranger, on the opposite side, leaving them alone.

Iorgo appeared at the table with their dinner. There was more silence while each one of them got their plate. Then the father turned to Mirella.

"Then the two of us will go. They can stay behind. I'm happier that way."

And almost before he had finished that sentence Monica started crying.

"Stop it," her father snapped.

It was incredible, Emma thought, how she could turn her tears on without warning, just like opening a faucet.

"Monica, you can get up from the table if you are going to behave like this," he said.

She left the table, sniffing. This was pretty bad; he had never been this angry with them. Luca looked at Emma, searching for her complicity, but she was hating him now and wouldn't give in. Mirella motioned as if to go after Monica, but the father pinned her wrist down to the table.

"Nobody moves," he said. "Just eat your dinner."

So they did, and nobody said another word.

.   •   .

The father and Mirella left early the next morning and the kids took the first solo breakfast of their life. They were euphoric: they drank coffee instead of tea, had cake instead of bread and butter and forgot entirely the previous night's drama. They couldn't wait for lunch to come to repeat the experience: playing the capable and independent orphans, traveling and dining out on their own. Emma for a moment thought it was uncanny, this sudden desire she had to see both of their parents dead and out of their lives.

"What should we do now?" Monica asked, eagerly.

"You do whatever you want. I'm going to go swimming in a little while," Luca said, looking around for a sign of Nadia, although she never emerged before eleven.

"You can read a book on the beach. Get your towel and go over there," Emma told her, slipping away from the table. "I'm going for a walk."

"Can I come with you?"

"No, you stay here."

"I don't want to."

"You are going to be fine. Just stay here and read until I come back."

Monica gave her a sullen look, but Emma didn't relent.

"If you need anything just go into the kitchen and ask Maria, okay?"

When Emma turned around she saw that Luca had left as well and Monica was sitting alone, elbows on the table, holding her round face between her hands. Luca had Nadia, their father had Mirella, and Emma had the English boy as a distraction to cling to. But Monica was still too much of a child to be interested in anybody outside her own family. Emma knew her little sister was probably on the verge of tears again and she felt a pang of guilt for leaving her behind. But she didn't turn back. She had only a few hours of freedom and knew she needed to take advantage of them.

· • ·

The door to the villa was open, so Emma peeked inside. The kitchen was silent, on the big table the usual array of rusty spanners and bolts next to half-eaten plates of congealed scrambled eggs, magazines and sandy towels strewn over chairs. Then she heard footsteps and Penny appeared, a towel wrapped around her head, wearing nothing but a tiny acid green bikini bottom with two minuscule strings tied on the hip bone. Her small breasts were just as tanned as the rest of her slim body. She welcomed Emma.

"Hallo, darling!"

She didn't bother to cover her breasts but grabbed a pack of cigarettes from the table and lit one.

"Are you looking for the boys? Sorry for the clutter, dear, we are terribly disorganized, as you can see."

Penny sat down at the kitchen table, crossed her legs and blew out the smoke. She looked around the room and sighed.

"God only knows why, no matter how hard I try, it always looks like a pigsty in here."

Emma wasn't sure it was okay to keep staring at her breasts but Penny seemed fine with that because she smiled and gestured for her to sit down.

"Jack is with Peter, they went to the hardware store in town. Let me call David for you."

She called out his name a couple of times, in a prolonged lilt, then whistled as if calling a puppy.

"He's still asleep, I'm afraid. I'd better wake him up, he needs to get out in the sun and breathe some fresh air before he positively rots up there."

Penny got up and left the kitchen.

Emma felt her disappointment rise into her face and settle there; she had hoped to be alone with Jack today and to seize this opportunity to try and touch him. She had envisioned their fingers brushing by accident at first and then their hands clasping. Imagining the feeling of his palm against hers had stirred something in her stomach. She didn't dare imagine anything further although she knew the next step would have to be kissing. It was still too big a step for her, but it was inevitable they would get there. But now Jack was at the "hardware store" (Emma didn't know yet what the word *hardware* meant, but it sounded impor-

tant and she gathered he must be on a serious mission) and she
was going to get David instead. But perhaps David, being his big
brother, would at least carry a bit of Jack-ness with him while at
the same time giving her the opportunity to practice her English.
Then—barefoot, slightly puffy and dazed—David appeared in
his swimsuit, as if he had just been dragged out of his bed.

"Hallo, Emma," he said and smiled so sweetly that Emma felt
instantly much happier than she expected. Penny reentered the
room, still topless and still perfectly at ease. She ran her fingers
through David's blond, matted hair.

"Darling, do you want to have a piece of toast before you go?
Otherwise get a cheese pie at the bakery on your way, that's much
easier, here's some change, luv. Get one for Emma as well. Now
off you go, you two, it's such a glorious day, I don't want you
hanging around the house!"

Penny kissed David on the cheek and puffed out the smoke
of her cigarette from the other side of her mouth. David grunted
something inaudible and Emma followed him outside into the
bright midmorning light.

· · ·

They walked along the main road, nibbling their fragrant cheese
pies without exchanging a word. It was very hot, there was no
wind. Nobody was around at that time of day. David took a turn
toward the beach, and stopped in front of the jetty.

"Should we go to the island?" he asked her.

Emma had feared this moment all summer long, though she
had prepared for it. Yet when the time had finally come, the task
seemed colossal. She looked at the island in the shimmering light.
It had never looked so far away.

"I don't have my flippers," she said, hoping that David might
change his mind and come up with a different plan. But he pulled
his hair behind his ear and smiled at her again.

"Okay, we'll take it slow getting there, then."

. . .

Emma prayed as she slowly advanced in her imperfect crawl. She prayed for her breath not to run out, for her legs not to get a cramp, for the water to keep still, for the wind not to rise, for the panic not to overwhelm her. There were so many elements— natural, physical and psychological—that had to be controlled and synchronized in order to avoid her drowning. The island loomed in the distance, looking hopelessly far, each time she opened her eyes. She prayed and prayed to an unknown God to keep her afloat and breathing. David was always slightly ahead of her; every now and then he turned to check that she was still behind him and raised an arm from the water to signal his presence. Emma tried to wave back, but the movement caused her to drop down, lose her rhythm and drink. The bitter taste of the sea in her mouth felt like the taste of her death and she decided to spare any extra movement. Her heart rate was speeding and her breath was shortening. Just past what seemed the midpoint, she felt a mix of desperation and rage building inside her chest. This would be the end of her, she knew. Just then she opened her eyes again and suddenly the island seemed much closer, almost reachable. She could see David, this time on terra firma, on top of a rock he had just climbed. She could hear him whistling a tune. Then, after only a few more strokes, her feet touched the rocky bottom.

. . .

It was done; she had made it. A gust of wind and the drone of the cicadas' chorus welcomed her to safety. She emerged from the water, her chest still heaving, rivulets of water streaming down to her feet, elated from the exertion like an athlete who has just won a race.

David whistled again, this time to signal his position. He was crouched on a slightly higher rock, looking out. His legs were long and thin like a stork's, so that his chin came to rest on top of his knees without having to bend. Scrambling up a couple of flat rocks she came up and sat next to him. David remained silent, as if he didn't want to be disturbed in his contemplation of the stretch of sea between them and the beach. She wondered whether it was up to her to start a conversation but decided it was more grown-up to be quiet. She was catching her breath, and anyway it still required an effort on her part to speak English. She had to pay a lot of attention to the sounds; often it felt like guesswork, pasting an unknown word to one she knew, and figuring out the meaning of the phrase that way. In order to keep pace her brain had to quiz and buzz at maximum speed. This was nice, to be quiet in this light breeze, the only sound being the bells of the goats. David lay flat on the rock and closed his eyes. Emma, still sitting upright, gazed at the white strip beneath his belly button, where his skin had not been exposed to the sun and his hip bones jutted forward; there was a thin shadow of fuzzy hair pointing down toward his crotch. Emma took her eyes away guiltily. She looked toward the beach opposite, toward the blue chairs of the taverna, where she could just about make out Monica's tiny shape sitting on the sand all by herself. She was a good girl, she'd stayed put, as she'd been told to do.

David sat up again.

"How did your mother die?"

Emma froze. She decided she had misunderstood the question.

"What?"

"Your mother." David spelled it out. "She died last year, right?"

Emma nodded.

"How?"

"It was an accident."

She turned her head down and tried to concentrate on her toenails. There was another silence, but this one was charged with tension. Emma held her breath, feeling David's eyes on her profile.

"Is it true she killed herself?"

Emma stared at him, speechless. David stared back with his big blue eyes widely set apart, waiting for an answer.

Emma's hands were shaking; she shook her head vigorously.

"No," she said. "She was in a car. It was an accident in a car."

"Penny said she drove off a bridge," he insisted.

"No, no," Emma said in one breath.

"She said it was a suicide," David pressed. Emma glared, and looked the other way. She felt her face turn red.

The idea that Penny might have had this conversation with her children and her husband at the kitchen table filled her with shame. When had the English boys learned about this? And why did David feel entitled to discuss this with her?

"It was an accident," she repeated forcefully.

"What happened?"

"I don't know—"

She searched for the word *exactly* but she couldn't find it anywhere. She knew this sounded dumb and unbelievable, despite its being the truth. So she added:

"I don't remember."

There was another silence. David seemed perfectly comfortable, as if they were having just any conversation about their favorite music. He hurled a couple of pebbles in the water, attempting to make them skip and bounce on the surface. Emma fixed her gaze on the tiny shape of Monica across the water. Her silhouette was moving up and down the beach mechanically. She could be playing something—maybe she was running after a ball—or might she be panicking, desperately looking for help? Monica didn't speak any English or any Greek and there was nobody around who could understand her if she was having a crisis. Emma felt that pang of guilt again, reminding her that she shouldn't have left her little sister all alone. If last summer Monica had seemed lighter—happier even—despite the tragedy that had just happened, this year she seemed more frightened, as if something darker had begun to sink in and bury itself inside her. Maybe she feared that they too—Emma, Luca, their father—could abandon her and leave her stranded in the blue taverna, because that was just what happened once you grew up. People left you.

David threw another pebble and this time it bounced three times.

"My mother died too," she thought she heard him saying.

Emma turned. This obviously couldn't be right. What had he said? His accent was harder for her to understand than Jack's.

"What?"

"I said that my mother also died."

Emma shook her head, as if to say she was confused. Maybe she had misunderstood the entire conversation.

"I am adopted. Penny is not my real mother."

"Oh. I'm sorry," she said awkwardly.

"She died when I was two and my real father had disappeared before I was even born. I was taken into an orphanage and Penny and Peter adopted me a few months later."

He paused. "But I don't remember any of that because I was too small."

Emma stared at him, stunned. Actually it made sense: he looked nothing like Penny or her husband. This whole story was so unexpected, it turned around the whole image she had had of the boys.

"And Jack? Is he . . ."

"No, Jack is their real son. He's four years younger than me. I was there when he was born, but I don't remember that either."

There was a pause. Emma felt she had to say something positive.

"You were lucky. Penny and Peter are very nice people."

It was a silly remark, but she didn't know what else to say. She resented David's confession. She didn't want him to think they shared a common destiny. Because they didn't.

A dark and unsettling feeling was beginning to creep in, like the first hint of nausea after eating a fish that didn't smell right. It was the forewarning of something more dangerous. She kept her eyes on her little sister, who now seemed to be running back and forth, like a crazy marionette.

"I need to go back," she said.

"Wait. We'll go in a minute."

And then without warning he was all over her. He grabbed her by the shoulders and sat on top of her on the flat rock, wrapping his storklike legs around hers. Emma felt the heat of his body, the pressure of his hips against hers, his foreign, bitter smell, enveloping her. His mouth pressed so hard on hers that her lips hurt against her teeth. This was so sudden and unexpected that she didn't have time to react, though in that fraction of time Emma managed to observe how inconceivable it was that this should be the right way to kiss: she had never expected it would be so wet and messy. His tongue was trying to pry open her lips, and Emma understood she was supposed to let it in—which she did—though she had no clue as to what to do next. His tongue started swirling around hers and she tried to cooperate by imitating the movement, despite finding everything about the kiss uncomfortable and slightly disgusting. The idea was for their saliva to merge— why on earth would one want to do that, spittle not being anybody's favorite thing? Something else was going on while she was busy moving her tongue in a circle, trying to escape David's—a difficult task in such a contained space—and it was happening in the lower part of her body. He was pushing against her hips and she began to feel his hard-on. She thought again of the thin trail of fuzz against the whiter area of his skin that she had glimpsed earlier, how it disappeared under his swimsuit heading toward what she knew was the most secret part of a man's body, a part she had never properly seen but only heard about. And there it was, swelling and pushing, clearly demanding something from her, which she had no idea how to reciprocate. Despite the discomfort and the terror to be treading on such uncharted territory, there was something Emma was enjoying in all this. It was difficult to tell what it was exactly: it was a warmth in her lower belly, an undistinguished longing, like a desire to open up, to allow him inside (but where? how?), mixed with the distant knowledge that this was the line that separated everything that she had been from what she was going to be from now on. That's when she felt David's hand fumbling inside her swimsuit, right between her legs. This was absolutely unheard of and was supposed to be terrifying. Half of her stiffened, the other half began to melt away.

· • ·

There had been a little pain, some blood and an unknown slimy substance glued to her legs that had made her uncomfortable. They had not said anything specific once it was over, they had just looked at each other, surprised, unsure as to what had happened and should be said or done next.

"I really have to go now." Emma had stood up, only then realizing how much her back hurt after lying on that rock with all that weight on top of her.

"Let's stay another minute. We can walk to the top. It's nice up there," David offered.

Emma's heart was still beating wildly; she had been a little scared throughout—she hadn't been able to see much, just quick flashes of skin, and was still unsure of the mechanics of the act itself—but now that it was over and done with she felt somewhat excited and proud. She was anxious to get away from David, and back to the beach to her brother and sister.

"Another time. My sister is waiting for me."

"Okay. See you later then," David said, quietly disappointed. He had gone back to being the slightly shy adolescent he was.

There was no trace left in him of that determination that had possessed him only minutes earlier. He sat back on the rock in the same position as before, chin on knees, looking out into space. He seemed used to being left behind.

Swimming back took no time. She skimmed the water like one of the pebbles David had hurled.

As soon as she jumped in, the goo and the blood between her legs washed away. She fixed her gaze on the beach. At every stroke the blue tables and chairs of Iorgo's taverna got closer and so did Monica, sitting at the head of the table where they had their meals, a small child all alone, waiting for her family to reappear and rescue her. Emma's breathing was steady, her strokes synchronized. The fluidity she had been pursuing all summer just came to her. She found herself gliding through the water effortlessly, as if her body had always known how to do it. The fear she'd had of drinking water or drowning had vanished. Getting to shore as fast as she could was all.

·　•　·

The crisis occurred that same afternoon, with the same abruptness of the downpour that marks the end of the summer.

The father and Mirella came back from Epidaurus in the early afternoon, earlier than expected. Luca and Emma were playing a game of backgammon at the table under the bamboo roof while Monica watched them. They could tell something had gone wrong by the way the father slammed the car door. He didn't even wait for Mirella to get out of the red Fiat but came straight to the table where the kids were playing, while she emerged from the passenger seat with her head slightly bent down and went straight up to her room without even saying hello to the children. He looked distraught and didn't say anything about the amphitheater, the beauty of the road, anything. He pulled out a cigarette from his crumpled pack and wiped the sweat from his brow with a handkerchief. When at last he looked at them, and asked how everyone was and if they'd been okay while he was gone, Luca and Emma just nodded, keeping their eyes on the board, rolling their dice.

"Emma swam to the island and back with the English boy," Monica said. She had been waiting all along for her retaliation to take place. The father turned abruptly to Emma, astonished.

"Did you?"

Emma feigned a smile; she wasn't sure whether his question meant he was proud of her feat. She nodded. He slapped her. Hard. Then turned to Luca.

"And where were you?"

"I . . . I was . . ."

"He was with Nadia in Kastraki. They both left me here," Monica said.

The father slammed his fist on the table and stood up.

"I've had enough of you two. I'm sick and tired of this!"

Emma covered her burning cheek with her hand. The father took Monica by the hand and left Emma and Luca without another word.

They looked at each other. Emma felt a terrible loneliness overcoming her all at once. She and Luca had been drifting more and more apart all summer to the point of becoming almost estranged. She understood something frightening was happening. Without their mother, there was no more center, no focus to hold them together. Pulled by an unknown centrifugal force, they were all breaking away from one another. Nadia, Mirella, the English boy, were only the beginning of their disintegration.

She opened her hand and moved it across the table. Luca took it.

·   ·   ·

Later that evening Mirella reappeared at the restaurant with the hesitant step of a convalescent. She looked around, sluggish and pale. Emma saw her approach in her peripheral vision, while she was letting Monica win at backgammon. The father was sitting next to them, immersed in his book. Peace and order had been silently restored. The girls exchanged a glance when the father reluctantly put his book away and stood up as if he had been summoned. Emma watched him and Mirella as they moved away along the beach into the blue light of dusk. She remembered being startled by the same image a year earlier, but now the scene had converted itself into a quieter, somber version of the previous summer. They were walking with caution, heads down, careful not to look at each other. Mirella seemed to be insisting on something the father would not agree with. They suddenly stopped and faced each other. The father made a couple of exasperated gestures, while Mirella, pleading and submissive, had the air of an obstinate victim. He took a step forward, leaving her behind. Mirella ran after him him and touched his arm. He shook her away. The father's gesture seemed so harsh and yet so intimate that Emma had to pull her eyes away from the scene. It pained her to see how desperate a woman could become.

It was late when the father came back. He was in a black mood and didn't make any effort at concealing it. He said he was sorry he had hit Emma earlier, though what she had done was dangerous and irresponsible. He said he needed her and Luca to look after Monica and he also needed them to help him with domestic tasks, as they were not children anymore. They were to be a team now. He articulated each word carefully, like someone rehearsing a speech. The way he was addressing them made them feel important, as if they'd been offered a promotion. He then said he felt it was time to head back home. He realized it was only mid-August and they were supposed to stay till the end of the month, but he was tired of the village. He didn't bother to come up with an excuse, a lie about work or some pretense emergency.

"You should please pack tonight so we can leave early tomorrow."

The children didn't protest. They had been brought up to

do what they were told. Mirella didn't show up for dinner. They would never see her again.

· • ·

Later that night Emma and Luca sat on the wooden floor of her room while Monica was fast asleep in her bed. Emma watched him open a tin box and pull out a cigarette. He lit it, blew out the smoke in one go and coughed.

"Since when do you smoke?"

"I do it only after dinner."

She watched him inhale again. He was such a beginner and the gesture made him look silly, just the opposite of how he was hoping to look. She decided not to tease him.

"That English boy. David, the blond one. He said something," Emma said. "Something crazy."

"What?"

"Something about Mom."

Luca tensed like a cat arching his back.

"Why was he even talking about her?"

"He said he'd heard a story."

"From whom?"

"His . . . his mother. You can't repeat it, though."

Luca's voice softened, like he knew what was coming.

"I won't. Tell me."

Emma knew that once she'd actually said the word, it would be between them for the rest of their lives. But there was no reason to keep it a secret anymore at this point. Everyone knew, they must. The aunts, the schoolteachers, the neighbors, even Penny and the English boys, Nadia and her large Greek family. And the father, of course. She knew Luca knew, just like she did. They'd just agreed never to say it out loud.

Emma glanced over to the bed where Monica was sleeping. She didn't know yet, Emma was sure of that, but in a few years she too was going to find out. Luca noticed Emma's fleeting look at their little sister. He gestured toward the door.

"We should have this conversation on the beach," he whispered.

Outside it was pitch-black, save for a sliver of moon high in the sky. Nobody was around and the only sound was the gentle lapping of the water. They sat very close on the cool sand, their shoulders and arms touching. They did need air, space—they needed darkness, to be able to talk about what they'd been avoiding for so long.

"Yes, it's much better out here." Emma smiled at Luca, grateful that he was her brother, that he was there, close again.

· • ·

It was early morning; only the birds broke the stillness, swooping underneath the bamboo roof in their search for leftover bread crumbs. Emma was sitting on top of her duffel bag outside the taverna's door while inside the father was settling the bill with Iorgo. The chorus of the same *sirtaki* song that had played all summer echoed from a speaker inside the large empty room despite the early hour. From where she was sitting she could see a portion of the two men leaning over a table where Iorgo scribbled numbers in his hesitant handwriting. She knew this was the last time she was going to see the beach and the island and wasn't quite sure what was required of her for an appropriate farewell. She felt languid and sentimental about leaving and wondered about performing some kind of ritual of goodbye.

"Oh, you're here."

In his travel clothes, dark shades, faded blue Lacoste shirt and long trousers, the father looked particularly efficient. He patted his pocket for his cigarettes.

"I'm going to load the car and we'll be ready to go in twenty minutes. Give me your bag, I'll put it in the trunk."

He seemed cheerful, now that his plan was being put into action. Emma stood up and let him take her duffel. She walked over to the water's edge with her flip-flops on, letting her feet sink a few inches in the soft sand. The water curled at her ankles.

"Hallo Emma . . ."

David had come up behind her in his slack swimsuit, holding his flippers. He stared at her dress, puzzled.

"Where are you going?" He shielded his eyes from the brilliance of the early-morning sun.

"Home. We are leaving now."

"Oh," he said, and looked away toward the island. Emma fixed her gaze on his bare chest. It was unreal, what had happened between them. She absolutely refused to understand what could have moved her. To allow him. To do *that*. It was unthinkable now.

"I thought you were staying till the end of August," he said, feigning indifference.

"My father wants to go home."

She knew he had come for her, eager and full of hope. She saw his long stork legs, his bony shoulders, how they were beginning to droop just a little. It should have been Jack, not him.

"Will you write to me?"

Emma looked the other way.

"I don't know. I don't have your address."

"Just wait a minute, please," he said.

David dropped his flippers and ran inside the taverna. He came back a few seconds later. He'd scribbled his address on a piece of the paper tablecloth and had put only his name on it: David Gallagher, 49 South Hill Gardens, London. So was that it? Because of what happened he now was the one who'd been able to claim her? She had obviously miscalculated the consequences and she had lost Jack without her knowing.

Luca appeared, with a heavy bag strapped across his shoulder, sweaty and agitated.

"Em, what are you doing still here? We are ready to go, get moving!"

Emma was relieved she had an excuse to leave David there. His hungry look repulsed her. Crumpling the note in her hand, she moved away and followed Luca to the car.

.   •   .

They never went back. Only Luca did, many years later while traveling with a girlfriend he intended to marry. He had made a point to detour to show her the village of his childhood. He sent Emma a postcard in flashy colors painted over a black-and-white photo. He had drawn an arrow pointing at an ugly five-story building: "This is where Iorgo's used to be. Nothing looks the same. Don't bother!!" Emma showed the postcard to her father. He put on his reading glasses and scanned the picture for a good thirty seconds, as if he were trying to single out someone he knew among the tiny figures crowding the beach in neat rows of umbrellas and sun chairs. The father had aged, put on weight, remarried. He handed the postcard back to Emma and made a face.

"He's so right. Never go back. It's always a disappointment."

In all those years the father had never found the right moment to discuss the accident with his children. At first because they were too young to be burdened with such an unforgiving truth, and once they were old enough he gathered that none of them wished to discuss it anymore. He assumed that by then they'd had enough time to process and digest their own version of the story and there was no need to dig any deeper. It wasn't true of course, but the children felt protective of him now; they'd become the ones who wanted to shield him from that memory, so they refrained from asking. In the course of time they worked secretly, collecting evidence that they exchanged and pieced together. Reconstructing the picture, finding the missing pieces, became part of the bond that held Emma and her siblings together. Each one of them brought something back to the puzzle—fragments, traces that they managed in time to extract from their aunts, their mother's closest friends, from letters and photos they found. Yes, Eleonora suffered from depression; yes, she was seeing a psychiatrist; yes, she was taking medication. No, it hadn't been anybody's fault. And no, it had not been an accident.

Although the information they'd collected was more than they needed to know, it didn't solve or settle anything, or help to soothe them.

·　•　·

In her early twenties, Emma fell in love with a young American biologist she'd met on a train to Florence. They had corresponded for a few months and then she had followed him to Boston. He lived in a dusty north-facing apartment in what she mistook for a nice neighborhood. She had momentarily dropped out of university in order to follow him—she was studying architecture, but without passion—and she got a job in a vegetarian restaurant to make some cash and get out of the house while he was at work. She thought she'd eventually get her working papers once the biologist married her and she'd be able to get a proper job. It was just a matter of time and patience. In the meantime she made delicious vegetable casseroles for dinner, which they ate while sprawled on the carpet in front of the fire. She admired the ease Americans had with their bodies, how they used objects and moved around the furniture with a freedom Europeans never had. How they took their work to bed, ate take-out food in the car, how they put their bare feet on the table, walked inside a bank in their shorts, used their cars as a cluttered closet where they could toss in just about anything. In Europe people had meals only if sitting at a table, only worked at their desks, hardly ever sat on the floor, never walked around the house in their bathrobes and socks. She wrote enthusiastic letters to her family and friends, describing her new life. She felt she had finally become the person she had always wanted to be. Someone who thought, dreamed and made love in a different language, who had acquired different habits and conformed to different rules of behavior.

By then her English was fluent and flawless, and she hardly had a trace of an accent. She made sure to pick up every mannerism and colloquial expression that might polish her new identity. Whenever someone asked her where and when she'd learned to speak such good English, she said something about a summer in Greece and an English boy named Jack she'd had a crush on. This tale, from which David had been conveniently omitted, had become the standard answer to the question and everyone always agreed with her answer: falling in love was surely the only way to learn a language properly. The fiction of Jack as her first love grew more and more solid. But it was impossible to completely erase David from her biography. He had the unshakable position of the boy to whom she'd lost her virginity.

Her happiness with the biologist didn't last. Within a year Emma fell out of love (she later admitted that she had been more in love with the idea of becoming an American than in love with him) and she moved to New York. Initially she had little hope of sustaining herself, but soon enough everything fell into place. Friends of friends offered her a place to stay; she got a part-time job with an architectural firm, moved into her own place and obtained a work visa. Three years later, on the day she received her green card, she got drunk on Champagne at eleven in the morning and declared to her friends, "It was my destiny. I always knew I belonged somewhere else."

.   .   .

A few months later, Emma flew to Rome to visit her family, where she lectured Luca and Monica on the benefits one had living in America. It was the usual litany about efficiency, good service, being able to return a clothing item even if already worn, getting your phone service up and running in a matter of minutes, being able to FedEx anything for a pittance, etc., etc. They resented being spoken to as if they were still living in the Middle Ages (they'd been subjected to her pro-America rhetoric before and were in tacit agreement that Emma's obsession to become an American was, to put it bluntly, pathetic).

Shortly after her arrival in Rome, Emma sat on a bench in the Piazza Navona eating a gelato while waiting to meet an old friend for a movie. It was a beautiful evening, warm and clear, and the large oblong square was busy with tourists taking pictures of the Fountain of the Four Rivers, while swifts flitted overhead. She was early and had a little time to contemplate the scene. She observed a crowd of Korean women in floppy hats, dark shades and with short legs entering the church of Saint Agnes in an orderly line; a mime with a face plastered in white set up his portable speaker, getting ready for his act; and children riding their bicycles in circles, oblivious to their mothers' calls. Emma felt buoyant, something of a tourist herself, able to look at every detail with a fresh eye.

The mime's sound track boomed from the speakers. It was, predictably, a frenzied piano score from a silent film. He was dressed in a business suit and his gig was about having to lift a very heavy suitcase. His efforts seemed titanic. The suitcase wouldn't move. He signaled a child to step out of the circle of onlookers and gestured for him to lift the suitcase for him, which the child did, effortlessly. People cheered and laughed. Emma smiled at the naïveté of the performance, and slid back into her musings. She saw that now that she lived in another country she had been able to develop a completely different affection for Rome. She no longer felt responsible for any of the things that had humiliated her in the past. The graffiti on the walls, the garbage on the streets, the potholes, the hideous traffic, the cheap tourist menus, the cheeky café waiters: none of it concerned her anymore, it was pure folklore.

Suddenly Emma felt a shift of energy around her and realized the circle of onlookers were now looking at her. The mime seemed to have zeroed in on her as his next assistant. She shook her head a couple of times and mouthed "no, no" but he ignored her and leaped forward, stretching his hand out. She spoke under her breath.

"No. No, please. Someone else, please. I can't."

But he already had her by the wrist and was pulling her in. The audience signaled their approval with applause. It was too late, he was already pointing at the suitcase. Obediently Emma lifted it: it was empty and weightless. The mime feigned bewilderment; he scratched his head like a clown and gestured for her to carry it over to his left. She did. More head scratching, more laughter from the audience, then he pointed to his far right. Emma complied, wanting to be done with it as fast as possible. He stood next to her and tried to lift the suitcase in vain. It really did look as if the suitcase weighed a ton. People clapped and cheered. Before she could take her exit, the mime grabbed Emma's arm and whispered in English.

"Wait. I think I know you."

"What?"

"Are you Emma?"

Emma stared at the white mask, the eyes penciled in black. A panda face.

"I'm Jack. Don't you remember? Jack from Kastraki beach."

.   .   .

He asked her to wait for him to finish his gig but she told him she had only fifteen minutes, she was supposed to be somewhere.

"Fifteen minutes. I need to wash my face. I can't talk to you with this stuff on."

"Yes. Sure. Fine. I'll wait for you over there." She pointed to one of the cafés bordering the square.

She kept an eye on him from where she sat. She watched him close his act in a hurry, gather his things and store them behind a potted plant. He washed his face with a sponge, at one of the water fountains.

When he sat at the table she recognized him. It was Jack all right, but a deflated version of younger Jack, his skin no longer so taut, some creases in his forehead. Still handsome, brown-eyed Jack, though, with a full head of hair. In his haste to meet her he'd left some smears of white makeup on his face. He stared at her, bewildered.

"I just knew it was you the minute I touched you. Your eyes. I never forgot them."

They each ordered a glass of red. He told her he had been studying with a famous French mime in the south of France, that he lived in Marseilles and he did street shows—that's what he called them—to make some cash when traveling. To justify this rather vague description of his life he said the previous year he'd performed at Avignon's theater festival with a Belgian company Emma had never heard of; she pretended to be impressed.

She told him she lived in Manhattan and worked for an architecture studio. No, she wasn't married and no, she didn't have children. Yes, she lived by herself, in a small one-bedroom apartment downtown.

He seemed relieved and smiled. He had bad teeth now, she observed. They were jumbled and yellowing, the teeth of a person who hasn't been taking care of them. Yet he didn't seem self-conscious about his smile.

"Do you still have your house in Greece?" she asked.

"Oh no. Mummy sold it years ago. She and Dad divorced. The money from the sale was part of the settlement."

"I'm sorry to hear that."

"Don't be. They'd been fighting like cats and dogs for years; we actually couldn't wait for them to divorce."

Emma took a small sip of wine. It was the kind of cheap Chianti they served in those tourist traps. The conversation seemed to be heading nowhere. She thought of something to say to relaunch it.

"How is David doing?"

"David died. Six years ago," Jack said.

Emma felt something in her chest, a sinking feeling.

"What happened?"

"Drugs, I'm afraid." He made a face and tilted his head sideways.

Emma closed her eyes for a second.

"Oh my God."

"Yeah."

They stared at each other for a few seconds, not knowing what to say. Emma thought she should grab his hand across the table. But Jack gulped his wine and looked away, above her head.

"Well, David always had problems. Dyslexia, depression, then drugs."

He paused, then tried a smile, to lighten up the mood.

"They all start with a *d,* like his name. I wonder what that means. Doom and disgrace, maybe?"

Emma didn't know how to answer; she was feeling increasingly uncomfortable. It all sounded so hopeless.

"You know, he was an adopted child, and maybe that was part of the problem," Jack continued. "He never felt he fit anywhere. At least that's what Mum thinks."

There was a silence. Jack seemed to be thinking about something, while he contemplated the froth of the Bernini fountain across from them. Emma was desperately trying to come up with the right thing to say. He turned to her.

"He had a huge crush on you, you know?"

She said nothing.

"He used to talk about you quite often. Every summer he'd say, 'I wonder if Emma is coming back.' He didn't know how to find you. I guess you hadn't exchanged addresses."

"No. In fact. We didn't."

Jack looked at Emma intensely, then smiled.

"And here I am, running into you by chance in Rome. He would have been so chuffed to know that I'd found you."

Emma smiled and nodded. Then she managed to squeeze in a quick look at her watch.

"I'm so sorry Jack, but I'm afraid I have to . . ."

"Sure. How long are you here for? I'd love to see you again, so we can catch up."

"Of course, I'd love to."

They made an appointment for the next evening at the same café.

"Afterward we could go for a pizza. If you have time, I mean," Jack suggested.

"Yes, why not? I know a good place around the corner."

She grabbed the outrageously expensive check and left some change on the table. Jack protested.

"No, please. Let me take care of it."

"Don't even try, this is my turf."

They hugged awkwardly. He smelled of sweat and wine. He held her an extra second, just as she was about to pull away.

"God, I am so happy I found you, Emma," he said, close to her face. "You have become such a beautiful woman."

Emma held her breath, fearing it might be possible that he would kiss her. They lingered for a few seconds in that dangerous proximity, then he let her go.

She turned around once more to wave goodbye from a secure distance. Jack was still sitting at the table. He lifted his wineglass in a toast, leaning back in his chair, his legs wide open, like a satisfied man enjoying his place in the world.

She walked away fast. She had already made up her mind not to show up the next night.

· • ·

Many years later she told the story of this chance encounter to the man she had married. He didn't understand what she was trying to convey. He was a furniture designer, a person with a strong practical sense—who found Emma's penchant for introspection both charming and alien. What was the point of the story? People did run into each other. It happened all the time.

"A mime," she said. "He was a *mime*."

They were driving a rented SUV through the Arizona desert. She had a map on her lap and was in charge of directions.

"Yes, I got that," he said. "But what made you feel so bad? Didn't you say you had been in love with him? Or was it the brother? I'm not sure I understand."

"No, not in love exactly. Although . . ."

She didn't know how to explain why the story had stayed with her all those years and why it still pained her. It had to do with many things at once; the passing of time marring Jack's once beautiful teeth; David's expression when she swam off the island, the look of defeat and resignation of a child used to being left behind. And the expression on Jack's face as he toasted to their reunion, when it was she who had turned her back to him in Piazza Navona.

"I guess what I mean is . . . in some ways I wouldn't be who I am today if it wasn't for those two. I wouldn't even speak English. I doubt I would have married you," she said.

She looked out the window at the vast expanse of the desert dotted by cacti under the cobalt blue sky, at the long trail of clouds hanging over the horizon, as if in a scene from an old western.

"They were my inspiration," she said, and realized she was almost on the verge of tears.

"That can't possibly be it," her husband was saying.

"Why not?"

"We should've taken the left at the gas station fifty miles back. I knew it."

He flapped his hand impatiently and pulled the car over.

"Just hand me that map, Emma."

Chanel

It was early September, the air still balmy, the perfect weather for a Venetian escapade. Caterina and Pascal were sitting in a café across a canal divining their future, in a quiet *campo* off the beaten track, away from the tourists and the film crowd who had invaded the city for the festival. They sipped their frothy iced cappuccinos, basking in the sun, their eyes fixed on its refractions dotting the greenish canal with specks of glitter. They felt that for once things were beginning to look promising for both of them.

Pascal had just fallen in love with a man in Paris and was going to move there in the fall. His intention was to get a job in a restaurant at first, give himself a little time to learn French well enough so he could find an agent and start acting in French films. This was of course an utterly delusional plan, but Pascal suffered from a very particular kind of blindness: he never took into consideration potential obstacles that might be looming ahead of his designs. It wasn't clear whether he simply ignored them or had a special technique for dodging them; the fact remained he did find success with most of the crazy schemes he pursued. Whereas Caterina—due to a more pragmatic approach to life or perhaps to a lack of self-confidence—didn't trust her resources enough and spent much of her time worrying about futile things. Recently she had been worrying quite a lot about Pascal moving out of the apartment they'd shared for almost three years. Not only because she was going to miss him terribly and she'd have to replace him with another roommate (although nobody could replace Pascal), but because she feared that, along with Pascal, the scent of his positive take on life was going to fly out the window and follow him to France, abandoning her.

Then, unexpectedly something miraculous happened.

Only a week earlier, while she was stuck in traffic in Via Nazionale on the 64 bus, Pascal had rung her.

"Cate, you are there! I am looking at your name right now in the paper! No joke!"

She couldn't scream or jump up, firmly lodged as she was between a large West African woman with a complicated hairdo and a man in a shabby jacket who was exhaling garlic fumes into her nostrils. She managed to wiggle out and get off at the next stop, bought the paper and, standing right in front of the newsstand, flipped through the pages. She skipped the earthquake, the war, the fall of the government, the catastrophic financial page and went straight to Entertainment.

There it was. Her name. She had been nominated.

She had played with the word for a few days. It felt like such a prodigious thing—to be *no-mi-na-ta*!—something akin to King Arthur touching her forehead with his sword and turning her instantly into a knight. Actually she had been nominated along with another four directors for a minor category—best short film—for the David Awards, the Italian version of the Oscars—like the Césars in France, the BAFTAs in England and whatever it's called in Spain, all Cinderella versions of the real thing. But, because she'd never been nominated for anything before in her life, this felt like her greatest achievement so far.

Her short was a documentary about a team of synchronized swimmers training for the Olympics. Young girls who composed amazingly intricate patterns in the pool—six-pointed stars, budding flowers, comets and rainbows—but who, once in the locker room, became savagely antagonistic toward one another. The concept was harmony versus disruption, discipline versus unleashed emotions—a sensual, stark portrait of female competition. The short had hardly any dialogue: Caterina had concentrated mostly on the composition of the shots, lighting, angles and a carefully engineered editing. The film was only thirteen minutes long, its budget just fifteen thousand euros, a surprisingly low amount that had been painstakingly put together by herself and her producer, Marco Guattari, a thirty-something energetic film buff and Ritalin addict with amazing focus and determination. Caterina had sold her vintage Beetle for four thousand euros and Marco had managed to borrow the rest from his cousin—an obsessive comics collector—who'd just won quite a crazily vast sum on a TV quiz show, answering a tricky question involving a lesser known Tintin adventure. The idea was to pay the cousin back once they sold the film to a network, but at the moment they didn't feel pressed to oblige, as the cousin had vanished somewhere in Brazil, where he was apparently spending money left and right without a care in the world.

According to a few seminal bloggers, Caterina's short had an uncanny quality. Her filming had been described as "stark and illuminating." Another brief account was nestled in *Corriere della Sera,* within an article about upcoming filmakers. "The manner by which Caterina De Maria exhibits the female body in water—in a flowing ballet that alternates between gracefulness and herculean exertion, elegance and cruelty—has an almost Wagnerian quality. Are we meant to think of her swimmers merely as athletes, or as marine monsters? De Maria's subtle and unusual work here marks a promising debut. Next time we hope to see her name linked to a full-length feature."

· • ·

To celebrate the sudden turn their lives had taken, Caterina and Pascal had decided to spend a long weekend in Venice, for a full cultural immersion, combining the Art Biennale and the Venice Film Festival on the Lido, two events that coincided that September and attracted voracious international crowds. They shared a large double bed in a tiny pensione near Le Zattere that, despite its funereal lighting, the musty walls and the yellowing curtains, was outrageously expensive. Just as expensive as the stale prepackaged sandwiches they were forced to live on, sold at every corner to desperate tourists, and as the tickets for the Biennale and for the vaporettos that shuttled them back and forth between Venice and the Lido. But they'd decided to ignore the money issue, since this was a time of celebration. Although they hadn't succeeded in eliciting a single invitation to any of the star-studded parties held nightly in glamorous and often secret venues, not even for a mere Bellini offered by a film distributor or for one free lunch, they still felt entitled to be there. Caterina's nomination had upgraded both of them from outsiders to quasi celebrities.

Venice, of course, was playing its subliminal part, its time-honored postcard soul contributing to lift Pascal and Caterina beyond the realm of reality. The minute they stepped off the train onto the vaporetto at Piazzale Roma, they agreed—as absolutely everyone else does the minute they step off the train—that Venice was incredible, so incredible that one forgot it did exist and had a life of its own outside films and novels. The transition from the train ride in a stuffy second-class compartment to Venice sliding past in its algaeish green and gilded glory was so fast that all the clichés inevitably crystallized within that first nautical ride: there it was, a dissolute and dissolving city built on water, impervious to passing centuries, moldy and decaying, its canals strewn with gondolas and paddling gondoliers, where slow barges carried loads of wood, boxes of fruit and vegetables or stacks of furniture piled up high as they had for centuries, its skyline of palazzi and bridges identical to Canaletto's and Turner's paintings. A place where nobody could escape the cheap fantasy of one day renting an attic overlooking the Grand Canal to do something artistic, like writing a novel or beginning to paint at last.

. • ·

Pascal and Caterina had spent the first day strolling through the Art Biennale in the Giardini. They went from pavilion to pavilion following an orderly geographical sequence: France, Italy, England, then Germany and Scandinavia (Pascal had method, nothing was random under his direction). He was in a state of overexcitement, determined to gorge himself on as much art as he could in one go. He believed in expanding his knowledge with the hunger of a connoisseur constantly searching for yet another enriching item to add to his collection. Pascal believed in knowledge per se, as if the sheer act of recognizing an artist, his or her particular style, and therefore being able to cast him or her in the correct mental file, would contribute to bringing more order to the universe. He flew through the large pavilions in a state of ecstasy, naming different artists Caterina had never heard of, pointing out the differences between their old works and the new ones (derivative! fresh!), rushing her to see abstruse videos she didn't really understand (staggering! so modern!), avoiding some installations like the plague (jejune! pathetic!), forcing her to sit for fifteen minutes in silence in front of an inexplicable sculpture (breathtaking!).

After a few hours Caterina began to experience a sense of overload, the first symptoms of art fatigue. The works started blurring together and her receptors weakened, like batteries dying out. She was jealous of the way Pascal seemed to be impressed by each work like photographic paper in a bath of acid. For long minutes at a time, she studied the elusive installations, longing to be fed the same nutrient, but she felt nothing other than a sense of being excluded. All she could think of was resting her aching feet and having a slice of pizza. Pascal gestured for her to follow through a small door and they entered a cubicle. The space was bathed in a lavender light. It wasn't clear what the medium was: swaths of color that weren't a painting as in a Rothko or Flavin's fluorescent tubes, but pure diffused light coming from above, as if the artist had managed to take a portion of the desert sky at dawn, and pour it into the cubicle through the ceiling. There were two other visitors sitting on the bench right in the middle of the room, completely silent and inebriated. They had clearly been in there having their own mystical experience for some time and they looked at Caterina and Pascal with scarcely repressed resentment, as squatters trespassing on their land. Caterina whispered an apology and sat quietly on the floor. She let herself drown in the pale blue mist that filled the room like a vapor. Soon she felt mesmerized by its nothingness, its lack of complication. A cloud of peace—that was maybe the idea. Pascal stood behind her, silent and impenetrable, but Caterina could tell he too was moved. Moved by what? she then asked herself. Was it the absence of structure, of subject; was it just its mystery? She knew better not to say anything. Nothing annoyed Pascal more than other people compelled to ask the meaning of contemporary artworks.

. . .

The next day Caterina and Pascal were patiently waiting in line at the cashier in a crowded café outside the Palazzo del Cinema after the midmorning screening. This was the busiest time of the day, when everyone's blood sugar level was at its lowest and people were ready to pay up to nine euros for the crappy panini with congealed cheese that looked like melted plastic. They'd just seen a three-and-a-half-hour-long documentary about an aging rock star from the seventies, who had retired from the stage at the peak of his career, vanishing somewhere at the feet of the Himalayas searching for answers and then retreating to an island off the coast of Spain.

While Pascal was waiting to order their sandwiches, Caterina felt an undertow of despair envelop her for no apparent reason. She tried to shake it off, but the feeling clung to her like a spiderweb. It definitely had something to do with the documentary they'd just seen. She kept thinking of the mega rocker's last interview. It was a time when he already knew he had cancer and only a few months to live. He was speaking directly into the camera, staring straight at the audience with a bold expression, seated on a stool in the middle of his vast, beautiful Spanish garden under the shade of a tall walnut tree. Right behind him soft clumps of different grasses lay beneath a bamboo grove, their silvery and purple plumes dangling in the breeze. Here and there dots of bright color—anemones, daffodils, alliums—glinted among the flickering grasses so that the wild, open feeling of the garden suggested it had grown spontaneously, as if designed by nature itself. The man called it "my last and everlasting oeuvre," which he had created in the last twenty years of his life. He had explained how looking after it had made him as deliriously happy as all the music he'd written over thirty years. It was a continuation of the same creative impulse, the only difference being that it hadn't made him any richer. Here he had laughed.

"If anything, the money only kept pouring out. I guess that is karmically fair, isn't it?" he asked, staring into the camera with his deep-set eyes.

One could see why just by looking at the magnificent landscape behind him: his garden brimmed with life just as his music had. Caterina felt a terrible sorrow for the man's death, for his absence—the world needed more enlightened people like him—and sorry for herself, for getting older, for being mortal, for all the music she still wanted to hear, the books she intended to read, the places she had meant to visit, the things she had promised herself she'd learn one day (the history of Egypt, French, raku pottery, sign language, violin) and probably never would because time was beginning to feel like a fast express train that no longer stopped at all the stations.

The rock star, his beautiful garden, his lovely songs, the pale blue room at the Biennale and the stark, pristine feeling it inspired,

the Turner brume over the Venetian canals in the evening—it all
came tumbling back like an ache. Caterina was surprised to realize that all the beauty she'd been exposed to in the last forty-eight
hours had piled up inside her and had turned itself into a burden
that now was weighing on her chest. Something began to give
deep inside, like a building crumbling in slow motion, folding
gently onto itself. Pascal had almost reached the cashier.

"Do you want prosciutto and Brie or tomatoes and mozzarella?" he asked her.

"Prosciutto and Brie, thank you. Oh, and a Diet Coke."

True beauty eluded her and made her feel lonelier because she
knew she would never be able to access it or grasp its fabric. It
wasn't something one could either pull apart like a doll, or study
its components and reproduce. You couldn't just learn it. The
dying man had always had this gift and he had been able to pass
it on to others, in different forms, throughout his life. This was
probably why—though he had only a few months left to live—he
was able to stare straight into the camera. He had given all that he
had taken, his accounts were even.

Pascal placed the rubbery sandwich in front of her, tightly
sealed in its plastic wrap.

"My gluten-free regime has gone out the window." He sighed
as he bit into his sandwich. "I feel so bloated already."

Her short film was a laughable attempt at creating something
poetic. She had been nominated, but what did it mean? Wasn't it
all a farce? A mediocre, worthless farce?

Right there and then, as her heart sank even deeper, her
gaze landed on a handsome face. A young man holding a
glass of Champagne standing at the counter next to a couple
of interesting-looking women who spoke Italian with a heavy
French accent smiled at her. Thick dark hair tied in a short
ponytail, impeccable gray suit over a black T-shirt, round glasses
with a thick frame. A studied Johnny Depp look. He excused

himself, moved away from the women and maneuvered through the crowd toward her.

"Caterina!"

"Hey!" she waved joyfully. She had no idea who he was, though she had a feeling she ought to.

"Congratulations. I'm really happy you made it with the nominees."

"Thank you, thank you so much. Yeah, that was a big surprise . . . ," she said shyly, her brain still in a blank.

"I just wanted to say that I loved your short and that I voted for you."

"Oh my God! Did you? I'm so . . . ," she gasped, wishing his name would pop up any second, so she could relax. Was he on the jury panel for the awards? His face was vaguely familiar; she frantically scrolled an invisible contact list but nothing showed.

"God, thank you so much. Wow. Really. I mean . . . what can I say? That's so generous of you."

The handsome man smiled, leaned a tiny bit closer and Caterina was enveloped in an expensive aroma of leather, cedar, musk.

"You have an unusual eye. Your short reminded me of Jane Campion's early films."

"Oh my God! That's like . . . Jane Campion? . . . She's my favorite director ever. That's the biggest compliment. Thank you so, so much."

She could feel Pascal staring at her with reproach. Surely he meant to flag that something in her demeanor was bothering him. She had a feeling it must be the way she kept wriggling and squealing. She was aware of doing something funny with her feet, pointing them inward and twisting her ankles, an annoying reflex that came up whenever she was anxious.

"I'd love to talk to you about something. Which hotel are you staying at?" the man asked.

"Hmm . . . we are staying at the . . . at the . . ." She turned to

Pascal for help but he signaled a nearly imperceptible no with his head.

An ascending cymbal ringtone floated between her and the man. He took out the phone from his pocket and glanced at the display.

"Sorry, I have to take this. I'll tell you what, just give me a call at the office when you come back, that'll be easier . . . It was really lovely to see you, Caterina."

He turned around and walked toward the exit.

Pascal shook his head, frowning.

"Why do you start every phrase with *Oh my God*? You sound like a twelve-year-old. You've got to stop doing that. It's really bad."

"Who is he?" she asked.

"Are you kidding? Giovanni Balti."

"Oh my God!"

"You see? It's like a tic. And stop acting like you are an impostor. It's so irritating. He voted for you because you are good at what you do."

"I was confused, I kept thinking who the hell is this guy? I just couldn't concentrate. Balti? I wish I had remembered. I had no idea he was so attractive."

Balti's aroma had made her dizzy. The reflective, elusive, desirable producer so many people she knew, including herself, dreamed of working with. Somehow, in that crowded café, among the tinkling sounds of cups and spoons and the hissing of the espresso machine, she felt a gentle shift take place under her feet. It was a physical sensation, like the harbinger of a fault running horizontally, severing her from the life she had been living till then. Caterina felt a combination of panic and exhilaration.

Yes, her new life must be waiting just around the corner from that crowded café, ready for her to slip into it. There was nothing to fear, all major changes tend to come in a flash, unannounced—like floods and fires.

. • .

So there they were the following day, their last in Venice, divining their future over iced cappuccinos, basking in the tepid September sun. The waiter brought the check on a plate.

"Fifteen euros," noted Pascal, arching an eyebrow.

"I'll get this," she said, feeling famous and beautiful again. She picked up the check and left a five-euro tip. She stood up, triumphant.

"What shall we do now? No more art, please. I'd say we've seen enough," she said, excavating some authority over Pascal from the depths of her soul.

"Fine. Let's go try on some clothes, then," Pascal suggested.

Pascal loved fashion in the same way he loved art. He thought of clothes as beautiful objects to be looked at, sampled, felt, experienced. Designer shops to him were the equals of galleries. One should walk in and try on whatever one wanted, just to enjoy the tactile experience.

It was a game they'd played before and there were rules that had been established. Pascal had mastered the technique to the point of perfection. Caterina had watched him walk with a confident stride into Christian Dior, Louis Vuitton and Hermès on the Via Condotti in Rome and ask for a jacket, a pair of trousers, a coat. Salesmen flocked because of his confidence and good looks, certain he must be a celebrity. The way he went straight to the rack, testing the fabric, shaking his head—at times even grimacing—as if nothing truly convinced him, was admirable. He would then ask for something *more* formal, with less of this and more of that. Money clearly wasn't the issue, he was careful never to ask the price.

Once, at Gucci, he had tried a black evening coat lined in wolf fur. He looked fabulous and impossibly dramatic. The salesmen surrounded him while he studied himself in the mirror showing the usual dissatisfaction. Caterina had kept quietly in the background (she was always nervous whenever they played the game) but that once, taken by a sudden inspiration, she felt confident enough herself and had stepped in closer.

"This would be perfect for the St. Petersburg concert," she had said out loud, looking straight at him through the mirror with an amused expression. She expected a sign of recognition or gratitude from Pascal for her brilliant idea (an orchestra conductor, of course! Who else would need a wolf-lined evening coat?). Instead he had glanced at her with an icy frown—as if to say, "That was ruinous, why did you have to do that"—and immediately took the coat off.

"I don't like anything in this shop," he declared and dropped the coat in the hands of a young man with a perfectly shaped goatee and a diamond earring.

For her part Caterina never possessed the guts to look sufficiently dissatisfied with the clothes so that she and Pascal could leave a shop making the salespeople feel inadequate and not the other way round. So, whenever it was her turn to try on something, Pascal would have to support the act by playing the irritable costume designer, the fussy buyer, the purist. He knew exactly when it was time to end the game and had his own exit strategy figured out. He would look at each dress with an air of exasperation that bordered on disdain, to show how unimpressed he was to begin with. If he felt the salesgirls were getting in any way pushy by praising the dress too much, or saying how becoming it looked on Caterina, how it perfectly fit her svelte figure, he would stare thoughtfully at her reflection in the mirror, incline his head to the side, tapping his chin with a finger, and say nothing for what felt like a long time. Then he'd turn away.

"Sorry, darling, but it just isn't you. And I'm afraid we are running late for our next appointment."

Caterina would have to change back into her clothes and he would lead her outside the shop in a rush, as if they'd wasted another hour of their precious time.

"Your turn," Pascal said, stopping in front of the window of the Chanel boutique in a corner right behind Piazza San Marco.

Caterina laughed. Sure, why not. On a day like this even she could brave Chanel. To her it spoke of *Breakfast at Tiffany's,* of the impossible dream of the penniless but eternally chic girl.

. . .

The shop was empty. Thick carpet, soft lighting. Sweetly scented. Pascal had sunk onto a white armchair and leaned back like a director before an audition he doesn't believe in. Someone had brought him an espresso in a tiny porcelain cup with pebbles of brown sugar in a silver bowl. Two salesgirls in shiny ballet pumps and little black dresses with golden chains, hair tied back in chignons, presented themselves. How could they help?

"We are looking for evening wear. Something soft, chiffony. It has to be luscious and light," Pascal said in his husky voice.

"Of course, sir. Black?"

"Yes, but not just. Surprise me!" He winked at them.

The salesgirls beamed, enraptured. They loved a whiff of petulance, it was so Chanel. They scuttled off.

The dressing room was like a private boudoir, with enough space for lounging and even taking a nap on the velvety couch if one felt like it. Soon it filled up with organza, feathers, sequins. Clouds of silk and tulle, in black, peach, cream, azure and jade green, hung on the walls. Caterina slipped out of her skinny jeans and T-shirt. She stood in front of the mirror in her bra and panties, slackened from too many harsh detergents, and looked at her pale, unmade face, her red tousled hair pinched on the tip of her head with a plastic hairclip. She regretted not having done her face up a bit that morning, and wished she'd remember to always have at least her Rouge Noir lipstick handy.

One of the girls in black knocked lightly at the door and slid inside, holding two boxes. She pulled out two different pairs of shoes from the crinkly paper. A shiny black patent leather sandal with a five-inch heel and a powdery pink one with a grosgrain bow on the tip.

"This one for the black and the other for the pastel colors."

Caterina nodded and took the shoes, one pair in each hand. They were truly exquisite objects.

"These are the sandals from our cruise collection," the girl said with a solemn expression.

"Please, let me help you with the dress. Shall we start with black?" suggested the other one.

Getting inside the first dress was like diving through a shimmering substance, each molecule of the fabric caressing her skin. She felt fresh, exuberant, feminine. Her skin flushed.

The two girls in black zipped her up, fastened hooks and buttons, fluffed the fabric, tucked the silk, slid her unpedicured feet into the shiny shoes and sent her out with moans of approval. Each time she wobbled out in front of Pascal (sprawled on the candid armchair, now munching a tiny buttery croissant), she attempted to do an ironic pirouette and in doing so caught a fleeting reflection of herself in the multiple mirrors.

Each time Pascal would stare at her for a few seconds without moving a muscle. The two girls in black would be waiting for the verdict, holding their breath. Pascal invariably shook his head slowly, smiling at them with a hint of disappointment.

"Shall we see something else, please?"

Once the black dresses came to an end, Pascal asked to see the pastels, letting transpire that despite the fact that his faith in the cruise collection was beginning to fade, he was still willing to give the Chanel girls another chance. He glanced at the time on his watch, to suggest that he and Caterina didn't have all day.

The girls helped her out of a gorgeous pleated chiffon affair, and into a lacy, vaporous pale yellow, shortly followed by a light blue, then pink, then peach, then white variations of the same ethereal idea. Pascal, sipping a glass of sparkling San Pellegrino, remained inscrutable.

It was getting late; the girls in black had lost some of their initial composure. A film of sweat shone on their upper lips and their immaculate hairdos were beginning to lose structure.

The last dress was simpler than all the others, less constructed, sleeveless and knee-length, but the color was a shade of azure green so perfect it almost didn't exist in nature. Maybe an alpine lake reflecting the woods on a pale morning would come close. Tiny feathers in the same delicate shade floated at the hem and trimmed the collar, giving it a sense of lightness. Caterina walked out once more on the powdery pink heels, in a more assured stride, and again she looked at the multiple images of herself in the mirrors. The aquamarine shade of the dress enhanced her copper hair and the whiteness of her skin. Pascal stared at her and this time his silence had a different quality. She remained still, a hand bent backward resting on her hip, as she'd seen models on the catwalk do. The girls in black were right behind her, hopeful.

"That's stunning," Pascal said.

His words filled the carpeted space. The girls in black sighed.

Yes, the dress was *stupendo, meraviglioso, elegantissimo*.

Caterina glanced at Pascal, a quizzical look on her face. He stood up and moved toward her.

"No, I really mean it. It looks fantastic on you. You should get it."

The girls in black were already chirping behind her. Of course, of course, they too agreed this was the best dress of all, the color, the shape, *tutto assolutamente perfetto*.

"How much is it?" Pascal asked, with the authoritative tone a man uses when he has finally made up his mind.

·   •   ·

Caterina had shot out of the boutique like a bullet, after an excruciating five minutes attempting to extricate herself from the enthusiasm of the girls in black. Pascal hadn't offered any help. He had let her deal with them, keeping two steps behind, while she blabbered the usual excuse (I have to think about it) and headed for the door. Outside the light of the afternoon had turned into a golden yellow, the shadows of the buildings had stretched to the edge of the canal.

"You broke the rules! Why did you do that?" she said, burning with shame.

"Because I do think you should buy it."

"Are you out of your mind? It's three thousand four hundred euros!"

"It's the least expensive of all. The black ones all cost around ten. Some even fifteen."

"So what? I can't spend that much anyway."

"It's an investment."

"I don't need that kind of investment."

"You do. You sure do, my dear."

Pascal turned around and started to walk away, leaving her behind. He did this to annoy her. She sprang behind him.

"Oh yeah? And how many times would I wear it? Once, twice tops, in my entire life!"

Pascal stopped in his tracks and swiveled toward her.

"You have just been nominated for a David Award. An award that will be nationally televised. I happen to know exactly what's hanging in your closet, Cate. And I know you have absolutely nothing to wear, other than rags."

"I already thought about that and I will borrow a dress from my friend Tina."

"You are twenty-nine and you still live like a student. It's pathetic."

"I can't afford to spend that much money on a dress. It's fucking crazy!" she exploded.

"That's exactly what I mean. This is the kind of attitude that reflects on every aspect of your life. Your film is going to win, I know it for a fact. And you are going to step up on that stage in someone else's dress, a dress that won't fit you right, in a pair of ugly shoes, and you will look just like another charmless, scruffy independent filmmaker. Fine, if that's who you think you are."

Caterina turned white with indignation and shock. This didn't deter Pascal, who went on.

"You keep thinking anything you achieve is by fluke, by God's gift or by some random benevolence? That you don't deserve the attention, that you are an impostor in a world you don't belong to? Great. Then keep on behaving like this and people will start believing it too. Their excitement about you will taper off, they will see you as less talented, less interesting, less *special*, because this is exactly what you project. Sorry."

He made a move to cross the street but Caterina grabbed him by the arm.

"What people? Who are you talking about exactly?"

"I don't know. *People.*"

"You mean a producer, like Balti?"

"Possibly." He put on his dark glasses. "Forget about it. Let's just go, okay?"

Whatever energy they'd just been floating on a few minutes earlier was gone. She had pierced the balloon with a pin and it had popped.

"What would you like to do now? You want to go back to the Lido and watch another film?" she asked.

"I'm starving. I need something to eat." Pascal looked the other way.

She hated to have disappointed him. Suddenly she knew their time together in Venice had peaked inside Chanel, and that from now on things would go downhill. The rest of the adventure would turn into endless bickering over the tiniest choices.

"Wait."

She reached up and slid his dark glasses off his nose with the tip of her fingers so she could see his eyes.

"You know it would be complete madness, don't you?"

"Not at all. It means raising the stakes. It's about feeling good about yourself and stepping up." Pascal slid his glasses back against his brow.

Caterina took a deep breath. There were moments in life that were like thresholds. Caterina distinctly felt that she was crossing one right there, outside that beautifully designed shop window that spelled elegance and charm.

"Let's go back inside then."

·   ·   ·

The transaction took less than fifteen minutes. As they reentered the empty store they were met by such a show of gratitude from the girls in black that Caterina was instantly persuaded she had done the right thing. She and Pascal were made to sit down while one of the girls disappeared to retrieve the green gown in the dressing room while the other served them another espresso in their exquisite porcelain cups.

"How about the shoes, madam?" she asked "They looked so right with the dress . . ."

Pascal and Caterina exchanged a glance. He shut his eyelids and nodded imperceptibly. It was too late to turn back, and besides, six hundred and fifty euros sounded like a pretty good deal compared to the dress. Any three-digit number would have, at that point.

Caterina had made a few calls before reentering the shop, in order to avoid going into the red. There was a small check she was expecting from her producer, and a bit of credit she could juggle with the bank, plus her sister—bedazzled at the prospect of a real Chanel coming into the family—agreed to lend Caterina some money that she could pay back in installments. There was a moment of panic when Caterina's card was denied, since the total amount was way beyond its limit. Pascal came to the rescue, offering his own credit card as added support, so that between the two of them the payment could go through. They waited for the slip to buzz out of the machine, and smiled to each other with relief.

Caterina realized she was sweating profusely, adrenaline shooting through her bloodstream as if she had just robbed a bank. She had to sit down, dizzy with excitement and fatigue, while the girls wrapped and hung the dress inside a black zippered bag with the white Chanel logo, and folded it inside another giant paper bag tied with a black silk ribbon.

The ride back to their musty pensione was enveloped in a daze, as though Caterina were coming down from a powerful drug, its energy now reduced to a softness that turned every muscle to mush. The people seated next to them on the vaporetto—a mix of tourists laden with bags and cameras, old Venetian ladies in housedresses and slippers, young mothers coming home from the supermarket—all appeared to be staring with timorous awe at the gigantic shopping bag with the two Cs entwined.

It was getting dark. Caterina turned to Pascal, who also appeared to be exhausted by all the emotions they'd gone through in the last hour.

"I hate that you are leaving me," she whispered in his ear.

· • ·

The Chanel dress, safely stowed on the train rack and then in the trunk of a taxi, made it all the way to the dreary neighborhood of Ostiense, where Caterina and Pascal lived in a two-bedroom flat above an electronics store and a cheap hairdresser.

As Caterina unzipped the bag, the silk organza unruffled itself, billowing like a flower in bloom. Gingerly she took the dress out and laid it on the bed. She held it for a moment, incredulous. She still couldn't quite believe this ethereal, otherworldly thing belonged to her now. It looked so foreign, in its feathery splendor and exquisite details—the minuscule mother of pearl buttons, the silk lining, the bias cut—sprawled over the frayed bedspread, next to the old couch, the threadbare rug, the cluttered desk, the tangle of electrical cords on the floor. She felt bad for having kidnapped it from the plush environs where it had lived till then. Surely a dress like that had never lived in such a dingy place.

There was only one solution for the dress to fit in with the rest of her life, and that was to upgrade its surroundings. Out with the plastic hairclips, the worn-out shoes. Out with the slackening underwear, the faded T-shirts, the ugly knickknacks, the dusty magazines piled on the floor, the Ikea rug. In with fresh flowers, room fragrance, a cleaner desk, a new expensive matte foundation. As a precaution, she kept the dress well zipped up in its bag, so that it wouldn't be contaminated by the lifeless clothes hanging next to it.

She made a few phone calls.

"Hey, you want to hear something crazy? I bought a Chanel dress!"

Her girlfriends flocked to the apartment, bewildered, as though she had bought a Matisse. Each time someone came for a showing, Caterina unzipped the bag slowly, letting some tiny feathers flutter out first, delaying its full revelation, like a stripper teasing the audience before unfastening her bra.

Not everyone knew what *cruise collection* meant, so she had to explain—being the haute couture expert now—that it was a mid-season collection that came between winter and spring. In the old days it meant exactly that: a line designed for wealthy customers going on cruises in warmer climates who needed extravagant clothes for their encounters on the deck. Think dancing in the ballroom of the *Queen Mary*. The cruise aspect made the dress even more romantic to her and her friends. Caterina associated it with Scott and Zelda, although she wasn't quite sure if the Fitzgeralds had ever taken a cruise in their lives.

Invariably her girlfriends begged her to model the dress for them; they too wanted to get a reverberation of its glamour. Wobbling on the powdery pink sandals, strolling up and down the bedroom, which lacked the softness of the lampshades inside

Chanel's boutique, Caterina believed she looked amazing, despite the merciless light of the low consumption bulb.

· • ·

Two days before the awards ceremony, while Caterina was washing her hair in the sink, the phone rang. A nasal voice announced herself as someone's assistant who was in charge of the event.

Caterina felt a thrill go down her spine, managed to grab a towel and wrap it around her dripping hair, while the woman was saying something about arrangements for a pickup in a limo. She struggled to find a piece of paper and a pen to jot down the details. The thought of the limo, the image of her waxed and bronzed legs stepping out of it in her powdery pink high heels, occupied her mind for a handful of seconds, obliterating what the woman was saying.

" . . . pick you up at eleven fifteen, so we'll make sure you'll get to the theater by noon. Do you think that will give you enough time?"

"Yes, sure. Forty-five minutes will be plenty."

She was about to add "It's not like I live in the jungle" when her brain did a quick rewind.

"What do you mean *noon*? Why noon?"

"I'm sorry, I forgot to tell you this year we'll be running on a different schedule. The ceremony takes place at noon."

"Why?"

"We changed it to daytime this year. It won't make any difference, really."

Caterina tightened her grip on the phone.

"No difference? Well . . . you mean . . . Is it no longer black tie?"

"No, it's a daytime event," the woman said gaily, "so no worries on that score, it'll be a much more relaxed dress code."

There was a pause.

"Hello? Are you there?" the woman said.

"Yes, yes, I'm here."

"I said you don't have to worry about getting all dressed up," the woman reassured her. "The ceremony this year won't even be televised."

"What? Why?"

"Budget cuts. It'll be a smaller affair. But we think it'll be a much warmer ceremony without the TV presenter, the cameras getting in the way and all the tension that comes with a live event."

"Sure . . . yes . . . of course."

"The car will be downstairs at eleven fifteen, then. Congratulations again, Ms. De Maria, we will see you there."

Caterina hung up but didn't move from the chair.

· • ·

That year, due to the disastrous financial situation of the Italian economy, was in fact the only year in its history when the David Awards ceremony was downgraded to daytime, an untelevised, wholly unglamorous affair. Because of this, the nominees for major categories, used as they were to receiving their awards in tuxedos and evening gowns, were incensed. In return for the affront, none of them dressed as if they gave a hoot at all. Men showed up in crumpled linen jackets and sneakers, women in unassuming dresses and flats. It was a kind of "fuck you and your pathetic award ceremony" attitude that people had as they walked up onto that stage. In the absence of a camera nobody bothered to make a speech, to smile, or to thank his or her producer or mother. Even the statuettes looked like trinkets that year.

Caterina's short did indeed end up winning for her category. She was one of the very few who didn't restrain her enthusiasm. She held her statuette up high, like she had seen actresses do at the Oscars, smiling to an imaginary audience, in her friend Tina's flowery dress and a pair of old platform espadrilles.

Pascal sat in the sparse audience (less than half the usual guests had attended given the inconvenient time and the lack of a red carpet) and he took several pictures with his phone of Caterina holding her statuette (the next day, when Pascal and Caterina Googled her name linked to the David Awards ceremony and found no images, they realized that his were the only existing shots of that glorious instant).

Once it was all over, the nominees and the press were offered a cocktail backstage—another sad ordeal of tiny plastic containers filled with microscopic sushi and cucumber mousse—but everyone dashed off in a hurry. Balti was one of the first to leave. Caterina saw him wave a hand in her direction from the other end of the room, but she wasn't certain it was meant for her. She waved hers back, just in case, and watched him disappear, arm in arm with yet another interesting woman who looked both brainy and sexy. After their encounter in Venice she hadn't yet summoned the guts to call him, and at that very moment she decided she wasn't going to.

After a boozy late lunch with Pascal, Caterina came home and opened the closet. She unzipped the Chanel bag for the umpteenth time and looked at the dress. Despite everything, there it was: still hers. She quietly closed the door. One day she would wear it. She knew she would. Now she needed to work hard, to make that day happen. She refused to think of that day in Venice as a missed opportunity or, even worse, as the biggest shopping mistake of her life.

The following year, thanks to a clever financial maneuver, some funds for the arts flowed back into the budget and the awards ceremony resumed its original grandeur, along with the live TV show. The prior year's austerity had been a hitch, a single interruption in its long history, and soon everyone forgot that it had ever happened.

In the years that followed Caterina managed to shoot one more short film about a community of Sikhs tending cattle near Bologna, and tried to get her first long feature off the ground, but she never succeeded.

· · ·

In the course of the following years potential occasions for wearing the Chanel became fewer and fewer. It was either too warm for summer, or too green for winter. There had been a couple of weddings but the dress always looked too dazzling for a simple civil ceremony or a reception in a country restaurant. There had been a few film premieres, the opening of a play or of an exhibition in a museum, but none of the people who went to these events would wear anything as shockingly elegant, so each time she opted for a more comfortable outfit. With time she got so used to the Chanel bag hanging in the closet that it became just another thing living in there, so familiar that it had become invisible. It became part of the furniture, and with the furniture it followed her to another apartment when her new boyfriend, Riccardo, asked her to move in, and on to another one when, three years later, he asked her to marry him. For a moment she considered wearing the dress at her own wedding.

Her sister and her friend Tina had studied the ensemble of dress and shoes while she modeled them once again in the bedroom.

"It looks a bit funny. I am not sure why," her sister had said, tentatively.

"Maybe a bit tight on your hips?" Tina had suggested.

"And anyway, you should wear something brand-new the day of your wedding. What the hell, right?"

Caterina hurried out of the dress self-consciously. It was true she had gained a bit of weight, especially around her midline, but at the time she didn't know yet that she was pregnant with the twins.

Whenever she checked the dress—more and more rarely now after the twins were born—she noticed how the feathers had lost their softness and had become brittle, how the fabric had lost some of its luster. She began to think of the Chanel as an old virgin—untouched but no longer fresh. Every time she zipped up the bag, it felt as though she were laying it back in its coffin.

It took a while before one day, sitting in her kitchen and feeling particularly depressed, she rang Pascal in Paris and told him she felt like a total failure. In the meantime, shortly after he'd moved in with his lover in the Marais, he had been cast for a minor role in a successful TV series as an Italian maître d', and that had been the beginning of a steady career as an actor. She told him she couldn't think of herself as a filmmaker anymore, but just as a mother of two.

"You are not a failure," Pascal said while munching on something. "Maybe you are not meant to make another film. That's all."

It felt like a shock and a liberation at the same time to be hearing this.

"Wow, I feel like I just received a punch in the jaw," she said, uncertain as to whether she should agree with him and accept this truth or try to fight it a little longer.

"It's not the end of the world, you know, there are other things in life you can do."

"What are you eating?"

"*Fromage* and crackers. I think you'd be brilliant at a million other things."

"Such as?"

"Darling, I'm not a tarot reader. All I'm saying is that if in all these years you haven't been able to make another film as impressive as your first, then maybe you should move on."

Pascal could always be brutal, but wasn't that exactly the reason she had called him?

"I still have the goddamned Chanel!" she cried. "I feel guilty every time I look at it."

"Why guilty? Just wear it."

"Where to? I doubt I'll be asked to go anywhere that formal ever again."

"Caterina. You should wear it to the supermarket and have fun with it."

"That's ridiculous and you know it."

"You are making too much of it. It's just a dress, it's not a coronation mantle."

Caterina thought of herself wearing the Chanel through the aisles of the Esselunga supermarket, or when going to pick up the twins at kindergarten. Of wearing it nonstop till it became a uniform, so that people would begin to think of her as the woman in the green dress. She would be considered an eccentric, of course, though by wearing the dress to death out of sheer willpower, she would not only extract from it every euro it had cost her, but also exhaust its fibers till it would have to simply give out and die of consumption, lose its feathers, become more humane, turn into a lifeless threadbare rag and no longer intimidate her. She would win by humbling it. It was an idea, a way of looking at the dilemma.

But she knew she didn't have the guts to engage in that kind of battle.

·　·　·

In her forties, working as a freelance editor for TV commercials, Caterina spent most of her time inside a darkroom off Via Cavour, cutting three-minute ads for luxury cars or perfumes. She had made peace with what she had become: she wasn't an artist but an artisan of sorts. There was no dormant Jane Campion inside her, there had been no misunderstood talent and there was nobody to blame. The twins had turned into bright, witty little boys with remarkable imaginations, well behaved and fun to be with; she and Riccardo were still good together and their marriage still felt like a safe place to be. In that, at least, she had been successful. The statuette she had won for her short now served as a doorstop and as a joke in the family.

One day, across from her office, right next door to the Pasticceria Paradisi, she saw that a stylish young woman had opened a vintage clothing store. Caterina browsed through the racks during her lunch break. The labels were all quite exclusive and prices were high.

"I have a vintage Chanel," she found herself saying. "Would you be interested?"

The woman raised her head from the book she was reading.

"Of course. As long as it's in good condition."

"It's perfect. It's never been worn."

The woman seemed skeptical.

"Bring it and I'll give you an evaluation," she said, lowering her eyes to her book again.

Caterina rang Pascal in Paris—he was about to direct his first play—and told him that she was finally getting rid of the Chanel. He replied without hesitation, saying it was blasphemy to sell it to a secondhand store.

"I need the money. It's not a hand-me-down, it's a very exclusive vintage store right across from the studio in Via del Boschetto. I'm tired of keeping this corpse in my closet."

"Whatever," Pascal said. He was busy, or perhaps tired of the game, which by now was more than ten years old.

· • ·

"It's gorgeous," the stylish young woman from the vintage store said as Caterina freed the dress from its body bag. "Is it yours?"

"Yes. I bought it almost a dozen years ago. It's from the cruise collection."

The woman brushed the fabric with her fingertips and delicately fluffed up the feathers.

"May I ask you why it's never been worn?"

"Oh . . . it's a long story. Actually that's not true, it's quite a simple story. Every time I tried it on it never looked right."

The woman smiled. She had beautiful black hair piled up high on top of her head and wore a dark red lipstick that contrasted with her very white skin.

"I can hardly believe it didn't look right on you. You have such a nice figure."

"Thank you."

"And the dress is a masterpiece."

"You think you can sell it?"

"Of course. It'll sell like that." She snapped her fingers.

"And how much do you think we could . . ."

"I can get more than a thousand for sure, but I'll have to check online. Probably it'll be the most expensive item in the store. If I had the money I would buy it from you for myself," she said with a hint of regret, gazing at the gown with longing.

"I have clients who will fight to have it. Costume designers, maybe a couple of actresses . . ."

She caressed it again and under her delicate touch the fabric rustled as though it were coming back to life.

"Are you really sure you want to part with this?" the young woman asked. "I feel a bit bad selling it. You might regret it afterward."

"No. Thank you. But I don't think so. Really. I kind of want to get rid of it. Actually I've been wanting to for years."

The woman was silent for a few seconds.

"Do me a favor. Just try it on one last time. Please."

When Caterina came out of the dressing room sheathed in the alpine lake cloud, the woman just stared at her and said nothing. She then brought her thin hands to her face, like a stunned child.

"What?" said Caterina.

"I beg you. Don't make the mistake. Keep it. You can always sell it later on."

"When? On my deathbed?"

The woman laughed.

"No, seriously. I won't take it unless you wear it at least once.

It would be—it would really be unethical of me. It looks too good on you, trust me."

Caterina looked at herself in the mirror. She knew what the dress looked like on her—she had lost count of how many times she had tried it on—but now she saw something different.

"Please," whispered the woman, behind her now. "I know clothes. You keep this one."

"I can't believe it. This thing just won't let go of me," Caterina said out loud, and sank onto a chair in front of the mirror. The dress had never looked so good. As if it didn't want to leave her.

. • .

She took it back under the livid light of the metropolitana, holding it in her arms like a child. She felt a special tenderness now, similar to the joy someone experiences having just rescued something that seemed forever lost. She had been on the verge of making a terrible mistake by disowning the dress as something she didn't need, or worse—something she didn't deserve and never would. How could she not have seen it? The dress was a talisman—her own talisman—the gift that she must always treasure, like the gold dust that she feared would fly out the window and follow Pascal all the way to Paris.

She resurfaced into the sunshine at the Garbatella stop and straightened her back, walking briskly toward her street. She clutched the dress bag closer to her body, feeling the glorious softness of the fabric inside, the faint crackling of feathers under her fingertips. Perhaps she just needed to remind herself more often how that gold was still floating above her head, its minuscule particles visible only when pierced by a certain light.

Big Island, Small Island

The swallows keep darting back and forth across the roof like shooting arrows. I think they must be playing a game—a kind of hide-and-seek—because they don't seem to get tired of it. I am not used to seeing birds fly through airports. It's quite a stretch to call this thatched roof standing on pillars an airport and I'm worried about the size of the plane we are about to board. If this is the size of the airport of the Big Island and we are going to the Small Island, how big can the next plane be?

I look around at my fellow passengers. We are not more than ten and that worries me too. There are large men clad in white *kanzus* (I'm already using the local language thanks to the *Teach Yourself Swahili* booklet I bought in Dar es Salaam) and *kofia*, which I just learned is what their finely stitched cap is called. Judging from their potbellies and thick gold watches they seem rather affluent. A couple of them have small-sized wives sitting next to them, wrapped in the black cape they call *buibui*. The men talk loudly, mostly among themselves or on old-fashioned Nokias—only a few have smartphones—whereas the wives don't flinch. They are as still as pillars of salt surrounded by hefty bundles and boxes. I can see baskets brimming with mangoes, cartons containing some household appliances, an electric fan, a kettle, a DVD player. They must've been shopping on the mainland; I didn't see any shopping opportunities for such items as kettles or fans on the Big Island. Just a few gift shops and a desolate, half-empty supermarket. A crackling voice on the intercom speaks in Swahili, and the man next to me shakes his head with disdain.

"Delay," he says, meeting my eyes.

"How much?"

"One hour."

It could be worse, I think, so I pull out my book.

I've been to Africa before—to Egypt and Morocco—but never south of the Sahara and never to such a remote place. During my travels I rarely ever mix with the locals, sealed as I am in my work bubble, always surrounded by colleagues. We end up spending most of our time inside conference rooms, in line at those ghastly buffet lunches, or in our anonymous hotel rooms watching the news. Since I've been on this particular detour I've been feeling more vulnerable but also more adventurous. I think I'm beginning to get the hang of traveling solo. For instance, whenever I am the only white person within a contained space, I find that reading is the best thing to turn to. It's actually an act of courtesy, I realized; it allows people to stare and even point at me if they need to—usually it's the women who find something ridiculous about my clothes and tend to giggle with hands over their mouths. My reading gives them total freedom to examine me without creating unnecessary embarrassment.

"Are you Italian?" a voice asks me in English.

I lift my eyes from the book. Sitting across from me is a man in his early fifties. He's clearly been looking at the cover of my book. He must have just sat down; I hadn't noticed him earlier. He wears a white linen shirt, nicely tailored cotton trousers in a shade of ocher, Ray-Bans and soft loafers without socks. This last detail, more than anything, tells me he must be Italian as well. Those are expensive car shoes, the kind Mr. Agnelli made famous. Only Italian men wear loafers without socks with their ankles showing this much beneath the trousers.

"*Sì,*" I say, and I shake the hand he's already holding out.

I am not sure whether to be relieved or disturbed by this

chance encounter. He lights a Marlboro and begins to chat amiably in Italian, ignoring my desire to read on.

His name is Carlo Tescari, he's been living in Tanzania for the last ten years. He's built a couple of luxury safari camps near Ngorongoro. Before that he lived in Kenya, where he built more luxury camps and sold them for a fortune. Twenty-five years in East Africa, he says, as though it's a record of some kind. Funny, because he looks as if someone had just lifted him from the Via Roma in Capri and landed him in this tiny airport on the Big Island, on his way to another, smaller island not many people have ever heard of.

"Are you with the NGO?" he asks me.

"No."

"Just visiting?"

"Yes."

"There are no hotels, you know. Not even a guest house."

"I'm staying at a friend's place."

"Are you?" He looks at me with a hint of suspicion. "Is it an African friend?"

"No. An old friend from Italy. He has been living there for fifteen years."

"Is this the man who works for that NGO?"

"Yes. That's him."

"I thought so. Someone at the embassy in Dar suggested I see him to get some advice. I've got his contacts somewhere."

He opens his leather briefcase and flicks through his documents.

"Here it is. Andrea Nelli, right? I spoke to him last week on the phone, he's expecting me. Well, that's quite a coincidence, isn't it?"

I nod, politely.

"Then I'll come along with you to his place. We can share the cab. If you don't mind."

"No, I don't," I say, even though I do, actually.

"I just need to ask him a few questions, it's not going to take long. He's the only *mzungu* that lives on the island, other than Jeffrey Stone. I'm staying at Jeffrey's, I know Jeff from Nairobi. He's the local veterinarian and hates it there. Apparently your friend has been on the island for, what did you say, fifteen years?"

"More or less, yes."

"Jeffrey has been there only three months and he's desperate to leave. Not much company."

"No?"

"No. And it's a dry island. No booze. The death of an Englishman. Very traditional Muslim community."

That, I'm aware of. Andrea has instructed me over the phone "long sleeves and no bathing suits. You can swim in a dress if you *really* have to."

Carlo Tescari seems eager to extract more details about my host.

"What's he like? He wasn't very forthcoming on the phone."

"I haven't seen him in ages. Since he moved out here."

"I see."

He takes a good look at me.

"So is this a happy reunion?"

"Yes."

"A sort of 'Dr. Livingstone, I presume' moment." He chuckles, then adds, "I hear your friend has become very local."

"I wouldn't be surprised, given that there are only locals, as you say. Except for your unhappy vet, of course."

He grins, showing a crown of teeth so white they might even be false.

It troubles me, to arrive at Andrea's house in the company of this man. I had envisaged a completely different scene when I decided to track him down a couple of weeks ago. And now, after such a long journey, I am nearly at his doorstep, about to show up with exactly the kind of person he will loathe.

. . .

This part of the journey, from the Big Island to the Small Island, was a last-minute diversion from my original itinerary. I'd been invited to attend a conference in Dar es Salaam on ecosystem disturbances and the management of protected forests. It was only once I was on the plane to Tanzania, while perusing the map of East Africa, that I realized how close I'd be to the place where Andrea had disappeared. Not exactly close-close, but certainly closer than I'd been in all this time, when it seemed he had vanished somewhere unreachable and exotic, never to be found again. None of us—not any of his friends—had ever heard of this tiny island in the Indian Ocean, which at the time of his disappearance was mentioned only in passing in guidebooks; later, when we'd all become expert Internet surfers, all I could find online in relation to the island were a couple of blurred photos of the ruin of a mosque, as though no travel writer had ever cared to explore it.

I'm a biologist with a doctorate in agriculture and food sciences and my specialty is biodiversity in Central European forests. At the conference in Dar I spoke at length to a sleepy audience on the effects of atmospheric pollution on lichens. Afterward, in the half-empty conference room, a mix of scientists from different parts of the world exchanged mild comments about my talk over watery coffee and stale biscuits. Before I could say anything they had already switched subjects, and were discussing the heat, the malfunctioning of the air-conditioning in their rooms and the poor reception on their phones. Once in my hotel room, instead of giving in to my resentment, I decided I still had a chance to give this exhausting trip a more significant purpose. To finally get hold of an ex-lover I hadn't heard from in ages seemed a much more rewarding task than introducing rare species of lichens to my colleagues. I Googled all the local airlines till I found a connection that could take me to the island where Andrea supposedly still lived. From Dar I'd have to fly to the Big Island and from there the only way to the Small Island would then be to get on a rusty ferry that takes a day and a half. The Indian Ocean tends to be choppy—at least that's what I read on Trip Advisor—so I opted for a twelve-seater plane. Before I bought the tickets I Googled Andrea's name in various combinations with the island name till I found a number for an NGO. Someone picked up the phone after the first ring. It was him. I gasped.

"Andrea? You are not going to believe this. It's Stella."

"Hi, Stella, where are you?"

He sounded wholly unfazed.

"I'm in Dar es Salaam. Not too far from you."

"What are you doing in that horrible city?"

"I am a speaker at an international conference on biodiversity."

"Sounds like you got your Ph.D. after all."

"I did."

Silence. I thought maybe the line had been cut off. Then I heard him clear his throat.

"Come see me. I haven't spoken Italian in so long."

"I was thinking I actually might do that. I could come for three or four days. If that would be okay . . . I mean, if you are not too busy."

"Just come."

There was another pause. I then tried a more familiar tone.

"Andrea? It's wonderful to hear your voice again. It's been such a long time. How are you?"

"I'll tell you when I see you."

· • ·

Naturally Carlo Tescari sits next to me during the short flight on our tiny plane and continues with his entire life story and his future business plans. Apparently our shared nationality gives him the right to treat me like an old friend and there is very little I can do to fend him off. So I learn the real purpose of his trip. On the east side of the island where the main village is situated, the coast is just mangroves and muddy shores. But on the northwest side, beaches as white and as soft as talcum powder stretch for miles and miles. He surveyed the coastline from a Cessna a couple of months back. He opens the briefcase and shows me a map. On a half-moon-shaped cove he plans to scatter a few thatch-roofed huts (he calls them *bandas*), with a larger common area built in natural materials and to be exquisitely designed by a Dutch architect. A minimalist, ecological, yet stylish and highly comfortable retreat for people seeking complete privacy in the wilderness. Of course he'll need to bring a road and water, but he doesn't think it'll be that hard.

"Building the road is going to be the most work of all, but I think I can get some politicians involved," he says. "Hopefully your friend can give me some advice as how to oil the right people."

From the sky the landing strip looks like a narrow slit cutting through the dense foliage. I close my eyes and hold my breath till we touch ground. The ride in an ancient blue taxi corroded by rust is just as bumpy as our landing; the roads on the island are packed dirt scarred by large ruts. It's baking hot, the earth is a deep vermilion and there's a film of orange dust shrouding the trees lining the way. I keep my eyes on the window, looking straight ahead, while Carlo Tescari goes on and on about the difficulty of dealing with old-fashioned Muslim politicians who don't welcome foreigners.

· • ·

As we approach the town, an ugly tower looms over the tops of the trees. Its concrete structure is covered in blackish mold, the plaster is flaking, the window frames have rusted badly and have come off in places. Strings of faded laundry adorn the squared balconies of apartments that look as though they were intended for the Russian working class. The tower—designed in the seventies by an architect in Leningrad? A gift from the Communist party to the president of this corrupted republic?—is rotting away in the sticky weather. We keep on driving, past the town on a winding road snaking through coconut and banana trees, random patches of vegetable gardens, ugly cinder-block houses. Women carry yellow plastic buckets on their heads sloshing with water. I intercept their corrugated brows and suspicious looks as they peek at the white people inside the car without smiling.

So this is where he has been all these years, while we, his friends, fell in love with other people, moved to different cities, got our degrees and found jobs. Some of us had children, some of us died in car accidents, some overdosed, some became famous, others did nothing with their lives.

In the beginning, when he first left, we often wondered why Andrea had stopped answering our letters. Then, as the years went by, we ceased to think about him, as though it were pointless to keep track of his existence: he'd simply gone too far and had fallen off the radar. If we mentioned his name, it was always only to say how lucky he was, to be living in such an exotic place, to have fled from our pasty, predictable, urban lives.

Funny, how we assumed the island he'd escaped to should be a setting out of a Graham Greene story: we pictured a small colonial town on the edge of a harbor in a lush, tropical landscape, its narrow streets winding through a lane of wooden buildings with lacy balconies, latticed verandas, with a touch of romantic decay.

·   ·   ·

He's waiting for us on the porch of the house—another no-frills cinder-block box with a blue door and small windows—standing erect, with arms crossed, in an assertive posture that demands respect. He's wearing a starched white *kanzu* and a *kofia* and, because of his dark hair and tanned skin, he doesn't look that much different from the local businessmen I flew in with. He's put on some weight and grown a short beard. He's quite stocky, actually, and his curls are gone, though his green eyes flicker for a moment when he sees me and that flash of mutual recognition gives me a jolt in the stomach. I feel a light resistance from him, a rigidity, when I fling myself into his arms. He moves his face slightly to the side, so that I miss his cheek and end up kissing air. He steps backward and smiles shyly.

"Hey, Stella" is all he says.

"I can't believe I finally got hold of you!" I almost shout, unable to repress my enthusiasm.

"Wait a minute, let me deal with him first," he says calmly, almost dreamily, lifting his chin toward Tescari, who has stayed behind, talking to the taxi driver, possibly telling him to wait for him.

It's disappointing, of course, that joy for this reunion should be put on hold and mitigated by the presence of a stranger.

Tescari sprints onto the porch baring his white teeth. He offers his hand.

"So very pleased to meet you at last. I can't stand communicating via e-mail or phone; one has to be able to look people in the eyes when talking business, don't you think?"

I catch a flash of surprise in his eyes as he takes in the white *kanzu* and *kofia*.

Andrea doesn't answer, he simply shows us into a small room, empty save for a green couch sheathed in plastic, a makeshift bookcase with a few paperbacks, and a sisal mat on the cement floor. On the bare walls hangs but a single picture, Arabic calligraphy. Tescari takes in the ambiance, then throws me a reproachful glance, as if I have lured him into a trap. Andrea shows him the couch.

"Please sit down."

Andrea instead sits on the floor, folding his legs in lotus position. Tescari slides uncomfortably onto the very edge of the couch, as though he wants to avoid contamination, and the plastic cover makes a screeching, embarrassing sound under him. He opens his briefcase and pulls out the drawings. I stand, as I've not been asked to sit down yet, glad to keep a distance from the position that Tescari has been given on the couch.

There is a moment of uncomfortable silence. Andrea and Tescari stare at each other as if neither one wants to be the first to speak. Then Andrea makes a gesture with his hand, signaling that Tescari should begin.

Tescari fumbles through his documents, then unfolds a large drawing.

"As I told you on the phone, I have investors in Europe that are extremely keen on this project. They are ready to come in as soon as I let them know the permits have been secured. Here, take a look at the plans."

Tescari hands the drawing down to Andrea, who takes a cursory look at it and says nothing. I hear a noise in the next room. Someone is splashing water on the cement floor.

"We're planning to fly the clients down from Dar to make it easier for them to reach the camp. All we need is a landing strip for a Cessna, that's not a problem, but we'll have to build a road to carry building materials and so on."

Tescari taps his shirt pocket.

"Can I smoke?"

"No. You can go outside if you wish."

Tescari leaves the pack of cigarettes in the pocket.

"How far is the beach from the main road? From the plane we couldn't see, the foliage was too thick. And how about water? Do you have any idea how deep one has to dig?"

Andrea doesn't answer. Just sits there with his legs in a knot. Tescari is puzzled but decides to ignore the awkward silence.

"You are the first person I am talking to, here. I will see the Ministry of Land and Forests as well, of course. But before I do I wanted to have a clearer picture of the technical aspects. I was told you're the best person to talk to since you know everybody on the island."

Tescari watches as Andrea folds the map shut.

"I've lived in East Africa long enough," Tescari says. "I know it can be tricky to start a project like this if you are an outsider. That's why I came to see you first. To get a sense of—"

Andrea hands the plan back to him. He speaks, slowly, enunciating each word distinctly. His tone is steady, unwavering.

"You can rest assured you will not get any permit, nor any help, to build this resort. The people on this island are not interested in facilitating this kind of project so that you and your investors can stash your clients' dollars into a Swiss account. If anything, I will do everything in my power to prevent this from happening."

There's a moment of silence. Tescari clears his throat.

"I'm afraid there's a misunderstanding. We are going to hire locals. Everyone will profit from this venture," he says. "By which what I really mean is that it will give jobs to lots of people. I'm sure that you, more than anyone here, realizes that this island needs some—"

Andrea raises his palm to stop him.

"This is a traditional island. We won't allow foreign speculators to wreck our customs and offend our values. We don't want half-naked tourists on our beaches smoking and drinking. The people here don't need jobs, we grow our own food and catch our fish, and this is the way the island has lived for centuries." Andrea's voice is quiet, unperturbed. "We don't need you. Is that clear enough? Now you can go. Please."

And he stands up, gesturing toward the door with a sweep of his arm.

Tescari shoots up, holding his folded plans to his chest, stunned. He turns toward me. "This man is crazy."

"Please go. I see your taxi is still waiting for you," Andrea insists, standing by the door.

"Crazy," Tescari says to me, a finger to his temple. "Honestly, if I were you I wouldn't stay here."

And then he's out the door.

I hear the engine start and the taxi pulls away. It is a relief and yet part of me feels abandoned.

"Wow," I say.

I'm waiting for Andrea to remark, waiting for him to erupt in a roaring laugh and utter something outrageous. For him to undo the monastic posture, get out of the starched *kanzu* and declare that what he just said was a joke, a performance he played on the Italian with loafers.

Instead he keeps very still and suddenly I feel uneasy.

"What are you?" I ask.

"What do you mean?"

"What are you here, anyway. Are you some kind of mullah?" I say, with a nervous laugh.

Andrea strokes his short beard and thinks for a moment. He doesn't get that my question is meant to be humorous.

"No. Although I did convert to Islam years ago."

"Oh. I see," I say, as though that explains everything.

We stare at each other uneasily. I look around the empty room and I wonder many things at once: whether he has a guest room for me or I am to sleep on the screeching plastic couch, whether he might in fact have gone crazy or even be under medication, whether coming here was a terrible mistake. It has nothing to do with his converting to Islam. It's that he just seems so much slower. Numbed.

"That guy," he says, "isn't the first one to show up here with a plan. I've told them all to fuck off. One by one."

Here he gains a bit of speed. He's more animated and that feels reassuring.

"I know how their plans work. They build what they call an *eco-friendly self-sustainable* camp in the wilderness for a pittance, so that for five hundred dollars a night millionaires can take a crap under the stars. Then, slowly but very very surely they declare the beach off limits, they deny access to the local fishermen because their clients need their 'privacy.' As though this has been their land for generations. Over my dead body they'll get in here."

"Absolutely!" I cheer. I'm relieved: he's sounding like himself at last.

It's only now that I realize that since I first arrived Andrea still hasn't really looked at me. And I cannot tell whether he's happy to see me or not.

· · ·

His body used to be lean and taut. Hip bones, ribs and knee caps showing under baggy jeans and faded T-shirts. Long hands and nimble fingers that touched things gently. I loved his feet too. Once I told him, "You have the hands and feet of a dancer," because there was a special gracefulness in the way he moved in space. He never brushed his hair, which was a tangle of light brown curls, often shading his eyes—those green, bright eyes that changed with the weather—and I suspect he didn't wash it often. Whenever we'd be all together—me, our friends—discussing something we'd read, whether it was politics, literature, ethics, he'd sit back while we made our loud arguments. His silence made us edgy, we felt observed and judged. We wanted him to level with us, so we'd turn to him and say, How about you, Andrea, let's hear what you think, and often what he said was just the opposite of what we'd so fervently maintained till then. He always seemed to come at things from another perspective, and what we had thought was right suddenly seemed wrong, what we thought was daring seemed banal.

We all wanted to be a this and a that: a writer, a photographer, an actor, an architect, a political activist, whereas he didn't seem to strive to be anything. He was good with his hands, he knew how to fix things and work with wood, he worshipped his motorcycle and spent hours adjusting and calibrating its mechanisms. We were aware that he knew a lot—more than us—that he loved to read and the books he chose were unusual and difficult, as though he had already read and digested what we were reading and was way ahead of us. He read essays, literary criticism, obscure play- wrights and poets, but he never lectured, never quoted from them. I think he found it pathetic, the way we showed off, always keen to sound wittier, more well read, more up-to-date.

We never met his parents and knew very little of his back- ground. He was an only child and apparently his father was a strange man who drank too much and didn't seem to have a real job. His mother had left the family when Andrea was a teenager and he didn't like to talk about her. Once he said he thought Freud had given all of us an alibi to whine.

At a time when we all strived to be reckless, he was the most fearless with drugs, though he never seemed high, only more con- centrated, sharper. We made love the first time under a shower, while tripping on LSD. I still remember how the yellow mosaic of the bathroom glimmered, and how I was convinced I was inside an Egyptian palace, shimmering with gold and sunshine. I don't remember whose apartment it was, and why I was alone under the shower—the sprinkling water felt like a cascade of yellow diamonds—but suddenly there he was, smiling, getting out of his clothes, entering the magic circle of gold with me.

I was already in love with him by then and I wasn't the only one. We all fought to get his attention, to spend time alone with him—men and women alike—and some of us fought harder to become his lover. There were jealousies and treacheries, though he never used the power we had given him to manipulate us.

One day he announced he was going away. Someone he knew had offered him a place as a volunteer to teach English to children in Africa. He mentioned the name of the island, a name so dif- ficult to pronounce that it became impossible to remember.

The last time I saw him it was on a winter day on the street right below my apartment. He had come around to say good- bye right before getting on the plane. He must have buzzed the intercom and I had come down. I was living by the Via dei Riari then, in a small studio at the end of the street, at the foot of the Gianicolo Hill, and I remember the feeling of sorrow clinging to my clothes as I walked out on the street. It was drizzling and cold and he wasn't wearing a coat or a jacket; all he had on was a thick black turtleneck and his old leather gloves. I also remember how he was leaning against a brick wall next to his motorcycle and how the wind ruffled his hair.

· · ·

He has a wife.

She must have been the one throwing water on the floor. She is only a girl—a very thin, very young girl like so many I saw along the island road with sloshing buckets balancing on their heads—who looks frightened to see me. She wears a threadbare *kanga* wrapped around her waist and another one with the same pattern over her shoulders. As she advances, she pulls its edge over her hair, which is braided in thick cornrows, as though she needs extra protection. Andrea speaks quickly to her in Swahili, and she whispers something inaudible. She lowers her eyes to the floor as she stands before me like a schoolgirl in front of the principal.

"This is Farida," Andrea says. "She hasn't met many Western women."

I stretch out my hand and she hesitates before moving hers tentatively toward mine. I rush to grab it. It's limp, and still wet from the washing.

"Hello, Farida, very nice to meet you," I say in English.

I realize my voice has taken the hideous inflection I sometimes can't help myself from having when talking to Africans. I tend to stretch all my vowels, in an unconscious effort to imitate their accent.

"Women don't shake hands here," Andrea warns me.

"Right. Sorry."

"Don't be sorry, foreigners don't always know."

Farida has beautiful eyes with long, curled eyelashes and her skin looks soft, flawless. She must be eighteen at the most. Her pupils dilate with apprehension, so I let go of her hand.

"She doesn't speak any English," he says.

Farida whispers something to him, he nods, releasing her, and she rushes off, back where she's been hiding.

He shows me where I am to sleep. It's a small room in the back, behind the kitchen, with a Spartan four-poster bed and a mosquito net. He stands by the door for a moment and I feel his eyes on me for the first time. I look at him and again, for a split second, I feel that flicker of recognition, a tiny leap of the heart, as though we both know what the other one is thinking. Snippets of the past are hovering between us. I am about to say something—I am not sure yet as to what—but I need to say something that will shorten the distance, make us close again. He cuts me off before I open my mouth.

"I'm going to the mosque for prayer, then we'll have dinner. You must be hungry."

· • ·

It's beginning to get dark outside when he comes back. I hear more water splashing, this time from the plastic bucket he showed me in the bathroom we are meant to share. When he knocks at my door to call me for dinner he has changed into a pair of cargo pants and a faded T-shirt. We sit on the mat under a bright fluorescent light and Farida brings out our dinner. Andrea scoops up rice, fish in coconut sauce, thinly cut greens mixed with sweet potatoes and chapati from warm aluminum pots covered by lids, while Farida retreats again to the back room. He hands me a full plate and begins to eat skillfully with his fingers, using the chapati to gather the food and mop up the sauce. I take a moment to study his technique. No food reaches past his first knuckle, I observe. A trick I'm unable to imitate.

"Would you like a spoon?" he asks.

"That would be great, actually."

He says something in the direction of the kitchen, and after a moment Farida reappears with a spoon, then departs again.

The food is not bad but it is bland. I am disappointed; I was counting on some delicious surprises coming out of that kitchen. Instead it's an unhappy sort of food, without zest, like one finds in hospitals or schools. And the buzzing light overhead washes everything in a deathly pallor.

"Isn't Farida eating with us?" I ask.

"No. She eats later."

"Why?"

"It's just the way it is."

"Women eat later?"

"Yes."

"That's absurd."

"Relax, Stella. It's okay."

He throws an amused glance at me.

"And trust me, she much prefers it that way when there are guests."

"Why? Am I that scary?"

He smiles. "It's very likely she thinks you are."

There is tenderness in his voice when he speaks of her. I see now how protective he is of her and that he won't let me intimidate her more than is necessary. I am the stranger here.

"So," I say, suddenly eager, as if it's time to get down to business, "where is your office?"

"Which office?"

"The NGO you work for."

"This is the office. Right here."

I look around. There is no trace of a desk, file cabinets, papers. Only an antiquated telephone sitting on the bookshelf.

"We've lost a few big donors because of the recession, like everyone else, and we had to get rid of staff. I'm alone right now. In fact, there's not much activity at the moment."

He explains how for the past five years he's been working for this NGO that offers microloans to women. He was hired, he says, because of his expertise with the local culture. He says all this with an ironic tinge. I tell him I've heard a lot about microcredit and how very successful it's proved in developing countries. He says that yes, it is a good template, but it needs to be adapted from place to place. Here on the island, he says, the idea is to give the women two goats each to start with, so they can slowly build a herd and sell the milk. They can also get chickens, for eggs. Theoretically within a few months they should be able to repay the loan and start saving some capital.

"Why theoretically?" I ask.

"Stuff happens all the time. Either it's the animals that die of mysterious diseases, or they're stolen by neighbors. Or the husbands take the money and use it for whatever they need. So actually most of the women have failed to repay the loans."

"That's disappointing."

He nods and keeps eating in silence. Somehow I had expected him to feel more passionate about this project. That he'd find it a rather noble task to devote one's life to lifting women from poverty.

"So, what happens now?" I asked. "Are you out of a job?"

"No. They have kept me on a salary while they try to figure out how to change the modus operandi."

"Who's 'they'?"

"A bunch of Norwegians," he says. Now I do hear a bit of passion—just shy of a sneer.

He shrugs and looks into his plate.

"As if they'd have any idea of how to operate it. They show up twice a year and they don't even speak the language."

I resist asking more. Though I have so many questions, clearly he doesn't particularly like to talk about any of this; he must know that this bare room looks nothing like an efficient NGO. Maybe there will be another opportunity, later. Maybe we both need a little time.

He fills my glass with water. I wonder if it's filtered but I don't dare ask. I could do with a drink, actually. It would really help me to soften up the edges and get through this more smoothly.

· • ·

When I retire to my room in the evening I discover that Farida has scattered pink frangipani petals on my bed. The scent is sweet and heady. I would like to take a photo of it, but the power goes off just as I start fumbling inside my bag for the camera. A couple of minutes later, Farida knocks lightly at the door and brings in a kerosene lamp that fills the room with a warmer glow. Now that we are alone, she covers her mouth, repressing a laugh, and reaches for my hair. She holds a strand between her fingers for a moment, testing its texture.

Later, once the sounds of closing doors, splashing water and coughing have ceased next door, I lay awake on the hard mattress, lending an ear to the other side of the wall. I am not ready to handle any intimate sounds that might seep through their bedroom walls.

· • ·

Time here moves as slowly as inside a dentist's waiting room.

I am trying to figure out what Andrea's routine is, to get a sense of his existence, but his life keeps eluding me. There has been a procession of visitors throughout the whole morning, all of them men who sit out on the porch with him and talk very loudly in Swahili. I watch Andrea as he slaps his thigh and raises his voice, joining the chorus. He's a different person in this new incarnation—that cool aloofness, that lightness of touch he had when I knew him, seems gone. Swahili sounds like a language that needs a strong vocal emission, wide gesticulation and theatrical facial expressions. The men wear shirts over colorful *kikoys* wrapped around their waists, bantering and laughing on the stone bench that I've been told is called *baraza*. It could be local gossip, or perhaps they are just recounting a fishing expedition; I notice one of them is moving an open hand like a knife slicing his forearm, perhaps demonstrating the size of his daily catch. Andrea hasn't introduced me to any of them.

After lunch—another disappointing meal of plain white rice and fried fish with too many bones—I tell Andrea I'd like to go out and take some pictures of the village. I have begun to feel hostage to the house, as though—inexplicably so—there's an unwritten rule that I am to stay put and not wander out. It is decided that Farida is to accompany me in my wanderings. Apparently it doesn't look good for any woman—*mzungu* or local—to be out on the streets by herself. This has of course not been openly stated, but somehow I get the drift. Farida reappears clad in her black *buibui*, showing an unforeseen eagerness for the assignment she's been given, and off we go. The minute we are alone she urges me in sign language to enter a neighbor's house. I try to protest— I've had enough of being shut inside—but she won't relent. Evidently she's no longer so scared of me.

·　·　·

We enter another squared house with a small inner courtyard where an old lady wrapped in a bright pink cloth sits quietly next to a goat with her withered legs stretched out in front. She looks blind, and strangely beautiful. Farida ignores her and we enter a dark, stuffy room. I hear giggles coming from its depths. There are two young women about Farida's age who get up from the floor and come toward us. Farida shows me off to them with pride, like a girl with a new doll. I have a feeling that news of my arrival has been spreading and the neighbors are expecting to get a glimpse of me. There is a brief discussion, then the young women decide I have to follow them to the next room, darker than the first one.

Here they pat the floor mat till I sit down. More women, both young and old, join us now, appearing from the recesses of what looks like a big house, and sit across from me, making sounds of appreciation. I am surrounded. The room smells of cheap lotions, cloth, sweat, boredom and sleep. Farida must have told them it'd be okay to go ahead and touch me, because now they tug at my hair, at my clothes, they inspect the fabric, grab my wrist, discuss my rings, my watch. The room is stifling; my clothes stick to my back as sweat rolls down my spine. I glance at my watch and I see it's only half past three. The end of the day still feels a long way ahead.

· ● ·

After two more visits in the neighborhood, we are back on the road, although the way Farida grips my arm enhances the feeling of being her prisoner. We walk past the mildewed Soviet tower, toward what looks like the center of town, but soon I realize there is no center, no pretty square as such, no leafy gardens, no latticed verandas, no bustling heart of the village, but only more cement buildings decaying among heaps of trash. The market—the destination I have so eagerly prepared for—sits underneath yet another concrete structure, built by the same ghastly planners. At this time of day it's half empty except for packs of stray dogs wandering through the leftovers of market day.

I look around, searching for a view of the ocean. It comes to me that since I've landed I haven't seen a single shade of blue. I look in every direction, walk this way and that, but the sea is nowhere to be seen. How can this be possible? How can an island—especially such a small island—conceal the water surrounding it? My anxiety mounts. There must be an outlook, a promontory, a belvedere from which one can see water. I pose the question to Farida. Where is the sea? The sea! I ask in an almost desperate tone. Water? But she shakes her head, amused. I try with Italian. *Mare? Acqua? Eau?* No, she doesn't understand a word, and I didn't carry my *Teach Yourself Swahili* with me. Suddenly I must see water. My heart pounds. This must be what a real attack of claustrophobia feels like.

It is then, from out of the corner of my eye, that I get a glimpse of khaki. My brain registers the shade, the texture of the fabric, and instantly flashes a message. Your tribe. It is indeed a man in his thirties, in a light blue shirt and shorts. Right behind him are the loafers of Carlo Tescari. He and his friend Jeffrey Stone—tall, with thick blond sideburns and round across the waist—are chatting as they come out of the fishmonger's with a parcel wrapped in newspaper.

My brain flashes again. I know exactly what's happening here. They will have delicious peppered shrimps in chili sauce for dinner. I raise my arm and yell.

"Hey!"

.   .   .

It has not been easy to get rid of Farida. She was very upset when I began to smilingly signal "You can go home, it's fine, I know the way. Just go home now, I'm okay." But the stubborn girl didn't want to move.

"Who is she?" Jeffrey Stone asked. We had just been introduced by Tescari, who had rejoiced when I had invited myself for a drink.

"You need a break from that madman, eh?" Tescari said, and I think he winked, too. "What did I tell you?"

"Who is this girl now?" Jeffrey Stone asked again.

I didn't reply and Farida didn't budge.

"Can you speak to her in Swahili? Please tell her she can go home, that I'll be fine, I know my way back."

Both Tescari and Stone spoke to her with the brisk tone people use with servants in this part of the world. Farida seemed hurt. She gave me a look under her long eyelashes, perhaps expecting me to explain her role to these men. She was my hostess, her face said, she was responsible for me. We must go home together. But I didn't obey her silent request. Instead I moved my hand again toward what I figured was the direction home.

Please. Please go.

Then a couple of words from the Swahili book resurfaced.

Nyumbani, tafadhali.

Reluctantly she turned and started walking away.

·   •   ·

Jeffrey Stone lives in a slightly nicer concrete box than Andrea's, although no building on this odd, seemingly seaviewless island meets any of the requirements that might elevate it to something even remotely romantic. Stone has made an effort to make the place look cozy, though. He has a few colorful throws scattered across his sofa and armchairs, a Moroccan rug on the floor and a few coffee table books with old photographs of hunting expeditions or East African interiors. We sit outside on the veranda on plantation chairs and an older man with a severe expression in *kanzu* and *kofia* brings out a tray with iced gin and tonics and freshly roasted cashew nuts. Apparently Tescari has brought the booze all the way from mainland Tanzania and, judging from what's left in the bottle, they've had quite a lot of it already.

Tescari has an appointment tomorrow morning with the Ministry of Land and he's pretty optimistic that he'll get his permits without a problem.

"Despite," he adds, turning to me, "what your friend claims."

I ignore his remark and say yes to a refill of my glass.

"He has married a local, right?" Jeffrey Stone inquires as he pours.

"Was that her?" Tescari asks.

I nod and feel both men's eyes on me. I know they expect me to make a remark or to crack half a joke as a sign of solidarity to the white man's cause when stranded on such unfriendly land, but I keep my straight face and ignore the question, asking Jeffrey what his job involves and whether he's planning to stay here much longer. He isn't, he's applied for a post in Uganda. Come the end of the year and he'll get the hell out of this hole.

This short parenthesis in the colonial world on the island has had the power to rejuvenate me, probably because of the alcohol intake, but I walk home strengthened, and full of ideas.

· · ·

Andrea's on the porch, crossed-legged on the *baraza*. Pretending to be looking into some miraculous cloud formation in the sky. I know he's been waiting for me, but when I walk in he just says hi, as though he's not interested in where I've been. I move to sit next to him and he scoots over to make room. We sit quietly for a moment, though I am not quiet inside. I am energized and determined to pierce through the armor with which he has been shielding himself. We enjoy a moment of silence, then I begin.

"How come one never sees the ocean on this island?"

"On this side of the island it's more difficult to see it."

"Then take me somewhere where I can. Otherwise I'll never believe this *is* an island."

He stares into nothingness.

"Come on. Let's go. Just you and me this time." I make my voice sound as conspiratory and commanding as I can.

But he looks up at me, as if weary.

"Why?"

"Because I've come all this way to see you, and you, Andrea, haven't spent a minute with me. You've either handed me over to your wife, or talked to me like a stranger."

He doesn't reply and looks away. I can feel him retreating, curling up. I raise my voice.

"Come back!"

He looks at me, startled, almost frightened. "What do you mean, *come back*?"

"Just come back, for God's sake!" I shout. "Come back into yourself! Come back! I feel you have turned into an alien."

"Have you been drinking?"

"It doesn't matter and who cares? It's exactly what I think. This *person* you are pretending to be—is not you."

"Oh really? And who am I then?"

"I've known you a long time. Longer than anybody else here. I know this is not you."

He stares at me and doesn't say anything. I hold my breath. Does he hate me?

"No you don't," he says coldly. "You think you know me, but you don't."

He glances toward the door of the house. "And please lower your voice."

Fifteen years of never eating fresh vegetables, but only rice, chapatis and fried fish in coconut oil have modified his shape, the texture of his skin, the molecules of his inner organs. Fifteen years of not having access to decent books, but just airport paperbacks snatched from the few foreign visitors, must have starved his mind, shrunk his intellect. Fifteen years of not speaking his mother language, forgetting its poetry, its songs, its sonorities and rhythms. And how about going to prayer five times a day, kneeling on a mat, his forehead touching the ground? In which way might that strict discipline transform an agnostic, a free spirit, a biker with long curls?

"*Why* are you still here?" my voice breaks. I had no idea I'd be so crushed.

He doesn't say anything.

I think about my boyfriend of five years, Gregorio, whom I'm not sure I'm still in love with but who has become my family, our sunny two-bedroom apartment in Monteverde Vecchio, my old dog, Olga. My daily morning run in the park, my small, cluttered office at the faculty, a couple of my brightest students.

The list of my life's highlights is not that long and maybe not that interesting.

Who am I to judge? Maybe Andrea didn't come here seeking adventure. Maybe he has chosen this place to venture inward rather than expand, since everything here—the people, the buildings, even the geography—lacks beauty and brilliance. Maybe he was relieved when he found a place where he could shrink and settle into a smaller life, away from the eyes of others. From all our expectations.

"I am here because this is my home now," he says, looking up again, to somewhere far away, above the mango trees across from the house.

"Don't you ever miss Rome?"

"Rome?" he asks, as baffled as if I'd said Mars. "No. Never. I never think of Rome."

"And us? Don't you ever think of us?"

He shakes his head slowly.

"No I haven't. In a long, long time."

That's fair, I think. I hadn't been thinking much about him either. I hadn't truly missed him till now.

"Take me to see the ocean, Andrea. Just the two of us."

He stares at me and something shifts in his eyes— is it tenderness? Or maybe just a spark of it.

· • ·

We drive for almost an hour in his battered Toyota with the NGO's logo painted on the side, heading north through a thick forest and then turning west, toward the setting sun. We walk on a sandy path through the bushes and suddenly it's as though a curtain has been lifted. Miles and miles of open view, of deep blue sea and sand lined with the vibrant green of the forest. The sand is as fine as talcum powder and snowy white, just as Tescari's brochure described it. I fill my lungs with the salty air, exhilarated by the open space.

We sit, and watch the sun go down. It's low tide and the water has just started to retreat, its rivulets are sculpting wavy furrows in the sand, the crabs running obliquely on its translucent surface.

"This is beautiful," I say.

The sun looks like an egg yolk ready to plop into the sea. I stand up and quickly strip off my shirt and unbutton my trousers.

He stands up, too, alarmed.

"What are you doing?"

"I'm going for a swim."

"No. You can't go in like that."

He quickly picks up my clothes and hands them back to me.

"Yes, I can. There's nobody around for miles and miles. And you've seen me naked before."

"Stella!"

I drop my panties on the sand and I slide off into the velvety, lukewarm water. I dive in and swim until I'm almost out of breath. When I reemerge I see him standing on the edge of the water with my clothes crumpled in his hand.

I swim out and out, where the sea gets bluer and darker, and after the last strokes I can muster, I wonder if I should worry about sharks. Suddenly, I make out a shadow, as a dark, elongated shape darts past me. I shoot up screaming, and he emerges from the froth, like a shiny dolphin, stark naked.

· • ·

We drive back in silence. It's a good kind of silence, as if the swim has exhausted us but also washed something away. The opaque film that has shrouded my days here has dissolved and now everything looks brighter.

By the time we reach the village it's night; there has been a power cut, and the house is wrapped in darkness, but for the faint glow of the kerosene lamp flickering through the windows. I can tell that Farida has been looking after our supper, there's a smell of curry wafting onto the porch. Before entering the house Andrea stops for a moment and rests a hand on top of my shoulder.

"You are the first person from my old life who has come to visit. It was a shock to see you. It was a shock to be speaking Italian again. I am sorry if I've seemed distant. It just felt like—well, like a lot to contend with."

"Of course. I understand. Don't worry."

"The day you arrived I was up all night, I just couldn't go to sleep. I was reminiscing, you know—all this stuff that I thought I had forgotten started coming back."

"I'm sorry I barged into your life just like that, I didn't—"

"No. No, it's great. It's really good to see you, Stella. Yes."

I reach for his hand, which is still resting on my shoulder, and I wrap my palm around it.

"Do you see me as a failure?" he asks. "Like some kind of beached hippie?"

"No, I don't," I say, and I squeeze his hand in mine, hard. "I really don't."

We enter the house and in the semidarkness I discern Farida sitting still on the floor, slightly slumped, her head hanging low. Only now I realize how worried she must be, seeing that Andrea and I have disappeared together. After all I am an impenetrable mystery to her—an older *mzungu* woman—an enigma she cannot even converse with or maybe even begin to grasp, like all of Andrea's life before her.

But as she hears us coming in, she leaps up and comes forward, and her face lights up. Maybe I'm wrong again here, I keep misreading the signs. From the way they look at each other, the way they gently exchange a few words, I see their bond is even stronger than what I'd glimpsed earlier. I look at Farida again. No, she isn't concerned after all. I'm not a threat to her. She knows her husband intimately.

And far better than I.

· · ·

The next morning they drive me to the airport in the NGO's car. I'm flying back to Dar and from there on to Rome. Gregorio is coming to pick me up at the airport with Olga. Strange, how home has never felt so blurred.

For the occasion Andrea and Farida have put on their nice clothes—immaculate white *kanzu* and embroidered *buibui* because there will be people they know leaving or arriving on the small plane from the Big Island and there will doubtless be polite conversations and exchanges of news. Andrea moves around the tiny airport with ease, he weighs my bag on the scale, has a chat with the man in overalls who checks my ticket and passport, greets the people he knows. Farida has once again been holding my wrist tightly all along and now that Andrea has gone to get me a bottle of water she keeps repeating something to me in a hushed voice, something urgent, which he's not meant to hear. She repeats it two, three times and I turn my palms up. I don't understand. She reiterates the same words, more forcefully this time, but I widen my eyes.

"*Nini?* What?" I ask.

She laughs. And then Andrea comes back and tells me it's time I go, they are about to board the plane, so I am going to have to leave without knowing what Farida so urgently wanted me to know. Though I'm aware this is not the right thing to do here, I hug her and kiss her on the cheek. And yet I don't shake hands with Andrea because I've been told that's another taboo, one I don't wish to violate as my parting gesture.

"Wait! Just a second!" I call out, before they get back to the car. I have pulled out my phone. Farida immediately strikes an awkward pose, as I take the picture of the two of them. This is the only picture I've taken during the whole trip. I peer at the tiny screen. It's a good one.

I know they will have beautiful children.

·　●　·

"Same flight again, eh?" I hear a voice behind my back.

"Yeah, same flight," I say to Tescari. Today he wears another freshly ironed blue shirt and orange trousers, hair still wet from a shower.

I see Jeffrey Stone in the lot, too, standing next to his brand-new SUV into which he'll soon climb and drive off.

"I bet you're happy to be heading back. At least I know I am," Tescari says under his breath. "This place would drive anyone nuts. Mosquitoes, crazy people, no booze, mangroves. It's hope-less."

I know that Carlo Tescari will sit next to me and talk nonstop for the entire length of the flight. He'll feel even more entitled to do so now, given our newly born comradeship, which we'd sealed earlier with gin.

After all, haven't we come from the same place, and aren't we headed in the same direction?

The Presence of Men

The bells woke Lara up at seven. When she opened her eyes under the tall vaulted ceiling, for a split second she felt as though she were inside a church. It had been her first night in the new house in the village and she'd slept beautifully.

She was emerging from the shower in her plum-colored, Moroccan-style bathroom when she heard a vigorous knock at the front door. Still dripping wet, she ran down in her robe, crossed the courtyard and opened the old wooden door, which had been painstakingly sandpapered and waxed. A small woman of indefinite age, with an old-fashioned perm, her body shaped like a box, was staring at her.

"You are the person who bought this house?" she asked, her voice loud as a trumpet. She was a local, as Lara could tell from her accent. She nodded.

"Ha ha! At last you are here in person!" the little woman said with a cruel smile and slid herself inside the courtyard like an eel.

"For months all I've been seeing are your builders. Very rude people. Where do they come from?"

"Martano, I think. Why?" Lara wondered if the small woman had come to give her some kind of fine, although she wore no uniform.

"I knew it. Martano people are all thieves."

"I'm so sorry, signora. Was there a problem?"

The woman ignored her and proceeded to take a long, critical look at the potted plants that filled the courtyard, at the indigo blue table and matching chairs that Lara had spotted in a magazine and bought online. She closely examined the pale dusty mauve of the walls, a hue that had cost days of trial and error.

"I see you have changed everything in here."

Lara wasn't sure where this might be leading.

"Well, I have restored the place. It was a ruin."

The woman ignored her and peered some more. "My great-aunt lived in this house," she said.

She brushed the smooth surface of the wall, then moved swiftly toward the glass door of what used to be the barn and glanced inside.

"She used to keep her donkey in there," she said, pointing at the space.

"Oh yes? Well, that's the living room now."

"She never married, she worked very hard all her life. She was a very clever woman."

Lara tried a friendlier expression. All this might be pretty sweet, after all. "So you knew this place from the time she lived here? How nice. Would you like to see what it looks like now?"

Lara opened the glass door, which gave into the ex-barn-now-living-room, but the woman was already snooping inside the kitchen on the opposite side of the courtyard.

"I knew this place like the back of my hand. We used to play in here all the time when we were children."

She stepped into the kitchen and Lara followed her. There were still unopened boxes on the floor; the stainless steel surfaces of the brand-new appliances glinted in the shady room. The woman gave a yelp.

"See! I had heard from people you had done this, but I wanted to see for myself."

"Had done what?" Lara asked.

The woman was glaring at the opposite wall.

"*This* thing you have done in here, is a mortal sin."

By now, had she been in Rome, Lara would have normally

lost her patience and asked her to leave, but it was her first contact with any of her neighbors in the village and she sensed she'd reached a delicate intersection that required some caution.

"A mortal sin!" the little woman repeated in a thundering voice.

"Please have a seat. Can I offer you a cup of coffee?"

"No."

"Okay. Then please, what is it that I did?"

"The *forno*. You tore it down."

Lara crossed her arms.

"Yes I did, the architect . . . my friend," she said, but immediately regretted bringing an architect into the conversation. "It was as big as a room. It took up too much space, it took half the courtyard."

But the woman was right; when, a year earlier, Lara had bought the house in the heart of the village, she'd taken Silvana, her architect friend, to see it. She was a towering woman in her forties with flaming hennaed hair who on principle never came off her high heels, especially when marching through building sites ("height gains you respect, it's Pavlovian"). Silvana had paced inside the old building not uttering a sound, with an air of concern. Maybe it was just her way, or maybe she didn't approve of the house. Lara had begun to worry. Silvana had taken one look at the opening of the gigantic wood oven in the kitchen and before Lara could say anything she'd climbed inside it with the speed of a crab, holding her flashlight.

"It's gigantic. And totally useless," her voice had boomed from the dark interior, like Jonah's from inside the whale.

She'd reappeared, her clothes coated in blackish dust, then effortlessly slid out of the oven mouth. She had a big grin on her face.

"Good. We can gain some space. I feel a lot better now."

So the *forno* went down, and what was once a dark chamber was now a third of her courtyard.

The little woman waved her index finger at Lara like a mad evangelist.

"You tore down the last oven of this village to gain a little space for your plants. That *forno* was a public monument. It was part of our history!"

The woman shook her head with disdain.

"Yes, I was told this room was the village bakery. But as I told you the wood oven took half the space of the courtyard. I mean, it went from here all the way to . . ." Lara made a sweeping arc with her hand across the expanse of the courtyard.

"This was not a *bakery*. It was a communal oven. An oven where people could bring their own loaves of bread. Bread and pies, so that my aunt could bake for them. She only charged ten, twenty liras a piece. We all came here as children with our tins, everyone did, every Saturday . . ."

"Did you? How nice. So, what did . . ." Lara loved stories like this, it was part of what had drawn her to the village in the first place. But the woman was talking right over her question.

" . . . And in winter, when it was really cold, this was the warmest room in the whole village, so we sat in that corner, see? My aunt used to have a wooden bench right there."

The woman gestured to the wall where now sat the dishwasher still sheathed in its cardboard box.

"My aunt would give us sweets while we waited. In the summer we'd wait outside in the garden, and we'd play with the donkey. This is how things were in this village up until only forty, fifty years ago."

The little woman grabbed a chair and slumped on it, hands entwined on her lap. Her feet barely touched the ground. Lara was beginning to feel it had been a mistake to let this creature in. Obviously this was only the beginning of something far more serious than Lara had envisaged.

The little woman went on. "But of course, what do you care? You people come from the outside and assume everything here is up for sale and you think you have a right to take it down, rip it all up as you please. You even bring your own *architect* to destroy our history!"

Lara stared at the little woman, shocked. This was truly a disgrace. She'd come to this village with the best intentions, eager to learn and respect the local culture and traditions. And now—barely twenty-four hours after she'd moved in—she was already facing the enormity of her first mistake.

"*Senta signora,* I'm sorry about the wood oven," Lara said. "I had no idea how important it was. In fact nobody told me. I'm really sorry, I . . . I wish I had known before, is all I can say."

It was true: the local real-estate agent—a young man with overly gelled hair and two cell phones constantly ringing—hadn't said a word about the oven being part of the village history, had made no mention of the old lady with a donkey who baked for the community; he didn't mention village women and children taking their tins of pies and bread into what was now her stainless steel kitchen.

"Why did you buy a house here?" the woman asked, a prosecutor for the defendant.

Lara widened her arms, resigned.

"Because I love this village and I wanted to preserve this beautiful house." She breathed in a bit and continued, "Which by the way would've crumbled had I not bought it."

The woman didn't balk; she shook her head.

"You people don't come here to buy property because you love it. You come because it's *cheaper.*"

Such was Lara's welcome to her new life in the house she'd bought right after her divorce.

· • ·

The truth was the little woman had a point. Tuscany was ridiculously expensive. Umbria was sold out. The Aeolian Islands were for millionaires. Whereas in this exquisite and undiscovered village in the depths of southern Italy, the house plus the cost of its renovation had equaled almost exactly the money Lara had managed to extract from the settlement. She'd thought of the quaint house in the heart of the village not only as a good investment or a summer holiday escape, but more like a second home where she could retreat all year round, and start over. She wanted it to look fresh and simple like those photos in *Elle Décor,* with handwoven baskets brimming with lavender sprigs or vegetables just picked from the garden, with linen tablecloths thrown over lovely old tables, secluded gardens and mosquito nets shrouding immaculate beds. Lara couldn't deny she'd seen the opportunity of a little side business as well, maybe involving buying/fixing up/selling properties. It was impossible not to, given the prices of local real estate. In the course of the previous year, Lara had come up to the village several times to oversee the restoration work, often enough to notice how old people seemed to be dying at a worrisome rate—at least according to how often church bells tolled announcing yet another funeral. During the time it took for the workers to finish, she saw more and more old houses go up for sale as younger people kept migrating up north. The new generation refused to work in the fields and the olive groves in favor of more appealing opportunities, like opening a cell phone store in some northern province with ghastly weather. Lara felt she'd stumbled on a pot of gold. All she needed to acquire a piece of property was a modest amount of capital. She didn't have any access to it at the moment, but she had always tended toward the unrealistic. The future, from underneath her high-vaulted ceiling, had seemed full of hope and potential.

· · ·

Lara felt she should look into the *forno* issue right away. That same afternoon she went online and found a posting on medieval communal ovens in France and England. There was no mention of the same in the south of Italy, which suggested she could add her own entry on Wikipedia if she ever decided to. According to the website they were called bakehouses and they were places *"where women and children would bring their tins of bread and biscuits for baking. Meeting at the bakehouse was also a way to exchange news and local gossip. Each woman marked her bread loaf with a distinctive cut to make sure she got back her own bread after baking."*

Reading all this made her feel even more at fault. The next day she walked to the city council, an unattractive modern building that sat like a shoe box on a parking lot and asked if she might see the historic plan of the village. She was shown inside the office of a skinny man with clearly dyed hair, semihidden behind piles of papers. He looked through the files and pulled out an old map. He showed her several locations, all marked with an *F*, which stood for *forno*. One of those capital *F*'s stood right over her building. It turned out that yes, she had indeed taken down the village's last bakehouse, which was "protected" and should have never been touched.

"I never meant to have done that!" Lara blurted out. She believed in karma and felt as though, by following her architect's advice, she had demolished an Egyptian tomb, with all the consequences that the sacrilege might entail. The skinny man behind the desk reassured her. Yes, she had actually broken the law, but it could all be fixed by paying a little something. It was going to be a small fine. Nothing much. Not to worry.

"I'll pay, of course. That's not the problem, it's just that . . . it's that I feel really bad that we . . ." Her voice broke a little. "That *I* did this. It was totally unintentional."

The skinny man seemed surprised by her concern. Obviously the oven didn't mean as much to him as to the little woman with the bad perm.

Lara rang her architect and told her about the communal oven.

Silvana cut her off. "We gained twenty square meters of walking space. It's an added value to the property."

"I know, I know. But—"

"You are just being sentimental, Lara. Just forget about it."

"I feel like we committed a crime. Which by the way we did. Apparently we actually broke the law."

But Silvana just laughed. "Well, Lara, it seems to me that everyone else did too, since you say it was the last remaining oven in the village."

"Yes, but it was a protected monument."

"What were you going to do with it anyway, bake loaves for the masses?" Silvana laughed. "This isn't the eighteenth century, everyone *has* an oven now. Anyway, let's talk about this later, I'm with a client now."

Lara realized how, until that moment, the politics of her street had completely escaped her, wrapped up as she'd been with only the builders and her architect. Up until now the neighbors had been to her only extras in the background, blank faces she hadn't paid any attention to and couldn't remember. Owning a house in a village was clearly very different from moving into a new apartment in a city, where anonymity was not only okay but an asset. She had moved into a community that had lived so closely together for years and years, where everyone knew every little thing about one another. Now this foreigner had shown up from out of the blue; for months she had been coming and going, ignoring their existence, interested only in her building work, and not once bothering to say hello or goodbye. Another mistake that needed immediate correction.

She decided the right person to ask would be the young man with plucked eyebrows—a distinctive trait she'd observed in the local male youth—who served her cappuccino every morning at the café in the piazza. The little woman's name was Mina, he told her. Everyone knew her: she was a dressmaker, the best in the area. She'd had a good elementary and high school education, a bit of money she'd saved, and although she'd never married she was self-sufficient and, according to the village standards, successful. Figuratively speaking, she was the mayor of Lara's street.

The following morning Lara knocked at Mina's door, presenting a box of chocolates. She saw the sewing machine, a stack of fabrics, a cat curled up on the table where Mina had been cutting a cloth, licking his paws.

Mina grabbed the box.

"Thank you," she said without smiling.

There were wisps of thread floating like dragonflies in the breeze blowing from the open windows. Lara smelled the heat rising from fabric that was being ironed.

"I was just wondering, Signora Mina . . . ," she said. "If I brought you a shirt, could you copy it for me?"

. . .

Apparently Mina had first gained her stature because of her closeness with the local barons, Donna Clara, Don Filippo, their children and later on to their children's husbands and wives. She had measured waists, bellies and breasts of three generations of barons and baronesses, brushed their bodies with her nimble fingers, draped cloth around their hips and buttocks. She knew how the women of the family tended to grow heavy around the thighs and thin in the torso, how the men would stay thin but put on love handles after forty. She suggested—discreetly—which cut or length would best suit them. The family had worn her perfectly tailored clothes at first communions, weddings, baptisms and garden parties, season after season. Whenever she would run into them on her way to the grocery shop, or at one of the many processions or funerals that ran along the main street, she would check out their dresses, jackets, trousers and whisper to a neighbor walking alongside her, "See how nicely it falls in the back? Look at the way I did the pleats, the pockets, the lapels. How becoming the cut on the shoulders, the collar, the way it's pinched at the waist."

By the time Lara bought the house on Mina's street, Donna Clara and Don Filippo had been dead for ten years at least and their children and grandchildren were scattered between Rome, Milan, Paris and Madrid. The second generation of barons worked as doctors, lawyers and financial consultants; one had become a successful shoe designer and was in a happy gay marriage in Spain. Things had changed a lot since the time of their parents; they no longer cared to use their titles and hardly ever came back to their eighteenth-century palazzo in the village square. It was too expensive to keep and none of them wanted to live there anyway, so they rented it out for weddings in order to pay for its maintenance. From April to October, young brides from the nearby villages wrapped in the cloud of tulle they'd always dreamed of would get photographed leaning from the balcony of the palazzo against a wall of ivy, or under a cascade of wisteria. By then even the people in the village had begun to shop at the OVS, the ubiquitous cheap department store where one could buy clothes for thirty-five euros. The epoch of tailored clothes was officially over.

· ● ·

Leo, the house is finished (I officially moved in three weeks ago!) as you can see from the attached photos. It's actually a lot larger and more spacious than it looks in the pictures. The ceilings are spectacularly high, I just can't get them all in the shot because I don't have the right lens. I walk to the beach every day (twenty minutes, walking briskly), I swim, I read a lot, I pick my rucola and fresh zucchini from the garden (did you know they grow overnight? They turn into monsters if you forget to pick them) and soon the figs will be ready on the tree. My neighbors are all supernice old ladies (not a man in sight, they must have all died or run off) and I've done all I could in my power to make them feel comfortable having me here. The other night I had a party for all of them. I baked spelt banana bread (which they had never had), made buckwheat cherry muffins (which they had never heard of) and

made tea (which they never drink, this is espresso nation).
However I made them try everything and after a few awkward moments and many laughs I have a feeling we bonded.
Mina is my favorite one; she's an amazing seamstress, she's
made me two beautiful shirts and a dress that cost me next
to nothing. It's incredible: you just bring her a Prada shirt
and she makes its identical twin for 25 euros! This is part of
what is so lovely about living here: everything is simple, easy
and cheap. When are you going to come? You did promise,
remember? Can't wait to spend a bit of time with you!

It had taken almost an hour to compose an e-mail to her
brother. It was important that she sounded funny and light, and
that she gave the most alluring description of her new domain. He
e-mailed her back ten days later. Late and economical, as always.

Hi, thanks for the pix, very martha stewart. I'm coming to visit
in august for a few days, I'll be with a client I'm representing,
ben jackson (have u seen "the man at the door"?), the guard-
ian published a big spread last week on yr area, it looked
really cool, then we go visit friends in pantelleria, talk to u
soon. Does skype work from there?

. . .

Six years earlier Leo had moved to London, where he'd begun his
career as an assistant to a film agent. Recently he had followed
his boss to Los Angeles and become a partner. All of a sudden
younger stars were flocking to him. He was perfect for the job;
taking care of others had been his number-one specialty since he
was a child. He seemed to possess a bottomless reserve of charm
that he was able to shower on anyone he encountered. He was a
natural. People came away from their first encounter with him
certain to have made an indelible impression and a dent in his

heart, a certainty that Leo was careful to keep feeding. His charm was his secret weapon, ensuring he'd be loved back, even if falsely or temporarily.

Thus it was odd how one of the very few people left out of this tight circle of love was his sister. He seemed to have lost interest in Lara, as if time spent in her company was not as rewarding as with everyone else. Yes, his life had taken a sharp turn and was now very different from hers—he attended exclusive parties, flew business class to film festivals, had his expensive meals and hotels paid for with a corporate card and was followed by an endless string of girlfriends without names. He was capable of sending a gift via iTunes to a particularly nice salesgirl with whom he'd had a casual conversation about a band while trying on clothes, or sending flowers with a thank-you note to an older lady he'd met on a plane ("For the wonderful conversation that made our flight last only minutes!"). But he hardly ever remembered to call his sister. Whenever Lara rang him he always happened to be in a meeting; if they succeeded in having a conversation he endured prolonged pauses during which she could hear him tapping on computer keys, and her own metallic voice reverberating in the room on speaker phone. Lara had begun to fear that he might be thinking of her as a loser. The Martha Stewart remark only confirmed this worry.

You can't come with Ben Jackson, this house isn't grand enough for him!! Let me book him a place where he'll be much more comfortable. There is a fabulous palazzo converted into B&B only six km from me. Jodie Foster stayed there. Please don't let him come and stay! No Skype from here, sorry. Signal is too weak.

Leo's response came, surprisingly, just two hours later.

Ben is cool. The house looks fine. Stop fretting.

. . .

The shirts and dresses always came neatly folded inside a plastic envelope, crisp and skillfully pressed, then wrapped in a sheet of newspaper sealed with tape. The package felt solid and as full of promise as a gift box from an exclusive boutique. Mina's work had a Victorian quality. It was flawless in every detail; the collar, pleats and buttonholes were stitched as if by an invisible hand and the buttons were either mother of pearl or covered in the same material as the dress. Lara's full name was always embroidered inside the collar in lovely childish lettering. Each time Lara had to insist that Mina quote her a price, but she would turn her head, reluctantly, the other way.

"I don't know. You give me what you think is right."

"Please, Mina. Otherwise I cannot ask you to make me anything else. Please."

This would go on for a while, till Mina would finally relent.

"Ten, fifteen, you decide. Whatever you think is right."

Lara would put a twenty on the table and Mina would snatch it without a sound the minute Lara took her eyes away. Clearly it was part of village etiquette, this pretense that money wasn't the issue. Outside of what she paid for the house itself, this felt like the best-spent money of her entire life. Lara, in her new clothes, looked in the mirror and saw herself slender and pretty again.

"Mina, you are a genius."

Mina cocked her head, beaming. Since the day Lara had become such an enthusiastic client, the issue of the *forno* seemed to have been forgotten, or at least put temporarily behind them.

. . .

For two years now Lara had seen her own body progressively lose its contours and definition. It wasn't age, it was the divorce that had caused the implosion and slackened her from within. Her whole being had lost muscle and core, as though what she'd assumed was her legendary physical strength, her lean muscular body trained by years of running, and then practicing and teaching yoga, had turned out to be only a secondary effect of the safety of her marriage, a reflection of her domestic stability. The minute her husband was gone, so too fled her body. Since then, clothes had had the purpose only of covering up what she feared about herself.

· • ·

At first there had been boredom. It had seeped into their marriage like a fume. Suddenly there was nothing to talk about, it was as simple as that. Nothing in the news worth discussing, nothing worth watching together on TV, no Caravaggio exhibit worth standing in line for, nothing they could share and use as a conversation piece. Just "Would you like another coffee? Are you coming back for lunch? Did you pick up my jacket from the cleaners? I am so tired I think I'll just go to bed." Their life had shrunk to a sequence of polite questions and answers that only served to make sure the mechanics of their cohabitation kept on working.

Then came the rage. It hit them like a tornado, it blew away the fume of boredom and shook their household from the foundations. In fifteen operatic minutes on one Sunday night everything came down and shattered. Rage made them feel alive and strong, gave color to their cheeks, lit their eyes. They were, for a fleeting moment, beautiful and sexy again. Of course it was a younger woman—a French one—whom they'd met at a dinner party three months earlier—a fact that gave Lara the chance to replay and revise all the instances when her husband had told her he wasn't coming home for dinner/was going to see his brother in Genoa/ meet in Paris an investor for his green technology firm, etc., etc. Lara stood up from the kitchen table, where they were eating a spinach and beluga lentil salad, and hurled the plate across the room. She saw the crumbled feta scatter in slow motion, then land on his shirt like snowflakes. She detected a flash of terror in his eyes and knew that at last she'd gained some power over him. She immediately furthered the opportunity and slapped him in the face. The gesture felt artful and precise as if, along with the shock, a supernatural force had just lodged inside her and was going to stay for good.

Sadly, rage turned out to be a bad drug; it never tasted as good as the first time and when it dissolved it left her limp on the floor like a used dishrag. She had tried to recapture its magnificence by summoning him again the next day for a further explanation (by then he'd checked into a hotel) but the force was gone, her fury was only a repetition of a stale act that led her nowhere. Now that he had abandoned the house, her husband seemed to have become invulnerable as if, after nine long years of marriage, he had, overnight, learned the trick of how to become a stranger. He was no longer scared of her reactions, but accommodating like a doctor with a difficult patient, ready to file for divorce, willing to take care of the bills and let her have the apartment. He was simply in a hurry to leave her behind.

"Is it because of the sex? I just need to know," she finally asked, wincing at the predictability of the words she was saying. It was the last time they saw each other alone, before the lawyers became their permanent bodyguards.

"No," he said.

"Then what is it? Does she make you feel younger?"

"No," he said, drawing out the syllable into two and moving his gaze toward her with a hint of mercy. "Actually, she makes me laugh."

Months later, once she had adjusted to the situation, the thing she regretted the most was having asked this last question. She could easily have lived with the version everyone had heard a million times, which required no translation, being the same in Chinese and Icelandic: man leaves wife for a younger, sexy girl

who adores him without discernment. But no. He had left her
for someone he simply had more fun with. She had visions of her
husband and the girl driving through Provence in a convertible,
laughing their heads off, as their hair blew in the wind.

Had she lost her sense of humor along the way, or—and this was
what she feared the most—had she never had one to begin with?

· · ·

Her brother texted her three days before arriving:

How many bars?

Just one in the main square.
They don't serve fancy cocktails, I warn you.

I mean bars as in reception for iPhone.

Ooops. 2. Sometimes 4 if u go up on the roof.

· · ·

Ben Jackson had gained at least twenty pounds in the last few
years. He was on the verge of fat, but because of his height he
looked Orson Wellesian. He emerged from the rental car sweaty
and pale in wrinkled linen pants, a faded T-shirt and flip-flops. He
stretched his arm out to Lara with a standard paparazzi-friendly
grin, then changed his mind and gave her a brief hug.

"Hey Lara, thanks so much for having me."

Leo was getting their bags out of the trunk. He and Ben were
wearing the same expensive-looking sunglasses. Their bags were
identical too.

"What are you, twins?" Lara said to her brother in Italian. She
was eager to show off her funny side.

"Gifts from the Cannes Film Festival. We were there last week."

Leo threw his eyes toward Ben and whispered, "Watch out. He had an Italian girlfriend, he speaks some."

Lara had been scrubbing the house all day and moving furniture around; she'd thrown pillows this way and that, tried a couple of different bedspreads for splashes of color. She had scattered issues of *The New Yorker* and *The Week* here and there, with a couple of *Vanity Fair*s for nighttime reading or in case the conversation languished. She guided them from room to room, telling a story for each one (we had to take down the wall here, see the floor? these are very old tiles, this used to be the barn, the kitchen was in the old days a communal oven, isn't that interesting?). The two men nodded and hmm'ed in turn and when she sensed they were beginning to get restless she cut the tour short and opened a bottle of cold Leone de Castris rosé.

They had dinner in the garden, where she'd strategically strewn a whole bag of tea lights. She served a lemony Middle Eastern salad, and calamari drowned in parsley. Leo and Ben didn't comment on the food, engrossed as they were in dissecting a number of the films they'd seen at Cannes. It was a lot of "I loved that bit, hated the ending, she was great, he sucked, oh, she is in rehab." Lara was eager to contribute but didn't find an entry into their tight Ping-Pong. The minute they mentioned an Indian director she managed to veer the conversation away from films. Somehow she found herself talking about the Hugging Mother, an Indian guru she'd gone to see in Kerala the previous year, right after the divorce. After only a few sentences she felt their attention waver and their silence go hollow, but it was too late to turn back. She braved it and kept on going.

"I thought, if it's true that she can make you feel better with a hug, why not? I was going through a very bad patch, anything to make me feel saner."

"Right," Ben agreed politely, helping himself again to the calamari. He sure had an appetite.

"There were thousands of people waiting outside the ashram under the sun. But we Westerners had a separate, much faster line."

"That's total bullshit," Leo interjected. "Why would you have a separate line?"

"First-class and second-class hugs?" Ben suggested, rounding his eyes in mock innocence.

"Whatever. I was happy, it was sweltering. Anyway, finally it was my turn and there she was, this small, round person waiting to hug me!"

Lara suddenly realized she didn't have a punch line, an unexpected twist or a satisfactory ending to the story. The anecdote lacked a tidy structure—a bit like her life, she thought.

"Did it work?" Leo asked with an undertone of sarcasm.

Lara avoided the trap.

"No. It was just a hug, really. It didn't change a thing."

Ben looked at her with what she took as sympathy. He surely had put on too much weight but he still had those eyes—honey-colored killer eyes and thick eyelashes that, luckily for him, would never go away.

"I'd love to be hugged by an Indian guru," he said. "God knows I need a hug these days."

He and Leo exchanged a look as if they were privy to a secret. With that the conversation tapered off and turned into a long stretch of silence.

"Hey Lara, I love your shirt," Ben said at last, uneasily, as though he felt the need to fill it in.

"Thank you. My next-door neighbor made it. She's quite a character, actually a fantastic—"

"I already told him about her," Leo interjected, as if to say, Please don't start with another cute tale.

Lara wished she'd let them talk about their movie life and movie friends and had never brought up the subject of hugs. Perhaps it would have been better to play the brooding, slightly eccentric recluse, a much more interesting character to embody than the eager, chirping hostess. Was it too late now to change her persona? Why had she agreed to have a movie star under her roof? Had Leo said they were staying a week? A whole week now seemed an enormity to bear.

She began to clear the table. Ben stood up to help her collect the dishes.

"Oh God, please don't," she said.

"Please, I always do it at home."

"No way. Really."

"But why? I want to help."

Lara gave a little laugh.

"I can't have Ben Jackson load the dishwasher in my kitchen. I just won't allow it."

Ben sat down obediently and pulled out his phone. He had been checking it a few times already. Leo lifted his index fingers toward the sky.

"On the roof," he reminded Ben.

.   •   .

The moon had just come up behind the church tower. The night was sweet and jasmine-scented. She loaded the dishwasher with exaggerated attention. She had read somewhere that, even when loading the dishwasher, paying attention to every tiny movement could be counted as a Zen practice. Apparently all one had to do was be aware and stay in the present moment. Despite all the yoga she had never been sure what being in the moment really meant. Yet she tried to savor sliding the plates into their slots one by one. She waited.

Adjusted her breathing.

Yes.

Maybe that was it.

The moment.

As precious as all the others that she had let go by without noticing, and now so stark in its uniqueness and unrepeatability.

She stood still in front of the dirty plates and concentrated harder, waiting for further epiphany. The breeze carried Ben's voice whispering sweet somethings into his phone while Leo sat in the dark smoking a joint and she could hear him exhale.

Then the moment passed.

. . .

Leo stumbled into the kitchen around ten the next morning, puffy and unshowered, just as Lara had finished laying the table for breakfast. She'd placed a couple of hydrangeas and English roses in a glass. It looked so lovely that she snapped a photo.

"Buongiorno! Il caffè è pronto nel thermos."

Switching to Italian with Leo made her feel more at ease, as it seemed to create the kind of intimacy she was craving.

He slumped in the chair with a sleepy grunt and poured half the thermos in his cup. "Where is Ben?" she asked.

"He's in the shower. Or on the phone, I'm not sure. Can you turn that thing down a bit?"

Lara lowered the volume on the radio: it was her favorite morning news program.

"That's better. So, what's up?" he asked, using the affectionate voice of family.

"What do you mean exactly?"

"What are your plans? Are you going to live here now?"

"Not all year round. But spend as much time as possible here in the warmer months, yes."

Leo looked around, as if taking in the place for the first time.

"And what are you planning to do for a living?"

He meant now that her divorce had been settled, and there was no more alimony coming her way.

"Oddio . . . that's a big question so early in the morning."

"Well, that's the question Mamma keeps asking me, which I have no answer for."

"You two discuss my future when she calls you in L.A.?"

"Not always. But she wonders, you know."

"Well, I was thinking I could get into a bit of real estate. You can buy property for next to nothing here."

"That sounds good. Do you have the money?"

"Not right now. But it's something I could get into in the near future."

Leo gave an unconvinced nod. Lara searched for an alternative.

"I was also thinking I could go back to teaching yoga. I could organize retreats here in the summer. People would love it. They could practice early in the morning and then go for a swim. This place is ideal."

Leo didn't say anything, waiting for more.

"I also thought—this sounds a bit like a crazy idea but I think it could work—I could start a little flower shop. I could use this kitchen as the store. It already has street access. You know, this was the *forno* in the old days, where people—"

"Yes, you've already told me that."

"Right. Sorry. But look how pretty this combination is." She brushed the flowers in the glass with her fingertips. "I could make really pretty arrangements using the flowers that grow all around here. Wildflowers."

"Yoga and flowers?" Leo said, studying the list of ingredients on the box of organic cookies Lara had put on the table. "That sounds a bit optimistic . . ."

"Well, I'd have to figure out the costs. I've only just started thinking about the future."

He put the box down and grabbed a *cornetto*. "It worries me that you have no safety net anymore."

But more than worried he sounded annoyed, as if this concern was something he didn't want to feel responsible for. Since her divorce, Leo had strayed even further away from her. Could it be that, now that she was on her own, she had become too much of a liability?

Ben's voice reached them from outside. He was, as ever, murmuring on the phone to someone, his conversation punctuated by a mix of short laughs and whispers.

"Is he still married?" Lara had a faint memory of a wife pictured next to him on a red carpet, a small brunette wearing sensible shoes.

"Yeah." Leo bit into a second *cornetto*. "They're having a bit of a . . . I'd say better not mention the subject right now."

"Okay." She looked around the room, searching for inspiration. "Hey, would you like me to take you two to see the cathedral in Otranto? It has an amazing floor, the largest Byzantine mosaic in the world. Would Ben like that kind of thing?"

Leo shrugged.

"I don't know. It might be too hot for sightseeing, and I think he wanted to just chill while he was here—"

Ben walked into the kitchen. His hair was wet and combed back like a schoolboy's. He was wearing just a faded sarong tightly wrapped around his waist. He had a big, glowing smile on his face and was still clutching his phone as if his joy was directly connected to the device.

"Good morning! What a glorious day!"

"I'll make some more coffee," Lara said, looking away; she found his big naked belly disconcerting.

Ben sat down and whispered something to Leo with a grin. Lara watched them as they spoke furtively. Their childish secrecy was making her uncomfortable.

"What are your plans for the day? Shall we go swimming?" she suggested. "I can take you to a lovely beach only ten minutes away, if you feel like it."

"We were thinking . . . ," Ben began, eyeing Leo, as if needing his help.

Leo immediately took charge.

"How about that dressmaker you mentioned? Do you think

she could make us something? We actually brought some material and shirts to copy."

"Mina? Of course. She'll be thrilled."

And so was Lara. Not only to share with them that gift but also, she realized, to be rid of them, even if only for an hour.

.   •   .

They entered Mina's breezy room with the cat and the flying wisps of thread. She was sitting on a tiny chair with her reading glasses perched on her nose, intent on stitching something. She stood up immediately the minute she saw Ben and Leo.

"Come in! Welcome! Please, sit down!" she said, grabbing a chair and a stool. "And who are these nice *giovanotti*? Are they both your brothers?"

Lara had never seen her so excited before. Oh, the presence of men, she thought. The difference it always makes.

Leo shook her hand, yes he was Lara's younger brother, and Ben introduced himself as Beniamino, *un amico*. He handed Mina a couple of shirts and patted his stomach.

"I'm afraid I'm bigger now," he said in his broken Italian.

"He means he's put on a little bit of weight, since he bought those," Leo intervened.

Mina took a professional look at the shirts and at Ben's waist-line. She grabbed a measuring tape.

"Lift your arms, please," she ordered.

Mina looked like a dwarf hugging a giant as she slid the tape around him. She scribbled measurements with her childish hand-writing on a scrap of a used paper napkin.

"Now your shoulders. Turn around."

Clearly she had no idea who Ben was—his films were a bit too highbrow for the local cinemas—and this seemed to relax him.

"I guess I'll leave you two in Mina's hands," Lara said, relieved. "I'll be home if you need anything."

The introduction had been a success. She ran back to the house and turned up the volume of the radio, just in time to catch the tail end of her favorite show.

. • .

In the days that followed Mina must have been working nonstop because the packages kept coming. She knocked at the door twice a day to summon Ben or Leo for yet another fitting. She had needles already threaded pinned to her shirt, scissors in her pocket, strands of fabric stuck to her skirt and she always looked frantic, as if high on something. Ben and Leo kept ordering more clothes and buying more fabric. Mina knew of old shops in the nearby villages that still had great leftover cloth from the seventies, or stalls that sold bolts of material at wholesale prices at the farmers' markets. They got in their car and drove incessantly following the directions she drew on her paper napkins. They always came home with rolls of soft percale cotton, pure linen, light cashmere wool under their arms, exultant and rewarded as if they'd been on a great outdoor adventure.

A few days later Lara came home from her midmorning swim and found the house empty. She set up the table for lunch, mixed a couscous salad with eggplant, fresh mint and fennel. Two hours later Leo and Ben came back, Ben waving enthusiastically and mouthing a hello, phone glued to his ear, as he went up the stairs leading to the roof in search of the fourth bar. Leo placed a woven basket filled with muddy potatoes and zucchini on the kitchen counter.

"This is from Mina. She has an amazing vegetable garden in the back of the house. Have you seen it?"

"Nope."

"Ben had a go at digging out the potatoes. It was hilarious."

He went straight to the fridge and poured himself some water. He glanced at the table.

"Don't bother with food, we just had something to eat at Mina's."

"Did you? Did she make you lunch?"

"Yes. *Supplì di riso* with saffron."

Lara cleared away the plates, napkins and her tastefully constructed salad.

" . . . and *carciofi fritti*."

"Wow, pretty fierce, cholesterol wise. And what did you talk about?"

"Lots of stuff. That woman is so much fun. The stories she tells. She told us about an old house right outside the village, past the railroad crossing. Nine rooms, vaulted ceilings, a huge lemon orchard."

"Really?"

"Some relatives of hers want to sell it. She said she could get it for us for something like two hundred."

"Us?" Lara stopped putting the plates away and turned toward her brother. "I had no idea you were interested in real estate, Leo."

"Well, Ben is."

"But why?"

Leo looked at his sister, surprised, then his tone shifted as if he were trying to handle someone irrefutably obstinate.

"What's so strange? He likes it here."

"He hasn't seen anything. All he's done is run back and forth from here to Mina's or up on the roof to talk on the phone."

"Ben has traveled all over the world. He can tell pretty quickly how he feels about a place. And nobody knows who he is here. That's a big plus for him."

Lara sat across from her brother at the kitchen table, discouraged. This little vacation wasn't going at all the way she'd hoped.

"It could be a good investment as well. Ben is pretty shrewd when it comes to business."

"Is he?" she asked, trying to sound neutral.

"Of course. His father was a mega investment banker. Ben has learned a thing or two from him."

"How convenient."

Leo ignored her sarcasm.

"We're going with Mina to look at the house later this afternoon," he said, without inviting her.

Lara felt gloom wrap itself around her like a fog. When she had mentioned her plan about buying property only a couple of days earlier, he hadn't shown a flicker of interest. Why couldn't they ever connect on anything? She had missed her brother and now that she was on her own, she needed him more than she had in the past.

They both remained silent for a moment across the table from each other, suddenly uneasy at finding themselves alone with each other in such a small space. Ben's intense phone flirting came down through the open door in bursts. It had become the musical score of their days together.

"Is this his lover?" Lara asked.

"I don't know."

"Of course it is."

Leo didn't say anything. He stood up and made a move as if to leave the kitchen, then turned back to her.

"Don't you open your mouth."

"As if I could give a shit. Honestly."

"He's in love, okay?"

"Good for him."

Then Leo moved closer, lowering his voice.

"He's *madly* in love, Lara. I've never seen him like this before."

Leo seemed sincerely moved, as if Ben's new happiness had changed things for the better for him as well. Actually, it was generous of her brother, Lara thought, to give some dignity to all those extramarital phone calls.

Lara was beginning to see what her problem was: she wasn't ready to accommodate other people's joy yet, she didn't have enough room in her. Next summer, maybe. It had been a mistake, this desire to share her space so soon. She heard herself saying, "It's a phase. It doesn't last. It never does."

Leo frowned. "Jesus. Why do you have to be so negative?"

"Actually only the other day you called me an optimist. Anyway, it's lust, Leonardo. It's a drug. You know that perfectly well, we've all been through it."

"Maybe we all need a little help for the initial boost," Leo said.

She thought about this for a moment. Yes. Love was a drug, a rave. People got high on it and within half an hour were capable of doing anything in its name. No place was too far to reach, no phone number too expensive to call, no decision faster to make. Lara envisioned a gigantic diptych in the vein of Michelangelo. It would be called *The Last Misjudgment*. Two frescoes on opposite walls: on one, a crowd of people would be engaged in all sorts of crazy activities—jumping off cliffs on Olympic trampolines; getting ready to sail the Atlantic solo or kneeling all the way to Santiago de Compostela, all in the name of love. On the other, the same crowd would be trapped in the debris of their marriages: slumped on couches, snoring in front of TV screens, overweight, dressed like slobs, eating in murderous silence at a pizza parlor.

Was Leo right? Had she really become negative? Hostile? Jealous? God, did she feel awful.

Ben barged in from the roof staircase grinning and made his announcement.

"Green light. We can go tomorrow!"

"Excellent!" Leo stood up, beaming.

They gave each other a high five. Then Ben turned to Lara and said, "We're going to visit a friend in Pantelleria. Do you know how to get there from here?"

"I have no idea. But I'm sure your phone will tell you," Lara said, her voice blurred, as though she'd just woken up from a feverish sleep.

Neither Leo nor Ben seemed to notice her grumpiness, and Ben was already tapping away on his beloved touch screen.

"I'll get Allison to take care of this. She's a whiz when it comes to travel," he said to Lara, smiling his fat boy smile.

· • ·

They left at the speed of a Special Forces operation. There were phone calls to L.A., with Ben's assistant booking tickets to Pantelleria via Rome, bags were packed and more phone calls were made to arrange the details of their arrival at the other end. It turned out that Ben's lover had rented a villa next to Giorgio Armani's on the secluded, volcanic, inhospitable but extremely chic island that lay halfway between Sicily and North Africa. Probably a husband, boyfriend or a not-so-trustworthy friend had just left, so that Ben and his faithful buddy Leo could make the final leap across the Mediterranean. For a moment Lara contemplated saying to her brother "I get it now: basically you two sat in my house as in a parking lot optimizing your wait by working on your wardrobes" but she was tired of being thought of as hostile, negative or, in this case, completely paranoid.

Mina's last package came an hour later, still warm from the ironing board. It was a beautiful linen jacket in a cream color. While Leo was busy loading the car, Ben unfolded it and held it in front of Lara with the tips of his fingers, as if he were showing her the Turin Shroud. Mina had come herself in case last-minute alterations were needed. She helped him slide his arms into the sleeves, frowning slightly as she adjusted the lapels, pulled the front, brushed the back with her palms, straightened the collar. Her light touch had a magic; she made the fabric do exactly what she wanted, till it flattened and fell just the way it was supposed to.

"It's a beauty," Ben declared in front of his audience. *"Come Prada, no?"*

Mina nodded, pretending to know what he meant. She

adjusted the front of the jacket once more and stepped back to look at her finished *capolavoro.*

"*Sembri il principe di Inghilterra.*"

Ben laughed. He turned around in a pirouette and grabbed Mina, hugged her tightly and kissed her on both cheeks.

Mina turned scarlet. For a moment she was so disoriented— how long since a man had touched her, let alone kissed her with such impetus? Perhaps she was used to receiving from men only the damp, marble-cold kisses that people exchanged at funerals. Her schoolmistress mask dissolved and in its place came the face of a ravished awkward schoolgirl with a bad haircut.

That night, after Leo and Ben left, Lara stood alone in the kitchen by the sink eating a nonfat yogurt as her dinner, her gaze fixed on the opposite wall. She ate slowly, savoring every spoonful, just as her book on meditation described. The yogurt tasted especially pure—how could anything white be harmful?—then she opened the fridge and looked at the massive food supply she had hoarded for her guests over the course of the previous days. The vegetables were neatly grouped by color on the bottom shelf, leftovers in identical glass containers were stacked in the middle, jars were arranged by size on the top, whereas all the dairy products were confined in a box with a smiling cow on the lid.

· • ·

The summer heat gradually intensified and reached its peak in mid-July—the scorching sun forced the whole village behind closed shutters for a good part of the day. Lara realized one had to be sturdy to endure that kind of temperature and that she probably didn't have the required stamina. There were days when she felt she was hiding from a raging war. The thick walls of the house protected her, but the moment she opened the door the sun scalded her skin like a burn from the stove. It didn't even feel like heat, it was more like nuclear radiation, an assault of mysterious force from outer space. The true nature of the place had emerged at last and its face was merciless. Her hydrangeas, roses and clematis, which had looked so happy until June, now lay incinerated in their pots. Her pretty courtyard had turned into a cemetery. She finally got it: this was cactus country, all thorns and spikes; it had no patience for anything soft or pastel.

She went swimming at seven each morning, when the small pebbled beach was empty and the water still retained a hint of coolness from the night. Already by eight there would be lines of people, streaming antlike from every direction, holding children, inflatable mattresses, folding chairs, umbrellas, plastic coolers, and by nine the place was swarming with people crammed in a small space, surrounded by their ugly, brightly colored belongings. The mingling of their thighs, hairy chests, stomachs, flabby arms smeared in lotion, plus the loud chorus of their voices, was unbearable. How was it possible that the oasis of peace and solitude she had experienced at the onset of summer had turned into this living hell? Was the dream of her new life in the village yet another mistake she'd made?

When the *farmacia* opened again after the afternoon siesta Lara pleaded with the chemist to let her have a Xanax even without a prescription.

"I wouldn't have the nerve to ask you if this wasn't an emergency," she said quietly.

· ● ·

Toward the middle of August the glare began to dwindle, till it dimmed, anticipating the soft September light. Lara could open the shutters and let the breeze in at last.

Curtains, she thought. Some billowing linen curtains were what she needed. She should have thought about this before when the light had been harsher. She decided it was time to pay Mina a visit—she hadn't seen her for weeks—to ask her where she could get the right material.

She waited for the bells' toll to announce the end of the evening Mass, then opened the door and went outside, watching the procession of her street's *signore* walk back together from church. The evening prayer was their one big outing of the day. It was not to be missed.

The same ladies who, only a couple of months earlier, had populated her vision merely as extras in the background now had names; they were Lina, Ada, Teresa and Assunta. Lara greeted them one by one. The women all had the same rectangular shape as Mina, they all wore similar housedresses in various shades of brown and gray, hair cut short, and held their small handbags close to their chests. They smiled back and waved; they probably didn't approve of the fact that she never attended Mass, not even on Sunday—but Lara felt she had gained their trust in other ways, and that they were even beginning to like her. She waited for Mina to appear, but there was no sign of her within the slow procession, which was unusual, since she was a devoted churchgoer. So she walked over to her house. The door, as usual, was open.

There was fabric all over the place, folded cuts of light merino wool, thick tweeds, dark blue cashmere; shirts, jackets, trousers, coats in various stages of their making were hanging from the backs of the chairs, from the open door of the armoire, from nails on the walls. The proprietor of this vast winter collection was unmistakable: his initials were embroidered inside the collar, on the inner pockets, in a royal swirl. The *B* and the *J* entwined in a knot, in golden thread. Mina sat by the window, sewing, barefoot and disheveled, gray roots showing on the top of her head, a big oily stain on her shirt just above her left breast. The house smelled stuffy and unclean.

"My God, what have you been up to?" Lara asked.

Mina gestured toward the clothes hanging about the room.

"Ben has been sending me the fabrics from America. With DHL."

She pronounced *DHL* with particular pride. International

courier service was clearly a novelty for her (the truck with the logo, the guy in uniform, the printed shipping envelope, how exciting was that? Surely nobody in this tiny village had ever DHLed anything anywhere).

Lara touched the merino wool spread on the table next to a couple of DVDs. She noticed they were both Ben's old movies.

"I've had no time to do anything else but work. No time to water the garden, look . . . everything died, tomatoes, eggplants, peppers. *Tutto morto.*" Mina shook her head, pretending to be worried, but Lara could see that she was gleaming underneath.

In the adjacent room, through the half-opened door, Lara glanced at a flat TV screen. She could swear it had never been there before.

"Ben has to go to Venice for the film festival and he wants this ready for the press conference," Mina said, holding a light gray linen jacket. "I have been up two nights in a row, the courier comes to pick it up tomorrow."

Things had changed indeed, in the brief space of one summer: even Mina knew about film festivals and press conferences now.

Lara lowered herself into a chair. "That's very exciting, Mina. Listen, though, do you think you could make me some curtains? Very simple job, I'll give you the measurements and all you have to do is the hem at the bottom and—"

"Are you kidding? Eh no, *bella mia*!" Mina stopped her in mid-sentence, raising her hand. "See how much work I have to do? Look, he sent me a coat he wants me to copy. I'll show you, it's very expensive, *molto signorile,* it's made in America . . ."

She opened the armoire and pulled out a huge black coat on a wooden hanger. She turned to Lara and brushed its lapels with an automatic gesture.

"He wants me to make him two of these—two!" She laughed. "He says all his friends compliment him on the clothes I make and now he wants me to stitch his whole winter wardrobe. Look at this . . ."

Mina put the ends of the sleeves of one of the jackets she'd made under Lara's nose, pointing to the minute work around the buttons.

"These days nobody hand stitches like this anymore, it's all machine work. By Chinese people! Ha!" She waved a hand in a dismissive gesture.

"Right. I see. Well, I guess you have no time for the curtains, then."

"How? Look at me: I haven't had time to do my hair, cook a decent meal. I am so tired, sometimes I fall asleep right at the sewing machine!"

Her throaty laugh went up an octave.

Lara stood and made a move toward the door.

"Okay, well . . . I guess this is good for you, Mina. I mean, it'll bring you lots of work."

Mina stood up from her chair and grabbed Lara's elbow tightly. She lowered her voice. "Ben is going to buy that house I told him about. I had my cousin take pictures and I sent him the photos— you know, for his architect to see. He calls me and says, 'Mina, I don't need to see it again, I trust you, how much do they need for down payment? Ten percent? No problem.'"

Lara didn't say anything.

"I made him cut a very good deal. He's getting a local price, no tourist price."

"Mina, he's a millionaire!" Lara cried.

"Yes, of course. He's very elegant, very stylish," Mina replied, not picking up on the irony.

Lara stood motionless for a moment. She felt betrayed in a way that was difficult to explain. It wasn't just the curtains. It seemed unfair that, while she had been lying in the shade of her rooms, feeling weak and indolent, just trying to stay in the moment, everyone else's alliances had been speeding forward. And in her very own backyard at that. She disentangled her elbow from Mina's grip.

"Okay then, see you around, Mina."

Mina was already back at the table, her glasses sliding down the bridge of her nose, threading a needle. She barely looked at Lara when she said goodbye. She didn't seem interested in her anymore, now that she had found a suitable replacement for the barons of her luminous past.

·   ·   ·

Ben Jackson's film won the Special Jury Prize at the Venice Film Festival. It was a harrowing drama about a father who kills his child's mother by accident and the difficult relationship that ensues between father and son. The critics raved about Ben's performance ("at last Jackson seems to have found his maturity and gravitas"). The German director was a young, controversial, good-looking guy and the press had fallen in instant love with him because he was new and nobody had a reason to hate him for anything yet. By accepting a part in such a low-budget project, Ben had gained a brand-new innocence. The two of them made a cool pair: young independent European director and Hollywood star, each shining his own particular light on the other. Lara watched clips of their interviews, which ran for days on cable, the major networks and YouTube. Lara had to admit Ben looked slimmer and happier. Mina's shirts and jackets fit him like a glove. Sure enough, there had been no sign of the wife with the sensible shoes anywhere on the red carpet, nor in any of the photos.

Every now and again Lara spotted a small portion of Leo hovering in the corner of a shot, behind a photographer's camera or obscured by someone else's arm or head. It would be either a fraction of his profile or the back of his head, at times just one eye and some lips. Only a percentage of him showed—10 percent or 20 percent of his body at the most—the same percentage, she thought wryly, as an agent's commission. It was disturbing to see him only in fragments, though she couldn't really tell exactly why.

He hadn't called her since they'd left her house for Pantelleria. He had only sent a brief text message.

Thank you for the grand hospitality, dear sister!
Can u give me mina's phone number?

In mid-September early one morning, her mother rang. More than concerned, she sounded exasperated.

"Do you have friends staying with you? Don't you feel a little lonely, all by yourself?"

Ironic that her mother would be worried about her being all alone, Lara thought, since she had asked her a few times to come and see her new house, but she refused to leave her air-conditioned apartment in Piazza Mazzini, claiming the trip took too long.

"No. I'm loving it here. I don't need anything."

"What's there to do? Haven't you done enough holidaying?"

"This is not a holiday, Mamma. It's my new life. I read, I study, I plant my vegetable gard—"

"You need to get a job, Lara. We are worried about you."

"Who is *we*?"

"Your brother and I. You need to come back to Rome, it's time you think of your future."

Future? What future? The future was so not what she'd been concentrating on. She was actually trying to focus on thoughts that went exactly in the opposite direction: "no past, no future; live in the moment; one breath at the time."

"I already told Leo, I'm going to start teaching yoga again, here. I'll be fine. Don't you start micromanaging my life, I beg of you."

"Micro what? What are you talking about, for heaven's sake?" her mother said.

.   .   .

Lara pulled out her old copy of *Shivananda Yoga Teacher's Manual* from the bookshelf. She skipped the introduction because she felt she only needed to refresh her memory on how to build a sequence. She skipped chapter one, then two, then three. She kept skipping. Nothing in the book seemed to hold her attention.

The breath, the names of the postures, the mantras, the anatomy, the names of the bones: she felt she knew it all already. She just flipped the pages, glancing over the pictures, and zoned out. Then she went out for ice cream.

A couple of days later she drove to the bookstore and bought a couple of gardening books; then she started with the cooking books. She gazed at all the photos. It seemed enough, for the moment. "I get it, I can do that," she would say out loud, without actually going through any of the text. The thought of studying any actual technique exhausted her.

Her best friend, Anita, who'd made a fortune breeding rare Chinese dogs, rang. She'd been in Beijing all summer long, dealing with puppies and kennels, and was back in the city.

"What are you doing still there? Are you not coming back?"

"Not immediately. And besides, September is so . . . so sweet here."

There was a silence.

"Lara, should I come get you?"

"Why? I can drive back whenever I want."

"I know, but just in case you didn't feel like it, I'm happy to come and get you."

She laughed. "It's not as if I'm being held hostage here, Anita."

"I know, I know, you sound just a little . . . I don't know. How should I say this?"

"Say it."

"Depressed?"

After this phone call Lara decided the time had come to test her flexibility after more than a year of neglecting her yoga practice. She sat for a while in cobbler's pose then settled into Janu Sirsasana, when something snapped in her knee with a loud pop. She waited a few seconds, then cautiously straightened her leg. She felt nothing, everything seemed to be in order, but she knew better. That kind of injury, she knew, was subtle and treacherous, the pain starting only the minute you believed you'd gotten away with it.

Delayed pain was the story of her life: it was exactly for this reason some people had called her an optimist and others a fool.

. . .

Sure enough, the knee swelled up and it began to hurt. A couple days later she limped across the street to Mina's, holding a Gertrude Jekyll rose she had picked up at the nursery outside the village. Mina came to the door, looking splendid. Her hair had been dyed a darker chestnut shade and was nicely done up in a smooth bouffant. She wore a pleated skirt and a starched pink shirt. The house smelled of lavender floor detergent.

"Oh! It's you! Come in, quickly!" she said, giddy with excitement.

Lara heard hushed voices and the screech of chairs coming from the back of the house.

"Do you want to join us?" Mina asked. "It's about to start. We'll have a little something afterward. I've made *parmigiana di melanzane* and *lasagne con le polpette*."

Lara peered through the half-open door into the next room. The ladies of the street had congregated in front of the flat screen in two neat rows. They were chatty and restless like children eager for a movie to begin. They greeted Lara cheerfully. One of them stood up, offering her a chair. Lara shook her head, mouthing "no thanks," and stepped back. She had been told that the local channel aired the evening prayers daily for older people who couldn't make it to church for the *vespro*.

"No, thanks, I've got a million things to do at home, I'm going back to the city early tomorrow. This is for your garden. It's an old English rose, it's called—"

Mina grabbed the Gertrude Jekyll and set it on the windowsill.

"Thank you. When are you coming back?"

"Soon, soon, I just have to take care of a few things. I hurt my knee and I need to see a doctor . . ." Lara peeked again into the room. Someone had closed the shutters and the women looked like ghosts lit by the bluish light of the TV. The music didn't sound like church at all. Credits were rolling over the dark screen.

"What are you watching?"

Mina looked surprised, as though Lara had asked a silly question.

"One of Ben's films is showing on Channel Two!"

"I see. And . . . you are having a party afterward?"

Mina lowered her voice, pointing her chin toward the other room. "They want to watch it with me. You know, these people are very provincial, they keep asking me all kinds of questions about Ben, they want to know this and that, what does he really look like, is he a nice person or not . . . they won't leave me alone. What can I do? They are my neighbors, I cannot simply shut them out the door, can I?"

"No, of course not. Well . . . have fun. I'll see you in a few weeks, I think. I'll come back soon, I don't really want to go back to Rome but I have to. I'm going to miss this place a lot—"

Mina didn't pay attention to this last comment. She was busy rummaging through the clutter on the table, lifting fabrics and packages till she fished out a gossip magazine and opened it. She hit a page with the back of her hand and showed Lara a spread of blurry photos. Reclined on a chaise longue on the edge of an infinity pool was a topless blonde with oversize dark glasses and earphones. Sitting on the edge of the same chaise, almost hovering over the girl's taut, tanned body, was Ben—the same faded sarong that he had worn at Lara's wrapped around his belly. There were palm trees and a stone and glass building in the background. Someone's legs entered the side of the shot. They clearly belonged to Leo, Lara knew instantly; she recognized a portion of his swimming trunks. Yet another fragment of her little brother.

"These people have no shame," Mina was saying. "To intrude

like this on Ben's privacy. I told him: when you buy the house here, you'll see, nobody is going to bother you. You'll be able to go as you please, live as you want, in broad daylight. There are no paparazzi where we live."

"I'm afraid they'd follow him no matter where he—"

But Mina wasn't listening. She clasped Lara's wrist and again lowered her voice to a whisper, checking behind her shoulder that none of the neighbors was in earshot.

"He wants a divorce. He's very unhappy with his wife."

"Really?" Lara glimpsed at the photo spread again. The girl had perfectly erect, Champagne cup–shaped breasts. She must be twenty-five at the most.

Mina nodded vigorously. "Oh yes. Apparently she's very cold, very selfish. He pays for everything: house, clothes, servants. Everything. He says his wife has a heart of stone . . ."

"Did he actually talk to you about that?"

" . . . and now they publish these photos. This woman here, she's just a friend, she has nothing to do with him but . . ."

"That's his lover."

" . . . with these pictures the wife will take him to the cleaners. It's going to be a big problem with the divorce case. She can take all of his money, you know?"

"It's his lover. I know that for a fact," Lara reiterated, louder this time.

Mina slapped the magazine shut and put it back on the table. She looked insulted. "Oh, no. She's just a friend. He told me he doesn't want to get involved with anybody for a while. He wants to think, to be left in peace."

"Wait. How do you . . . Do you speak to him on the phone?" This was crazy.

Mina issued her shrill laugh.

"Yes, he calls me almost every day! That man needs to rest. Yes, he has to have his peace. He works so hard, he deserves it."

"What language does he speak to you? He speaks to you in

Italian?" Lara was bewildered. When did Ben decide to pick Mina as his confidante? Didn't he have more suitable friends in Hollywood?

Mina nodded distractedly.

"These pictures are going to cause a very big problem with the wife . . ."

Lara sighed. Why was she engaging in this anyway? It was hopeless.

"I have to go now."

"Yes, yes, go," Mina said and glanced into the TV room.

Ben had just made his entrance on the screen—a few years younger, a few pounds lighter, in a police uniform.

·   •   ·

Lara's apartment in Rome was the same one in Via Plinio where she'd lived with her husband. After nearly three months of absence it looked foreign, abandoned and dreary. For a few days Lara moved around the rooms with circumspection, unsure as to what to do with her body, where to park it. She tried the couch, the green armchair, the desk, but couldn't find a spot where it felt natural to be. She asked Anita over for dinner and realized she no longer knew how to cook in that kitchen. All the dexterity she'd had all summer long with food, her ability to throw together extravagant recipes in just a few minutes, was gone.

"They say having two houses is like having two wives. Neither one has the whole of you," she said gloomily when Anita arrived. She'd shown up in a slinky Sue Wong dress and with a bottle of Prosecco, ready for a bubbly night of gossip and laughs. She pulled a minuscule puppy out of a tote bag and proudly announced, "And this is Carmen. A hairless Chinese crested."

The tiny dog was as ugly as it was hairless—except for the long, soft tufts of white hair that flowed from the top of its head. From this very ugliness came its adorableness, Lara supposed.

But she was in no mood to discuss Chinese puppies with Anita. All she wanted to talk about was her restlessness; how her previous life in the city seemed impossible to resume, how she couldn't find her center anymore, how hurting her knee had clearly been a sign, and not a good one. Lara barely gave the puppy a glance.

"It looks like a rat with a wig," she said, pouring Prosecco in the glasses.

Anita stared at her, puzzled, then lifted the glass in a toast with one hand while settling Carmen back in the bag with the other.

· • ·

The next morning Lara rang her ex-husband. They hadn't spoken in almost a year. She said she wanted to see him.

"It's important to me. I don't want to think of us as enemies anymore, okay?"

"We are not enemies. I never felt that way, despite what you think, Lara," he said, peacefully. A bit too peacefully, in fact.

"That's great, then. One more reason to see each other, I'd say," she insisted.

She struggled to find a sensible place to meet. A café could be hazardous—too many people, tables too close, what if she ended up crying? Her mind raced.

"How about the bar at the Excelsior?"

Her husband hesitated; the venue sounded dangerously romantic. Lara could feel a small panic rising in him.

"It's comfortable, it'll be quiet. And they make great martinis," she reassured him. As if she went there regularly for expensive cocktails.

The day of their rendezvous was a premonition of fall, with a heavy sky and a constant drizzle, perfect weather for meeting an ex-husband. She wanted to surprise him by looking more glamorous and mysterious than she had ever been while with him, so he'd assume that a major event—a man, a new vocation?—had turned her into a different person, or, even better, allowed her true nature to emerge. She longed to be anything but the same woman he'd wanted to leave.

A few minutes after six, she limped into the lobby of the Excelsior a few minutes after six in a light beige raincoat and large dark glasses, her hair pulled back in a chignon with a vintage Hermès silk scarf folded and tied as a headband—in the vague hope of resembling Grace Kelly in one of those movies with Cary Grant.

Her ex-husband was waiting at a table in the far corner of the wood-paneled bar, among soft cushions and elaborate Japanese flower arrangements. He looked more attractive than she remembered and, like her apartment without him, oddly foreign. The memory of their physical intimacy—even its subtle scent—had vanished as though someone else (the woman with a sense of humor?) had erased it for eternity. He asked why she was limping and when she told him about the Janu Sirsasana incident, he couldn't keep back a condescending smirk.

"Yoga. You didn't give that up yet, did you?"

"It's not like I'm doing heroin," she said breezily, yet she regretted having mentioned the word *yoga*. He'd always found the subject—with its obsessive concerns about hips, knees and shoulder openings, breathing techniques, mantras and especially the smugness that came with an advanced practice—deeply irritating.

The conversation floated without a purpose for a few minutes, aided by the intervention of a young waiter who took their order. Her ex-husband asked for a pot of green tea but Lara felt she ought to order a martini. She tried to sum up the past year, giving a joyful picture of all that had happened without him. She was happy with her choice of the venue; it had just the right atmosphere: the bar was quiet, almost empty, the muted colors soothing, the decor minimal yet cozy. The drinks came, and there was another awkward silence while he juggled with cup and teapot. He then broke the silence with a studied casual tone.

"It's great that you're happy in your place down south. Where exactly is it again?"

"It's just a tiny village south of Lecce. You wouldn't have heard of it."

Because she'd bought it with his money she felt protective of it, as if he could lay claim to what was now only hers.

He smiled encouragingly. He only wanted to be nice and friendly.

"It sounds good, your life. I mean, you used to be such a city girl. I never pictured you in a small village growing vegetables."

Lara wasn't sure this was the kind of recognition she'd been looking for, and the eagerness he showed in approving her life without him was beginning to unnerve her.

Suddenly, in the richly upholstered, orchid-filled bar, her ideas about growing her own vegetables and making fig preserves sounded naïve, even pathetic. She looked at her ex-husband, in his superbly tailored pin-striped suit, who kept smiling at her as one would with a crazy person. Now that she had him in front of her it wasn't clear why she'd wanted to see him again. She didn't love him, didn't hate him or want him anymore, and certainly she didn't care to be his friend. Maybe she thought that seeing him again would help her make sense of the nine years spent in his company. She needed evidence that those years had been mean-ingful for both of them but, the more she looked for that evi-dence, the less she found it.

"You look good. I like this look. The raincoat," he said.

The martini was beginning to have its effect. She hadn't had a stiff drink in ages and had a feeling her eyes were beginning to spin all over the place without a focus and her voice had started to slacken.

"Lara," he said calmly.

"Yes? What?" Had she been staring at the wall too long? She quickly regained her posture in the velvet armchair.

"Nicole and I are getting married next month."

There was a long pause. She collected herself again.

"Nicole? Oh. Is that her name?"

He nodded, with a hint of impatience. She knew her name, of course.

"We are going to have a baby in January," he added as he sipped his tea, so that the cup would conceal the lower half of his face.

There was another silence. He took a deep breath.

"I meant to call you. I wanted you to know but you beat me to it. I didn't want you to learn it from someone else."

She kept still, her eyes fixed steadily on him.

"Lara? Are you okay?"

"Yes. Totally. Why? Well, that's very good news. Really good. Congratulations. I mean it."

"We'll be moving to Paris next month. GreenTech has hired me as a consultant."

"Paris? Wonderful."

She smiled. He smiled back. Sipped more tea.

"I'm glad I got to see you. I really am. You seem good," he said and then chuckled. "Except for your knee, of course."

"You never made me laugh," she blurted out.

"What?"

"You were never funny. You have no fucking clue as to what humor even is."

His face morphed into the more familiar expression of hostility and alarm.

"Please, don't let's start."

"Start what? I am so done." Her rage had unleashed itself like a vicious animal. "I am so bored with you I cannot bear this conversation another minute."

She stood up and wobbled across the creaky wooden floor without turning around. She asked for the ladies' room and when she came across her image in the mirror—half drunk, her hands still shaking from adrenaline—instead of Grace Kelly what she saw was a dull, unattractive woman in a frumpy beige raincoat with a ridiculous scarf around her head.

· • ·

That fall Ben Jackson was listed in *Vogue* as one of the Ten Best Dressed Men of the Year.

Leo sent her a link from his office in Los Angeles.

Check this out. How cool is that?

Vogue had posted several photos featuring Ben either attending different exclusive events in eveningwear, caught on the street fidgeting with his car keys, or walking with a take-out latte in his surfing shorts. Lara scanned the pictures one by one: nine times out of ten he was wearing one of Mina's creations. The clothes had a distinctive, classic Italian cut with a slight retro look, which felt new and original because of the gutsy nonchalance he had in wearing them, thanks to the way he turned up the stiff collars without wearing a tie, or left the shirt cuffs dangling unbuttoned.

The other nine celebrities on the list had gone to great lengths to praise their favorite labels and designers, whose clothes they were wearing, whereas Ben told the press he detested labels and that his entire wardrobe had been cut and hand stitched by a single seamstress in a small village in the south of Italy. A true talent, he was quoted as saying, like those gifted dressmakers Balenciaga or Dior at one time had had in their *maisons*—a rare, endangered species that should be protected. The whole thing sounded fabulously exclusive and rare, and the writer tried in vain to obtain at least the name of the obscure Italian seamstress, which Ben refused to disclose. "I'm a no-logo, and I want to remain a no-logo," he stated vehemently, like an anarchist standing on a barricade.

Lara e-mailed Leo back.

I hope he's sent Mina a present. A ticket to Tahiti? A big fat check?

There was no answer. She re-sent the message as a text and got an instant reply.

what are you now, mina's agent?

Lara put the magazine in the post to Mina and rang her brother at his office. She got his voice mail instead and resigned herself to leaving a lengthy message in which she listed all the things she most resented in their relationship. It was a long list that got cut off by the end of the tape.

· • ·

The days were getting crisper and shorter, the light through the trees projected starker shadows on the sidewalk. October came, the month of enterprises and plans. Everyone around Lara had one, even her mother—she had enrolled in the Elders University, resolved to get a degree in anthropology. Anita was looking into a rare breed of Balinese dogs—even smaller than the hairless Chinese cresteds—which were all the rage in California (you can stuff them inside your coat pocket and fly with them everywhere, she'd exclaimed) and she predicted they would soon hit Europe. Leo was finally getting an office of his own—he had enough clients now to have a company with his name. Her ex-husband and Nicole were probably unpacking boxes in their new Parisian flat. Her belly must be pretty big by now.

Lara sat in her apartment in Rome, thinking about all this. After three weeks of gentle physical therapy, her knee was fine again, she had printed flyers and made a few phone calls advertising her yoga class, but only two people had called so far. She sat around the house unable to think of an alternative. What had happened to her? Nine years of safe marriage with a steady flow of cash assured by her husband's salary had turned her into an incapable, paralyzed human being. It had been a steady flow of unlearning all that she'd known before. But it was late now. Too late even for being mad at herself.

.   .   .

The tourists had gone and with them their ugly plastic paraphernalia of inflatable mattresses, flippers and flip-flops that all summer long had crammed the exterior of the *tabacchi* shop and the grocery store. The village had regained its sober style and had gone back to looking like what it used to look like: an undisclosed secret, just a village nobody had ever heard of, with a small but perfectly proportioned square, a pretty clock tower, a baroque church and a grand palazzo once owned by a family of barons.

Lara had taken an early flight and arrived at the house just as her neighbors were sweeping the street outside their doors, as they did every day. When they saw her get out of the taxi they called out her name. They seemed happy to see her back, off season, just like a regular neighbor, like someone who lived there.

"I came for this evening's procession. *Per la Vergine della Tempesta*," Lara announced proudly, wanting to confirm that she had, in some way, become one of them; that this particular day—when the Virgin had appeared to a group of fishermen in the midst of a storm and had saved them from drowning—mattered to her as well.

"*Brava! Brava!*" The women in slippers with brooms in hand nodded and laughed.

.   .   .

Mina's house had gone through a radical transformation. Everything was in its place, no more wisps of thread flying around, no bolts of fabric or clothes hanging off nails. Surfaces were clean and clear, there was no trace of work, no electricity or stuffy smells of sweat and fatigue in the air. Even the orange cat looked different, stretched on the windowsill next to the Gertrude Jekyll rose. Lara peered in the next room. The big TV screen was gone. But the change was owing to something deeper than just a cleanup. Something was gone from Mina as well: her mad exhilaration, her electric excitement. Now she looked older, more austere.

"It looks so neat in here."

"I'm on holiday," Mina said drily.

"That's good. You deserve a bit of rest. You did so much work this summer."

Mina didn't answer. She was sitting on a chair and fiddling inside her tiny handbag. She pulled out a handkerchief.

"Too much work." She gave Lara a crooked look and blew her nose.

"You mean . . . the work you did for Ben?"

Mina scowled. "Do you have any idea how much material I had to use for that big a man?"

"Of course. More fabric, more sewing. More everything."

"Not more money, though!" Mina cried with unexpected force, which allowed Lara to dig deeper.

"You don't feel Ben paid you fairly?"

"Ha!" Mina turned her face to the side with spite. "Those people, they have big mansions in England with swimming pools and servants but when it comes to—"

"Actually he lives in America, he doesn't have a—"

"—squeezing money where they can, then . . . you should see them! Do they know the difference between something expensive and something truly beautiful? No, they don't!"

Lara replayed the last sentence in her mind and double-checked its meaning. That was a sharp observation.

"Did he not pay you what you asked?"

Mina shrugged again, and turned her face away, as if the question didn't even deserve an answer. Lara pressed her.

"Didn't you tell him upfront what you were going to charge him?"

But, clutching her handbag and rising from the chair, Mina ignored this. For the occasion she had chosen to wear her pleated skirt and a funny blue jacket with golden buttons. She eyed her tiny wristwatch.

"We'd better go," she said. "The procession starts at six and we need to find a good parking spot, one by the harbor."

. . .

In the car—the small Subaru she had bought secondhand from a local dealer when she had first moved down south—Lara hoped Mina would release more information about what had happened with Ben, but she was wrapped in silence. Lara had to poke at her again.

"Have you heard from him lately?"

Mina shook her head.

"I thought he used to call you on the phone like every other day."

Mina looked out the window, pretending to be absorbed by the landscape.

"Oh yes, he called, what, three weeks ago? 'Mina, I'm flying down to see you for two days,' he says, 'I need you to do some more work for me.' I say, 'Of course, come, you are always welcome, and we must speak about the deal on the house.' You know, the house of my cousin. So he arrives in a black car with black windows and a driver in a black suit. It looks like a funeral car, everyone got so frightened. People thought I was dead."

Lara laughed, but Mina didn't.

"With this blond woman. The one in the photograph."

Lara stopped at a red light and turned toward Mina.

"The one by the swimming pool?"

"That one. He walks into the house, hugs me, kisses me like I am his mother," Mina said with disdain. "Then he introduces this woman who doesn't speak a word of Italian. She's almost naked, in a little camisole that shows everything underneath. He says,

'Mina, this is my fiancée and she loves your work, look, she has brought some clothes for you to copy.' And this woman opens a suitcase filled with her flimsy dresses, and then she throws them on my table."

Like she was his mother, Lara thought. Could that be what had hurt her the most? But how could Mina have been that deluded? But—she reminded herself—it was also true that Mina now knew Ben's body like a familiar map, its exact measurements; she'd cut and sewn the fabric that would envelop him and keep him warm. She'd touched him on the shoulders, around the waist, along his legs. She had memorized every inch of him. Wasn't that some other, extraordinary kind of intimacy?

Mina didn't say anything more. She sat stiffly on the edge of her seat as the small harbor came into view. She indicated a slot between parked cars.

"There. You can fit right in there."

There was another long pause during the parking maneuver.

"And then?" Lara kept checking her rearview mirror, pretending to be only half interested.

"I told him I was on holiday," Mina said bitterly. "I gave him the address of Jolanda, in Ortelle. She's not as good as me, no. But she can make their clothes."

· · ·

Slowly, gingerly, they made their way with the crowd down the steep winding road that led to the small harbor. Whole families marched together, fathers carrying their children on their shoulders, old ladies holding on to the arms of their daughters, kids eating their gelati. They walked briskly, with festive smiles, grown-ups and children equally eager for the music and the fireworks that were to follow. Below, on the small piazza by the water's edge, there were stalls selling sweets—caramelized almonds, chocolate nougat and Nutella crepes—and Chinese-made toys that lit up, buzzed and shrieked with *Star Wars* sounds. The local band in their uniforms was tuning the trombones and the tubas under the pagoda-shaped gazebo set up in the piazza. In a few minutes the door of the white church would let out the procession bearing the statue of the Virgin. The oldest and strongest fishermen decked out in their Sunday clothes would bring her down to the pier, haul her onto one of the boats. Mina's gait wobbled on the steep descent. She grabbed Lara's arm, making her slow down.

"I am not stupid," she hissed. "If one's name is printed in that American magazine—whatever it's called—one becomes famous all over the world. Why couldn't he say, 'Write this down: all my clothes were made by Mina Corvaglia from Andrano'?"

"He totally should have told the magazine," Lara agreed. Part of her was rejoicing. She was going to recount it all to Leo, word for word.

"Perhaps he thinks he doesn't need to give my name because I am just a—a peasant, from the sticks," Mina said, shaking her head. "But we don't live in mud huts here."

.   .   .

Mina knew exactly where they needed to position themselves in order to get the best view of the boats and the fireworks. She stopped on top of a stairway that went steeply down all the way to the square, unfolded a large handkerchief and spread it on one of the spotless steps. She sat on it with care, and kept brushing her pleated skirt, making sure it wouldn't touch the pavement. Lara sat next to her and remained quiet for a few minutes, as the procession slowly approached the harbor. They watched as the statue of the *Vergine della Tempesta* was carefully placed inside a palanquin on the prow of a larger boat adorned with flowers and candles.

"What about the house he's buying?" Lara finally asked.

Mina was busy making sure her skirt was in place. She then closed her arm around her knees.

"My cousin, he changed his mind. He's decided to keep the house for now."

"Really? How come?"

"Too much confusion. Paparazzi will come to steal photos, more foreigners will come to buy property, prices will go up. We don't need that kind of pandemonium here."

·   ·   ·

The evening light was dimming and turning everything into a watercolor with runny edges of lavender and blue. The boats had grouped around the biggest one, the one that carried the Virgin, and they started to move away from the shore in the twilight. The big boat led the way with its palanquin in a triumph of tiny lights and the fishermen's boats followed with their flickering lanterns. Somewhere, someone was lighting small hot air balloons made of paper that ascended in a slow, billowing flight, one by one. They were dotting the sky with their orangey glow, illuminated by the boat lights below, forming a dazzling constellation.

Just then the moon emerged from the strand of haze sitting on top of the horizon. A big, apricot moon, pinned against a lilac background. Everything went quiet, the band, the birds, the children's voices, the Chinese electronic toys. It was as if for a moment everyone felt what it was like to be present, all together, and alive.

Lara held her breath. She had hoped for this feeling for so long. And now, without her aiming for it or practicing toward it, here it was, epiphanic, timeless. She knew the feeling would last only another handful of seconds. But somehow, hadn't she earned it? From now on she'd at least be able to call it back and it would unfold, replay itself.

She looked at Mina and their eyes met. For whatever seconds were left of that knowing, they were together in it and nothing needed to be said. Then the first of the fireworks sprang up in a cascade of gold that streaked the darkening sky, then fell with a soft crackling noise into the water.

. . .

After two hours of fireworks and deafening explosions, their lungs and eyes filled with so much acrid smoke it was as if they'd just escaped a battlefield, Lara suggested it might be time to leave. They'd eaten pork sandwiches and Nutella crepes, bought the nougat and a plastic parrot on a branch that chirped every five minutes, which Mina was planning to hang on her lemon tree. Her digestion upset, but nevertheless satisfied and happily exhausted, Lara steered Mina up the hill, back to where the car was parked.

"Does it get very cold in the winter months here?" she asked, as she drove them back, breaking the sleepy silence in the car.

No answer came, so Lara took her eyes away from the road and turned to Mina, who shook her head, her eyes half closed.

"You know, I was thinking . . . ," Lara went on. "How much do you think it would cost to rebuild the *forno* at the house?"

"I don't know. I can ask my cousin."

"I had this crazy idea. I was thinking I could turn that room into a small bakery. I'm a pretty good baker, you know? I used to make my own bread."

"You could make pizza too," Mina murmured.

"Exactly! I could also bake muffins in the morning. I think it would work, especially in the summer months, for the tourists. Don't you think?"

"If you made good bread, even the local people will buy it all year round. Nobody makes bread the way we used to anymore. Everyone is using that chemical yeast now."

"Absolutely. And there are no good bakeries around us for miles."

Mina yawned.

"I could give you my aunt's recipe."

It had started to get dark much earlier now. Lara could smell the woody scent of fall coming through the half-open window.

"Maybe you and I could go into this together," she offered.

There was no answer.

"You know what? I think we'd make good money," Lara said almost to herself and threw a glance at Mina. She was snoring lightly, her head abandoned to the headrest, the plastic parrot clutched to her chest.

Lara drove on in the pitch-dark, the brights shining on the twisted olive trunks shaped like gnomes. But it was easy; by now she knew the way home like the back of her hand.

An Indian Soirée

The crow woke her up with a start, ripping her away from the dream. Every morning at seven sharp, the stupid bird tapped its beak on the window demanding to enter, each day unaware that he was knocking on a pane of glass. Its relentless cawing was the most disagreeable sound to wake up to.

Her heart was still beating fast from what had just happened in her sleep. She glanced at the pillow next to hers. Her husband gave a moan directed at the crow, then turned over and continued to sleep. Better that way. She needed some time alone.

She lay still, in an attempt to extricate herself from the shreds of her dream. She had just been passionately kissed and made love to and the lovemaking had stirred such a strong longing, she was still overwhelmed and aroused. Apparently she and her ex-lover had met again at a party somewhere. There were people standing around with drinks in hand. He had pressed her gently against the wall, his forehead on hers, and that's how they'd looked into each other's eyes, like two stags locking antlers. She had felt they were being observed and for a moment had thought, This is impossible, we can't, not in front of everybody. Instead all she said in the dream was "I have missed you so much," and it felt as though such an uncomplicated phrase had instantly commanded a truth that had been buried for years. The words had taken on, as often happens in dreams, a special power, as if they'd meant so much more than just that. As she pronounced them she had felt a surge of relief. From that moment on, she knew it would be impossible to hide this simple truth again: it was true, she *had* missed him all these years, despite having refused to admit it, so that the dream had come as a revelation, an awakening of sorts. Just then he had leaned in to kiss her, pressing his mouth to hers with an incredible will, in the same way he had with his forehead. And then, still in the dream, of course, she no longer cared if others were watching and word would get out. Yes, it would be public. Her husband would have to know. It was inevitable. They had found each other again and discovered that their passion was intact. In fact, it had never faded. How astonishing was that?

She got up slowly, entered the bathroom and looked at herself in the mirror. She hadn't seen him in almost fifteen years. She didn't even know where he was anymore, whether he was married or had children. Then why, she wondered, *why* would he come in her dream so forcefully, so completely out of the blue? She splashed her face with cold water. Her eyes looked puffy again, she noticed with dismay. It felt almost as if he'd ambushed her, leaping out from the depths of some repressed memory. And what was the dream meant to be? A secret message? A prophecy? How about telepathy? Could he have been dreaming of her too, on the very same night? Was this some kind of message she was meant to pick up and do something about? After the kiss, when he'd made love to her, the feeling was so visceral, she couldn't accept it had been just something she'd fabricated. She must have had an orgasm or something, it just wasn't possible to feel this way other-wise. She looked at her face, more closely this time, till her breath fogged the mirror. Puffy eyes, crinkly at the corners.

This was insane. Yes, insane. But she wanted him back now—how did that happen?—after years of not even thinking of him. She would have to track his number, his Facebook page or search his username on Skype. Nobody could disappear entirely any-more. She unscrewed the cap of jasmine bath gel, one of the luxu-rious ayurvedic products offered in the hotel, and turned on the shower.

. • .

He knew exactly what was going to happen to her hair. As it thinned out—and it would, eventually, with age—it would go limp and disclose the unseemly shape of the back of her head, which was flat. He knew it would happen, because of her mother. That's exactly what had happened to her head and he found the detail deeply depressing, as though this plane at the back of her mother's head, its lack of roundness, signaled a weakness. It made the older woman look even more helpless, especially since she was unaware of this particular flaw, being at the back where she couldn't see it. He had never liked his mother-in-law. She was a petulant, self-centered and uninteresting woman who relentlessly talked rubbish. Often he'd had to stop himself from shouting at her to shut the fuck up. That was another problem with marriage, you were stuck for life with people you didn't care for.

Why these days did he always wake up to unpleasant thoughts such as this one? They'd come just like that, surprisingly clear and specific. His wife's hair issue wasn't a particularly bad one compared to others. Most days the first thought he'd have would concern his own death. It was like a message flashing an alarm just as he was floating back to the surface of consciousness. A little voice would warn him, getting louder and louder till he had to open his eyes: "Good morning, you are going to die! It will occur soon, every day it'll be a day sooner!"

He'd started having these deathly reminders since he'd turned thirty-five. It was the age when he'd became physically aware that half of his life had gone past him. Once he'd heard a well-known writer at a dinner party, much older than him, say that since he'd turned fifty he'd had the distinct sensation that he had more past than future, as on a scale that tilts the other way. The concept had terrified him. These unpleasant thoughts, such as his wife's hair eventually flattening with age (which he put in the same death department as this idea, too, had to do with the passing of time and the loss of youth), would greet him as soon as he opened his eyes with a frightening punctuality, like that damned crow cawing so loudly outside the window, that horrible sound that always woke him with a fright. There was nothing to do. Crows, he had told his wife since the day they arrived, were the sound track of India. And so was death. According to the clichés.

He stumbled out of bed and went into the shower. There were signs of his wife having just left: a damp towel abandoned on the floor, the bottle of shower gel uncapped, covered in droplets. His wife was an early riser and her morning routine was always a fast one. It was one of the first things he'd observed about her when they'd first started sleeping together. She could be ready in fifteen minutes and look perfect. He thought that it was an attractive trait in a woman; he hated having to wait around and didn't like women who put on too much makeup. The shower was pleasantly hot, the bath gel's fragrance was sweet. As usual, sinister thoughts were washed out under the forceful jet. They were not to come back again, at least until the next morning.

· • ·

He had been to India before, loved it, and had enjoyed playing the India expert for decades. This time however, he wasn't sure he loved it as much. Maybe he was just in a bad mood, and India could be difficult if taken the wrong way. Things that had never bothered him were now beginning to take a toll. The pollution, the ugly malls sprouting everywhere in the big cities. Even the food was tiresome. When they had gone up north in Rajasthan two weeks earlier, nothing had felt authentic, it had all seemed a circus, a façade for the wealthy tourists. When he had traveled through the same regions back in his twenties, he had felt as though he had continuously stumbled upon fairy tales happening before his eyes. The magnificent *haveli* in Jaisalmer that cost only two hundred rupees a night where no other guests were staying, seemingly open just for him and his friend; their room with

exquisite wall paintings and a balcony carved in sandstone overlooking the desert. The lovely country residence of a local Thakur
outside Bikaner who had taken him horseback riding through the
plains and led him inside a thatched hut, its mud floor swept
clean, walls painted in bright turquoise lime, where they'd been
offered opium tea by the Bishnoi, a vanishing tribe over which
the Thakur family had ruled for centuries. Now the *haveli* looking
out on the desert had been badly restored and was on Trip Advisor and the Thakur had handed his family home over to a hotel
chain, so that now travel agents offered guided tours in the huts
of the Bishnoi with "opium tea included in the price." It all had to
do with time, of course. That was then, when he was young and
India was poor, this was now, when he could afford a seven-star
hotel and India's economy had grown at a stellar rate.

His wife had never been to India before and she loved everything she saw unconditionally. Before they left she had devoured
guidebooks, Indian novels, essays on Hinduism and Jainism, and
was determined to get the most out of this trip. She was an enthu-
siast, a firm believer in the glass-half-full theory. He had married
her partly for that reason: he knew that as long as he held on to
her, she would save him from the gloom that haunted him at
every corner.

During the trip she noticed things he no longer saw or that
didn't interest him enough to notice.

"I love the way everything happens on the floor. How good
people here are at doing things we can do only on tables."

"Like what?"

"Eating. Ironing. Lots of stuff. Have you seen how the tailors
squat and hold the material down with their big toe when they
cut it?"

Images like that stuck. Now, whenever they happened to see a
tailor at work on his haunches, he couldn't help checking his feet,
how deftly he was using them to clasp the fabric.

"Do you realize these women drape six meters of fabric around their bodies with only one pin, if any? They tuck the pleated fabric of the sari into the petticoat. No buttons, no stitches, nothing. And the way they put those flower garlands in their hair? It takes one second for them to do, and yet they stay on for the whole day."

She had wanted a garland in her hair too, and women in the temple during a *pooja* had pinned one in her short ponytail. It didn't look as good as theirs. For some reason it kept dangling wildly in a way that it never did on Indian braids or buns. After twenty minutes, she lost it.

"See? That would never happen to them," she said, defeated. And immediately added, "I must study the way they clip this thing on."

She was constantly figuring out how things worked or why they didn't, compiling her own India instructions booklet. This attitude she had of being always on the outside, looking inside, mildly irritated him; he'd always disliked the idea of being a tourist. He believed in that quote by Paul Bowles—how did it go again?—the one that made the distinction between a tourist and a traveler. Of course he wasn't a traveler. He was just a tourist who hated to be one.

· • ·

The first week she had worn her own clothes, light fitted shirts and cotton pants, her nice sandals. It turned out that these had too many straps and were an inconvenience to put on and take off each time they entered a shop or a temple, so she got herself a pair of *chappals*. That was the beginning of the transformation. Then came the kurtas, the long shirts women wear over their *shalwar* pants. She found them so comfortable that soon she had to get the pants as well, in matching colors, and then the *dupatta*, the scarf that women so artfully throw across their chest. The *dupatta* for him was the last straw. It turned her outfit into a dress-up costume, plus it kept falling off her shoulders so that she was read-justing it every five minutes.

He loved her—that went without saying—but they'd been together for almost sixteen years and it was normal to find her tiresome at times. He had to admit that it was lovely, the way she found so many things interesting and worth being investigated; it was a sign of her vitality, and he cherished that. He only wished she had stuck to wearing her own clothes instead of those Indian outfits that were slowly multiplying inside the suitcase, which she didn't know how to wear.

.   .   .

He came out to the garden terrace, where they served breakfast. It was still chilly in the morning. A thin fog had descended over the river, blurring the contours of the forest on the opposite bank. Its outline, with its wide canopies and dangling roots, reminded him of a faint watercolor on the jacket of a Kipling novel he had owned ages ago, painted by one of those nineteenth-century Brit-ish women artists who'd traveled all over the East in search of exotic flora to draw. The river was still, unperturbed, save for a slim boat, a *shikara*, slowly breaking the surface with its oars.

There she was, alone at the table under the trellis, wrapped up in the new pashmina dyed with natural pigments that had taken the place of her black sweater ("Black? Who wants to wear black anymore, once you see all these vibrant colors?").

"Hi, darling," she said, smiling. She was usually in a good mood in the morning. She always said that it was her happiest time.

"Would you like to see the paper?" She slid *The Hindu* across the table. It was another ruse she had taken up, this pretense of being interested in Indian internal affairs, with all those intricate party names and corrupt politicians. However, in only a couple of weeks she'd become an authority. She knew the candidates for the next elections by name and had even picked the one they should root for.

"No thanks, not now," he demurred. Every now and again, he resisted her voracious curiosity; it was his way of keeping her in check.

What about his own enthusiasms? Why had they dwindled, why did he no longer take pleasure in discovering new things? He feared there might be only one answer to that, and it was age. He was only forty-seven—just three more years to go before the old writer's epiphany—yet he felt his scale had already tilted over to one side. Surely the portion of future available to him as a youngish-looking, energetic and still attractive man was much smaller than what he had put behind already. Shouldn't he make an effort, make the best of it? Why could he not gather the energy to feel passionate again about what lay outside his own head?

He had figured he no longer did because by now all he really cared and worried about were the books he still needed to write before it was too late and he'd have nothing more to say. "Egotism—necessary/essential trait," he'd once scrawled in a journal, thinking that one day he might use the idea in an essay. At this point in his life all he actually longed for was to be able to sit still in one place with as little disturbance as possible in front of his computer, waiting for the words that would, line after line, compose the unformed story in his head. He knew he wasn't alone in that; every other writer had said the same thing when asked about the mystery of their profession in any interview: the act of writing was a sedentary, solitary work, where no other people were needed. He had stashed away enough experiences when he was a younger man; now he just needed to elaborate on that material, organize it. He didn't need to live it again, did he?

It was either that or depression, this lack of want for life.

Secretly, a year earlier, he had seen a psychiatrist, a friend of a friend whom he'd met at a party. "Only half an hour of your time is all I really need," he had told the kind-looking doctor. But the minute he sat across from him in his luscious, book-lined studio, he poured out his unpleasant thoughts of death, how his appetite for life seemed to be tapering off. The older man, with his gentle face and sympathetic expression, had said he didn't sound depressed—depression being a serious clinical condition. But he'd be happy to prescribe something mild if he felt he needed "just a little help." He said he didn't need it and came out of the doctor's studio both relieved and disappointed. The idea of "a little help" was humiliating; he'd somehow wanted his mental condition to be either all or nothing.

He realized in the taxi home after his session that what he forgot to tell the psychiatrist was that his novels didn't sell nearly as well as they had in the past. There were reasons, of course. New, younger writers for one, to whom people were more drawn because of their looks, their reckless lives, the wordplay they used. There was also the fact that he, along with so many other writers of his generation, had lost his luster (the author's photos on the jackets had had to change, no more leather and ruffled hair, but tailored suits and receding hairlines). And lastly, possibly, he had to admit to a certain repetitiveness in the plots of his novels. Like most writers, he'd always had a specific theme and followed the same thread (wasn't that a quality rather than a flaw? Didn't great writers essentially always write variations of the same book over and over again?). His particular theme had revolved around the existential musings of a character who had been the protagonist of most of his novels. Throughout the years the character had kept the same name, the same job, he had grown, aged, lost his hair, just like him. Somehow though, as of late, his readership too had thinned. Not dramatically—he still sold enough to keep his publisher happy and enough money coming in—but the phone calls from his agent to keep him up to date on the sales were not nearly as effervescent or as frequent as ten years earlier.

· • ·

The trip had been her idea. He knew he owed it to her. It was only fair for her to demand they spend time alone together, have a few weeks with nothing coming between them. Yet he couldn't help thinking of it as a duty rather than a gift. She'd proposed that after handing in the last draft of his novel he take her to India. Since they'd been together, he'd promised just this. But something had always come up and the trip had always been postponed.

"I'll divorce you, otherwise," she'd said jokingly.

In the fall he rang an expensive travel agent who organized upmarket tours in the vein of Paul Bowles followers. Then he wrapped the itinerary and tickets in a golden envelope and gave it to her for Christmas.

They'd been at the Fort three days now and so far they'd been the only guests. She had instantly fallen in love with the place and had asked him if they might lengthen their stay instead of moving on to their next destination. He was relieved at the idea of canceling what was left of their exhausting itinerary and settling down somewhere. He didn't mind that some of the hotels had already been paid for, he'd never been fussy about money. What was more important was the relief of no more hours spent driving on those terrible roads risking their lives, always too close to the HORN PLEASE signs on the backs of those overly painted trucks; no more dark temples with sticky floors, *poojas*, milk poured on shiny lingams, no more beggars, fumes, swarms of motorcycles carrying husband, wife and two children squeezed on one seat with no helmet; no more ghastly bazaars selling dusty junk, no more haggling with rude rickshaw drivers. They could sit still, make this beautiful place their home, so that he might be able to jot down some lines at last while his wife read and went looking for the handloom textiles the region was famous for.

The hotel had been the family home to a dynasty of maharajas for four hundred years. It was an impressive fortress perched on the edge of a cliff overlooking the banks of the Narmada River. It had only a handful of exquisitely furnished rooms open to guests; the rest was still the maharaja's private home. He was the last heir to the dynasty, a handsome man in his midfifties with a slender, elegant figure, who spoke fluent French, Italian and English with a pleasant American accent, due to the years he'd spent there in college. He joined them every morning for breakfast on the terrace in the rampart, overlooking the river, in a beautiful coat cut in Mughal style, and he reappeared in the evening in a starched kurta and woolen vest and a ruby on his little finger. The maharaja had a Danish wife, who was in Copenhagen at the moment, but they'd seen a picture of her in a silver frame on one of the tables in the drawing room. She was beautiful and wore her sari like she'd been born into it.

Being the only guests had enhanced the feeling of being at home and allowed the fantasy of owning the place. They dined each night in a different courtyard lit by hundreds of candles that flickered in the dark, designing graceful geometric patterns. Every night his wife engaged in conversation with the maharaja—she was of course enraptured by his elegance, his knowledge of the local traditions, but also by his worldly manners and his wit. She was delighted to have the prince all to herself.

· • ·

He joined her at the beautifully laid breakfast table. There were flowers arranged in small clusters, linen napkins and silverware polished to a glossy shine. An attendant immediately came to pour his tea.

"Where is our prince?" he asked his wife.

"He just left. We had a lengthy discussion about food. He wanted to know about fried zucchini flowers, believe it or not. Apparently he had them in Rome once and has never forgotten them. He wants me to teach him the recipe. Isn't it hilarious?" She laughed. "You must come and take a picture of me in the kitchen while he and I cook together. Will you?"

He nodded absentmindedly. They both knew that he'd find an excuse not to and that eventually she'd find someone else, either a waiter, the cook or the woman who swept their room—people whose names she'd already memorized—and hand over the camera. It was the kind of photo she most sought to have and to show: immortalized in her *shalwar kameez*, next to her charming prince, intent on cooking in his kitchen! That would show their friends how far inside real India they'd managed to reach.

"Tomorrow he's organized a classical dance performance on a tiny island upriver for a group of friends who arrive tonight. We're invited, of course. Would you like to go?" she said.

He nodded vaguely.

"Let's see how the day goes."

"His friends are from Delhi," she added, as if to stress that the level of familiarity they'd accessed with the prince wouldn't be offset by the arrival of a bunch of foreigners. It was an all-Indian soirée they'd been asked to.

"It's an Odissi dance performer. Apparently she is the best in the country, he said. The number one."

She waited for him to show some interest.

"Odissi is the classical dance we've seen in the temple sculptures. In Puri, remember? Those beautiful bas-reliefs?"

"As long as it's not a four-hour-long ordeal. You know how entertainment can drag on forever here."

"It won't, I'm sure. I'm sure it'll be fantastic. He's so good at creating fabulous sets using just lights and flowers."

"Do we have to answer now?" he asked. There was a hint of impatience in his voice.

"Not immediately. But I think it would be polite to let him know by tonight, don't you?"

"Fine. We will. Can you pass me a piece of toast, please?"

He began to butter the slice of brown bread and she went back to *The Hindu*.

She still looked beautiful, despite her age. She was already forty-two. Good bone structure—that, she had. High cheek-bones, a straight aquiline nose, lips still full and thick eyebrows. It was a handsome, strong face. There were lines, of course, there was sagging and creasing in places. But she was still holding on graciously. Men still looked at her and found her attractive.

"You look ravishing today," he said, feeling guilty. He knew he had been unpleasant.

She immediately touched her face.

"Really? I can't look at my face, it's so drawn. And my hair is a horror."

"Don't be silly. You are glowing."

She rested her hand on his.

"Thank you. That makes me feel a lot better."

· ● ·

He needed a little time alone, he'd said as they finished their breakfast. They would meet again for lunch, after the zucchini flowers experiment. She was used to this kind of announce-ment, it had been such a big part of their marriage, the off-limits zone he declared at random that had to be immediately cleared. Whenever he said he needed to be alone it meant he had to think and when he had to think it meant he had to walk. Apparently moving at a fast pace produced a parallel flow in his mental pro-cesses, facilitating an entryway into the story he was beginning to shape in his head. This rule she had learned to observe with respect, even awe. The first few years they were together she took it as a sign of his artistic temperament and had been proud of his mannerisms.

He left her reading the paper at the table and walked down the steps that led from the Fort to the *ghats* below. The riverbank was quiet in the early-morning light. There were only a few women washing clothes or bathing in their saris, slowly combing their long, wet hair. The water sloshed quietly against the steps, lapping at the feet of the small marble *nandis* that lined the bank. Each one of the divine bulls carved in stone had an oil lamp at its feet, and at night people would light them. He had seen their glow from the Fort's terrace at night. Who took care of that? And since when? Perhaps those oil lamps beneath the feet of the *nandis* had burned nightly for centuries and there would have been someone attending to this ritual every night. Even at this time of day, so early in the morning, the white marble bulls had already been laden with garlands of fresh jasmine and marigolds. He also wondered where all those flowers came from. Every morning all across India, from the north to the south, whether there was snow or desert, people bought garlands to crown their gods. He assumed thousands of tons of flowers must be strung in garlands every day. Yet he never saw flowers growing anywhere, all he had seen in weeks of traveling was red dust, burned grass, yellowing reeds. How did all the flowers travel, how many trucks drove across the country at night, loaded with marigolds and jasmine? How come these garlands always looked fresh, undeterred by dust and heat? Surely his wife would love to research this conundrum.

He walked some more, all the way to the Shiva shrine at the end of the *ghat*. He had had no useful thoughts about the story he was trying to crack. India wasn't a place conducive to creativity, he decided; it occupied too much space with all its unanswerable questions. Despite his efforts not to be distracted, he too had been encumbered by India's too many layers, its multiple souls, by the myriad messages it sent everywhere one looked.

· • ·

She went back upstairs to their room and sat on the cushions by the bay window overlooking the river. She was relieved to be alone again. Looking through the latticed shutters she was able to make out the silhouette of her husband walking slowly on the *ghat* right below her, heading toward the Shiva shrine. In his blue polo shirt and khaki pants, he stuck out like a sore thumb among all the women standing knee-deep in the river. As usual, he walked with his head down, looking only at his feet. He didn't look happy, or inspired by his walk, that much she could tell. She wished that every now and then he'd make the effort to look up at what was around him rather than gazing constantly inward. They had been three weeks on the road by now and she'd begun to feel how tiresome it was to travel with someone who never seemed to enjoy himself. As usual, she had had to do all the work, like a puppeteer moving all the characters across the stage, or a ventriloquist doing all the voices, in order to keep the audience entertained. Sometimes it became too demanding. Though she knew that if she stopped working at it they would both sink into a silence and that could get scary. Once she had tried it: she had allowed herself to plunge into a wistful silence and he'd begun to question her relentlessly, not because he sincerely worried about what might have upset her, but rather, she felt, because he was alarmed at the idea that his private jester may have gone on strike.

Although she hadn't formulated this thought in its entirety, she knew exactly why she'd come up to the room and what was going to happen next. She watched herself open her husband's laptop and go online. Watched her fingers tap her ex-lover's name. She just wanted to check how difficult it would be to find him. She could look for his name on Skype first. That would be easy and quite innocent. No need to call or send a message. All she wanted was to find a way to get in touch with him, so that someday—and only if she wanted to—she would know how.

.   •   .

At lunch the two of them sat in the shade at the table by the pool. He was relieved to be alone with his wife, so they wouldn't have to sustain a polite conversation with strangers. Thank God the prince never joined them at lunch, only at breakfast and dinner.

Evidently two meals with his guests were more than enough for him as well.

The waiter brought a plate of golden fried zucchini flowers. A starter, he announced.

"You and the prince made these?" he asked his wife.

She nodded.

"Very tasty. The batter is nice. What is it?"

She was looking beyond the pool, beyond the trees, somewhere out of focus.

"Chickpea flour, I think."

He waited for her to say more, but she didn't. They ate in silence. The waiter took away the plates and presented the main course, shrimp sautéed with chilis served with mango slices over arugula. The food here was tasteful, understated and the staff didn't wear funny turbans or garish Bollywood-style outfits. They had a simple uniform like that of the staff in a house where one didn't have to show off or pose in front of a camera all day long.

"Did you have fun?" he asked.

She turned to him, surprised, as if shaken from a thought. "What?"

"In the kitchen. With the prince."

"Yes, we did. It was a lot of fun."

"Are you all right? You look tired."

"Maybe. I didn't sleep very well last night. I might take a nap after lunch."

"Good. Then I'll do some work. I think I've just had an idea I want to get down."

She didn't ask him what the idea was. She just smiled with a blank expression, not having listened to what he'd just said.

·   ·   ·

When he came down from the room around seven, the guests from Delhi were sitting on the terrace around the low table set for the evening drinks. He had a hard time getting their names right when the prince made the introductions, the names being always so complicated in India. One of the guests was an older playwright—our living legend, the prince had said—a thin, elongated man who resembled a stork, with fine birdlike features and an impressive mane of flowing white hair. The playwright stood up and shook his hand, emanating a subtle aroma of sandalwood. He wore a finely tailored silk kurta that reached his shins and had a very fine, soft shawl wrapped around his shoulders. His wife, an ex-dancer, was a beautiful woman in her early sixties, draped in a blue and gold sari. Her ears and nose were studded with diamonds. There was a middle-aged choreographer, a tall, bald, bulky man in loose white pajamas and tunic who had lived in New York in the seventies (and had danced with Martha Graham and then performed with Peter Brook, it was explained). His friend, or perhaps his companion, was a younger man, a translator, who was the only one wearing jeans and a black T-shirt and had longish, uncombed hair. Unfortunately the translator spoke with a very thick Indian accent that was hard to understand, so he made sure to sit at the opposite end of the table, in order to avoid having to decipher him.

The bald choreographer had just come back from London and had brought a rare bottle of gin infused with cucumber and rose petals. Everyone was having cucumber gin martinis, so he agreed to have one and found it deliciously refreshing. In order to include him in the conversation the group was eager to know what kind of books he wrote and whether they could read them, had any of them been translated into English? Yes, a few had, so everyone made a mental note of the titles so they could look for them in Delhi. They mentioned names of the few Italian writers they'd read (Eco, Calvino), then mentioned Fellini and Antonioni's films so that the conversation could seamlessly shift from them to him and he could take the lead. He felt at ease, well liked, especially after the second cucumber gin martini. This was what it must be like to live here, he thought, to have a normal conversation with people who do not address me just as a foreigner but as an intellectual: these people could easily be my friends as well. Then he asked them about Indian literature, a subject to which he—unlike his wife—hadn't given much thought until that very moment, but the company inspired him and he wanted to return the courtesy. They discussed the problem of translation, how Indian literature was written in so many different languages and so much of it couldn't be read by the rest of the country. There was an immense amount of excellent literature bound to remain unknown. It was so unfair. The young translator with the impossible accent was indicated as one of the best, if not the best, translators of Tamil literature into Hindi. He had translated epic novels, contemporary essays and poetry that would have been lost otherwise to all the Indians who didn't read Tamil. There were twenty-two major languages, and most of the regions that spoke them had their own flourishing literature. What to do? He mentioned the few Indian novels translated into Italian he had read and praised them, to show them that not all Indian literature had been lost to foreigners. They pointed out that those novels were of a different kind, though, as they were originally written in English by writers who no longer lived in India or were born abroad and either wrote about their parents' origins or wrote about the discovery of their roots as adults.

"We have a word for them, you know . . . ," the playwright said with a hint of a smile. The choreographer joined in and finished his sentence.

"We call them Indonostalgics," he said, and everyone laughed.

Indonostalgics, he repeated, savoring the word, and making a mental note. That was exactly the kind of inside knowledge he enjoyed.

"Isn't your wife joining us tonight?" the prince asked.

He had completely forgotten to mention her. She had decided to stay in the room. She said she wasn't in the mood to talk to lots of people tonight.

"Unfortunately not. She wasn't feeling too well. She might come for dinner, otherwise she'll order room service, if that's not a problem for the kitchen."

And as he said that, heads turned toward the opposite end of the terrace. A woman had appeared and was walking toward them.

The men stood up.

"Ah, here she is, at last," the prince said and went over to embrace her.

There was a suspension, while everyone in turn greeted her.

"This is Ushma Das, our greatest dancer. She is to perform for us tomorrow night," the playwright said.

The woman wore a short red cotton sari over green *shalwar* pants. The sari was neatly pleated in the front, as in the temple sculptures. She was barefoot and her anklets made a lovely sound as she moved.

"I've just finished a brief rehearsal with the musicians," she was saying. "I was going to bathe and change before joining you, but then I heard your voices and . . ."

She turned to him, surprised to find him there.

He introduced himself, and she looked intently at him with her big, almond-shaped eyes penciled in black kohl.

"Very nice to meet you," she said, and let him hold her cool, bony hand.

"Please have a drink with us now, dear. The light is so lovely," said the older ex-dancer with the diamond studs in her nose. "You can freshen up later. We are having cucumber martinis."

"You know I am not supposed to drink, Auntie," Ushma said with a little smile. Everyone rebutted at once. Of course she could have a small drink after rehearsal. It wasn't going to get her drunk at all. They would make it very light. She took another look at him; he was standing speechless in front of her beauty.

"I'll have a club soda, that's all."

Then she sat down in the chair, erect, with royal gravity.

"And where is home, for you?" she asked, tilting her head toward him with what he took for sincere interest.

. . .

Earlier in the day, while her husband was on his inspirational promenade on the *ghats,* she had been staring at his laptop screen, open to Skype, while beads of sweat ran down her neck. The sun came straight through the bay window and the old-fashioned ceiling fan didn't help against that heat. She had typed the ex-lover's name in the space that said "enter name or e-mail address of the user you're looking for" and had clicked on *search.* Only three names like his had appeared, and next to them a green icon with the + sign. One lived in Buenos Aires, but the other two were actual possibilities. One in Paris, the other in San Francisco. More likely, he would be the one in California, but she might send the same message to both. She had been staring at the green icons for a while now. What if he was happily married with kids and his wife would intercept her message? Would that be a problem? She should write something so neutral and blameless that even his wife could read it and think nothing of it. The wife could ask him, "Who is that?" And he might say, "Just someone I knew ages ago when I lived in Italy." He might reply to her innocent message in a similar tone, something like "Hey, how've you been?" although he wasn't the type that would ever write "hey." After a lot of composing and scribbling on a scrap of paper in order to get it just right, she typed the message into the space. She stared at it. Then erased it. This was a mistake. He'd probably completely forgotten about their affair. But then she thought, What if he wasn't married, what if he had had the same dream or he had been thinking of her too? What a wasted opportunity, right? She typed the message again. It read, "Are you the Tyler I think you are?" signed with her name. She stared at the words again, then, after what seemed an agonizing amount of time, she said out loud, *What the hell,* and clicked on the green icons next to both Paris and San

Francisco. She jumped up from the chair as if it burned. She felt exhilarated, as though she had just sent a missile into space from Cape Canaveral.

Since that moment she had been feeling hopelessly anxious, as if time had taken on a completely different speed. After lunch by the pool she'd waited for her husband to leave the room so she could check her Skype page. She could've easily checked the same page on her cell phone but she just couldn't make herself do it with him in the same room. He had decided to read his book in bed, had fallen asleep, and woken up and ordered tea, which they took on the terrace together. He asked her to take a walk with him in the village, after which he took a shower and changed for evening drinks. Finally she had gotten rid of him, if only for a few hours. The minute he was out the door she ran to check the laptop. A tiny red light was blinking next to the Skype icon. Her heart leaped.

"Yes, it's me," the message said. "When can we talk?"

.   •   .

In the meantime, he'd learned quite a lot about Ushma Das. Once the older guests had retired for the night, the two of them had lingered at the candlelit table in the courtyard and then moved onto the terrace to watch the moonlight over the river. He had had a couple of more drinks to oil his conversational skills, whereas she'd stuck to tea. He asked her about Odissi dance, wasn't it one of the oldest forms of dance? Yes, she said, dancers are found depicted in bas-reliefs dating from the first century BC, and the *Natya Shastra,* the oldest surviving text on stagecraft in the world, speaks of this dance style. He told her he had seen the temple sculptures of the dancers in Puri only a week earlier, as if it had been his idea and not his wife's. He also said he'd been moved by the gracefulness of the postures depicted on the bas-reliefs, although he only vaguely remembered them. Ushma seemed pleased by his enthusiasm. She explained how the *devadasis,* or temple girls, at the time of those sculptures were highly educated courtesans who lived with kings and held an elevated social status. They had to learn music and singing, study poetry and scriptures. Under the moonlight, now that she had changed into a maroon sari and had combed her hair in a tight bun, she did look like an ancient courtesan from some rhapsodic Indian tale. She moved slowly, with extreme awareness, and he was completely engulfed by her beauty and her seriousness.

"Where do you live?" he asked her.

"In the countryside outside Bhubaneswar. I have a school there where I teach and live with my students. Dance is all we do. We wake up at dawn and dance all day. It's what I've done every day of my life for the last twenty years."

He showed surprise. Twenty years of monastic life? That seemed like a waste to him, for a woman this beautiful.

"You are not married?"

She gave a little laugh and turned her face away from him, as though the question had embarrassed her.

"No, how could I? I've been married to my guru and my students are now married to me. Ours is a never-ending chain, we have no time to devote to anything else. This has always been the way knowledge and artistic expression has been taught by our gurus for centuries."

"It sounds extremely demanding."

"It has been my choice. Of course it is hard. But we are rewarded when we dance."

She relaxed her face into a softer expression and smiled, as if letting him in on a secret.

"There is nothing like it."

"I am sure. It must be"—he searched for an appropriate word and then said—"pure ecstasy?"

Her face remained neutral, almost grave. "Not exactly. It's more like a feeling of oneness."

Oneness. What a beautiful thing to feel, he thought.

There was a moment of suspension, as if she were going to add something, but then she looked away.

"I am afraid I have to leave you now," she said. "Tomorrow we have a long rehearsal and I must go and get my sleep."

·   ·   ·

He had had way too much to drink, that was clear the minute he opened his eyes the next day. However, despite the hangover, he stirred in his bed, pleasantly excited. No trace of his daily dose of mortality awareness to greet him today. He got up, full of resolve and expectation.

His wife lay in bed, still asleep, which was unusual, but he took the opportunity to take a quick shower and sneak out of the room before she got up. He was hoping to run into Ushma Das at breakfast and be alone with her again, so they could continue the conversation they'd had the previous night. Actually, he realized, it was more than just hope—he was dying to see her again. She was nowhere to be found, but the faint sounds of a tabla and a bansuri flute wafted through the Fort's numerous courtyards and reached him as he walked into the terrace garden.

He sat at the empty breakfast table. He saw the prince cross-legged on a chair at the end of the terrace, facing the pale sun rising above the Narmada. He was taking his usual morning shave in front of an old-fashioned portable mirror. They said hello to each other but didn't engage in a conversation. Men, he thought, had far less need to affect unnecessary familiarity between themselves than women did.

He was restless, so he had only a cup of coffee and didn't bother to eat his fruit salad, but got up and began to walk around the labyrinthine courtyards of the Fort, following the sound of the music till he could make out Ushma's voice; it sounded as if she was giving sharp instructions to someone. He stumbled into a small open space he hadn't seen before, with a shiny red cement floor and wooden pillars. The musicians sat on a long pillow and three young girls, in the same shorter sari and pants he'd seen Usha wearing the day before, moved around the space with their hands entwined over their heads, their torsos tilted in a diagonal line. Usha was sitting next to the drummer, clapping her hands to the rhythm while giving the dancers the tempo in quick staccato spurts.

"Taka-taka-taka-tee-takatee-takatee-taa-taaa!"

He slid quietly inside the space and sat in a corner, attempting a semilotus position, though his knees hurt.

"Takateeta deena, takateeta deena, takateeta deen!"

He beckoned her, tilting his head in what he thought would be an appropriate gesture.

"Stooop!"

The music ceased, the dancers' poses came undone.

She rose quickly and came over to him.

How lovely she looked! A strand of fresh jasmine was tied to her braid, and she was wearing a green kurta and purple pants with a scarf around her tiny waist. Her cheeks were flushed, she exuded heat from the exertion and a subtle scent of musk.

"I'm sorry but you cannot watch the rehearsal."

He rose unsteadily and dusted his trousers. How foolish of him.

"I am so sorry . . . I had no idea. I am really sorry."

Then he saw that she was smiling.

"I don't want you to see any of this before tonight," she said quietly. "I want you to see it the way it is meant to be seen. With proper lighting and costumes."

There was a glow in her eyes, and an excitement. For a split second he saw she could even perhaps be insecure.

"Of course, of course. You are absolutely right."

"I want it to be a surprise for you," she added.

"Absolutely. Well, goodbye then. I'll see you tonight," he said quietly.

She nodded with her enigmatic smile. He moved away and turned to look at her one last time. She was standing by the pillar, watching him go, a foot curled on its toes crossing over the other ankle, in a pose similar to one of those miniatures he'd seen somewhere, in one of the museums—or was it on a bas-relief?—he couldn't remember which.

He spent the day aimlessly, waiting for the evening to come, elated and restless. Elated because of what Ushma Das had unexpectedly stirred in him. True, his body had responded to attractive women before; he'd had his random secret affairs, his brief sexual encounters, like all men his age who'd been in a marriage for more than ten years. It didn't make a difference, that's what all of them said the rare times the subject of extramarital affairs surfaced. They all agreed on one point: what really mattered was conjugal solidarity. That's what they'd invested in and were counting on. By rating their solid marriage as priority number one, they'd automatically given themselves permission to fuck around without thinking much of it. But this was a different sort of thing, it wasn't even carnal, or just carnal. This had a tinge of emotion, an undercurrent of real feeling. He didn't see Ushma Das just as an attractive woman, no, she was more like a goddess who had stepped down from those temple sculptures he had snubbed, which he now so regretted. She was quintessential, archetypal, inspiring. Yes, this was exactly what his life had been lacking for too long: inspiration, and, why not, an unexpected bout of romanticism. On the other hand, he felt a rising anxiety at the thought of what was going to happen that evening. He wasn't sure that Ushma Das was even aware he had a wife. He had almost forgotten it, too.

· • ·

His wife made her appearance at lunch in one of those ridiculous new ensembles that so embarrassed him. The choreographer was kind enough to compliment her on her harem-style pants and she seemed pleased.

He asked, in a casual tone, whether Ushma was going to join them.

"Oh no, Ushma never eats before a show," the diamond-studded lady said. "She's such a perfectionist. She will rehearse till one hour before going onstage, even for a small performance such as tonight."

"Dance is a devotional act," said the playwright. "It doesn't really matter to her how many people are in the audience."

"Indeed. Shouldn't that be true for every form of art?" he asked, more forcefully than rhetorically. "Of course, now its original purpose has been lost. But for millennia artistic expression has been a means to reach the divine within us!"

His wife lifted her eyes from her plate. She wasn't used to hearing such earnest talk coming from him about art's divine power.

Later in the day, after their usual postprandial nap, he woke up and found her sitting at the desk, in front of his laptop. She quickly closed the screen.

"What's wrong?" he asked.

"Nothing."

"You don't feel well?"

"No. I feel a little dizzy, I think."

"Is it the heat?"

"Maybe. I'm not sure. I don't feel a hundred percent myself," she said, massaging her stomach.

"Could it be something you ate?"

"I do feel a little nauseous, you know . . ."

This seemed an unexpected opportunity.

"Maybe you should stay in tonight and rest," he suggested.

She smiled, thankful.

"Actually I was just thinking that."

"Well then, by all means, stay put."

He stood up, relieved. She also seemed content.

"Are you going to see the performance anyway?" she asked with a hint of anxiety.

"I guess I'll have to. I believe the prince has already arranged everything counting us in. I'm afraid it's going to be rude if we both cancel, don't you think?"

"Probably. Yeah."

"Unless you want me to stay with you."

He held his breath, hoping it hadn't been a mistake to offer.

"No, no, of course not," she said. "I'll be fine."

"Okay then. I'll let the prince know you're not coming."

"Are you sure you don't mind going without me, love?"

"No, darling, I don't mind at all. They are nice people, and as you say I'm sure it's going to be interesting to see this performance."

"I'm sorry to be missing it, but I really don't feel like getting on a boat at night, you know? It gets so chilly out on the river."

"Yes, it does get quite damp at a certain time of the night, doesn't it?"

"I'd much rather cuddle up in bed with a mug of hot tea."

"You can watch a movie on my computer. That sounds blissful. In a way I wish I could do the same."

They smiled at each other, as if contemplating the possibility of that happening, and neither one said another word.

· • ·

Tyler had moved to Paris and had been working for a human rights organization that monitored the International Criminal Court. When they'd finally managed to speak on Skype he was about to catch a flight to The Hague so he had to be brief. Only a few hours before, the ICC had issued a guilty verdict against an African warlord for using child soldiers in the bloody ethnic conflict in the north of the Democratic Republic of the Congo. This was apparently great news since the trial against him had lasted a decade and it was going to hit the headlines in a major way. Tyler said he was literally on his way to a press conference that was scheduled that same afternoon.

There'd been no mention of a wife or children.

"That's wonderful, Tyler. You must be so excited," she said, though she had no idea who this particular warlord was.

"I am. But I'm very excited to hear from you," he said, in his husky, velvety voice, a voice she had nearly forgotten, which was coming back like a landslide.

"Me, too," she said, almost breathless.

"What took you so long to find me?"

"You didn't work too hard at finding me either," she said, grinning.

"True. But that doesn't mean I haven't been thinking of you."

She swallowed hard.

"Turn on the camera," he said.

She gave a light laugh.

"No way. I look awful. I'm not ready yet."

"I'm dying to see you. When can I see you? In person, I mean."

"I . . . I don't know," she said. She felt a slight panic, and made herself laugh. "Wow, Tyler, maybe we've got to slow it down."

She heard a loud buzz in the background of his place.

"Shit, I really have to go now," he said. "Can we speak later? I can call you after the press conference."

"Yes . . . but not too late. There's a time difference here."

"Okay, just hold on a sec."

She heard the sound of a chair screeching, then footsteps, then his voice saying *"J'arrive"* on what she assumed was the intercom.

"I've got to go, the taxi is here. What were you saying?"

"I said, there's a time difference . . ."

"Where are you?"

She was reluctant to say. Holidaying in a maharaja's fort sounded frivolous compared to where he was headed. And if she said she was on some sort of holiday, he'd know she must be with someone.

"I am in India, but I'll be back in Rome next week."

"Great. Come to Paris."

She laughed.

"Maybe I will."

"You must. How late can I call you back? I want to talk to you."

"My ten thirty? They turn off the generator after eleven," she lied.

"Va bene, mia bella," he said. He used to call her that when they were together, in that soft, rolling American accent she used to find so seductive.

· • ·

Hundreds of tiny lights advanced in the dark, floating on the river's surface like a mirrored reflection of the starry sky. They had appeared all at once, past the river bend, dotting the Narmada like sequins on black velvet while they were having drinks on the top terrace. Everyone stopped talking and just looked in amazement at the clusters of lights flowing downstream. They were told by a waiter that the *shikara* was ready to take them, so the group descended the steps to the *ghats,* their spirits lifted by more cucumber martinis and the knowledge that they were under the flawless stage directions of the prince who left no detail unattended. The boat slid silently on the smooth river surface (no engines were allowed on that stretch of the sacred river), parting the clusters of lights that were coming toward them. Now they could see there were lotus flowers and coconuts floating alongside with the oil lamps—were these offerings to deities?— that someone upriver must have been instructed to release at the appointed hour, in order to make their short trip unforgettable. The tiny island glowed in the distance. There were torches burning and more lanterns that lent the scene a warming glow. As they approached he saw, waiting for them on the bank, a few attendants dressed in white, who helped them descend. A white padded carpet as wide as a room had been spread on the ground.

They sat barefoot among the soft cushions and more scattered rose petals. In the darkness that surrounded the small circle of light he could make out the silhouettes of the musicians, who'd begun to tune their instruments, cross-legged on a wooden platform, right across from where they were sitting. For the first time since he had been in India, he wished he were wearing the same comfortable shirts and soft shawls as the other men in his company, which blended so well with the surroundings. Even the young translator had abandoned his jeans and T-shirt in favor of traditional clothes perfectly starched and ironed; now he too looked noble and sculpted. A light drumming started, accompanied by the violin and then the flute. The prince walked over to the stage and introduced with a few words the piece they were going to see, then he ceremoniously lit the oil lamps under a small bronze sculpture of Shiva and his wheel. The glimmering flames lit and revealed the depth of the stage and the shapes of the musicians.

He felt inebriated by the smells, the sounds of crickets in the trees, the quiet waves lapping in the distance. As the music began, a soft, beguiling tune, the dancers entered the stage in their elaborate silk costumes. Ushma was in the center, in a flaming orange sari, covered in rich golden jewelry. She moved across the stage in a slightly tilted stance, where head, bust and torso formed a curvaceous line in an S shape that made the temple sculptures come alive. She wore a sphinxlike smile, while her enormous black irises moved right and left in the blinding whites of her eyes, adding expression and movement to the dance; her fingers opened and closed, like petals of a lotus flower. Every part of her body flexed, creating opposing angles as she kept shifting her weight from right to left, in a geometric design that seemed impossible to accomplish other than in a drawing. It was a timeless image, as powerful and dense as only dreams can be. Ushma wasn't looking at him. Her face, her smile and her glances were set in the carefully constructed mask the dance required. But underneath the composure of her face she was, he knew, dancing for him.

Something softened inside and he realized he had tears in his eyes. What a relief and what a revelation, to be feeling something so deeply that it should bring tears. So there *was* something left in him that had been frozen and now was thawing. Might this be a case of Stendhal syndrome? he wondered as he dabbed away at his tears. It must be either that or the feeling of oneness with the universe that Ushma had described. Where else would this spellbinding emotion come from? This was exactly what he needed to reconnect with: the simple truth contained within a perfect act. If only he could tap into that source again, then he would be safe, as an artist and as a man.

When the performance ended Ushma came forward, followed by the three younger dancers. With their long hennaed fingers they touched first their heads, then their eyes, then their hearts, and bowed. Not to the audience, he realized—they didn't engage with them, or smile or come out of their composure—they were bowing to Shiva and to his cosmic dance. Then the three slender younger dancers, in one swift, deft move, knelt down in front of Ushma, placed their hands around her ankles and kissed her feet, touching their foreheads lightly to the floor. To each one Ushma gave a blessing, by touching their heads with her open palms. This exchange, performed with such delicacy, a daily ritual that didn't seem to surprise his Indian companions, astounded him. To kiss your teacher's feet. To be blessed by your guru. For a fleeting moment he thought that if he could only penetrate more deeply into this magnificent tradition and be part of it—no longer as a visitor or as part of an audience, but physically delve into it—then he might have hope to find a way back into his work. There was no longer any respect for serious writers in the West, only marketing. Appearances. Money. It was no wonder he was so disillusioned, no wonder his inspiration had waned. Now Ushma smiled, as the small audience kept clapping, and he was sure that she was looking directly at him. Yes, she had danced for him, and for him only. That he knew. How could he let go of such a miracle?

.   •   .

It took a surprisingly short time for sixteen years of marriage to come undone. Later, neither one of them was able to recollect how the sequence had unfolded—which phrase had prompted the next, nor how it had been possible that a mild irritation, an unpleasant remark, had unveiled truths that had seemed impossible to reveal until that moment.

The feeling they both had was of a tidal wave that kept gaining speed and had crashed upon them before they could take shelter. Just like any natural calamity, it happened without foresight, while they were having tea on the small terrace of their room, looking at the peaceful river bathed in the morning light. It is possible that during the night they both had been prey to the kinds of dreams they'd had since coming to India—dreams of unusual intensity—and were still under their spell. In any case, seconds before it started, neither of them had the perception that they were about to hack to death their marriage, nor could they foresee how quick and (apparently) painless this hacking would turn out to be. Everything had seemed possible, in that moment. Possible that they could put an end to their marriage, that they could go different ways (he would stay on, she would go back). The decision had sounded final and conclusive, as though both of them had been toying secretly with it until it had become so familiar that it no longer frightened them. Oh no, now they were both looking forward to what would happen next, when they would be without the other. It didn't deter them to think they would have to move out of their comfortable apartment, close their joint bank account, file for divorce, find a new place to live, maybe even move to a different country. Suddenly they were ready for change. In fact they'd never felt more euphoric.

They had to say things to each other that would make turning back impossible, and they obliged. *I don't love you anymore. I haven't been in love with you for years. I am still young, I want pas-*

sion. I need to feel inspired again. I want my life back, I have lived only in your shadow. How odiously clichéd it all sounded, and yet—at that very moment—so utterly real, so satisfying. It was as though with each phrase they were shedding years of dissimulation. They grew lighter, younger, more desirable, now that they thought they were about to take their lives back.

Before leaving the Fort, Ushma had given him her number and the name of a simple hotel he could stay in outside Bubaneshwar, not far from where she lived. He told the prince he would stay a couple of more days at the Fort, then he might go back to Orissa to look at the temples again. Plans were still uncertain, but he didn't mind, he said.

She booked her flight online and in two hours was packed.

He didn't bother to ask his wife why she was flying to Paris instead of Rome.

. . .

When, a few weeks later, they met again to discuss the details of their separation, their enthusiasm had already subsided (both their romantic fantasies had turned out to be unrealistic or disappointing) and they were faced only with the practicalities of dismantling what was left of their life as a couple. They were disoriented and afraid but also unable to repair the damage done.

Later, when they tried to explain to their friends why their marriage had fallen apart, within *"l'espace d'un matin,"* she'd said, they admitted they weren't quite sure how it happened.

They both, separately, used the same expression.

It was like being in a dream, they said. A strange dream, which seemed so vivid until it lasted.

The Club

Soon after her husband's death in 1995, Mrs. D'Costa moved from the big Mombasa house overlooking the Mtwapa Creek to a small cottage by the ocean, farther down the coast. She had lived happily in that house for more than forty years with her husband, a well-respected Goan doctor, and their three children. They had met in the fifties in Edinburgh, where they both went to college, and at the time young freckled Anne Munro could never have imagined that one day she'd call herself a white Kenyan and that she'd never set foot in Scotland again.

She had given most of her furniture away to the Salvation Army—her long teak dining table with its eight chairs, beds, lamps, paintings, the two old armchairs she and her husband used to sit on after dinner to do the crossword, various knickknacks of no value—and took with her only the strictly necessary to fill the two-bedroom cottage—whatever she couldn't live without. That included her cook, Hamisi, now gray at the temples, who had been with her for twenty-five years, and her aging Jack Russells, Pickle and Chutney, fond of biting strangers.

Among the things that had appealed to her about moving away from the city was the fact that two old friends of hers, Prudence and Lionel Wilton (she a former actress with the Little Theatre Club company in Mombasa, he a brilliant architect originally from England), had retired twenty years before to this remote stretch of coastline, on the edge of a thick forest that ran all the way down south. The forest was a sacred place to the local Digo tribe and it had been designated a national monument. Rare species of plants and wild animals still thrived in its thick shade, and the Wiltons claimed they'd had leopards cross their land up until fifteen years back. They lived on a leafy ten-acre property overlooking the ocean, in an airy white house Lionel had designed in a simple Frank Lloyd Wright style. Not far from their manicured garden that gently sloped toward the beach, one could see the remnants of other crumbling houses probably built in the forties and fifties, barely standing under the shade of gigantic flame trees, half hidden beneath the tangle of creepers and ancient bougainvilleas. Wild fig trees had sprouted in the cracks of the floors, their roots blasting the walls with their violent push. Their original owners had all left for mysterious reasons and had never returned, so for years now Prudence and Lionel had been the only residents—that is to say white residents—in that area other than the fishermen and their families who lived in thatched huts scattered in the bush at the back of the property.

The Wiltons were eager for their friend to become their neighbor. Now that they were reaching their seventies, they were beginning to feel lonelier and were longing for a bit of company. When he heard that her husband had passed away, Lionel immediately called Mrs. D'Costa and told her about the empty cottage next door to them.

· • ·

Without thinking about it twice, she'd enthusiastically agreed to move there. Actually she was relieved to let go of the big house and its happy memories now that her children had married and gone off to England, Australia and Durban. She had always tried to see change as a good thing and not to be afraid of it.

Her new landlord, a Mr. Khan who owned the hardware store twenty miles down the road, had agreed to have some work done to the cottage, since nobody had lived in it for a very long time and it was in a state of disrepair. He was quite relieved when Mrs.

Anne D'Costa showed up at the store, inquiring if he'd agree to rent it to her. Though what she could afford to pay was minimal, he was happy for the income, and that someone would occupy the place. She asked him to replace the thatch roof with tin, to whitewash the walls and have one of his workers cut the mangle of weeds and bushes that strangled the trees. He was pleased to find out that Mrs. D'Costa was an easy tenant with few demands. She didn't expect him to replace the old pipes or the haphazard wires that were snaking from the walls, nor did she seem to mind the yellowing Bakelite switches and fuse boxes dating back to the fifties. She had done enough maintenance while running a household of six, and now that she was alone she didn't feel like being fussy about housekeeping anymore.

· · ·

The Wiltons had welcomed Anne on her first night in the cottage with a strong vodka tonic. They sat on squeaking plastic chairs out on their veranda just as the full moon was about to bob up from the horizon.

"Welcome to our private paradise, my dear!" said Lionel, raising his glass. "You must come over for sundowners every evening!"

He still wore faded khaki shorts, knee socks and desert shoes, just as he did when she'd met him right before Kenya Independence, and he still combed what was left of his sandy hair on the side. But his body had shrunk and shriveled since then and his liver-spotted hand trembled slightly when he held up a glass.

"We'll see about that, Lionel. We'll see," Mrs. D'Costa said jokingly. "I am not going to inflict my presence on a daily basis, I wouldn't want you to get sick of me too soon."

"That's an order, Anne! I won't compromise!" Lionel said, adding a generous splash of vodka to her glass.

Prudence poked him lightly with her elbow.

"Lionel, please let poor Anne be. She'll do as she pleases. You'll scare her away if you insist." She shook her head and poured herself another drink.

"Don't pay attention to him, Anne. He has become such a bully, this husband of mine."

Prudence had put on quite a lot of weight since her days at the Little Theatre, but her roundness seemed to lend her a more youthful air. Men used to fall in love with her all the time, Mrs. D'Costa remembered. She had a lovely figure and a quirky taste in clothes back in the Mombasa days. Gamine, charming: that's how people described her whenever Prudence came up in conversation. And quite rightly; she had been a lovely girl indeed.

Now Prudence wore Bata plastic slippers and large caftans that helped conceal her frame. She had cut her thick hair short and let it go white. She had spent too many years in the sun, and her face was a web of wrinkles. It didn't matter, Mrs. D'Costa thought with relief: they had all aged in the sun and at the same pace so why should any of them mind the way they'd changed? They had known one another for so long, shouldn't they be like family by now? And besides, as far as she was concerned, she believed she looked better now than when she'd just met the Wiltons. She had been a flat-chested, mousy girl with thick glasses, just twenty-one years old. An alien, really, who had just landed in the heat of Mombasa from the Scottish fog.

· • ·

When Anne and her husband, Victor, met in college at Edinburgh, it was almost love at first sight. Victor D'Costa was a handsome, quiet young man. His family was originally from Goa, but in the thirties his grandfather had migrated to Kenya to work for the railroad company.

In those days in Edinburgh it was rare to see a student with brown skin on a university campus. Anne felt a bit of an outsider herself; she didn't have many friends either, coming as she did from a poor, uneducated family in Glasgow. She noticed how the rest of the students either ignored Victor or plain avoided him, and was drawn to him exactly for this reason. As she got to know Victor, she grew more in awe of his impeccable manners, his kindness and wit. Actually she found him far more sophisticated than most of the students who snubbed him.

In 1952, right after their wedding (a small affair, neither had money to spend on the ceremony), the couple had sailed off to Mombasa to stay with his family. She'd immediately agreed to follow him there; she wasn't leaving much behind anyway: a stuffy rented room that smelled of cabbage, her father's drinking and her mother's dreariness. There was also a surly brother she never got on with.

She wasn't ready for so much brightness.

The East African light was blinding as their ship approached the coast; even at eight in the morning the air was redolent of cloves and sweet flowers. She could smell water in that heat. The clothes clung to her skin.

"It feels like sitting in a warm bath," she said, leaning into her husband, minutes after touching land at Mombasa port. They had been at sea for seven days.

"Is it too much, dear?"

"Oh, no. This is lovely. Lovely," she said with a mirthful laugh. "I feel like taking my shoes off and running barefoot on the road!"

He clutched her hand and his eyes welled up slightly. He had been so worried that she might find the climate too harsh.

Her in-laws and her husband had decided it was better to take some time "to adjust" before getting a place of their own, so for a few months they'd lived with his family in the old town, in a big house full of relatives and children. Mixed marriages were a rare thing then, but the D'Costas immediately took her in as one of their own. It did help that they were Catholic Goans and they could all go together to church on Sunday, but in all respects

Anne felt truly welcomed from the very first day. Now she saw where Victor's kindness came from.

Her new family was right, she did need time to get used to her life in Africa. Her head was spinning with fear and delight every time she walked out the door of her new home. Not only had she gained a whole new family, but there was a new language to learn, new smells, colors, noises and very different rules to get used to.

· · ·

She asked Prudence whether she still liked to play mah-jongg.

"Mah-jongg? Oh dear, I haven't for ages, actually. But guess what? I must have that same old set we had in the Bamburi house somewhere, remember? Shall I retrieve it from wherever it's buried? We sure could play again on Sunday nights, like the old days. That would be so jolly."

Prudence's enthusiasm reassured her. It had been a good decision, to reunite with the Wiltons. They were such warm and lovely people.

Mrs. D'Costa and Prudence had met before Independence, in 1961. They'd been hired as typists in a British trading company's office on Kilindini Road, which was then called Prince Charles Street. But after only two months Prudence had left her desk to join the Little Theatre company, where, thanks to her charm and her looks, she'd been offered a much more exciting career—as well as a more rewarding payroll. Soon after, Lionel—a dashing architect from London who had designed several hotels on the south coast—had spotted her onstage playing Vera in *Ten Little Indians* and had immediately fallen for her.

That first night at the Wiltons' Mrs. D'Costa walked back home escorted by their night *askari,* Saleem. He flashed his feeble flashlight along a small path that cut through Prudence and Lionel's garden, skirted one of the crumbling houses standing in the plot right next to theirs and cut through the back of Mrs. D'Costa's compound.

The night was scented with frangipani and the full moon peeked through the rustling palm fronds, leaving a silver trail on the dark surface of the ocean. It reminded Mrs. D'Costa of an advertisment from the forties for cruises in the tropics. She wished good night to old Saleem and sat on her veranda with a nightcap before retiring to bed. She was certain she'd sleep soundly on her first night at the cottage, and she did, lulled by the sound of the surf breaking on the reef in the distance.

Only two weeks after Mrs. D'Costa had moved into the cottage, Prudence and Lionel's ancient Land Rover was hit by a truck as they were heading to Nairobi to visit their daughter, and they died on the spot.

It was a terrible shock, and for days Mrs. D'Costa avoided taking in the enormity of what had just happened by keeping herself busy. When the Wiltons' five children congregated in the airy house from different parts of the world with spouses and children, it was she who took charge of the situation. Without even asking permission to do so, Mrs. D'Costa supervised meals, went shopping for supplies and took care of logistics with military precision, as one does whenever a tragedy strikes and everyone else is walking around in a daze.

· • ·

Now, with Prudence and Lionel gone, she had been battling her loneliness in various ways. She'd started working daily in the garden—she had landscaped most of the garden at Mtwapa herself—and now with Hamisi's help she dug a small pond that they filled with papyrus, water lilies and tiny fish. She attempted to teach English to some of the children living in the bush behind her property and had gone to great lengths to organize a Sunday class in her house. Only a couple of them showed up, brought by their mothers, who squatted outside on the floor of the veranda while Mrs. D'Costa sat at the table with the children. She gave them notebooks and pens and started her first lesson conjugating the verb *to be*. The children—who had never sat at a table before and had never seen a house like hers—looked terrified. They were unable to follow what she was saying (despite the years she had spent in the country, her Swahili was still poor and too heavily accented), and as soon as one of them started crying, the other followed suit. The mothers apologized. The children were not used to *wazungus*. They were shy and they "had fear" of her.

That same year, during the monsoon, Anne spent endless afternoons under the pounding of the rain against the tin roof. She played solitaire over and over, reread cover to cover most of the yellowing paperbacks on the shelf—old thrillers, a couple of Daphne du Maurier novels, *The Field Guide to Birds in East Africa*. In between the daily power cuts she'd listen avidly to the BBC World or talk to her dogs, and one afternoon she finally resolved to teach Hamisi gin rummy so that they could play it together after dinner. He wasn't as engaged by the game as she'd expected he would be, so she let him win most of the time in the hope of luring him into playing another hand and then another. It was essential that she keep spirits high and not indulge in dark thoughts. It was too late to turn back. And besides, even if she'd wanted, there was no other place waiting for her to turn back to.

· • ·

Margaret Dobson—Margie to her friends—back in the days of old Mombasa had been a celebrated beauty, with the perfect marriage and the perfect children. A slender blonde with light blue eyes, she bought her wardrobe in England and always had a string of cultured pearls dangling around her neck. For Mrs. D'Costa she'd been just an acquaintance—they didn't belong to the same Mombasa circles—but Anne had always admired her style from afar. Thus it was with extreme pleasure and surprise that two years after the terrible accident she learned that Margie and her husband, Keith, were looking to leave Mombasa to retire on the south coast and were coming to look at the Wiltons' plot of land. News of their visit had reached her via Saleem, the old *askari* who still lived on the premises, looking after the empty house. He came almost every evening to drink a cup of masala *chai* with her cook, Hamisi, to shake off the loneliness. The two men sat on the *baraza* outside the kitchen talking in Digo. Mrs. D'Costa enjoyed the sound of their soft cackles that seeped from the backyard into the house while she read a book with Pickle and Chutney snoring at her feet.

As soon as she heard that Margie and Keith were coming to pay a second visit to the property, Mrs. D'Costa sent Hamisi over to the house next door with a note asking the Dobsons to stop by for tea. She then instructed him to bring out the nicer cups and to serve tea under the flame tree on the lawn, where they could have a good view of the sea. For the occasion she washed her hair, put it into rollers and wore a dress with a large floral print.

"It would be lovely if you came to live here," she said, pouring the tea into the floral porcelain cups. How exciting to have the Dobsons, of all people, sitting on her wicker chairs looking out at the ocean.

"Yes, it would. Wouldn't it, Keith?" Margie asked her husband, her face eager and cautious at once; she was clearly afraid to commit herself without his approval. He nodded briefly, seemingly impatient with this impromptu tea party, and looked the other way.

He was tall and imposing, quite handsome still. As a young man he'd had a classic appeal, dark haired, with a roguish face with thick eyebrows over green eyes. That wild Irish look that aged well. He had maintained his stature and bulk. Time seemed to have only made him more interesting.

Margie had been the one to keep the conversation alive. After commenting on the tragedy that had ended Lionel's and Prudence's lives she noted that it seemed that many of their old friends had followed a similar journey: from their society days at the club, the up-country safaris with the children and ayahs in tow, to retirement on a quiet beach, looking forward to silence and lots to read. Mrs. D'Costa agreed, out of politeness, despite the fact that she'd never been part of the "society days" at the club nor had she been on safaris with ayahs. Clearly Margie had no recollection of how distant their life had been from hers in the days when she and Keith had pink gin at the club every evening. In fact, so many years later, none of her white friends seemed to remember how different things had been before Independence, Mrs. D'Costa thought, but she wasn't the kind of person who would make a sarcastic remark. She disliked feeling any bitterness.

The sea glowed like an iridescent sheet of mercury. A heron flew low over its still surface, and one could hear the sound of its wings flapping. Two fishermen came walking from the other end of the beach in their tattered shorts, squatted on their haunches by the edge of the water and started to wash themselves, rubbing white sand on their dark skin, in the bluish light of dusk.

"Look at that reef, Keith," Margie said encouragingly in her lilting voice. "It's just like a gouache, isn't it?"

Her husband didn't answer.

"You could start painting again," she added.

Keith ignored her. He lifted a stale Barvita biscuit from the plastic tray but put it back. He'd never possessed good social skills, that much Mrs. D'Costa remembered about him. He was always brooding, intimidating; the rare times they'd met in the past she'd never dared start a conversation with him. But now that the Dobsons had landed on her turf, she was the one who was supposed to show them the ropes. If they came here they'd have to rely on her, at least in the beginning.

"It's *very* peaceful indeed, this beach," Keith finally conceded, perhaps with a hint of sarcasm.

"I hope peace is what you're looking for," Mrs. D'Costa said, an eyebrow raised, "because here you'll find plenty of it."

. . .

On the first of each month Mrs. D'Costa drove the twenty miles to the small junction that people proudly called town and stopped at the hardware store to pay the rent. The so-called town was a mix of moldy one-story buildings in need of whitewashing clustered around the post office, the hardware store, the gas station and the bank. A line of wooden stalls along the main road sold wrinkled vegetables and dried fish. The butcher's sign had ribs and loins drawn by a childish hand. Slabs of meat covered in flies hung on hooks against the bright blue wall. Young men shielded by cheap sunglasses and rasta hats were smoking ganja by the bus station, while the eternal Bob Marley song blared from a portable radio from one of the wooden shacks that sold fries, hard-boiled eggs and sweet masala *chai*.

Mrs. D'Costa didn't dislike coming to town, didn't think of it as charmless or ugly. The memory of European architecture for her had faded, and these days she couldn't recall much of the geography there and hardly ever thought about it anyway. To her the town was just any African town and she expected nothing more of it other than what it offered.

She actually had always looked forward to her visits to the hardware store. She enjoyed having a chat with her landlord and she liked the smell of sawdust, the dim light filtering from the skylight, the old teak cabinets filled with antiquated brass locks and hinges. Mr. Khan was a chubby man with thick tortoiseshell glasses who seemed always to be sitting in the large chair in the front of his shop, propped up by several pillows because of his bad back. The Khans were a wealthy Gujarati family who'd come to East Africa looking for opportunities and had been successful shopkeepers for generations. Mr. Khan was no longer the one in charge of the shop; his son Kublai had now taken over the business, but the old man still liked to sit by the cashier under the fan, just to sip tea and greet clients while wrapping a pound of nails in a scrap of old newspaper, give out some change, shout an order to one of the younger guys who sawed wood in the backyard. Though balding at the top, he wore dangling white mustaches and kept the rest of his hair rather long, so that he was beginning to look more like a Chinese sage than an Asian shopkeeper.

Young Kublai greeted Anne at the door, smelling of incense and Lifebuoy soap.

"Good morning, Mrs. D'Costa. How are things at the cottage? Did Hamisi manage to fix the faucet or should I send you one of my *fundi*?"

"No need to, Kublai, thank you very much. Hamisi and I managed. We have a pretty good toolbox. I'll let you know if it holds, otherwise we'll have to replace it, I'm afraid."

"No problem. You know that we are always here to assist you."

Kublai Khan bore his noble name graciously. Somehow he reminded Mrs. D'Costa of her husband when they'd first met. Kublai too had exquisite manners, a mane of jet-black hair and thick eyebrows. His English was perfect, his words always carefully articulated. He'd been an exceptional student and had spent a few years in England right after high school to study as an engineer but didn't like it there and had left.

The weather, he'd said laconically. And I missed my folks.

So he'd come back to the family's empire within the small perimeter that circled the gas station, the tire center and the hardware store, where members of his clan had been undisputed kings for three generations. A melancholic young man, one could have said of Kublai Khan, someone who at some point had followed an impulse in the belief that he could've become a completely different person than the rest of his kin. But that sense of a calling had never quite come through. That was part of the reason Mrs. D'Costa felt a special empathy toward him. Like her, he too, had a dent.

Right behind the lumberyard one could get a glimpse of the Khan women dashing around in their starched saris, scurrying back and forth from the kitchen of the house. The smell of roasted cumin, mustard seeds, turmeric and cardamom wafted through the dimly lit shop. A pale little girl with skinny legs brought a bowl of food to her father and grandfather. Fresh chapati and shrimp *jeera*.

"Would you like to taste some, Mrs. D'Costa?" Kublai asked, placing the bowl on the counter.

"No thank you, Kublai, Hamisi is waiting for me to take my lunch at home."

"Please. My daughter-in-law is a very good cook," the elder Mr. Khan interjected.

"I have no doubt about that, Mr. Khan! I can surely tell when a curry powder is homemade and ground with a mortar and pestle."

The old man laughed. "Of course, of course you can, Mrs. D'Costa. Did you learn your cooking from your mother-in-law?" he asked gently. He knew of course that her in-laws were Goans and that they'd lived in the old town in Mombasa.

"Yes, she taught me everything. When I first came over all I knew was meat, boiled carrots and potatoes!" She started laughing too. "And she was very particular, you know. We had to roast each spice separately, and make fresh powder every morning. She just refused to use the leftover curry from the previous day."

"That is the way. That is the way," Mr. Khan said. "In our house it was the same. My late wife also had the same rule."

He leaned slightly over the dark wood counter and lowered his voice in a complicit tone.

"She made sure the daughters-in-law didn't use the kind you buy at the *duka*. You know how the younger ladies now prefer to take shortcuts in the kitchen?"

"Of course. Everything comes in a box, these days. But it surely doesn't taste the same."

Mrs. D'Costa slid the envelope filled with banknotes over the counter.

"One day I'd like you to taste my Sunday curry, Mr. Khan. I

suspect you won't be disappointed!" she said in an unusually exuberant voice and, as she heard herself, she felt her cheeks blush as she hadn't in God knows how many years.

Mr. Khan took the envelope and joined his palms together over his chest.

"It's always a pleasure to see you, Mrs. D'Costa. And remember, if you have any problems at home, just give us a call and we'll send someone to fix it for you."

In the car, on her way home, Mrs. D'Costa thought about Mr. Khan. She felt so at ease in his company; he was such a nice, courteous man and she would've liked to get to know him better. She wondered whether she had been too forward mentioning Sunday lunch. She knew the rules, of course, when it came to Asian family etiquette. The upper and lower caste issue—although unspoken—still existed to some degree and her strict mother-in-law would have surely disapproved of her asking a shopkeeper to lunch.

Oh well, we're all outcasts here, after all. Which means we are all the same in the end, Mrs. D'Costa thought. The idea made her smile.

She left the paved road and turned left, on the winding dirt track that took her home through the coconut plantation. Every time she made that turn she was greeted by the sudden shift from the blinding light of the main road to the shady coolness of the bush. She loved the way the sun filtered through the branches of the mango trees lining the road, projecting dancing shadows on the red earth.

Thinking of what she'd said to Keith Dobson only a couple of days earlier, she nodded to herself: she was lucky to have found such a place to live.

· • ·

As the Dobsons were finalizing the paperwork for the title deeds up in Mombasa, Anne was announcing to Kublai their imminent arrival, telling him that they'd probably need to do quite a lot of repair around the house, and would most certainly place a large order of materials with him. She was actually savoring the moment when she would take Keith to the store and show him not only how well regarded she was there, but also what lovely people the Khans were. Hopefully that would help to make him like the place more. But when the time came and she offered to make the introduction Keith simply said that he didn't care to meet any shopkeeper from the village. He had already placed an order for everything he needed in Mombasa and it was due to be delivered any day.

"I hate that horrid little junction anyway," he said in his disparaging tone. "The less I'll have to go there, the happier I will be."

Six weeks later, once the walls had been repainted, the bathrooms renovated and the kitchen redesigned, the Dobsons moved into the Wiltons' old house, breathing new life into rooms that had been empty for more than two years. Mrs. D'Costa brought over a potted bougainvillea as a housewarming present and Margie showed her around the rooms. They were filled with sturdy furniture in blond wood, with bookcases for the large number of books that Keith meant to read, with a grand piano that Margie meant to play, with an astonishing variety of kitchen utensils, pots and pans, garden furniture and the usual array of paintings people collect during a lifetime in East Africa: there were buffaloes staring down from a ridge, Masai warriors on the hunt holding spears and blazing sunsets over the Indian Ocean. There were, of course, dozens of pictures of the Dobsons' progeny scattered everywhere, either sailing a dhow off the island of Zanzibar, trekking Mount Kenya or driving open cars through the bush in muddy safari clothes with a beer can in hand. They were two incredibly good-looking boys, tanned, blond, healthy, carrying the great mix of their parents' genes in their youthful bodies.

Mrs. D'Costa inspected every picture with great care. She was looking forward to meeting the boys when they would come to visit their parents. It would be so refreshing to have some young people around.

Her own children all lived too far away. For them to fly with wives and children just to see her was too expensive. The oldest was a schoolteacher in Brisbane, the other a chiropractor in a small town in northern England, and her daughter was a full-time mother of three in Durban. They all struggled to make ends meet at the end of the month, and though they always promised a visit, they kept postponing the trip and now it'd been close to three years since she had seen them. They often wrote letters (Mrs. D'Costa had firmly refused to learn how to use a computer and to write e-mails) and they called her once every two or three weeks, but she wished she could see the grandchildren more. These days children grew up so fast, one had a hard time recognizing them after only six months.

Looking at these festive family photographs she couldn't help but admit that her own children had had a very different life than that of the Dobsons. Not so much access to adventure. Well, and very different looking, for sure.

. . .

In early December the short rains ended and the weather finally changed. Every morning now the skies were clear, no more rumbling in the distance announcing another downpour. The nights were warmer, the fishermen went out in the evenings in their slim *ingalawas,* dotting the horizon with flickering lights.

But it turned out that, unlike Lionel and Prudence, the Dobsons hardly ever invited her over, and Mrs. D'Costa's gin rummy nights with Hamisi continued. One week shortly after they'd settled in she'd asked the Dobsons over to Sunday lunch and had extended the invitation also to her old friend Ada, an ex-nurse who still lived in Mombasa, whom she'd met through the East African Women's Society. Ada arrived almost an hour late, so that by the time they heard her battered car sputtering and clanking along the driveway, everyone was starved and jittery. They heard the car door slam, then Pickle's and Chutney's furious barking over Ada's high-pitched voice.

"So sorry! I had a bloody puncture and nobody stopped to give me a hand! Off you go! Off! You wretched creatures!"

Ada appeared on the veranda panting and puffing in faded baggy trousers and a strange shirt with a ruffled collar that didn't make any sense. White roots were showing under a faded hair dye.

They sat down to lunch at last and Hamisi brought his legendary curry to the table. Even before Ada had arrived, Mrs. D'Costa could tell that Keith found the company dull, as he didn't make any effort to participate in conversation and now ate his food in rapid, greedy gulps, shaking his leg under the table in a nervous tic. Ada began a meandering tale about how she'd just won the yearly contest of the society with her tomato preserves, and how the previous year the first prize had gone, of all people, to Mrs. D'Costa for a multicolored crocheted blanket. Margie half listened while sending quick, concerned glances across the table to her husband, probably gauging his tolerance level, which was clearly dropping by the minute. None of this escaped Mrs. D'Costa, who felt sorry both for Keith, who had to listen to all this nonsense, and for Ada, who was making a fool of herself. She was relieved when Keith suddenly stood up and declared it was time for his nap.

After this experiment Mrs. D'Costa had enough good sense not to ask them again. She thought it wiser to sit and wait for the Dobsons to return the invitation. It never came. If by chance she'd cross their car on the dirt road, the Dobsons would limit themselves to waving a hand and keep driving on.

Often in the evening the breeze would carry the sound of Margie playing the piano, or sometimes she'd hear Keith's voice calling for Justin, the houseboy they'd taken with them from their previous home, or laughing out loud about something. It was like receiving snippets of a parallel life she had no access to.

"Oh well," she said out loud to her face in the bathroom mirror. "If they want to keep their privacy, just let them be." But she knew better.

As the holidays neared, Margie showed up a couple of times by the cottage on her way to the junction. Sometimes she would just honk at the end of the driveway without even getting out of the car, with the engine running. The last few times Margie apologized for being always in such a hurry—she told Mrs. D'Costa that she was terribly busy getting everything ready for Christmas. Their two sons were coming with their wives and children, and there was so much to do. Where should she get the turkey for Christmas dinner? Was it necessary to book one? Would Anne know a good, reasonably priced *fundi* for repairing the thatch roof of the garage?

Mrs. D'Costa had prepared for Christmas well in advance, as she always did. Early in November she had mailed handmade cards to her children and nephews; with Hamisi she had collected doum palm fruits and all sorts of pods in the garden to make their own Christmas decorations. They'd painted them in silver and gold and scattered them around the house. They'd painted a few shells too, which they hung on the branches of the trees, and they looked really pretty. On Christmas Eve she'd attended the usual tea party at the East African Women's Society (she was a senior member) and the next day she had Christmas lunch with Ada, as they'd done for years.

Finally, early in the morning on Boxing Day, Justin, the Dobsons' houseboy, showed up at the cottage with a note. Margie was asking her for supper that evening so she could meet Tim and Mark, their wives and the children.

It was an extremely cheerful evening. Mrs. D'Costa found the boys as handsome as their photographs. The wives, Tara and Ruth, were charming and the children adorable. Mark, the older son, was a lawyer in London; Tim a cook in New York.

"A chef," Margie made sure to make the distinction. "It's much more than just a cook over there, of course. Tim was on Zagat's ten best chefs list last year."

Tim gave her a look, trying to silence her, but she ignored him.

"There was even a profile written on him in one of the papers, I think it was *The New York Times,* isn't that right, darling?"

Before leaving, slightly tipsy from the wine, Mrs. D'Costa kissed everyone except for the children, who wouldn't let her, invited them all to pay her a visit (you can come anytime, you're always welcome! Just walk up the stone steps from the beach), but they smiled and thanked her, without making a specific plan.

Before New Year's, the whole crew of youngsters had gone to the island of Lamu to meet other friends, Margie told her. They'd met by chance at the big Nakumatt supermarket by the Likoni Ferry.

"They fly to Nairobi on Sunday and then straight back home from there," Margaret said, pushing her cart along the aisle.

"That's too bad. I was hoping to see them again," Mrs. D'Costa said.

Margie sighed.

"I feel we've had such a little time with them, I've hardly realized they were here. I'm afraid that after a few days they get bored with us. Especially Tara and Ruth."

"Nonsense! They had a marvelous time on the beach. I could see them from my veranda playing and snorkeling. They loved it here. Who wouldn't? We live in paradise."

Margie nodded, only half listening, and kept searching the aisle. She examined the label of a pricey French coffee and waved the package in front of Anne's nose.

"Any idea what this is like? Ever tried it?"

"Heavens, no. I only take Nescafé."

"Oh well, I'll give it a try. Keith loves his morning coffee. Perhaps it will remind him of Paris."

She gave Mrs. D'Costa a faint smile and dumped the French

roast in the basket full of imported groceries. Margie didn't wait for her at the checkout, and Anne saw her Range Rover pull away.

. . .

Three weeks later, at two in the morning, Justin knocked frantically at the door of the cottage. He was shaking and tears were rolling down his cheeks.

"*Bwana Kee amekufa. Kugia nyumbani tafadhali, Mama naogopa sana.*"

Mrs. D'Costa sprang into instant action mode; she knew she was at her best when it came to emergencies. She put on some clothes, woke up Hamisi, asked him to get in the passenger seat of the car and drove to the Dobsons' at full speed on the bumpy dirt road.

Margie was in hysterics. Keith lay in his bed in his boxer shorts and an old T-shirt. He was dead. Heart failure, most probably. Mrs. D'Costa administered a Valium to Margie, gave orders to the house staff to make chamomile tea, sent for Dr. Singh and asked for Tim's and Mark's phone numbers. As it often happened, there was no signal at the house and the landline was down. Margie kept shaking her head between sobs, unable to offer a solution, so Mrs. D'Costa drove straight back to her own house and called from there. She found herself calling England and the United States, having to explain a couple of times who she was to the person on the other end of the line as they had no immediate recollection of her name. She then proceeded to explain in a steady tone that their father was dead, thank God he hadn't suffered, that she was terribly sorry but they needed to book the first flight out if they wanted to make it to the funeral. Then she added in her matter-of-fact way:

"With this heat we can't wait around too long, you see. As you know, refrigeration is a big problem here."

Part of her coveted moments like this. She had always maintained that, living in Africa, one always had to be prepared for anything to happen. And though perhaps it was wrong to feel this way in light of what had happened, she was now secretly enjoying the fact that she'd stopped being invisible to them, and that, even for a short interlude, she was needed again.

· · ·

Two days later, the whole Christmas crew reappeared at their parents' home, their faces bloated from too many hours of travel, still faintly tanned from the holiday they'd spent there only a few weeks earlier. Mark and Tim cried, in a manly way—silent, with a few sniffs—holding their mother in turns. She was sent to bed with another pill, as she was completely helpless, given the state she was in. Ruth and Tara were disoriented and jet-lagged, the children seemed frightened by the eerie atmosphere. The two brothers wandered aimlessly around the house—a house that was foreign to them, of which they held no memories—as if searching for an answer to what had happened so unexpectedly and so unfairly. They seemed resentful, as though their father had played a trick on them. Mrs. D'Costa watched them with sympathy. She knew well how one could get angry when an unexpected death occurred.

"There was nothing wrong with his heart. He was in perfect form for seventy-two. Absolutely nothing wrong," Mark kept saying, his voice raging with hostility toward anybody who rang to offer condolences.

Tim sat in the kitchen fiddling with his laptop while Mrs. D'Costa put the kettle on and spooned the expensive French roast into the pot. Once again she'd been the one to take care of the logistics: dealing with the British High Commission, getting the death certificate from Dr. Singh, straightening things up with the police and looking into the laborious paperwork needed to return Keith's body to Sussex.

"Are you sure you want to take him to England?" she asked Tim in a soft voice. "Your father lived in Kenya most of his life, why not put him under that beautiful baobab at the end of the property?"

"Because Mummy cannot possibly live here all by herself, so we'll have to sell this house," he answered bluntly, without lifting his eyes from the screen.

"Will you? I'm so sorry to hear that."

There was a moment of silence, but for the sound of Tim tapping on the keyboard. She waited till he was done.

"And where will your mother go from here?"

Tim rubbed his eyes. He looked exhausted.

"We'll have to see. Probably with my brother in the U.K. for the moment? I don't know, Mrs. D'Costa. We haven't had the time to think about it, to be honest with you."

The kettle started its furious whistling. Mrs. D'Costa took it off the stove, then she put both her fists on her hips and turned to Tim again. She wanted to sound determined in what she was going to say.

"Tim, I want you to know that I'm perfectly happy to look after Margie if you are concerned about her being alone. I could even move in here for a while if you think that would help. At least in the beginning. What will she do in England now? She doesn't know anybody there other than your brother."

"That's out of the question. My mother won't survive here on her own. She's never lived alone a day in her life. Mark and I were always against buying this house anyway. We knew it was a mistake."

"But I could—"

"It's spooky," he went on, without listening. "Someone told us there's a spell on the coconut plantation at the back. The coconut trees keep dying no matter how many times they get replanted. This whole place is jinxed."

Mrs. D'Costa stopped pouring hot water into the French press and put the kettle down.

"Where did you hear *that*?" she cried.

"One of the men at the gas station down the road. He worked as the watchman for some of the neighbors who left. He said that's the reason nobody has bought property around here in all these years. All those abandoned houses along the beach? Owners were either broken into or got into accidents. I hate the energy of this house. My brother felt it, too, the minute he set foot here."

Anne wouldn't have it. She pushed her shoulders back and replied, with as much resolve as she could summon, "What utter foolishness! That's a piece of ridiculous superstition! I'm surprised you took that seriously."

Tim ignored her and grabbed the kettle, taking over the coffee making. Next door a child was crying and they could hear Ruth soothing him. Tim poured himself a cup, stirred in an artificial sweetener and prepared another mug.

"The Wiltons first. Then Dad. It's enough deaths, as far as I'm concerned. Please excuse me, Anne, I have to take this to my wife. She needs a shot of caffeine, it's been a very hard day for her as well."

·   ·   ·

Tara and Ruth wanted to get the children out of the house. Too much talk of death upset them, so that evening Ruth asked Mrs. D'Costa if she might take all of them over to her place the next day, while the grown-ups dealt with more phone calls and paperwork.

"I'll bring some food, you don't have to worry about anything," she offered.

Ruth was a good-looking girl of about thirty, with strong muscular legs, a smooth complexion and long hair of an astonishing strawberry-blond color that fell in thick ringlets on her shoulders.

"Nonsense! I'll make some sandwiches, and we'll have a picnic on the beach," Mrs. D'Costa said. "Hamisi and I will get everything ready, please don't you worry."

She got up early and prepared cheese, tomato and avocado

sandwiches, then pulled some chicken out of the refrigerator, which Hamisi fried till it was golden and crispy. She sent him to the little *duka* on the main road to buy Fantas and Coca-Colas. She had been so looking forward to having some guests around, especially the young ones.

·   •   ·

Mrs. D'Costa was sitting on a mat in the shade of a doum palm, next to Ruth, who'd brought a fat paperback. For the occasion (she hardly ever went down to the beach anymore), she'd put on a large straw hat that flopped slightly on one side and a wildly colored sundress that she hadn't worn since the seventies; she also wore a pair of very dark sunglasses, so heavily covered in a film of dust that she saw everything in a blur. She looked like a blind woman. The children had once more been slightly intimidated by her strangeness and were splashing in the water at a safe distance while the dogs ran, barking madly after the herons.

Ruth lifted her eyes from her book. "Where are you originally from, Mrs. D'Costa?" She had a soft, rounded American accent; something about her had seemed more relaxed and easier than all the others.

"A little town near Glasgow, a mining town. That's so long ago, I nearly forget what it looked like."

"My grandparents came from the bogs of Scotland too. I've never been there. I'd like to go one day."

"It shows in your coloring that you have Scottish blood. Such beautiful hair you have."

"Thank you. And what is D'Costa? An Italian name?"

"Oh no, dear, that's Portuguese. My husband's family came from Goa."

Ruth closed the book, suddenly interested.

"Goa, you mean in India? How interesting. What did your husband do?"

"He was a pediatrician."

"And how did you two meet?"

"In college, in Edinburgh. I never got my degree, but he did. He was an excellent doctor."

"Did you have children?"

"Three, Dana, Philip and Ralph. They all got married and live abroad now."

"And . . ." Ruth lingered, uncertain whether it might be rude to ask. "Do you think they feel more Indian or more Scottish?"

"Neither one nor the other, probably . . ." Anne thought for a moment. "They've never been to either place. We no longer have any family there, you see."

Ruth nodded.

"They feel Kenyan, I suppose," Mrs. D'Costa said, even though she wasn't sure at this point what her children felt anymore.

"And have you known Margie and Keith a long time?"

"Yes, since the late fifties . . ."

She hesitated for a moment. Ruth kept looking at her, waiting for her to go on, as though she knew there was something else Mrs. D'Costa wanted to say.

"But we were never close friends. We belonged to very different worlds," Mrs. D'Costa said, and, looking back into Ruth's straightforward gaze, felt good saying it to her.

She felt strangely at ease with this young woman. Ruth seemed earnest, considerate. Mrs. D'Costa realized it had been a long time since anybody had showed interest in the story of her life. She looked out toward the water. It was lovely, the way the afternoon light skimmed the surface in shimmering sparks.

"In those days, if you were an expat, your life revolved pretty much around the Mombasa Club. That's where everyone met," she said. "Your whole social life took place there. Margie and Keith were a very popular couple, of course."

"Yes, they took us all to lunch there when we came one Christmas," Ruth said. "It still has that old colonial atmosphere. We had visions of people wearing white linen, drinking sundowners on the terrace under the fans." She laughed, as if to let on she'd found the place ridiculous.

Mrs. D'Costa took off the dark glasses and slowly wiped the sheen of dirt off them with the hem of her dress. She cleared her throat.

"The thing was that before Independence, if you were married to an African, or an Indian . . . actually to anybody who wasn't British, or white for that matter . . ."

She paused and then put the glasses back on.

"Yes?"

"Well, you couldn't be a member of the club, you see. It was a very . . . separate society, in those days. Well, we couldn't even go to the same restaurants," she said hesitantly, as if it still shamed her to admit that such a thing had happened.

Ruth's eyes widened. "Really?"

"Of course, dear. If we were sick they wouldn't take us at the Mombasa Hospital. We had to go to Coast General"—Mrs. D'Costa's voice hardened—"which was hell on earth. Oh yes, that's what it was like."

She felt some of her old anger rise to her cheeks. It struck her how certain feelings, no matter how deeply buried, would still come up in a matter of seconds, as if woken by a siren.

"That is totally insane," Ruth said.

Mrs. D'Costa tipped back the flopping side of the hat.

"Naturally everything changed after Independence. But by that point my husband couldn't give a flying hoot about getting into the club." She laughed. "We were never that kind of people, you know; I mean, having sundowners on the terrace under the fans, as you put it."

She smiled at Ruth. "We drank cheap vodka on our own veranda!"

"Good for you." Ruth shook her head in disbelief but didn't laugh or even smile. "Wow. But I didn't realize that even right before Independence it would be like that here. That in Kenya people in your situation would be so . . ." She paused, searching for the appropriate word. "Excluded."

Mrs. D'Costa recoiled slightly at the word.

"We did have some perfectly nice white Kenyan friends, and English ones of course, like Prudence and Lionel Wilton, who were more progressive in that sense. But in general, I'd say that white people weren't used to mixed couples, in those days."

"It must have been very difficult for you." Ruth spoke softly and turned to her with sympathy.

"Well, yes, but no. I had three beautiful children, a lovely house. A loving husband. He came from a very good Goan family. My relatives were super people."

"Of course, of course," Ruth said, aware that her reaction may have embarrassed the older woman.

"And we had other friends, of course. Swahili, Somali, Omani. Mombasa was—and still is—a very cosmopolitan town, you know." Anne paused for a moment, then added cheerfully, "We were constantly invited to their weddings. Fabulous parties, they lasted for days!"

Anne had learned back then, and had never forgotten, Victor's rule number one: never hold a grudge. We have each other, he used to say to her, and that was what counted.

How difficult had it really been for her? Mrs. D'Costa thought for a moment. She could hardly remember, so much of that past had faded already, and besides, she'd learned to keep the bad, hurt feelings to herself. She had always avoided talking about them to her husband or her children. It would've been a burden on them. And at the time she had no close friends who were in her "situation," as Ruth had put it. In fact, she hadn't known anyone who was.

There were things Ruth didn't understand about her British in-laws either, she was saying. All that talk about accents and public schools. She sometimes joked with Tim about how England to this day still had its own caste system.

"Scots versus Brits." Mrs. D'Costa laughed. "Such an old story."

"May I?" Ruth gently lifted the side of the hat, which kept falling over Mrs. D'Costa's eye.

"Thank you, dear. It's quite an old hat, I'm afraid."

"It's a sweet hat." Ruth looked at her with a kind of tenderness. "Don't you throw it out. It suits you, Anne."

There was a short silence. They both turned their eyes to the children, who were intent on digging a tunnel in the sand.

"I am so grateful that our kids are growing up in the twenty-first century in America," Ruth said.

"Yes," said Mrs. D'Costa, "it's a great advantage, isn't it?"

She often wondered about her own children. She and Victor had done everything they could to give them all they needed. And yet, she knew that their lives must have been more complicated than what she was ready to admit at the time. Maybe she had tried too hard to follow her husband's rule, to stick to the bright side of things.

There were questions she hardly ever dared ask herself. Why had all of her children left Kenya and gone to live elsewhere? Perhaps they had had to bury their hurts and resentments, when they were small. Had she made a mistake by never encouraging them to talk about it?

Maybe some of what she'd then called optimism would today be called denial.

·   •   ·

The Khans' store was busy: right outside, a few African men in overalls were loading bags of cement in the back of a lorry. One young man was weighing a thick coil of rope on a scale next to where Mrs. D'Costa was standing.

She handed the note with the measurements to Kublai and his father. The three of them remained silent for a few seconds, their eyes fixed on the scrap of paper.

"It has to be zinc," she said. "Sealed. That's the procedure required to carry the body on a plane," she said.

"No problem, Mrs. D'Costa. We'll get it ready by tomorrow," Kublai said, and scribbled something on a piece of paper.

She had offered to take care of this. It seemed a practical thing, something that she could handle easily, and she was happy to spare Mark and Tim the ride to the junction for such a gruesome task.

Mr. Khan leaned in over the counter and removed his reading glasses from the tip of his nose.

"Why not the Hindu crematorium in town? We could have helped them, we know the people who work there. Ashes would have been so much easier to carry. Once in England they could have whatever ceremony they wish."

"I couldn't agree with you more. But the family wants to bring the body back. To their home, and put it underground, in British soil. It's their way."

Later, as she was getting ready to reverse the car and head home, she saw Mr. Khan with his wobbly gait exiting the store.

"Mrs. D'Costa! Wait!"

She left the keys in the ignition and stepped out, her car idling under the midmorning sun.

"Yes, Mr. Khan?"

He held out his hand to show her the cluster of white flowers he was clutching between his fingers.

"In Gujarat we call them Barsoli flowers. My mother planted them in our garden when she got married to my father. She had the seeds sent here from India. Nobody else has a tree like this in all of Kenya. Smell."

The scent was deliciously sweet.

"My mother would wear one of these every night behind her ear. The flowers lasted only a few hours."

"What a beautiful habit," Mrs. D'Costa said.

"She planted the seeds in our garden so she'd have her personal supply in this country for the rest of her life." He held the flower

up to his nose. "And to remind herself that all things are imper-
manent."

He pulled a tiny envelope out of his breast pocket.

"I have collected some seeds for you. I know how much you
like gardening."

"Thank you, Mr. Khan. What a kind thought."

Then, unexpectedly, he lifted a strand of her hair and slid the
flower behind her ear.

There was a pause, then he bowed his head slightly. Mrs.
D'Costa brushed the flower with the tip of her finger.

As she drove back home she kept glancing in the rearview mirror to see the white blossom in her hair.

· • ·

She took the turn into the plantation at the back of her and the
Dobsons' plot of land. Yes, some of the coconut trees were dying,
it was true. She had been noticing more and more naked stumps
dotting the horizon. Tim's comment about the place being jinxed
had disturbed her. Trees die too when they age, and these coconuts were planted a very long time ago, she should've told him. It
was natural. Would that have silenced him?

Tim was right, Margie didn't belong here. None of them did,
Anne thought. It was a much better idea to take her back to England after all, even though she didn't know anybody there.

Once all the Dobsons had left and she'd be able to go back to
her routine, she would ask Mr. Khan to her Sunday curry lunch.
Maybe she'd inquire if he liked cards or mah-jongg and they could
sometimes play a game or two. It was such a comfort to know
someone like him and his son. He and Kublai were always so kind
and thoughtful. She turned into her driveway and immediately
heard Pickle's and Chutney's cheerful barking. Hamisi was waiting by the gate, ready to open it for her.

Such a nice, good family, the Khans, she thought. Just like the
family she once had.

The Italian System

Spring landed on her like an avalanche. Walking through Central Park she heard birds chirping in the trees, as though they'd just returned from a long voyage and now were busy-busy, getting their nests ready for the new season.

The buds on the cherry trees were ready to burst, the tiny leaves sprouting from the branches, so fine they were almost transparent, like a baby's fingers on an ultrasound. Everything around her was primed for rebirth.

She thought she too might be ready for a change of scene.

. . .

She had come to New York seven years earlier with a rather ambitious plan. While still in Rome, she'd applied online for a summer workshop in creative writing at the New School. It was an expensive course, but she'd saved some money just for that. She'd always had a notion that one day she'd write a novel but she knew she'd never start unless she developed a technique and got some encouragement. She'd always admired the pragmatic approach Americans took, even on those subjects—like art, literature, acting, music—that Europeans regarded as too elusive, or impossible to define, and therefore to teach. Americans believed there was a method for everything, and they were right; hadn't they succeeded in all those fields in which the Europeans, with their snobbish talk of talent and inspiration, were now beginning to fade?

As soon as she set foot in Manhattan she decided that she

didn't want to leave it, ever. It was a *coup de foudre*. She felt light, full of promise. In New York she realized she had no witnesses, no memories, just a brilliant, spectacular stretch of future in front of her.

The summer course at the New School eventually came to an end and she had no more money to invest in her education as a writer. She found a part-time job in a language school. It started as a way to pay the rent on the place in Brooklyn she shared with another girl. With time, teaching became her real job and she forgot about other aspirations; to her what mattered most was that she had found a way to stay in New York.

But lately she'd begun to feel an undercurrent nagging at her throughout the day, an insidious feeling of frustration that hovered above while she was asleep, and which confronted her first thing each morning when she opened her eyes.

· · ·

Ever since she'd arrived in the city she'd tried very hard to become an American, but it had proved hard to blend in. It wasn't just the accent or the mispronunciation of difficult words that singled her out, it was a question of attitude. Of posture, even.

New York was a city of foreigners, everyone came from some other place just as in Rome, where she had been born and raised. People had come to Imperial Rome to seek fortune and fame from its farthest colonies under Augustus, and exotic people had done the same in New York before the age of Abraham Lincoln. The flow had never stopped.

Yet a foreigner always remains a foreigner, no matter how long he's been away from his native place. Like the Chinese students at Columbia, the Korean grocers and the Latino hairdressers, like the Ukrainian waitresses and the Greek cooks, the Afghan and the Sikh taxi drivers, she still thought of her grandmother's food as superior to anyone else's, and like all of them, despite their perfect grasp of English, she dreamed in a different language. She knew that these people, even the ones who had been born on American soil, were prey to a nostalgia for faraway places, some they'd never even been to and may never even see. Such is the strength of the seed implanted in us at birth, she thought, as she exited the Q train at Lexington Avenue and waded through the late afternoon rush hour crowd on the way to teach the first class of the day.

·   ·   ·

Whenever she walked along the streets of Manhattan, she looked at all the different faces coming toward her and, despite their different features and colors, she regarded them all as Americans. None of them seemed a stranger to the city. How at ease they looked on the train, underneath their books, Kindles, iPods and iPads, at the wheel of the taxi, behind the counter of the coffee shop, at the gym or inside the beauty parlor! On the other hand, she, even after all these years, still felt self-conscious, afraid of making a faux pas. She came to feel that this was the inherent condition of anybody unmoored from the familiar, and living in a place that is home to others.

And yet here was a riddle she couldn't figure out: Why did that look of disorientation and vulnerability she knew was stamped on her face seem invisible on everyone else's?

·   ·   ·

That day in the park, sitting on a bench under the trees bursting with their promise of bloom, she felt a breeze of optimism caress her face.

All right, she thought, like those birds building a nest, I'm going to start something new.

Maybe, in the early hours of the morning, before going to work, she could try to jot down the introduction to the book she'd been thinking about for months. Her plan was still nebulous but at least she had a good title. It said it all, and though she had forgotten a lot of the rules she had learned at the creative writing course, what if she just followed her instinct and started from that?

Italians are always described as warm, stylish, fun, passionate, charming, life-loving people. What is their secret?

   How do they manage to look always so groomed and elegant even when they can't afford to buy expensive clothes? How is it possible that the most desolate trattoria on the back road of a nondescript town will serve you the best dish you've had in years? And how can Italians appear so confident and full of life despite the fact they live in one of the most malfunctioning countries, run by the Mafia and corrupt, shifty politicians, a country basically going bankrupt? So why, despite these failings, do Italians come across as positive, gregarious, always ready to laugh? This book is going to teach you how to make your life more enjoyable, how to gain confidence, taste and charm—without trying too hard. Nonchalance is the key factor: the less you try, the easier it will be to feel as stylish and charismatic as the Italians are, deep down in their skin. The secret is very simple. It's called the Italian System.

· · ·

She set the alarm for seven and wrote every morning till lunchtime, as she had planned. She usually reached the school by five. Let's Speak Italian was located in a small town house on the Upper East Side; it was sparsely furnished with folding metal chairs, Formica desks and cheaply framed photographs of famous Italian monuments and movie stars. Her classes started at five thirty—she taught evening classes to people who mostly had full-time jobs—but she liked to get there early, take time to look at the students' papers and have a cup of coffee with some of her colleagues. To be teaching Italian in a school, surrounded by other Italians who had the same poorly paid part-time jobs—some of them had come to New York because of a marriage, others had

had higher literary ambitions that failed—only enhanced her feeling of being trapped inside a circle of outsiders. All her students spoke with terrible accents and hated the *congiuntivo* and the *condizionale;* they were either coming to the school because of their line of work—fashion, wine, travel—or were affluent retirees who liked the idea of being able to engage with the locals on their next Italian holiday. And it was for their sake that she felt she was supposed to retain all of her Italianness while at work. Her students loved her accent, the way she moved her hands and certain grammatical mistakes she still made when speaking in English. The act of writing the book not only partly relieved her of the frustration she'd begun to feel, but also let her put that feeling of otherness to use, make something positive, anchoring, out of it.

For the very first time she was able to isolate small details that shone like jewels among the ruins, the corruption, the vulgarity of her country of origin. So many immigrants are embarrassed by the place they come from, she thought, it's probably inevitable. After all, it has to be a love-hate relationship. Without the hate there would be no voyage.

· · ·

Memories from her childhood started to come up like gnocchi in boiling water, at the most unexpected moments. Food always came up first, for her.

> *Stop being afraid of calories, they are not your real enemies. The problem is not the pasta, pizza, or your* cornetto *and* cappuccino. *It's not the carbs that will make you fat, but the complications that are the essence of the American meal. Just think of the endless layers that form a hamburger: bread, mustard, cheese, bacon, meat, onion, pickle, ketchup. Why so many ingredients in one dish? What's the point of such a crazy medley?*
>
> *The first time I checked the list of flavors inside an ice*

cream parlor in America my head spun. All I wanted was chocolate. But I was forced to choose between chocolate–chocolate chip, caramel-chocolate-pecan, double chocolate chip–walnut cookie, triple choc-fudge-pecan-walnut and choco-choco-superdark-almond-caramel-crunch. In Italy we grew up with chocolate, hazelnut, coffee, cream and vanilla. In the fruit department we had only lemon and strawberry. In the early days, that was it and we were quite content. These simple, straightforward flavors were superbly executed and delicious. They were like clothes in solid colors as opposed to some mad flowery psychedelic pattern.

There were things that suddenly caught her attention. Everywhere she looked now, wandering around the aisles of a supermarket, or on the Q train coming back from work, she noticed things that suggested another observation, another idea. The book was like a magnet that attracted the tiniest particle. Everything, no matter how small, stuck. She took brief notes on a Moleskine she tucked in her pocket. The notes sounded like a secret code, but she knew what they meant and she would decipher them later on, once at home : "gutting fish," "what's inside a chicken?," "lack of frontier."

A word about dairy. Our milk goes bad in five days. Mozzarella, ricotta? You have to eat it the same day. Forty-eight more hours and the cheese tastes like yogurt. We don't mind about the bacteria that the FDA army has ordered killed in every dairy product sold on American soil. That bacteria boosts our immune systems and no American tourist visiting Rome, Venice or Florence has ever contracted salmonella from a cappuccino or a caprese salad. It's a celebration and a ritual to buy something that will spoil in one day, knowing we are eating it only a few hours after it was made.

On the same note: every Italian knows how to gut a fish

234 · The Other Language

under the faucet and clean it, how to pull the gizzards out of
a chicken, how to tell liver from brains or kidneys, tail from
tongue in the butcher's display. Feathers, blood, entrails, every-
thing that is part of an animal is still visible and tangible, and
that means we are still in touch with natural elements at least
to a certain degree, whereas in America most children can still
barely grasp the connection between a steak and the animal it
comes from.

She was slowly gaining confidence. Her writing had become more fluid, more agile. It was like a muscle that stretched and gained speed. Dared she admit, even to herself, that a book like this could have a voice? And that she was actually beginning to find it? Now and again she threw in a funny line, a little humorous spark. She was getting bolder. One day, as she was having coffee with her colleagues before class, she mentioned that she was writing something. It felt good to come out and say it, as it would make her work real and stop her from treating it like a hobby, a secret pastime. There were words of approval along with a few patronizing smiles. When one of her colleagues asked whether she had a publisher, she laughed. It's an experiment, I'm just having fun with it, she said breezily. Later, on the train back home, one of the teachers—Clelia, a sad woman from Pisa who had married an Iranian in New Jersey and then had had a tragic divorce—asked her what her book was about. She answered vaguely, afraid that Clelia, with her thick glasses and old-fashioned clothes, might think she was making fun of her, that she might be making caricatures out of all of them—a bunch of Italians who still spoke English with thick accents, small people who lived in small apartments, who didn't have the glamour of the fashion designers, the visual artists or the famous architects who'd made their country such a salable commodity.

She went home that night and decided it was time to do something about the huge pile of laundry that had amassed over the kitchen table. Laundry was something she had always tended to postpone, as she found the whole procedure boring and unpleasant. She took the elevator down to the basement, and started loading the washing machine. Under the tremulous fluorescent light in that dark space she realized why doing the laundry in the city could be such a depressing chore.

The dryer.

We, as a people, are against it: no Italian possesses one. Dryers are the only bit of American culture that we still firmly and unanimously resist. We dry our sheets, towels, shirts, T-shirts, etc., on a clothesline, letting wind and sun take care of them. We still believe in the power of natural heat and we love the smell of bedsheets dried on a sunny, windy day. In any Italian city, you'll see our garments hanging on a line outside our windows, balconies, roofs or strung across an alley. We don't mind, we actually love the sight of our underwear flapping in the wind. Our eyes have gotten used to it, it's part of the landscape; tourists love to take pictures of it, they think hanging laundry is quintessentially Italian, the way it dots the landscape in bright colors. Sometimes their photos appear on Instagram or on Flickr, or as a lovely postcard, and we think that's quite sweet—our underwear, socks and panties have become a work of art!

There's another advantage that comes with hanging laundry on a line. Not only do we save energy, but our clothes don't get floppy and slack like they do in America because of that killer dryer spin that—it is common knowledge—destroys the weave of any fiber. Can't you see how dead and stale your socks and T-shirts, blouses and pants, feel on your skin after just a couple of spins? That floppiness soon translates into slovenliness, and before you know it you'll look like a slob if you don't run out and buy something new.

Part of what is internationally known as "Italian style" is simply a sense of crispness, which derives from the wind and sun that rejuvenates the very fabrics we wear. What I'm talking about is something deep and archaic, linked with a ritual that has been performed for millennia. To hang your clothes out to dry in the sun as opposed to throwing them inside the belly of a metal monster in the depths of your dark basement is a drastically different choice. If you agree that the world is made up of billions of particles aggregating in different shapes and forms, then you'll see what I mean when I say that dryers not only kill clothes but tamper with your energy and charisma.

A student of hers, a young corporate lawyer in love with Tuscany and its cypresses, asked her for private tutoring. They met twice a week in a coffee shop in Midtown near his office and had conversations over his lunch break. They always ordered a scoop of tuna and potato salad on a bed of lettuce and he insisted on paying the bill. It was awkward at first (having these dates with a complete stranger and being paid twenty dollars an hour in order to make small talk?) and she worried she might have nothing to say. Because the man was mildly attractive she felt shy around him and for both reasons early in the week she'd start making a list of possible subjects, in order to arrive prepared. The conversation languished at first, they struggled, pretending to be interested in the bland topics she'd picked—the weather, summer holidays, and, of course, favorite foods—then they became more comfortable with each other as the weeks went by and they began to talk about films they'd seen, music they loved, TV series they watched. One day he told her about a show in an art gallery in Chelsea he'd read about and asked her if she'd like to go with him on the weekend. They could do their lesson in motion and speak about art. She said yes, that would be a really good idea. Then he said he liked her style. What style? she asked, feeling her cheeks redden. I don't know. The things you wear.

Let me tell you about my mother.

Her number one rule is "meglio morta che in pigiama" *(better dead than in pj's). That means that even if she has nowhere to go and no one to see, half an hour after waking up, she'll be coiffed, dressed, lipsticked, in sheer stockings and patent leather shoes, a dot of perfume dabbed on each wrist. In my entire life I've never seen my mother in slippers, or what some people call a housedress or a nightie, past 8 a.m. I am not talking about a grand dame, but an ordinary housewife in her late sixties living off her dead husband's meager pension. What she wears are tweed skirts and low pumps bought twenty or thirty years ago that—according to her—never went out of fashion. And although they certainly did, if your average Americans were to see my mother walking with her shopping bag out for groceries on a side street of the* centro storico *wearing her old-fashioned dark glasses and cultured pearls, they would ask each other, "How do Italians manage to always be so chic? Just take a look at that old lady across the street." The recipient of this compliment would be wearing an ensemble worth no more than twenty-five euros max in a vintage store, one that any American would have thrown out fifteen years earlier. Italian style is not a matter of designers or labels or fashion, it's a question of details—of a certain formality. It's not so much about what we wear as what we don't. You'll never see an adult Italian walking around in shorts other than at the beach, or wearing a baseball cap. Sneakers made a brief appearance in the eighties, flip-flops are a no-no footwear other than at the beach or the spa. For Italians, comfort is not a value and has never been aspiration. Good construction comes with constriction, and we are perfectly used to being uncomfortable in our ingeniously tailored clothes. In Rome the only people in shorts, baggy T-shirts and baseball hats are the flocks of tourists wandering between the Forum and the Colosseum. They seem to be completely unaware of the fact that they look like slobs, especially when they are over sixty years old, dressed like fat teenagers. My grandfather wore hats and jackets till the day he died. To think of him, even as a young man, in shorts and a baseball cap is not only inconceivable: it would be grotesque. I am convinced that having the image of your ancestors in hats and jackets embedded in your memory will translate into a bonus—i.e., it must and will affect your behavior and ultimately your self-confidence.*

After the art show the corporate lawyer—his name was Matt—took her to dinner at an expensive Italian restaurant and after the first glass of wine they switched to English. They both relaxed and became their true selves now that they didn't have to speak like five-year-olds in simplified Italian. Back in full control of the language, he made witty remarks about the artist and the people at the opening. He wasn't wearing a suit like the ones she always saw him in, but jeans and an untucked checked flannel shirt. They both ordered linguine with shrimp and asparagus, and he said it was a relief to eat with someone who wasn't just going to have a salad with dressing on the side, and that he liked the way Italian women seemed to worry less about eating, drinking and smoking than their American counterparts. She took the cue and they both went outside for a cigarette after dessert. She told him she was writing a book called *The Italian System*. He momentarily switched back to Italian and asked, *"Cosa parla il libro?"* She corrected him: *"Di cosa parla il libro?"* Of what does the book talk about? They both agreed that it was funny the way, in Italian, a book "talked" about itself. Matt walked her home and as he said goodbye he told her his firm had done legal work for a publishing company some time ago and he could talk to some people about her idea if she wished.

. . .

Matt the lawyer never came back to her with news from the publishing company. Actually, after their date at the art show, he disappeared and there were no more lunches at the coffee shop. She didn't care. She didn't even bother to spend any time worrying about what might have gone wrong, whether he had found her dull or, worse, delusional. She had more important things to think about now than flirting with a corporate lawyer. These days on the train to work she listened to audiobooks. She liked the isolation that shielded her from the rest of the commuters. She avidly listened to the writers' prose with a different, more intimate attention, no longer merely as a reader, more like someone intent on stealing technique. She singled out adjectives and phrases and rushed to scribble them down in her notebook; random words ended up in her net like tiny prey that she meant to free at home, once in front of the computer. She was busy, she had a mission to complete.

Did you know that in Italian there is no word for wilderness? The only possible way to translate it is "natura," even though nature can be peaceful, tamed, a pastoral dream. From time immemorial—due to its shape and history—very little of the territory of Italy has remained unpopulated, uncultivated, undomesticated. During Augustus's reign, Rome already had a population of one million people, the whole country was a maze of paved roads that connected north to south, east to west, that went over mountains and rivers. Everyone was connected; ours has always been an unthreatening, user-friendly landscape. A small country, as lovely in its details as a miniature. We had no tundra, no black forest, no savanna, no desert, no endless plains or prairies to cross or wade through. We had palaces, libraries, theaters, spas, aqueducts, silks and jewels, people bought food at the market during the same era

that—in most parts of the planet—men still had to go hunt-
ing in the woods with bows and arrows to get their dinner.

How has this lack of wilderness affected us? It has given
us an innate friendliness, an open heart, and maybe a lesser
talent for extreme adventures. The Italian System is a mix of
civilized demeanor, and domesticity, coupled with the spon-
taneity deriving from our connection to the natural (we are
not the hunters of the world, we are the happy foragers!) with
its secret ingredient: lightness. Yes, we are a deeply superficial
people. And by deeply I mean that our lightness has complexity
and layers. La leggerezza, *as we call it, is the necessary quality*
to execute the flawless dive, the effortless pirouette. The nature
of anything truly enchanting has to be as light as a whiff of air.

·   •   ·

During the summer holidays she flew to Rome to visit her mother.
As soon as she got off the plane the first thing that greeted her on
the A91 were gigantic billboards of naked women advertising all
kinds of things that didn't require nudity—a luxury handbag, a
hardware store, a double-dark-chocolate ice cream. From the taxi,
once in the city, she noticed cracks in the asphalt, where wild grass
had sprouted and bloomed, potholes and cigarette butts strewn
on the pavement. At the traffic lights she spotted several men in
shorts and baseball hats, riding their mopeds. Some were middle-
aged and wore slackened tank tops, which showed drooping shoulders and flabby underarms. Most of the women on the streets had
a flat, opaque, orangey tan, the kind that can be acquired only in
a salon. Their slutty tops and boa constrictor jeans had nothing
of the elegance and formality she had conjured up in her notes.
The taxi driver kept the radio full blast on a local station where
a rowdy and drunken group of males were having an argument
about a football match. The sulking driver pretended not to hear
when she asked if he could please lower the volume because she
needed to use her cell phone. He swore without restraint for two

solid minutes when a driver swerved unexpectedly in front of him. He overcharged her.

When her mother heard she was on her way home from the airport she was caught by surprise.

"You are here already? Oh my God, I'm still in my night-gown!" she said.

"It's almost noon, Mamma! How come you're not ready yet? I'll be over in twenty minutes."

"I know, I know, but it's Sunday, and I've been taking things slowly on a Sunday."

She heard her mother rummaging somewhere, the sound of drawers opening and closing.

"Santo Cielo!" her mother said, in a frantic tone. "I have only frozen peas in the fridge. I totally forgot to shop for food last night. I could put together a pea omelette for lunch, though. Would you be happy with that?"

Lately her mother had become forgetful, and the smallest change of plan confused her.

"A pea omelette? I never heard of it," she said. "I think we should go out to eat and celebrate instead. I have so much to tell you."

The corner restaurant had changed owners and now was serving only fixed-price meals for tourists. Since they were sitting outside in the sun her mother had insisted on wearing a straw hat and a strange pair of polyester workout pants with a stripe down the legs, an article of clothing she'd never seen her mother in before. The waiter, after taking a look at the old lady's outfit, had addressed them in English.

"We are Italian! We are from around the corner!" she said, glaring at him with reproach.

She had a soggy plate of microwaved lasagne but decided to contain her resentment. When they were finished eating she raised her glass of Pinot Grigio.

"Mamma, we need to make a toast. I have something very important to tell you."

Her mother raised her Diet Coke. Apparently she was no longer drinking any wine.

"Did you find somebody, over there?" her mother asked, hopeful.

"No. It's much better than that. I've got a publisher. A big one."

"A publisher?"

"Yes, for the book I told you about, the one that I've been writing all year? They love the idea. They've given me a pretty nice advance."

Her mother's eyes lost their focus for a moment. Then she came back and smiled.

"That's wonderful, *tesoro*. I am so happy for you."

They touched glasses and each took a small sip.

"It's like a manual. How to become an Italian sort of thing. My editor says it has a lot of commercial potential. She loves the title."

Her mother seemed lost in thought again. She said, "I feel like having something sweet. How about you?"

She nodded distractedly. "The book is called *The Italian System,* Mamma. What do you think?"

"*The Italian System?*" the mother asked while engrossed in the dessert menu. She closed it and stared at her with the blank expression she wore when she wasn't really listening.

"Yes. *Il Sistema Italiano*. Don't you think it would work?"

"Do we have a system? I never knew we had one, actually."

Before she could say anything her mother raised her hand toward the waiter.

"The ginger-basil-walnut ice cream sounds very tempting."

It didn't matter that everything looked different. Maybe it had always been this way, a sort of uglier version of what she had recalled. But this is exactly what matters, she thought: it's the imprint that makes us who we are, no matter the land we're born to, or on what soil we walk.

"I'll have the same," she said.

Quantum Theory

I

Most probably Sonia's phone was lying somewhere in the gully amid the debris and the shards of glass; therefore she hadn't been able to contact anybody yet. Being incommunicado had actually been an advantage, allowing her a stretch of time, which she badly needed in order to adjust to the new scenario. Ever since the previous afternoon, when the stranger had appeared in her rearview mirror on the side of the road, an unexpected stillness had descended upon her, as though every familiar aspect of her life had suddenly come to a halt. This unusual pause, despite the equatorial heat, had a likeness to snow falling and padded footfalls. All that had seemed so pressing till then—the background buzz of her anxiety, the phone calls and e-mails that needed to be attended to, plus the heat, the headache, the mild sense of frustration that had been following her around like a sniffing dog for days—had dissipated, leaving only a vast, immaculate expanse in front of her. It was as though suddenly a curtain had lifted on an endless space that unrolled into the future. A promise.

. . .

They had been feeling quite jittery because of the proximity of their bodies in the front seat. As the car lurched and bounced on the rocky track, their hips, thighs and shoulders had kept making contact. She remembered how one moment there was music—something good, though she couldn't remember the name of the band—and the next came a deafening bang. It was like a sudden explosion, which, hours later, still rang in her ears. What followed was a suspension that seemed to stretch forever, during which Sonia had time to realize that the car's wheels were no longer on the ground, that they were actually falling off the parapet of the bridge, and that those seconds might be the last of her life. There was no room for fear, since the surprise that she should be dying like that, and moreover that she would be dying in the company of a stranger, was so overwhelming. Possibly because of all the vodka she had drunk, the only thought that had flashed through her mind during the car's slow-motioned flight was that their lives must have always been entangled and were clearly meant to end together. The thought seemed beautiful and somehow pure. Then, as they tumbled down the ravine and rolled over, she heard branches snapping and breaking. What followed was an eerie silence, except for the crickets that went on undisturbed through the clear night. The headlights illuminated a thick cloud of reddish dust that gently fluttered above, and slowly descended, giving the scene the aspect of a science fiction film, in which an alien spaceship lands in a clearing of a forest. The engine stopped, the headlights died, everything went quiet. The sequence of events had its own rhythm and beauty. The music, the bang, the silence, then just the crickets.

Life/death/life again, but quieter.

It was hard to figure out exactly where they'd fallen (a riverbed, a ravine?) and the position they were in (where was the sky? where the passenger door?), because the car had landed on its side. For a handful of seconds she heard nothing inside the car. Then she felt his hand touch her ankle in the dark.

They whispered, quickly, economically.

Are you okay? Yes, and you? Yes. Good.

He helped her out of the car from the shattered windshield. They eased through the broken glass, nimbly finding their way without getting a single scratch. Outside, there were stars and a sliver of moon peeking from behind the trees. She smelled something green and fresh rising from the broken branches. Eucalyptus.

He took her hand.

"Can you walk?"

"I think so."

"Good. Let's go then."

"Go where?"

"To the hospital. It isn't too far from here. We can walk there. They'll give us painkillers or something."

At the time, in the confusion of the moment, it seemed a perfectly logical thing to do, to walk barefoot in the bush (her right shoe was missing) in the middle of the night, leaving the car on its side like a dead elephant in the gully and thinking nothing of it.

"What about animals?" she said.

"What animals?"

"I don't know. Anything dangerous."

"I wouldn't worry about that now."

He put a finger under her chin and lifted her head just slightly, like one does to a child.

"We're going to be all right. Just follow me, okay?"

So they climbed out of the canyon and got back onto the road. He took her hand and held it tightly. The gesture startled her. They didn't talk much, so intent were they to experience the warmth of their hands, finally free to touch. They didn't seem to be frightened or surprised that they should be alive and unscathed on top of it. More than anything they felt euphoric that they should be together in this predicament.

"It's a beautiful night," she said dreamily.

He nodded and gave her a light squeeze on the fingers.

"We are still drunk, right?" she asked.

"We most certainly are."

The crash had finally splintered all pretense of formality between them, like a bomb annihilating what was left of barriers and trenches, accelerating the process of their coming together. The accident, more than all the alcohol they'd been drinking, had finally earned them an intimacy. After all, their bodies had been rolling together in the air, bouncing and dancing in the front seat in what had felt like slow motion—like bodies of astronauts in space, she thought—and had reemerged from the wreck intact. At this point they both felt they were allowed to be quiet and give a rest to the exhausting flirting they'd been engaged in, up until they had fallen off the road.

"We can take a nap and lie on a bed for a while. We'll take it from there," he suggested, as though, after lying in a hospital bed for a few hours, they would be presented with a variety of desirable options they could choose from.

· • ·

They reached the hospital as the sky was beginning to pale behind the trees.

The small building was an outpost built in the forties by the British for the white farmers and the officers who lived in the Northern District. It was a dainty cottage surrounded by flower beds and herbaceous borders blooming with agapanthus. It looked more like an old English lady's residence than an emergency room for people shot by Somali *shiftas* or mauled by buffaloes. It sat right outside the northern side of the town and marked the border between two worlds. Anything south of the hospital still maintained a resemblance to civilized life: there were irrigated farmlands, trucks that daily drove pea and flower pickers to the fields or to the greenhouses; there was a bank, a post office, a small supermarket. Even a hairdresser. North of the hospital lay the Great Nothing: an endless desert dotted by thorny acacias and dust devils, nomads who spoke an incomprehensible clipped language and whose cheeks and foreheads were marked by tribal scars. The electricity line and running water stopped there, the faint phone signal tapered off and vanished a few miles into the arid scrubland.

At the hospital they had been let in by the night watchman, then a sleepy nurse had medicated their superficial cuts and wheeled them into a cozy room, assuming they were a couple. The head nurse, a tall Kikuyu lady with an elaborate braided hairdo, had actually referred to the stranger as "your husband." Sonia had felt a thrill and didn't think of correcting the mistake.

· · ·

Now it was nearly eight in the morning, only a little time left before they'd be pulled apart and sucked back into their respective lives. In a matter of hours, long phone calls and complicated flight arrangements would have to be made, spouses and possibly children might appear to reclaim them.

Sonia glanced around the room. A stack of ancient videos sat next to a TV set, books in leather bindings were lined on a shelf, an old-fashioned cotton print on the curtains (shells? sweet potatoes? UFOs? She couldn't tell what those funny shapes were) matched the print on the bedspread. He followed her gaze.

"Astonishing decor for a hospital in the middle of nowhere, right?" she said.

He was lying in his cot across from hers in the sunny room with a cut across his nose and a small bandage on his temple. He didn't say anything, but looked at her long and hard.

"What?" Sonia asked, puzzled.

"We may as well do it," he said.

Sonia pretended to ignore him, though a rush of blood behind her neck rose slowly, warming up her cranium and her face.

"I see no point in prolonging it anymore, since we've done it a hundred times already in our heads," he said.

She swallowed hard. The blood now was rushing everywhere beneath her bruised skin, from the tips of her fingers to her toes, carrying a scintillating substance that woke up every pore. She had never felt this alert.

"No way. And besides, every bone in my rib cage hurts," she said, playfully.

"We'll do it softly," he said, dead serious.

Sonia raised her eyes to the ceiling and gave no answer.

She wasn't sure what to do with whatever time they had left, but she wanted to use it in a way that would be long-lasting. Having sex didn't seem to be the most useful option: it was going to be over and done with too quickly and it would drain all the luminous force they had accumulated during their short life together as a couple. She knew exactly what would happen: they would spend all the energy that had built up in one go and they'd be left with nothing. Despite this sensible argument, all Sonia could think of was his body. His bare legs were muscular and tanned. The shape of his knees was perfect. He had beautiful, strong forearms. She longed to see the rest of him and feel his touch all over her.

· . ·

The day before, her car had died on her way back from the village school. She had sat staring into the nothingness ahead of her windshield, with the resignation people must acquire when traveling through such remote parts of the world. She had tried to call the rental car office but there was no signal where she was. All she could do was sit and wait for someone to rescue her. It was about four in the afternoon and she figured that if nobody was going to drive by in the next couple of hours she would have to spend the night in the backseat, as it was unlikely that people would travel on that road in the dark. In her canvas bag she had a change of clothes and a warm jacket; she knew well how chilly it could get after dark in the desert. She happened to have a book, a torch, a half-full bottle of water and some chocolate biscuits she had bought in town on her way up, by habit.

When she was a child, way before cell phones came into the country, her parents were always ready for that kind of emergency when traveling in the bush: they never left home without food, water and a couple of blankets in case the car broke down. She did remember getting stranded a few times, having to spend the night on the backseat next to her little brother, to be rescued at the crack of dawn either by a group of park rangers in their khaki uniforms or by African farmers in a beat-up pickup truck. They would end up squeezing in their rescuers' vehicle till they reached the next village. These rides always turned out to be cheerful occasions, filled with Swahili banter and laughs, with a stop for *chai* and hot fried *mandazi* as soon as they hit the first tea stall.

After seven years of European life, she found herself smiling at the predicament she'd found herself in. It was a reminder that there were still places in the world where one could vanish, be lost, be found and rescued by strangers.

. . .

She had dozed off only for a few minutes in the driver's seat when the sound of a running engine approaching behind her startled her. The sun was low, about to set, and the first thing she saw in her rearview mirror were a man's faded shorts and long legs, unlaced leather boots, an indigo blue shirt. A tap on her window. A mop of unruly hair, shades, a maroon cotton scarf wrapped around his neck.

Yes, she'd had a problem.

No, it wasn't the battery. Yes, of course she had plenty of gas.

He insisted on lifting the hood and started screwing and unscrewing tops and bolts, rubbing the tip of the spark plugs with the corner of his shirt as men tend to do when presented with a broken-down car and a woman in the driver's seat.

I've checked those as well, she said, but he pretended not to hear.

She stood next to him looking at the tangle of wires under the hood and answered his third degree.

She had come to write a report on an NGO just north of Barsaloi.

Yes, she had been driving by herself all the way.

No, she didn't need a driver because she knew the road.

Because she had grown up there.

On a farm not far from here.

No, she hadn't been back in a few years. She used to come visit, but she hadn't now for a while.

She was heading to the airstrip outside the town to get on a six-seater back to the capital.

She was supposed to fly back to Europe the following day.

"Okay," he said, "hop in my car, I'll give you a ride to the airstrip. Forget the car. We'll send a mechanic tomorrow."

"Leave it. It's a rented car, I'll call them and they'll take care of it."

"Then get your stuff and I'll drop you off."

She sat next to him in the big Land Cruiser, filled with tools, carton boxes, muddy boots and towels covered in red dirt. They drove off and for a while neither one of them spoke.

· · ·

She remembered him, of course. She didn't feel like telling him, because it had been so long ago, at a time when she still lived in the country, and she didn't want him to think she still remembered their brief encounter after all these years. He had changed, but he looked more interesting now that he wasn't so boyish, with thin lines around his eyes. He lit a cigarette without asking her whether it might bother her.

"I remember you," he said, breaking the long silence.

"Really? From where?"

"We met in the bathroom at Jonathan Cole's house. You had on a pair of bright red sandals you had just bought in Italy."

She opened her mouth, feigning bewilderment.

"Come on. How can you remember *that*?"

"We had quite a long chat in there, and I tend to notice women's feet," he said.

She had been putting on her lipstick when he'd wandered in with a drink in his hand. They had flirted—mildly, in the oblique way people flirt late at night at parties—and shared his vodka tonic while sitting on the edge of the bathtub. Then Consuelo Gambrino, the alluring Argentinean eye doctor, had walked in.

"What are you two doing here?" she had asked them mischievously, shattering the moment. Consuelo had pulled up a stool and had started speaking nonsense to him in her thickly accented English, ignoring her. Sonia had left the room, meaning to catch up with him later, but somehow she'd lost sight of him, or maybe he had left without saying goodbye.

"Yes," she said, "I remember you now. You described in detail a scene from a book you were reading."

"Did I? That sounds rather boring."

"It was . . . it was the one with the lion and—was it the heart, the skin?—in the title. The part where the nun falls off the bridge. I actually bought the book afterward."

"Did you?"

"Yes, you made me want to read it."

"Did you like it?"

"I did."

He turned and looked at her and said nothing. She felt nervous for having said that, as though it had been an admission of some sort.

"Sorry if I didn't recognize you right away," she added after a short silence, wanting to sound casual. "It's been a very long time."

"No problem," he said and grinned. He knew she was lying and he liked that.

. • .

They asked each other polite questions, carefully steering away from the details of their personal lives, avoiding any mention of wife or girlfriend, children or husband. He said that for years he'd had a highly paid job for the UN, driving relief trucks into Sudan and Somalia. Now he worked as a manager on a sheep farm up-country. She suspected this change might have to do with having a family and settling down, though he didn't wear a wedding ring. She mentioned the name of the foundation she worked for and told him how sometimes she had to travel to assess the state of the projects they funded. They had just started to finance schooling projects for girls in the nomadic areas of East Africa and she had been assigned to report on them because of her knowledge of the place. She didn't delve into the details, knowing that he, having lived in the country for so many years, wasn't going to be impressed by her job. It was mainly her friends back in Europe who always introduced her as a kind of heroine because she had lived in a couple of African countries and was working for the poor.

"Do you ever miss your life here?" he asked.

"All the time," she said, and felt herself blushing. It seemed inappropriate to admit such a thing in front of him. A betrayal to the new life she had chosen.

. • .

When, almost eight years earlier, Sonia had made up her mind to move to Europe, it had seemed like a final decision. At the time she could no longer bear the corruption, the frustration of living in a hopeless country constantly on the edge of disaster where—if she was ever to have children—they would grow up like wild things without a clue about what was going on in the rest of the world and never adjusting to it. She convinced herself that she needed to live in a place where one would be able to go to a museum on a whim, see a movie, get proper clothes, eat decent food and be surrounded by people who could talk about ideas rather than dams, engines, electric fencing, wells and cattle. When she'd met the man who was to become her husband—a director of photography who'd come into the country to shoot a documentary on the Ndorobos, a disappearing tribe—she hadn't let him escape without her, holding on to him with the resilience of a castaway grasping a wide, steady plank of wood.

She had adjusted very quickly to her new life—after all it was much easier to go from bush to city than the other way around. The "how to" instructions were easy and written on every wall; the comfort of European life was strongly addictive, she discovered, and one immediately forgot how to live without it.

Now that she felt something of an exile returning to her homeland, she'd been assaulted by nostalgia, not only for the raw beauty of the country, but for her former self, a person happy to live with few clothes, who didn't wear makeup and who didn't think much of crossing a river in a four-wheel drive.

· • ·

Sometimes, in the city where she lived now, glancing around the crowd in the bus, she would single out a couple of faces. She recognized their shy smiles, the way they moved their open hands around their faces, the familiar singsong in their voices—certain words that she'd catch in the distance. Usually they would be cleaning ladies, sometimes they'd be young nuns or street sellers just arrived—she could tell from the clothes they wore. She couldn't restrain herself from moving closer and closer to them, elbowing other tired passengers until she'd find herself standing right next to them in order to catch the gist of their conversation. She'd wait for the right moment to barge in and they'd open their eyes wide, stunned to hear a *mzungu* lady in her nice coat address them in their language.

"I grew up there."

They would laugh and slap their thighs.

"So you are an African too!"

"Oh yes, *sana kabisa*," she'd say and join their laughter.

Often she would not get off at her stop, wanting to prolong the conversation; the sound of Swahili was like music to her.

· · ·

He hadn't been exactly present in her thoughts for all those years; she seemed to have almost forgotten him, to have lost track of his existence as if he hadn't left such a big impression after all. But the memory of that encounter on the edge of a bathtub must have been lingering somewhere beneath the surface—invisible, yet bobbing about. All this became clear to Sonia only once she sat next to him in the car, so that coming across him in such an unlikely circumstance seemed the obvious segue to their encounter of nearly ten years earlier, when she was still single, hadn't settled anywhere yet and still had a sense that the future was a sheet of white photographic paper on which her life was still waiting to emerge.

· · ·

They passed clusters of zebras, antelopes and small cattle herds led by men wrapped in red cloth, covered in colorful beaded jewelry. Just before it got dark they saw a leopard appear and cross the track ahead of them, its golden shape cut against the white dust. He turned off the engine of the car and they watched the animal move slowly across—a tight bundle of muscles and tendons—and disappear into the thick again. They looked at each other and didn't make a comment; they exchanged a smile, as though the leopard crossing their way had been a good omen, or a special signal sent just for them.

He glanced at his wristwatch.

"It's a quarter to seven. Can you still make your flight to Nairobi?"

"Oh. Forget it, it left two hours ago. I'll have to try to go tomorrow."

She could almost hear them both think, *Good, we have a little time.*

.   .   .

Once they left the track the landscape changed, turned greener and the air cooler. They knew that now that the desert was behind them they'd reach town within an hour. They became aware that they'd have to come up with some sort of a plan in order to prolong the encounter. Neither was ready to let the other one go.

Behind a gas station, at the intersection of a small cluster of shacks selling wrinkled vegetables and Masai blankets, they saw a *nyama choma* sign painted on the side.

"They have good food here," he said. "How about a snack and a drink?"

Sonia nodded, relieved that he'd taken the initiative.

The place was dimly lit by a string of red lightbulbs, empty except for a stocky man behind the counter, busy swatting flies away. He brought out what was left in the kitchen, cold chapatis, goat stew and *sukumawiki,* a meal that reminded Sonia of her childhood.

Suddenly a white woman with sandy hair walked briskly into the joint. She looked around and called his name.

"Hey, I saw your car outside, what are you . . . ," she said, and stopped, seeing he wasn't alone.

He stood up and hugged her warmly, like an old friend. The two of them stood by the table and spoke briefly, while Sonia kept looking into her plate. She overheard the woman say something about a ghastly group of clients whom she had just driven to the airport, a problem with the power line, a lunch she was planning to have on Sunday.

"Please come and bring the children," the woman said. "I've got to run now, give my love to Alexandra. Don't forget Sunday."

She moved away and quickly fluttered her hand in Sonia's direction. Throughout the conversation with the woman he had seemed perfectly at ease and not in the least embarrassed to be seen with her, a fact that mildly disappointed Sonia. He sat down and ordered another round of drinks.

They lingered over their food, sipping cheap vodka and lime soda. The alcohol had smoothed their conversation, which was sliding more freely now, without pauses or impediments. They spoke only of things they'd be allowed to share: it didn't matter what, anything that came to mind would do—a visit to the Prado, the beauty of Norwegian fjords, what had happened with Terrence Malick in his recent film, a cult book by Julian Jaynes they'd both happened to have read. They were like tightrope walkers on the same line, careful not to stray from their finely attuned balance. They had been given only one direction to go and the challenge was exhilarating.

The owner approached with the fly-swatting rag in his hand and began to wipe the table next to them. It was closing time.

There was a pause.

"Where shall I take you now?" he asked her.

"I'll get a room somewhere for the night," she said.

"There are no hotels around here where you'd want to spend the night."

"It's fine. I'm not fussy."

They walked on the gravel toward the car. A soft breeze enveloped them. The sky was like blue carbon paper. It felt so wrong to pretend to be indifferent.

"Wow. I'm totally drunk," Sonia said, stumbling, taking time, wanting it to slow down. It seemed to be ticking too fast.

He opened the passenger door and looked at her. He seemed perfectly sober.

"I like talking to you."

"Yeah. Me, too. That was nice."

She sat in her seat, not knowing what they would be doing next.

"I wish I had met you when you were still living here," he said as he turned the key of the starter.

· • ·

In the years that followed the accident Sonia thought often of that phrase. How her life would have panned out differently had the eye doctor Consuelo Gambrino never entered the bathroom and interrupted their conversation when they'd first met, had she not been too shy to follow him through the party crowd, had she pursued him, kissed him, made love to him that same night. Maybe she would've stayed on in the country and learned to cope with the hovering feeling of impending disaster, with her lack of sophistication, which at the time had seemed so unbearable to her. That way she would've had a good reason to go on living in the place where she belonged.

She also often wondered how it had been possible to fall like that. When exactly had it happened, this falling, this opening up completely? What was the connection, why him of all the people she'd come across? Clearly she couldn't talk to anyone about this without feeling pathetic. It sounded like some adolescent fantasy, material for a cheap novel, something her friends would laugh about.

She went quietly back to her life, and kept that feeling a secret, something stashed away in the folds of her memory that now and again she would turn to. She'd go back to it and there it would be, intact, unfaded, like a diamond ring that one cannot wear in daylight, that can only be taken out of its velvet pouch every now and again, just to make sure it is still as glittering and fabulous as one remembers.

The only tangible memory of the car crash was a tiny scar. Nothing more than a thin line running across her forearm. A discreet reminder, something she would see on herself every day, that had become part of who she was, a mark that people hardly noticed.

II

The list, dashed off in pencil on the back of an envelope, is quite long. It starts with a new set of pajamas and a few toys for the child that she will need in the days to come. There's lots of other stuff she has to get, like milk and vegetables, snow boots, medicines, honey, detergents, printing paper and converters for their European plugs, but Sonia has decided to start with the child's list, which is the longest and the most urgent.

Since they arrived in New York it has been nonstop rushing and fatigue. The moving, the settling in, the adjusting to the new space. She hates the new bed. She hates the view. A fire escape is not what she was expecting to be looking at, first thing in the morning.

It has been snowing for days. The brownstones in the Village are laced in a mantle of white, romantic as in an Edith Wharton story, but this morning Sonia struggles to see the beautiful side of things.

She walks very fast, making her way uptown. These days she cannot face the subway and prefers to walk; crowds make her nervous, she has been breaking out in cold sweats. It's just tension, nothing to worry about—after all, it's the least she can expect from her body given the circumstances—so she keeps some herbal remedy in her pocket. It's called Rescue Remedy and she likes the sound of its name. Every now and again she squeezes a few drops under her tongue to rein in any spike of anxiety.

Inside the department store the suffocating dampness mixed with the smells emanating from too many bodies feels like a lethal gas that will slowly poison her. She spends too long inside there,

unable to make up her mind between two sets of pajamas, incapable of picking the right kind of snow boots, feeling heady, hungry and weak. Too much to choose from, too many options, that's
always the problem with department stores.

She bolts.

.   •   .

Out on the street Sonia inhales the cold slap of air on her face and
quickly heads back downtown toward her more familiar neighborhood. The farther south she goes, the deeper into the West
Village, the more stylish the women: cloaked in well-cut coats and
fur-lined boots, extravagant head gear—a Mongolian-Tibetan
style with a contemporary touch—hands gloved in unusual shades
for a splash of color. Her own clothes feel limp and stale on her.
What seemed a perfectly decent coat only two weeks ago as she
was leaving Europe here feels threadbare, secondhand.

It's going to be tough to brave this city, she thinks. It would've
been easier, exciting, had they been in a different state of mind.
Had they come for a different reason. Her feet are freezing already
after only a few steps, the soles of her boots are too thin for the
hard, icy pavement. Had she been more patient in her shopping
attempt, she could've gotten at least the snow boots that were on
sale on the ground floor. At least she'd have ticked one item off
the list. Actually this constant postponing is a way to keep away
all that is in store for them in the coming weeks. For what feels
like a long time now she has been pushing the future—*any* portion of the future, regardless of its weight and size—as far away
as possible.

A bubble, a tiny capsule of time where nothing is happening,
no decision can be made, is all she wishes for.

.   •   .

A Starbucks beckons from across the street. Another whiff of hot
air welcomes her. Sleepy youths in cotton T-shirts lounge in the

ample armchairs holding laptops on their knees, busy with their Facebook pages, their backpacks and jackets spread on the floor as if it were their living room.

She sits by the window with a tall regular coffee, and along with the caffeine kick she injects her neurons with more drops of Rescue Remedy.

That's when her peripheral vision catches a slight movement on her left side. She looks over to the window. Someone is standing outside looking in and shading with a hand the reflection on the glass. It's a man in a leather coat. Their gaze meets in mid-air—a laser beam that pierces the glass and freezes the frame.

She jolts, her heart beating wildly in her throat.

·   •   ·

Neither one knows how to proceed. He has walked in, brushing fresh snowflakes off his scarf, with a big smile made to conceal a certain uneasiness. They hug, briefly, circumspectly, without kissing. He sits down without taking off his coat, as though he cannot stay for long. Clearly he's had to walk in, given the incredible coincidence, spotting her inside a Starbucks in an unlikely neighborhood, in a city of millions. They agree that once again they've met under unusual circumstances, though neither one pronounces the word *sign* or *destiny*. He has aged slightly, gracefully. His hair is shorter, he might have gained a few pounds, but his body still looks strong and muscular; it has the natural build gained by a life outdoors rather than the neatly sculpted physique created inside a gym. His clothes—such an African wardrobe—make him look incongruous, in a way rather unstylish; like a cowboy just landed in Manhattan. He glances over at the indolent college kids sitting next to them, at the mess of their used paper cups and half-eaten pastries on the tables. He seems fascinated, as though he's never been inside a Starbucks before.

He and Sonia are evasive as to their whereabouts—why they

both find themselves in New York of all places. He says he's there
for only another couple of days—business, boring stuff—and
he'll be flying back home on the weekend. Actually he might have
said *We'll be flying back*—Sonia tries to replay the phrase in order
to double-check the pronoun but her memory plays funny tricks,
it tends to blur words she doesn't want to hear.

"Business," she repeats, then asks, smiling, "Sheep business in
New York?"

"No," he says, "no more sheep in my life. More like big spare
parts. You don't want to know."

Then he rubs his gloveless hands and blows on them.

"What are you doing here? Are you waiting for someone?" he
asks.

"No, I was just . . ."

She stands up and gets her coat, gathers her bag.

". . . just getting a coffee. Come on, let's get out of here. I hate
this place."

Her hands are shaking lightly as she wraps the scarf around
her neck. Nothing has changed—the excitement, the fear, the
desire—it's all still there, unevolved, unexpired. Still dangerously
alive, as if it has only been asleep inside her.

.   .   .

Suddenly New York in the snow looks heartbreakingly beautiful. They walk along the small blocks around Greenwich Street,
where there are fewer people, less traffic. They don't have a plan
yet but she wants to be somewhere quiet, where they can have
some privacy.

"Are you hungry, you want to get something to eat?" she asks,
to let him know that she does have a little time.

"Sure," he says, looking slightly disoriented now. She sees a
Japanese banner farther up the street.

"Good. How about sushi?"

"Whatever you feel like."

She quickly writes a text on her phone and he discreetly looks the other way.

grabbing a bite, back by 2

She then turns the phone off.

· • ·

The restaurant has just a few tables, low lighting, wood-paneled walls saturated with a fishy aroma. There are no customers as it is still early. A rice paper sliding door is half opened onto a private room with a table and two simple benches. She points toward it and the waiter nods.

"Shoes, madam," the waiter whispers.

Slipping in the small room in their socks feels sinful, as though they are entering a bedroom.

The table is long and thin, meant for at least eight, low and slightly sunk in, so they can eat cross-legged facing each other.

They are too nervous to be interested in the food, neither one feels like looking at the menu.

"I'll take what you take," he says.

She orders soup, black cod with miso and tea. For a moment she fears it might have been a mistake to drag him all the way inside this private room; he might be feeling uncomfortable, trapped. He could've been on his way to a meeting, or maybe his family is waiting to have lunch with him somewhere after all. Yes, she might have been moving too fast, again, without thinking.

"What have you been up to since I saw you last?" Sonia asks, deciding to sound casual, with the tone people use when bumping into each other at a party. They have to start somewhere, after all.

"Uh, let's see . . ." He fiddles for a moment with the chopsticks.

"I've been thinking of you," he says, deadpan, "on and off since we crashed."

Sonia gives a nervous, artificial laugh.

"Well, I guess that was a hard one to forget, since we nearly died," Sonia says. It's the wrong tone of voice, she knows—casual, ironic. Yet she doesn't know how to change it.

He doesn't answer and keeps his eyes on her, intent.

"Did you ever recover the car?" Sonia asks.

"No, I had to buy another one."

"I'm so sorry."

"It wasn't your fault."

There is a pause as the waiter walks in with tea and soup in lacquered bowls.

She just can't bring herself to say what she has been waiting to say for all these years. Time keeps ticking away. Soon they'll be done eating, they'll find themselves out on the street and once again she will go home having said nothing. She knows she will not be granted another chance. On the edge of a bathtub; in the middle of the bush; now Perry Street in the snow. It's not going to happen again.

"What is this *thing*?" she blurts out at last.

"Which thing?"

"This thing between us. It's ridiculous."

"It must be what people call falling in love."

How shocking, that he should be the one to be so unfettered. Yet she's thankful, he has dared to say it out loud.

"I didn't say I *love* you," he says, defiantly. "I said I might have fallen *in love. In love* is a different phase, it doesn't involve all that love requires."

"What does love require?"

"Things like trust, affection. Solidarity."

"I like trust, affection, solidarity," she says. "I prize them enormously."

"So do I. But those need time, and a lot of work."

Sonia holds her cup with two hands, hiding part of her face.

"Okay, so what exactly is this?"

"It's the way we as a species came to be. Some billions of years ago, that's how life started to happen on the planet. I don't see anything wrong with that."

Sonia smiles. His humor is gentle, unthreatening. He sips his tea.

"We didn't just crash, you know," he says. "We *exploded*. From the . . . from the tension. That's an enormous amount of energy, what you and I conjured up that night."

"We fell off the bridge because we had had too much to drink," she says, and again regrets the way she's still keeping herself at a distance, feigning to be blasé.

He shakes his head.

"No, that's not it. I'm not making this up. It's physics. Like, you know, quantum theory."

Sonia knows that soon her husband will call her phone and find it turned off. He won't think much of that, he has no reason to be suspicious. There is trust between them, there has always been. The babysitter will leave in an hour. She really needs to go soon.

She looks at him and suddenly their eyes meet in that brief, suspended space where there are no more funny lines, no irony, but a seriousness they hadn't dared before. She knows that this is the only chance she has to cross that realm and say what she has been wanting to tell him; that, yes, she has, in some quiet way, loved him all these years. She just wants him to acknowledge the part he's been playing unknowingly in her life, as if, after learning that, they will finally reach a place of rest. And yet, she can't make herself say it. What would happen at this point, she thinks, once those words are spoken? Would they really be at peace? Wouldn't they feel they ought to do something with them? Take a room in a hotel?

And that, of course, would be insane.

"My husband has cancer." The words pour out fast, almost without her knowing. "We came here because they have the best doctors. I have no idea how long it's going to take."

He nods, waiting for her to continue.

"We had to sell our apartment back home because it's going to be horribly expensive to have surgery done here without insurance."

Sonia leans sideways. She lets her own weight pull her down and slides slowly, till she's reclining on the bench, under the table.

It's the fatigue, the weight of all the events and circumstances that she can no longer control, all the questions that have no answer, this venturing onward, through a darkness getting darker. It's the near future at the rice paper door.

At times it is so tiring, she needs to close her eyes.

He too slides and reclines on his side, coming into her view. Now they face each other under the table, supine on the benches, just like they did in those hospital beds six years earlier.

"We decided we'd do whatever it takes. So here we are."

He nods and then holds out his arm toward her.

"Tell me more," he says.

"We have a child, she's only three," Sonia says, her voice nearly breaking. "She needs her father. They adore each other."

Sonia needs him too. It's just that her mind refuses to register the likelihood that she may lose him.

She extends her arm till their hands find each other. It's the first real physical contact they have had since the night of the crash. She feels his fingers closing on hers, brushing them lightly. They remain like that, without saying anything for a while. And it feels okay to be able to be silent together, lying under the table, taking a break from all that is happening above it.

It's a relief. This resting place.

"What about your children?" Sonia asks.

"They're growing up fast. We have three now."

"You and Alexandra are still good?"

He nods.

"I'm happy for you."

"She's wonderful. I couldn't live without her."

This is a grace, Sonia thinks, to have this, to be able to look at it and say this is what we have, rather than this is what we can't have.

Love has many faces.

. • .

The rice paper door slides open and the waiter enters holding a tray with the food. For a moment he looks around—it seems as if his two customers have vanished. Then he sees they are lying on the benches under the table, facing each other. Holding hands.

He places the food on the table and steps out as lightly as possible, so as not to wake them.

Roman Romance

Elsa still had his letters in a shoebox somewhere. They'd been written in longhand on a yellow legal pad and on the backs of the envelopes was "drew barker 21 taft road kenosha wisconsin usa," all in lowercase.

Her mother kept suggesting she sell them on eBay if she needed cash.

"You know how much money you'd make? Enough to do your whole apartment, even the kitchen and the bathroom."

"Will you stop it? You're annoying me," Elsa said to shut her up.

She found the box one day while rummaging on top of an armoire. It was buried under some old sweaters she'd meant to give away. She sat cross-legged on the rug and read all the letters, one after the other, without stopping. They were sweet and melancholic; rereading his words after so long saddened her. They made her aware of all the things she had lost and left behind.

. . .

Elsa didn't own a car on principle. She rode her bike, a red Atala, everywhere across the city. Every morning on her way to work, she pedaled along the Lungotevere, under its thick canopy of plane trees, and then turned right into Via Giulia along the ivy-covered wall of Palazzo Farnese. The street was pretty much in the shade all day, and like similar streets in old Rome, it smelled of moss and mushrooms. The walls of the palazzo exuded damp; a whiff of cool air came from its vents even at the height of summer. It was a chilling sensation, this smell of death and cold stone mixed together. She had never had a good feeling about Via Giulia: too many cruel cardinals and scheming courtesans had lived in the palazzi that lined the street, too many murders and Machiavellian plots had taken place around its dark corners. As soon as she entered the wide-open space of Piazza Farnese, with its twin fountains and the gently concave cobblestoned pavement, a sudden warmth always lifted her heart. At that time of day the tables of the corner café were usually crowded with good-looking people facing the sun in expensive sunglasses, either busy texting, getting a tan or reading the paper. Past the square Elsa crossed the confusion of Campo de' Fiori, slowed down through the open market, skirted the stands of flower sellers, the mounds of vegetables piled artistically on the stalls for the benefit of the tourists, and parked her bicycle in Via del Pellegrino, another dark and murky street right off the piazza. The studio was on the first floor of a poorly maintained building. She had recently joined a group of graphic designers who built websites mainly related to art. They made catalogs for contemporary art galleries and museums. It was a good job, and she'd just been asked to become a partner.

She was parking the bike on the rack at the corner when she noticed the poster on the opposite side of the street. She'd heard he was coming; she just hadn't realized it was going to be that soon.

·   •   ·

When Drew and Elsa had first met, about twenty years earlier, they'd made fun of their respective names. Elsa was convinced that whenever she introduced herself to strangers, the image of Elsa the lioness—from a sixties film about an orphaned lion cub raised as a pet in Kenya—would pop up in their minds, obscuring her face. She told Drew she'd always felt as though she'd been walking through life with the head of a famous animal stuck to her body. He rebutted that she was the luckier of the two: if she was stuck with a lioness's head, he had been named after a past tense.

In his early twenties Drew was a skinny guy with a mop of dark hair falling on his face, which he was constantly tucking behind his ear, Mick Jagger lips and skin as white as milk. They had met one night in a club behind Piazza del Fico, where he was playing with a band—a bunch of young Italians who played indie rock. The club was actually just a small, smoky room where people barely paid attention to the live music, busy as they were picking up strangers and exchanging drugs in the bathroom. Elsa's friends wanted to leave after a only a few minutes—the music was so bad, they said—but she said go, I'll stay on a bit, because she liked the American singer with the milky skin and the hoarse voice. She waited patiently for the act to finish, determined to talk to him. By then it was past one thirty in the morning and Drew was pretty wasted, so they ended up groping each other in a dark corner without much of a preliminary introduction. They fucked standing against the wall in the club's storeroom, among stacks of empty bottles that kept rattling as they bounced. She couldn't go home with him because at the time she was still living at her parents'—it was her last year in high school—but he wrote her number on a packet of cigarettes and said he'd call her. He didn't, and for a week she obsessed about him, driving herself crazy with angst. When she finally gave up and decided he was just another asshole, the phone rang. It was him. And that's how it all started.

· • ·

About three or four years after that, when Drew was back in the States and on his way to becoming famous, he decided to use his last name only and morphed into Barker. Like Beyoncé and Sting, like Madonna, Bono and Adele, it seemed that rock stars didn't need a first and last name like regular people. Understandably so in his case, since Drew wasn't a name particularly fit for a famous person.

Since then Drew had become universally known as Barker and his face had been scanned, photographed, blown up on posters, banners and magazines all over the world so that everybody had access to every pore of his skin. He was forty-something now and he still looked great in every photograph Elsa saw, his waist small, his ass pretty tight. His handsome face had lost that boyish, fake innocence. The nose was stronger, the cheekbones more prominent, the hair short and still thick. Of course, being a millionaire must have helped as far as preservation goes. Stars like Barker could count on personal trainers, personal chefs, expensive spa treatments, yoga gurus and miraculous ayurvedic, Swedish or Chinese treatments.

She didn't feel possessive of him in any way: she had too much good sense to claim him as personal property just because she'd slept with him way before he became famous. It was actually kind of weird how Elsa—who felt pretty bland and unglamorous at thirty-nine—couldn't see in Barker what everyone else saw, but just saw Drew Barker, the kid from Kenosha, Wisconsin, who'd come to live in Rome to escape his provincial destiny and play guitar in a lousy band. During the time they were together Elsa was moved and at the same time embarrassed by the naive image he attempted to project—the Bohemian-artist-living-in-Rome, with the yellowing copies of *A Moveable Feast* and Allen Ginsberg poetry rolled up in his jeans back pocket. Drew Barker, who swore he'd never set foot in Wisconsin again because there was nothing beautiful or remotely cultural to look at there.

He was sweet and catlike in the way he made love to her, but he could also be mean, in ways so subtle that she often misread him. He would call her up late at night, from his rehearsals with the band, or from a noisy bar, saying, "I'll be home at midnight. Go over now and wait for me. The key is under the mat."

"Why don't I come and pick you up and we'll go together?" Elsa would ask—she longed to be the girlfriend who showed up at the end of rehearsals and was seen going home with him.

"No," he'd say. "I want you to go now, just go over to my apartment and warm up my bed."

She was only nineteen, she didn't know enough about men and their ways, and took his orders as flattery.

· • ·

Her new colleagues at the studio shared cool music files, bought tickets for contemporary dance and went to gallery openings all the time. They were busy people, working hard at keeping up with the buzz. Elsa didn't go out much after work, she listened mostly to classical music these days and didn't care about contemporary art. She was actually content to spend the evenings after work cuddling her cat while watching movies on her computer. Despite her aloofness people at work respected her—she was a brilliant designer, with a great sense of proportion and composition—though nobody seemed interested in becoming her friend.

It was a mystery how the rumor crept up on her. Elsa had no idea who started it or how it spread. But slowly and surely, spread it did, and she knew it had reached her the minute people gravitated toward her with a particular kind of curiosity.

The first one to show the signs at the office was Marta, the receptionist.

"Can I ask you a personal question?" she asked Elsa one morning with a knowing smile. It was a couple of months after she'd started working at Creative TechDesign.

Elsa blew on her pink polka dot tea mug, in which she had her special tulsi tea, and made a sound with her nose that could mean various things.

"What?"

"I don't know if this is true," Marta began. "But I was told that in that Barker song . . ."

Elsa glanced at the porcelain cleavage emerging from the low cut of the girl's black T-shirt, at the elaborate Japanese tattoo sneaking up her arm like a sleeve. At her full, plump lips, possibly injected, or simply inherited, it was hard to say. Pretty girl, twenty-something. Then Elsa blew on her tea again and started scrolling through her e-mail. The girl paused, taken aback by her indifference.

Elsa lifted her gaze. "You were, what, five, ten, when he wrote that song? How come you even know it?"

Marta grinned.

"Are you kidding me? We grew up with it. It's a—a hymn to love. I know all his songs by heart."

A hymn to love? *Please,* Elsa felt like saying.

She got up from her desk to signal that the exchange was about to be over.

"I think I know what it is you want to ask me," she said. "I get asked that all the time. And the answer is no."

"Oh. Oh. Sorry. It's just that . . . well, it's just that someone told me you were—"

"They were wrong," Elsa said, and that was the end of that.

· • ·

Apart from his very first CD, Elsa hadn't bought any of Barker's music. She pretended there wasn't a particular reason. Perhaps because of their shared past, she didn't feel she should have to pay money to listen to him; and in any case there was no way to escape his music, since it had been playing everywhere for so many years on every radio station, in commercials and supermarkets and at shopping malls. Elsa tended to stay away from it as much as possible, as though the amplified sound of his voice might blast the delicate mechanism over which she'd managed for many years to keep control.

Her mother was the one who kept bringing up the subject. She always phoned Elsa the moment she read anything about Barker.

Did you hear, he divorced the wife. He moved to London, he bought a three-story house in Notting Hill. He's given two hundred thousand dollars to a charity in Bangladesh. You should get in touch with him, Elsa, I'm sure he'd be happy to hear from you . . .

There was no way to get her off the subject once she started.

But Elsa didn't want to hear: she was wary of the past. She'd always had the good sense not to yearn for anything irretrievably lost. She and Barker had forked paths eons before—they had had such different lives now, there was no point in trying to draw a parallel between them. Especially now that she'd gained weight in all the wrong places, had allowed a streak of gray to grow out at the temples and was too lazy to color it.

. • .

Drew had ended their love affair brusquely one morning. Elsa had told her parents she was going to Florence with a girlfriend for two days. She had to lie to them, as they would never allow her to spend the night with a man while she was still living at home.

"I don't think I am in love with you anymore," he announced literally minutes after she'd opened her eyes, or at least that's the way Elsa remembered it. "I think you should go."

She looked at him, aghast. So he repeated what he'd said, this time more urgently.

"I think you should go. Like, *now*."

Elsa made a leap stark naked from the bed to the bathroom so that he wouldn't see her cry. She sank onto the toilet and began to sob, staring at her bare feet on the pink tiles while he begged her to open the door. They went on like that for a while—her sobbing, him knocking and begging. When she finally let him in, he didn't console her or say he was sorry. He only seemed eager for her to leave. He was probably waiting for someone else to call or show up; he seemed in such a hurry to get rid of her. Elsa picked up her clothes from the floor, put them on in a rush and ran down the stairs, still howling. She kept on howling while she ran across the river under a drizzling rain. Passersby stared at her with a pained expression. There's something terribly sad about a very young girl sobbing on the street without restraint. You just know she must have a broken heart.

.   •   .

She was crossing Piazza Farnese on her bicycle when the unmistakable curly head of Sandro Donati, the handsome photographer, slid into her peripheral vision. He was sitting by himself at the beautiful people's corner café wrapped up in a voluminous blue scarf and a tweed jacket with leather patches on the elbows, intent on reading what seemed to be *Corriere dello Sport*. Elsa had designed his new website only a few weeks earlier—the two of them had had a couple of meetings and exchanged quite a few e-mails discussing the layout and concept of the site, and by now she felt a connection of some sort because of the amount of time she had spent in the company of his exquisite black-and-white shots—portraits, still lifes—arranging the short poetic text that accompanied the images on the site, setting it in different fonts and so on. She felt a rush of shyness overtake her but, as she was about to turn the corner, she caught him waving in her direction. For a fraction of a second she thought she could actually stop and join him, but her reserve won out and she kept moving. In the fugitive space of indecision between accelerating and stopping, she caught his reflection in the café window, his head still turned toward her, his hand stuck in midair, so she made a quick decision and backtracked.

"Hey," Sandro said half jokingly. "I thought you were blatantly ignoring me."

"Oh no, I wasn't quite sure it was you. I am afraid I need glasses," she said, trying to laugh.

"Would you like to sit down and have a cup of coffee? It's so nice to see you, Elsa, actually I was thinking about you just the other day."

He waved to a waiter and pulled up a chair for her. It was so nice to hear him say her name.

. • .

After that shocking breakup, Elsa had heard that Drew was seeing an American art student from Texas. A leggy blonde with a
mane of long wavy hair who'd come to Rome to finish her Ph.D.
on the Italian Renaissance painter Artemisia Gentileschi. Just the
sort of thing Drew from Kenosha would suck up to, Elsa thought.
She had been trying her best to reestablish some kind of superiority in order to overcome the humiliation, and after receiving this bit of information she rode a train all the way to Naples
just to look at Artemisia's most famous painting—*Judith Slaying
Holofernes*, in the Capodimonte museum, a magnificent palazzo
built for King Carlo di Borbone in the mid-eighteenth century to
house his vast art collection. Never, she felt, had a painting been
so brutally graphic: Judith and her woman servant are holding
the struggling Assyrian warrior down on the bed with a forceful
gesture as though slaughtering a pig for the kitchen. Elsa knew the
painting well, from her art history classes—it was an iconic work,
embraced by several feminist critics—but up until that day she
had only seen it reproduced in books. Art historians agreed that
this work was Artemisia's most powerful because in choosing this
subject she had channeled her hatred for Agostino Tassi—a much
less talented painter who worked in her father's studio—a man
who'd raped her, dishonored her. Elsa stared at the painting for a
long time, fixing her gaze on every detail, taking in the way the
blood spurts from Holofernes's throat onto the mattress, noticing
the way Judith (whom historians had established was Artemisia's
self-portrait) has rolled up her sleeves to the elbows and keeps her
body slightly askew from the bed, so as not to soil her beautiful
blue dress. Elsa was in awe of the artist's cruelty, her determination. This was revenge at its best. Elsa moved away from the painting having filled herself with a righteous fury. Walking through
the rooms of what she felt was *her* gallery, giving friendly nods to
her museum guards sitting idly in the corners of the empty rooms,

gave her a renewed sense of authority, as if she had succeeded in reestablishing her ownership not only of Artemisia Gentileschi, but of the entire Italian Baroque and Renaissance period. Elsa rode the two-hour train back to Rome with her face against the window feeling that, despite the fact that it had been her first visit to the Capodimonte museum, her brief time there had allowed her to regain stature in the face of those foreigners who came from nowhere, assuming they could simply absorb by osmosis her culture and history, and transform themselves into someone else by grabbing, using and then spitting out whatever came their way.

· • ·

The letters started coming about a year after Drew left, completely out of the blue. Elsa was twenty years old; she'd left home by then and was sharing a flat with two friends from university. The first letter, mailed to her parents' address—an event, since nobody bothered to write with a pen on paper, buy stamps and find a mailbox anymore—didn't sound like Drew at all, it had absolutely no trace of his dark humor. Its tone was formal, old-fashioned, just like his neat handwriting: it was very specific and seemed concerned only as to whether she could forgive him for what he had done to her. Apparently Drew had gone back to Wisconsin after all; the letter claimed he'd now realized how "confused and unhappy" he'd been in Rome at the time of their breakup. What he'd inflicted on her was "unforgivable" and only now could he see what he had lost by breaking off their relationship so abruptly as if, he wrote, "you had been my enemy rather than a person I loved."

Elsa was puzzled by the saintly tone, and showed the letter to one of her roommates, a girl whose skills at deciphering emotional nuances she trusted. The girl declared he must be in one of those American 12-step programs either for booze or drugs or both. This letter, she said, was simply what step 8 required: making amends to all the people you've harmed under the influence;

Elsa surely happened to be just one in a long list of people to whom he owed apologies.

"I bet quite a few of these aerograms must be flying across the globe as we speak," the girl said with a smirk.

This obvious truth came as a mild disappointment and Elsa regretted showing her the letter.

But then, a couple of days later, she decided to jump at the opportunity and secretly constructed a short but effervescent reply, chiseling her words, cutting and shaping it more and more so that her letter would sound casual, affectionate and humorous enough in case he might be interested in continuing their correspondence. Drew wrote back a week later with the same humorless tone of the first message, confessing he'd just recovered from a very dark period and was now helping out his father in the hardware shop back in Kenosha. He was thinking of taking up playing music again with a bunch of guys from the neighborhood. He thanked her for putting the letter in the post rather than e-mailing him back. He said that seeing her familiar handwriting again made their contact "so much more valuable." It struck Elsa as odd, unlikely, the way these details seemed to be precious to him. As if he'd shed a protective layer and what was left underneath was too tender, too vulnerable to be attractive.

· ● ·

Sandro Donati ordered two cappuccinos and forced Elsa to try an almond croissant despite her protests. Nonsense, he said, you are not fat at all. Elsa couldn't make herself look into his piercing blue eyes, he was so much more attractive than she remembered when they were discussing ideas for his website. He then complimented her for the work she'd done and on the vintage leather jacket she was wearing. He asked her whether she also lived in the neighborhood.

"I see you often coming and going on your bicycle. I live right around the corner, in Via Monserrato," he said.

The fact that he was a neighbor as well as a client seemed to allow a significant shift in their relationship. Elsa found him easy to talk to—they compared notes about the new restaurant that had just opened in Via dei Giubbonari, discussed which one was their favorite vegetable seller at the market in Campo de' Fiori. Elsa was flattered when he asked her for her phone number.

"If you like, one of these days we could go to a movie or get a bite at that new place," he said, and rose to kiss her lightly on the cheek when she left.

Elsa rode her bike to the studio in a state of euphoria. Lately there had been little excitement in Elsa's love life. An affair with a married man had gone awry a couple of years earlier and she'd been sleeping on and off with an old boyfriend she was no longer attracted to just to keep her body engaged in some sort of sexual activity. Even that had come to an end for lack of purpose.

In the following days she caught herself checking messages and missed calls. When she finally saw Sandro's name on the display and he told her he'd been given two tickets for Barker's concert, she couldn't say no.

· · ·

It wasn't long before Elsa had lost interest in Drew's correspondence. He'd told her that he'd started to play music again but his life in Kenosha, apart from a couple of gigs in small venues with his band and idle talk of a contract with an obscure music producer, seemed to have shrunk into a dull repetition—early morning jog, nine to six in the hardware shop, evening practice with the band in the garage. He did mention attending weekly Narcotics Anonymous meetings—so Elsa's friend was spot-on there—and she suspected that getting off his addictions had probably made him a better person. But it had dulled the edge, killed the magic. All his romantic notions about art and literature, about living his life to its fullest, all that drug-induced passion that had possessed him and sometimes embarrassed her when she knew him in Rome, seemed to have faded and dispersed like fog, revealing his true substance. Reformed Drew was actually no longer worth yearning for, she told herself. And that's how Elsa was healed of her broken heart and eventually stopped thinking about him altogether.

· • ·

The posters were everywhere now. A black-and-white one was covering the scaffolding on the façade of the Andrea della Valle church, which was undergoing yet another restoration. As Elsa kneeled down to lock her bicycle to a lamppost across the street, she felt Barker's now universally recognized shape hovering above her. The shot caught him jumping midair in skinny jeans and cowboy boots, his sculpted biceps protruding from his T-shirt like some kind of superhero in flight. For a moment she wondered whether it was a good idea, to see him in the flesh again after so many years, even if only at a distance, while in the company of a man she barely knew and had a bit of a crush on.

Sandro had made a reservation at the restaurant around the corner so they could get a quick bite before the concert. Elsa found him sitting at a table, wearing a kind of English countryman's cap and a fluorescent orange shirt peeking out beneath a bright blue jacket. Did he look glamorous? she asked herself. Fashionable, perhaps, but also on the verge of ridiculous. They both seemed less at ease than they'd been at the outdoor café only a few days earlier, and struggled to find a subject about which they might both be knowledgeable enough to sustain a conversation. This was exactly what was so nerve-racking about going on a first date these days: one had to proceed on this slippery, egg-shelled ground that could crack at any second. They began their slow trek picking through the main headline of the day—the primary election for the new Democratic Party candidate—but their opinions turned out to be antithetical, so they quickly backed up and ventured onto a different theme, as they didn't want to—didn't care, actually—have a debate. Their point was to agree, not to differ, to find common ground rather than contradict each other. Elsa ordered a hamburger and he made a comment in passing about being a vegetarian, so they explored that issue temporarily—Was he a vegan? No, actually a pescatarian. Was it because of some Buddhist credo? No, he simply didn't eat anything that had a face. Ah yes, she could totally see his point, maybe she too should stop eating animals with faces. When that subject had been unraveled to its fullest, Elsa turned the conversation to summer holidaying. She said she enjoyed hiking the Dolomites in August, Sandro said he liked Ibiza in September, when the rave crowd had left. He said he always rented the same villa on the far side of the island—a very simple, very isolated farmhouse. It is so quiet, you'd never know you were in Ibiza. That's what everyone always said about Ibiza, Elsa thought, they all made sure to stay in the remotest part of the island, so remote that you would never know it *was* Ibiza. She wondered why people bothered going to a place where they had to make such an effort to stay away from everything the place was famous for.

The idle chatter was beginning to tire her. The problem was she wasn't feeling any vibe coming from him, there was absolutely zero chemistry now, which was maybe part of the reason it was so hard to find common ground. She wondered why on earth he'd bothered asking her for a date.

"Nice shirt," Elsa said at one point. She must have hit the right spot at last because he suddenly jumped up from his chair and stood, beaming.

"It's my favorite," he said, with unexpected fervor. He struggled out of the shiny jacket and turned around, showing the fluorescent white velcro stripes on the back of his shirt.

"Guess what?" He laughed, delighted.

"Tell me."

"I found it under a pile of junk at the Porta Portese flea market. This is the shirt men wear on road works. Five euros!"

"That's amazing," she said. "Amazing. I thought it was a Helmut Lang. Five euros? Pheeew! Who would have guessed."

. . .

Barker's first album came out in the mid-nineties, only a few years after he'd left Rome, and became a worldwide sensation overnight. He'd surprised Elsa once more: risen from the ashes of his detoxified, mediocre life, he'd bloomed into a star. Elsa just couldn't believe how fast he'd made the leap from the hardware store in Kenosha to the cover of *Rolling Stone*.

Then she read in a magazine the title of his hit song, the one that had climbed to the top of the charts.

"Roman Romance." And her heart skipped a beat.

So those letters had not been just a formality, a mandatory step to add her pardon to his list. The song had to be his tribute to her, long overdue. What a relief for Elsa to realize that with time and sobriety Drew—or Barker, whatever she was supposed to call him now—had been reminiscing about their love, that he had genuinely missed her. And to realize that she, well—that she had been in some way his muse.

Elsa ran to the music store in Via del Corso and bought the CD, but as soon as she got home and sat down to listen to the lyrics, she was mortified.

By then it was already too late, there was no way of stopping the rumor. Friends started ringing her up, people she only barely knew stopped her on the street, acting unusually friendly, her mother pestered her. All of them asking the same question. Is it you, the girl in the song? Is it you?

It was pointless to tell people that no, it wasn't her but a blond Texan art student. People just wouldn't hear, they loved the story too much. Knowing Elsa made them feel a step closer to Barker. By knowing her, they too could claim a piece of him. So the song kept following her. It became an albatross in C-sharp minor, another reminder of her humiliation.

· · ·

She hadn't been to a big rock concert since her twenties and never in such a grand auditorium. Crowds frightened her. People were streaming inside the stadium like ants, joyfully, expectantly. They walked with beatific smiles stamped on their faces, as if to confirm they were all there for the same exact reason, like a clan wearing the same tattoo. The place probably had more than twenty thousand seats and it was full to the brim. Sandro had been given VIP tickets, so they sat in a square section right across from the stage, cordoned off and slightly above the heads of those below. There were comfortable, nicely padded chairs, and complimentary mineral water with snacks. Elsa recognized a few faces in the VIP crowd, a couple of actresses and comedians, a young politician who had been recently involved in a scandal, fashion models with chopstick legs in impossible high heels next to orange-tanned football players. They were passing out Champagne in paper cups to one another, kissing and hugging and making their cordoned-off space their special private party, blatantly ignoring the supporting act. One of them—a beautiful dark-headed woman Elsa had seen in several films—came over and kissed Sandro Donati quickly on the mouth. I love your shirt, she said in a throaty, languorous voice, I am so going to steal it from you.

· · ·

As the lights went down, a ripple went through the audience and then—there he was, center stage, under one sharp cone of light, in black pants and a crisp white shirt. His face filled the giant screen behind him: the tiny crow's-feet, the two-day-old beard, the Mick Jagger lips, every intimate detail was so uncannily familiar to Elsa. She had actually touched those cheekbones, she knew the dots floating in those irises and the straight bridge of that nose. When the camera framed his hands picking the strings of the acoustic guitar, she recognized the shape of his fingers, his square nails and the flat shape of his thumb, which for some reason she had always found such an exquisite, manly feature. Those fingers had actually once explored every millimeter of her body, including cavities and hidden parts.

"Grazie di essere qui, Roma! Sono felice di essere con voi!"

His voice boomed in an almost perfect Italian accent as the band began to play the opening track. A roar, like a wave echoing and rippling, responded. They loved him. No, they were crazy about him. You could feel their adoration rise and fill the auditorium like a fog of sweat, love so thick you could cut it like cake. These were not casual fans, this was a crowd of diehards, faithful followers, the majority of whom seemed to be deep into their forties. They must have attended many of his concerts, because there was some kind of script they all knew and performed with uncanny discipline. They were doing funny stuff with their hands, raising them and flapping them loosely above their heads, so that the stadium seemed to flutter and vibrate as if filled by thousands of butterflies. They sang the lyrics of each song as soon as Barker gave them a cue, and stopped as soon as the chorus ended so that he could pick up from where they had left it. It was a dance, a well-rehearsed duet between him and a disciplined crowd of thousands responding as a single monstrous individual.

Soon even their cordoned-off VIP section was standing up, dancing like the rest of the audience, singing along with everyone, their arms up like a bunch of teenagers. Sandro looked at Elsa, in what seemed a hopeful way, as if expecting for her to say or do something that would confirm an expectation. He had taken off his jacket and cap, and was moving his hips to the beat. Two of those paper cups of Champagne had warmed him up and he was glowing. Elsa smiled encouragingly so he came closer and wrapped an arm around her waist, his femur thumping lightly against hers. Elsa accommodated his tentative steps, felt the warm dampness of his sweat through his shirt. By now everybody around them was touching and pressing against one another as Barker emitted an irresistible sexual energy, conducting their dance from the giant screen.

Sandro turned to her, his breath warm on her neck.

"Isn't he just the best?"

Elsa nodded, feeling the increased pressure of his hand around her waist.

"I am glad you came." Sandro blew softly in her ear. There was definitely a spark now, the chemistry of the night was beginning to take effect. It was a good feeling, though Elsa wondered whether it would have been wiser to come alone, in order to be free to focus on Barker's physical manifestation in all his glory, and on the unforeseen effects this manifestation might have on her. Hers was a completely different reading of Barker's performance from anyone's crammed in that auditorium. The crowd of VIPs were getting sloppy and slightly out of hand. But her experience was private, and one she couldn't possibly share with anybody.

The sax played a vibrant solo. Barker ran back and forth across the stage. The notes kept climbing higher and higher, driving the crowd to the limit. Until they became delirious.

. • .

Then the lights dimmed, the music seamlessly turned from rock mode to acoustic solo and the audience reacted with a giant intake of breath, a mix of wonder and delighted surprise. Flickering lights dotted the darkness. And then, as if on cue, everyone was holding up their cell phones as Barker began to sing "Roman Romance." The flashes and the lit displays turned the dome of the auditorium into a starry sky. The audience followed the lyrics in a hushed chorus, waving their bluish screens in a gentle motion.

It was an apotheosis. Most of the audience knew, from gossip, star mags, blogs if not from Wikipedia, that Barker had lived in Rome when he was young. There he had fallen deeply in love with a mysterious girl, so that now "Roman Romance" belonged to the

Romans by birthright. It had become their hymn to love, just as Marta the receptionist had said. And tonight tens of thousands of them were singing those lines with increasing pathos, till they became one fervent voice.

Elsa sensed a flutter around her, she could tell the VIP crowd was watching her, pointing, whispering. Sandro Donati studied her face but she pretended not to notice and fixed her gaze on the stage. Although she didn't remember all the lyrics (after hearing it that first time she had carefully avoided paying attention to them) she felt she should try and sing along with everyone else. It was a gesture of atonement, like an atheist attempting to remember the lines of a prayer. The words reemerged, unstrung.

> *Girl, girl,*
> *combing your hair*
> *You will need me,*
> *you will want me*
> *more than you think.*
> *Girl, girl,*
> *in a beautiful coat,*
> *you will be cold,*
> *you will be dead*
> *without me*

Elsa was suddenly overwhelmed, swept off in a giant wave as if by the rupture of a dam. A burst of longing seized her. All she had been able to see at the time had been Barker's ruthlessness, all that had mattered to her had been her broken heart and her revenge. Then, because of his vulnerability and his unexpected kindness, she had disregarded him, brushed him off as this Midwestern bumpkin without future or depth. How could she have been so unreasonably unforgiving, to the point of refusing to own a single track of his?

. . . golden light shines on your pillow,
Botticelli hair covers your face,
you are killing me even when asleep,
kill me, kill me
I saw you
My Renaissance queen
running toward me
calling me, calling my name
across the Ponte Sisto
I have loved you in Rome
Yes I have
Loved you loved you
In Rome

So many years later, in the gigantic auditorium, the melody of "Roman Romance" came as a revelation, as if her heart, throat and lungs had been plugged into a light switch and her brain had lit up. Yes, they were all connected: Barker, Elsa, the tens of thousands, the leggy Texan art student in the song, Artemisia beheading Holofernes, her past and present. They were all one big dot-to-dot constellation like those lights quivering in the dark.

Did it matter that it wasn't her in the song? And what difference did it make now? The song was no longer about anybody. It was just this beautiful thing that Barker had created nearly twenty years ago that would survive all of them. Really, she thought, what a waste of time. To have kept her distance, to have waited so long to see him in his full splendor. Why not rejoice and accept his greatness, his fabulous talent, and just love it, like everyone else?

Anyway, even the girl from Texas must be over forty by now, and maybe she, too, had gained weight and chopped off her Botticelli hair.

. . .

The gorgeous dark-haired actress was coming toward her. She spoke directly to Elsa, ignoring Sandro.

"We are having a small party at my place after the concert. Please join us, I'd love to talk to you."

Elsa nodded, almost condescendingly. Sandro held her closer to him as if to exhibit her as his private property.

"Are you going to go backstage afterward?" he asked, somewhat nervously.

Elsa was lost for a moment, then she regained control.

"It gets too crowded backstage," she said. "I'm going to see him tomorrow for lunch at his hotel. We always do that when he comes back. It's our little ritual."

Sandro looked at her with admiration and awe. He pressed his body harder against her, testing if he could still dare claim her after this last statement.

"How does it feel to listen to this song among so many people?" he asked.

He must have been waiting to ask this question since the day they'd met at the café by the Palazzo Farnese.

"It always feels sweet," Elsa said. She turned to him, feeling tall, mysterious. She smiled.

"Music is such a miracle," she said.

He leaned toward her and kissed her. His mouth was soft and his kiss had a delicious taste.

· ACKNOWLEDGMENTS ·

The writing of this book would not have been possible without the support of the M Literary Residency. My gratitude to Michelle Garnaut, Arshia Sattar and DW Gibson for the opportunity they've given me to write at Sangam House, to Lynne and June Fernandez, Bijayini Satpathy and Surupa Sen for their warm hospitality at Nrityagam, and to Jordan Pavlin for the poem. My deepest thanks go as always to my editor at Pantheon, Robin Desser, for her encouragement, enthusiasm and invaluable help, to Jennifer Kurdyla, and to my literary agent, Toby Eady.

A NOTE ABOUT THE AUTHOR

Francesca Marciano is also the author of the novels *Rules of the Wild, Casa Rossa,* and *The End of Manners.* She lives in Rome.

SS   Marciano, Francesca.
MARCIANO
            The other language.

$24.95   04/05/2014

DATE			
2/14			

BAKER & TAYLOR